TIME STAND STILL

A Novel By
John Misak

Published By
Barclay Books, LLC

St. Petersburg Florida
www.barclaybooks.com

PUBLISHED BY BARCLAY BOOKS, LLC
6161 51ST STREET SOUTH
ST. PETERSBURG, FLORIDA 33715
www.barclaybooks.com

This novel is a work of fiction. The characters, names, incidents, places, dialogue, and plot are the products of the author's imagination or are used fictitiously. Any resemblance to actual persons, living or dead, or events is purely coincidental.

Printed and bound in the United States of America

ISBN: 1-931402-18-3

10 9 8 7 6 5 4 3 2 1

This novel is dedicated to Haley, Jack, and Braden, my niece and nephews. Life can be a confusing, disheartening experience. You three show me it doesn't always have to be that way.

I'd like to thank my volunteer proofreaders: Brian Geiger, Barry Pearlstein, Joseph Persichilli, Karl Livigni, Vincent Sollitto, and Sharon Dickinson. Without your feedback and support, this novel would have been much harder to complete.

Read John Misak's Acclaimed First Novel

SOFT CASE

A city icon is dead…

A detective with nothing to lose…

A mystery you can't forget…

When software mogul Ronald Mullins is found dead as an apparent suicide, the entire city holds its breath. NYPD Homicide Detective John Keegan had asked for more excitement in his life. Having the high profile case fall on his desk gives him more than he ever could have wanted.

Over the course of the investigation, Keegan must handle an over-zealous partner, an upwardly mobile captain, and a hungry media just waiting for him to make a mistake. Along the way, Keegan discovers a web of corruption that goes from the top of the city government, right down to his own precinct.

When the entire police organization turns against him, Keegan takes on the case alone, armed only with his wit, and a handful of people he has no choice but to trust. In order to solve the biggest case the city has seen in years, Keegan must risk his job, his friends, and possibly his life.

"An entertaining, exciting, enjoyable read."
Brittan Barclay, Author of OFF PACE

Rated 5 Stars by Amazon.com and Barnes and Noble Readers

ISBN: 1-931402-10-8

Prologue

It took a lot of nerve to make the turn I attempted. Charging down 43rd Avenue at around 65 miles an hour in a car that excels only in straightforward speed, taking a sharp turn onto 7th Avenue was highly unadvisable, but I really didn't have much of a choice. A glance at my rear-view mirror displayed what the howling sirens behind me were saying—don't stop. Trying not to think too much about it, I cut the wheel hard to the right while not easing up on the gas, sending the already worn rear tires of my 1984 Camaro Z28 into a frenzy. The back of the car fishtailed left to almost 90 degrees, so I cut the wheel hard to the left while I bolted down an empty Seventh Avenue. The car then fishtailed right, left again, then finally settled down and let me concentrate on what I needed to do—get as much distance between myself and the proud men of the NYPD.

I stole a look at the back seat of the car, catching a glimpse of the nondescript beige box resting there. It had shifted quite a bit during my vehicular maneuvers, but it didn't seem damaged yet. Not that I cared. I actually wanted it damaged. If I had a choice, I would have thrown it out the window, but I didn't want anyone getting a hold of the components inside, in case any of them didn't break. My future—hell, my life it seemed—relied on that box being destroyed as if it never came into existence. I still didn't know exactly how I was going to destroy it completely, but I had it in my possession, and possession is two thirds of victory in my book. The men in the squad cars chasing after me saw it differently, of course, but they didn't know what I did. They didn't know how dangerous that box was. To them, it was just a computer, just a piece of someone else's property that I pilfered. They were right in that sense, but, as I said, they didn't know what I did.

The police were gaining ground, and they had a distinct advantage; there was really no way for me to exit the city. I couldn't take either of the tunnels—they were certainly road blocked. Water surrounded me, so any real attempt at an escape by car was pretty much ruled out. I briefly considered the 59th Street Bridge, and then realized they would have that road blocked as well. Then it hit me. I wasn't going to make it out of the city by car. I also didn't have much of a chance trying to hop a train. I could, however, destroy the computer and ditch the evidence for a short time. That was the thing; I technically had all the time in the world. If things went according to plan, the destruction of that computer would be followed by a return to life as usual for me, and my problems would be solved. At least, that was what I was hoping.

I cut another turn onto 22nd Street, and headed down toward the South Street Seaport. Luckily, the streets were empty, because I took this one a bit too wide. A metal garbage can lost its life in that collision, but nothing else. Though New York is certainly the city that never sleeps, it does take a catnap around 4AM. I got control of the car, which now was missing its right headlight, and burned down the street. The squad cars behind me took the turn more cautiously, and I had gained a little ground for the time being. I knew that wouldn't last, mainly because they surely had backup on the way to intercept me. The only way to avoid that, or minimize it at least, was to take the most indirect route to the seaport. This way, they would have no idea where to set up the interference.

For the people who think that high speed chases must be the coolest thing out there, let me dispel that rumor. Even though the adrenaline level during such an event is life-threateningly high, you are really too focused on staying alive to really get a rush out of it. If you've ever felt the bottoming of your stomach when you see police lights in your rear-view mirror, multiply that by about a hundred and you get the idea. On top of that, this was a mission for me. I was too concerned about failing to realize what I was doing. It didn't have the same effect a good videogame does, even. I guess I could equate it to receiving a phone call stating that a loved one has been rushed to the hospital, and you're racing there, not knowing what happened. Oh, and you just finished off about four lines of good cocaine. Not the crap that's been cut four or five times. I mean the good stuff.

I took another turn onto Park Avenue, running through my mind the routes necessary to get to the seaport. I heard the computer ram against the side of the car. Something probably came loose. I felt a little better about that. At least, if I was caught, the folks at the research laboratory would have their work ahead of them getting that hellish computer working properly. Even if I threw off their timetable, that would be fine. There were a few cabs on Park, so I had to be careful not to hit any of them. I didn't care so much about getting into an accident, but I was afraid of anything that would slow me down. I punched the accelerator some more, and the big V8 engine growled, as if to tell me it was getting tired of this. I looked at the gas gauge and saw I had just a touch more than a quarter tank, so I had plenty of fuel to dump this car into the East River. I just hoped I personally had enough energy to get out of the damn car.

I chose 18th Street as my final route to the seaport, and inched the needle on the speedometer over 100 down that street. I was acutely aware of the fact that any collision at that speed, even with the smallest of objects, would spell disaster for me. Well, disaster for me at that moment. I had a theory, a cockeyed one at that, which I hoped would protect me from danger. If I didn't rely on that theory, I wouldn't have tried to pull this stunt off in the first place. Theories, at least this one, are nothing more than elaborate lies we tell ourselves in times of trouble. Despite the fact that I knew this, I hoped to God, or anyone else who was listening, that it would work.

I raced through the streets with only getting away from the police on my mind. I had never been in trouble with the law before, so having what seemed like an entire precinct chasing after me didn't feel comfortable. I figured it wouldn't be long before they starting shooting at me. After all, at the speed I was driving, I could be considered a danger. I didn't know enough about police procedure in a car chase, but I did see enough of the reality cop shows to know I didn't have much time.

Just as I had the seaport in full view, I hit a classic New York City pothole at about 95 miles per hour that caused the steering wheel to go berserk. I felt control of the car slipping from me, and I mashed the accelerator and turned the wheel hard to wrestle control back. It didn't happen. The front right tire, the one that found the pothole, had shredded, leaving me with three working wheels and a slick metal rim. I did my best not to think about it. To put it plainly, I shit my pants. The car jimmied sideways, still moving along at high speed. I calculated as best I could whether or not I would have enough momentum to make it to the pier and thrust the car over the edge. There were a few boats, I noticed, and since I did not have any steering capability at all, I had to hope I hit a spot on the pier that was clear of them. I didn't hear or see the police behind me, but I knew they had to be close. I closed my eyes and awaited whatever it was fate had in the cards for me.

* * *

It might help to explain how I got into this situation—how I broke into one of the largest research facilities in New York City, evaded security, and walked off with a $100,000 piece of computer equipment. I'm sure that an explanation of why I chose to get into a high-speed chase with the NYPD and then dump my pride and joy of an automobile into the East River would help. Answers to such questions are not cut and dried, and I must admit, I don't know the exact answers for sure. I only know things from my perspective, which I guess will have to do. I know there is a saying about watching out what you hope for. Though this statement does apply to my situation somewhat, this is more about what sort of schemes you use to cheat the game of life. Some of us have no opportunity in this game whatsoever. Most people are victims of the game, hopelessly plodding along the bottom of the bell curve, knowing full well they are doomed to an existence of mediocrity at best. I thought I was one of them, one of the people who would never realize any of their potential because life had other things in mind.

Opportunity has the ability to surprise us all. I've come to realize that, though this is true, not all opportunity should be seized. Most opportunities are tests to see how gullible we are. Anyone can be foolish enough to take the bait. It is those of us who refuse it, and decide to continue our seemingly worthless lives instead of being caught in the allure of better living, that end up better in the long run. That's why I chose to tell this story. I want to offer a warning to the people who might get the same opportunity I did. I wasn't strong enough to turn it down. I didn't have the willpower to politely refuse.

I really can't imagine many people who could. But, if the information I give in the following pages helps at all, then I have completed my mission.

Book One - Jason's Ladder

Chapter 1

June 22nd, 2002

I fiddled with the tiny straw in my gin and tonic for what seemed like the millionth time. I tried to focus my thoughts on something far away, something removed from the tense situation I was facing. I sometimes like to portray myself as someone who confronts my issues, instead of turning to my half-empty drink for inspiration. I'm not saying the bottle doesn't offer inspiration for me from time to time, but I was angry with myself for not taking control right then. It's just when she's around, I lose that control. Throw anything at me, a disastrous situation that calls for a man of action, and I'm your guy. Yet, bring this blonde beauty that was sitting before me and ask me to be firm with her about how I feel, and my tongue turns to Play-Do.

I shouldn't have even been there. Not the place, the situation. I liked the place. Ruth's Chris Steakhouse in Westbury, one of my favorite restaurants. It was all dark wood paneling with a nice round bar, the sort of place you felt instantly comfortable in. Despite my liking the place, I didn't want to come. Well, at first I did. I thought I would sit right down at that table, look across at her, into those deep green eyes, and tell her there wasn't a shred of feeling left in my heart for her. To take it a step further, I even convinced myself that what I was doing was the best thing for both of us. I figured I would be freeing her. That might have been true, but the thought of my executing that was a dream at best. What gets me most is how much I wanted to do it, finally sever the last thread in a relationship I had

10

once thought would be the completion of my existence. I don't know how we went wrong. Such situations breed nothing more than opinions, and though I have one, I don't think it's the complete story. It's only my version, skewed this way and that in my hopes of justifying whatever actions I took that led to it's downfall. Throw a couple of drinks in me and bring up the subject and I will tell you she is a psychopathic bitch whose mental problems ccver the entire spectrum of an Abnormal Psychology textbook. Still, this was the woman I had banked my future on at one point, and right then, the sight of her instilled anger and despair in me, along with the thick sexual and romantic tension that always existed between us. *What went wrong?* I asked myself as I stared down at my half empty drink. Yet again, *What went wrong?*

I guess it's simple. Life went wrong. As much as I would like to find some cosmic reason for our demise, the truth is that things didn't go as planned. Between career problems and her emotional state, a distance was created between us, and one morning I woke up not wanting to have anything to do with her. I couldn't think of being emotionally involved with her anymore, and I had to stop it. So I did. We both actually thought this was just a temporary stop on our romantic highway, caused by an educational jackknife in my life. She blamed it on my inability to finish college, and that made sense. We thought it would pass. Well, it was seven years and countless new "first dates" later, and we were still going nowhere. Wow, seven years. It hit me then, sitting across from her, harder than it ever had. I'd wasted seven years of my life searching for something that I knew all along was gone, just because I couldn't look this woman in the face and tell her to get on with her life. God, was I a coward.

I glanced up at her, caught her eyes, and looked away again. I couldn't do it. Every time I tried, I felt that the words just wouldn't come out of my mouth. I think it was because I felt bad for her, that I didn't want to hurt her feelings. Maybe that's just a justification for my cowardice and that was fine with me. She was a part of this too, and dammit, maybe she should have been the one to see how I was struggling, and see the busted relationship for what it really was. It takes two to tango, they say, and if her partner has two left feet, then it's time for her to take the reigns and carry the dance. Hell, I've never even danced the goddamned tango before.

"You want another drink?" she asked me. *Yeah, like twenty*, I thought. Maybe under the influence of Tanqueray's best I might build up enough courage to do the job.

"Yeah. You?" Well, I could speak. The mouth functions correctly when discussing simple topics like drink orders. *Coward.*

"Are you okay?" I knew what she was asking, because even though I thought she might have been a little screwed up in the noggin, she did know how to read me perfectly well. She knew I was sitting across from her with something on my mind and I'm sure she was afraid to find out what that was.

"Yeah, fine," I said, watching a bus boy clean up a table. I followed him all the way to the kitchen instead of looking in her direction. *Sissy.*

"Hey, I'm over here," she said, reaching across the table and turning my chin to face her. I knew the look on my face was pure weakness, and I tried to hide it with a smile.

"I know where you are."

"But I'm not so sure about you. You haven't said a thing tonight. If you didn't want to come here . . ." She stopped herself mid-sentence like she always did when she was trying to add emphasis. Tanya (that's her name, if you were wondering) did this often.

"If I didn't want to come, I wouldn't be here." There's my token response when someone asks for a truth I think they don't want to hear. Of course I didn't want to be there. I never understood people who ask such forthright questions in sticky situations. It's like someone you don't like asking you if you like them. They must get the subtle signs about your feelings for them, but subtlety is lost on most people. They have to ask the big questions, and people like me, who don't want to upset anyone, have to make stupid comments in a creative effort to be nice.

"So, you don't want to be here." Remember, I said she read me well.

"It's not that." The waiter came over in what should go down as one of the best cases of being saved by the bell in history. "I'll have another gin and tonic and give her another Zinfandel." He nodded and left without saying a word. Maybe he sensed the tension between the two of us and decided he'd rather be telling someone else about the specials of the day than jumping into this pot that was coming to a slow boil. Regardless of his intentions, I did appreciate the timely interruption. Unfortunately, it didn't last.

"You were saying?" Tanya asked.

"You don't miss a beat, do you?"

"Taught me well."

"Maybe too well, if you ask me, but then again, you didn't ask me," I said.

"You're stalling."

"I am."

"What's wrong? Does sitting across from me make you that uncomfortable? Is it something you're not telling me? Don't even sit there and say that you can't tell me what's on your mind. It wasn't so long ago that you told me everything." Once she gets started, there's no stopping her.

I took a healthy sip of my drink, finishing it, and found myself waiting for the other one to arrive.

"You ever have one of those days where everything is bothersome? You wake up, you don't want to shower, don't want to brush your teeth, and don't want to eat? Not because you're depressed or because you are in a bad mood so to speak, but because it all just requires too much effort."

"No," she answered.

"Well, thanks for the help. You know what I mean."

"I don't know about that, but I can tell you that you must have that type of day every time you see me." It was right here that I hoped she was seeing the subtlety, that she had come to the conclusion I was leading her towards. You know what they say about bringing the horse to water. This mare wasn't thirsty. "Is everything okay with you? You and your father aren't arguing again, are you?" This last statement, above all, proves how out of time this relationship had gotten. When Tanya and I were dating, my relationship with my father was strained. I kept screwing up in college, and at least once a week my father would give me the mandatory father-son speech about getting my shit together and making something out of my life. The problem was, my father wasn't too good at this, and he probably hated the fact that he felt compelled to do it anyway. I, of course, didn't listen to a word he said and kept going on my steady pace toward expulsion. Tanya had been there for that, had listened to me bitch about how my father was breaking my balls, and how I thought he hadn't made much of his life either. What she wasn't there for was the repairing of the father-son relationship. Even though I had told her on many occasions that my father and I were like friends, she never really witnessed that because I refused to bring her around the house after the breakup.

"I'm fine," I said, avoiding the father comment. "I've just been under a little pressure is all." For the life of me, I couldn't figure out what that pressure was. Everything was going pretty smoothly in my life, and even though I really didn't like what I was doing or the fact that I was getting older, I didn't have too much to complain about, other than the task at hand.

"What sort of pressure?"

"The normal shit. Nothing important or life threatening."

"You're bored," Tanya insisted.

"I'm not bored."

"Yes you are, I can see it in your eyes."

"I have bored eyes?" I asked.

"You know what I mean. This detective thing isn't doing it for you, is it?"

Now there, she was dead wrong. You see, after I had gotten the letter from my college thanking me for four years of attendance but suggesting I don't bother to register for the next semester, I had no idea what I wanted to do. I thought it might have been a good idea to become a police officer. I took the test, and during my return to college, I got my call from the NYPD. I jumped at the opportunity, and was set to go to the academy in three months. That summer, I was playing a pickup basketball game, and during a near-perfect Michael Jordan impression, I came down on my knee in a way it wasn't designed for. The doctors called it a torn anterior something-or-other ligament. I called it pain. The NYPD called it "Medically Unfit." That was my brief tour in the line of police work. Still undaunted, I decided to finish my degree in police science and, after working four years for a scumbag detective, I got my P.I. license. Now, when people call me a dick, I can wholeheartedly agree with them.

"Everything is going fine with work. Hey, I'm not chasing down the most interesting people in the world, but I like it, and it gives me time to do other things," I said, figuring this would shut her up.

She frowned at this answer almost as if she wasn't happy that I am content. If I were depressed about my life, maybe that could explain away the way I had treated her recently. I've noticed this trend with women for a long time, and it is something I just don't understand. If a woman meets a guy who is fantastic for the first six months of a relationship, and then takes a drastic turn and starts treating them like shit, they think it is because something changed in their man's life. For the most part, this is entirely untrue. You see, ladies of the world, that first six months is nothing but a farce, a relationship sales pitch. Men and women think differently, but the male mind is easier to figure out. All you have to do is think of the simplest reason for why a man is acting the way he is, and odds are you'll be right.

"So what is it then?"

"What?" I asked.

"The way you are right now. I mean, you'd think you were sitting with a stranger," Tanya said.

"I told you, I'm having one of those days."

"Enough with that. Tell me what's really going on."

The waiter came back with our drinks, and again I was happy for the interruption. Sometimes, it's all about timing.

"Here's your drinks, sir," he said, giving me a look of understanding.

"I wish you would talk to me," Tanya said.

"What do you call what I have been doing for the last ten minutes?"

"Making small talk."

"That's talking, isn't it?" I asked.

"No, it's not. You know what I mean," Tanya said.

"Actually I don't. The only thing I know is that I might not be telling you what you want to hear. If I knew what that was, maybe I could be of more help."

"Jesus, you act as though there is nothing between us, that we just came here to hang out for a little while, shoot the shit, as you would say," she said.

"And?"

Tanya huffed. "What do you want from me?" she asked.

"What do you mean?"

"Darren, this has been going on for a long time. You know how I feel about you, but I have no idea where you are coming from. I mean, if I take what you say when you have been drinking, I'd think everything was fine. When you're like this, though, it's like you are all tensed up, and I can't get through to you. I think I'm wasting my

15

time." She touched on the truth so superficially she probably didn't even realize it.

"I don't get it. I mean, have I made any promises to you? Have I told you to stop living your life to wait for me? I've told you time and time again that I just can't see myself settling down just yet, that there are too many things going on in my life to make anything happen. I appreciate the time I spend with you, but I don't want the responsibility of anything else." Okay, there was some truth sprinkled in there.

"It's been years. How long should I wait for you?" There was the opportunity. She gave me an opening to deliver my message with the least amount of difficulty. It was just a matter of me having the balls to take it.

"I don't want you to wait. Hell, if there is someone else out there you want to be with, then by all means go for it."

It was Tanya's turn to look down at her glass. It seemed like she did that forever, but it must have been only about ten seconds.

"You're willing to just throw it all away? You'd risk losing me to someone else?" she asked.

"Hey, you're the one that talks about destiny so much. If you are certain we are destined to be together, then nothing can get in the way, right? The problem is, you keep trying to push things, make them happen on your own schedule. If there is such a thing as destiny, well, then, I am sure it has it's own timetable, and no matter how much pushing you or I do, nothing will change that."

"You're seeing someone, aren't you?"

"I'm not," I said. I wasn't. I wished I was. I wished I could find someone that could act as a living, breathing explanation of my feelings about my relationship with Tanya. Couldn't seem to find that, though.

"Then what is it?"

"Weren't you listening? I don't think it's right at the moment."

"Do you think it will ever be?" Opportunity number two staring me right in the face. I took a long swig of my drink to build up my courage and decided to leave it all on the table.

"I don't know. I have no idea what the future holds. But, if you are asking me if I think it will work now, that we could date and move forward, I would have to say no. Listen, I've never felt anything as strong as the feelings I had for you. I probably never will. I know what I am risking by telling you this, but I just can't see getting together with you when it doesn't feel right. We did that once, remember, and look what happened," I said.

She was near tears, and I felt like a shitheel for making that happen. It wasn't like I had a choice.

"So, what you are trying to tell me is that you don't feel anything for me anymore. Jesus, Darren, why couldn't you tell me this a while ago, so I wouldn't have wasted all this time on you?"

"It's not that simple. Part of me wants to be with you, but that part really wants things to be like they were, when all I could think about was you. If we tried to recapture that, it would fall short. I'd forever be comparing the past to the present. That wouldn't work."

"You can't live in the past, and you can't hold me hostage for the things I did back then. I'm different now. I'd give you your space. I'd let you live your life. God, you haven't even given it a chance. You don't know what I am like now. You can't say how things would be because you don't know. But you won't ever give it a chance, will you?"

I thought I would feel bad for telling her how I felt. I was wrong. I felt worse than bad. I felt like the biggest asshole on the face of the earth. A part of me was screaming not to do this, not to let her go. I knew that was the unrealistic part of me, the nostalgic part that wanted to relive the past. My mind knew better than that. It just had a real hard time convincing my heart to bury this whole thing and move on.

"I can't give you half of me, and that's all I could promise to try and give. We both deserve better than that. Doing something just for the sake of doing it will always end in disaster," I said.

"Tell me you don't love me right now, and I'll leave."

"Even if I could do that, you wouldn't believe it. Yeah, you'll walk out the door right now, but you would later think differently. I know you, I know how you think."

"Just do it." She looked right into my eyes, searching for something I guess. She must not have found it, because she frowned and looked away. "I don't know what's wrong with you, but I'll tell you this. If you keep going on lying to yourself, about everything, your job, your future, me, you're gonna wake up one day, and you'll be forty and have no idea what you want. You'll look back on nights like this one and wish you could have them back, but it will be too late. I'll have moved on, and all of your opportunities will have passed you by. I love you, with all of my heart. I want nothing more than to spend my life with you, but I can't force that to happen. We both know I've tried. It's up to you, and I don't think you're going to be able to do anything about it. It's sad, Darren, it really is."

Tanya got up from the table.

"Don't leave now," I said, for lack of anything else better.

"I have to. I shouldn't have come here. I knew it, too. I knew you would give me the same story. I don't know why I lie to myself about you."

"Maybe I keep telling you the same story because it is the only truth I can give you," I said, realizing the harshness of my words.

"If that's the case, then you are even sadder than I thought. Goodbye Darren. I wish you the best." With that, she turned and walked toward the door. I wanted to get up and stop her, but my legs wouldn't move. I was frozen in that booth, watching her walk past the waiter and out the door. The strange part was that, even though I had gone to that dinner with the intentions of letting her go, when she was walking out the door, I didn't feel so sure about that.

I sat at the table, noticing people trying to stare at me and not be obvious. There's really no way to recover from such a situation, so I just stayed at the table and gulped my drink. Without asking, the waiter came over with another one. He didn't say a word and I was thankful for that. He took the two empty glasses away and I went to work on the third, angry at life for dealing me such a shitty romantic hand. For the rest of the time I was there I thought about how things could have turned out differently. What happened to all the confidence I had hours earlier when I was sure letting her go was the right thing to do?

I came to the conclusion that there was no "right thing." As far as I could tell, nothing could ever be certain. I also knew that if such a thing existed, I was not about to see it. The fourth drink came, and my head was already feeling light. The waiter asked if I was going to be having dinner, and I shook my head. He didn't question me any further, and thankfully, despite the fact that the place was busy, he never said anything about me getting up from the table so they could use it for customers who wanted to eat. I thought that was nice of him, considering the situation.

After fifteen minutes, I decided it was time to free the table. The management was being nice by letting me occupy a prime table on a busy night, and I didn't want to abuse such niceness. I was about to get up when I saw a familiar face walk in the front door. I wasn't sure at first, but then I recognized the old man for who he was. Alan, my ex-step-grandfather had come in. I hadn't seen the guy in about 17 years, but I was certain it was him. I didn't want him to see me, though I didn't suspect he would have said hello. I knew it was him by the sheer size of the man, which was imposing even though the guy had to be in his eighties. Plus, he was wearing the same thick black-rimmed glasses he always wore. With him was a woman about twenty years younger. The sight of her made me want to throw up. Alan was a widow-hunter. He'd done that with my grandmother, and with several women afterward from what I knew. He would latch on to a woman who was single, get them to put all their money into a joint account with him, and then, from what I gathered, waited for them to die. I suspected sometimes he tired of waiting. He'd married my grandmother after she had been diagnosed with cancer, and after she passed, he waited about three months to move on to his next target. I didn't realize it back then, but after thinking about it when I had gotten older, I thought he might have had something to do with my grandmother's sudden death. I never mentioned this to anyone in my family, only because it had been years since my grandmother passed away when I figured it out, and talking about such things would only have upset everyone. On top of that, I had nothing but weak circumstantial evidence to prove my theory. Still, I hated the guy with a passion, and seeing him right there made me angrier than I had felt in a long time. If there was only something I could do about it all.

I stayed at my booth for about ten minutes, sipping my drink and waiting for the present asshole to be seated. Once he was taken to a table in the back, I fantasized briefly about going to his table and spitting at him, then decided the best thing to do was go to the bar, pay my bill, and get out of there, which I did.

Chapter 2

I guess my days started oddly back then. It had become a series of wake-ups and snooze button hits, all in an effort to catch enough sleep to feel alive. The problem was, no matter how much sleep I got, I still got out of bed feeling weary, as if my body was waging some sort of war at night and was exhausted from the battle. Everything ached and it took a good two or three hours before I shook the sleep away. For a while, I thought I had some sort of illness, something seriously wrong with me. Of course, I didn't go to the doctor. That would have been the smart thing to do. Instead, I plodded through each day constantly looking forward to the time that I could put my head on the pillow again. It never came soon enough.

The only thing I felt thankful for that morning was the fact it was Saturday, and I really didn't have much to do. I did handle cases from time to time on a Saturday, but I knew as soon as my eyes opened I was doing nothing that day. My head ached a little from the extra gin, and I walked across my cold hardwood floor to the colder tiled bathroom floor and swallowed a few Advil with some tap water. Content I had done a good deed for my body, I made my way across the apartment to my kitchen and whipped up breakfast. Well, I opened a can of Diet Coke, which was about all the "whipping up" I could manage. I took a long sip, and let the soda tingle in the back of my dry throat.

I did my usual morning scan across the apartment, noticing the blazer I threw across the couch and the half-empty bag of Doritos I had snacked from the night before. I can't say that I am a neat freak, mainly because if anyone who knows me heard such a comment, they might die of laughter. To give myself the benefit of the doubt, I'll say I'm disorganized. I really don't leave things dirty for too long, but not much has a place in my apartment, and there certainly isn't a place for everything. Compact disc cases were strewn all about the apartment, and I could guarantee that at least half of the ones that were sitting in the shiny silver rack I bought the year before were empty. I can't tell you how many CDs I've destroyed by leaving them loose in the car and then either stepping on them or scratching them one way or another. My music collection and how I handle it speaks volumes about my lack of organization.

So, I guess what I am trying to say was that my apartment resembled one which the FBI politely tossed. Saturday would normally be the day to get things together. Not this Saturday. Instead of doing some much needed cleaning, I decided to put something on other than the paisley boxers I was wearing and do a little Internet work. I went back to the room and changed into a pair of khaki shorts I only wore at home and a black t-shirt that came with some computer game I had bought. The shirt had some picture of a half-naked female computer character and it was also something that I would never wear outside the comforts of home.

I sat down in my overly expensive black leather computer chair, powered on the computer, and leaned back. This is what Saturdays were all about. I took the last swig of soda and waited for my computer to boot. Unfortunately, that took too long. When I bought the damn thing, it was touted as the fastest thing short of NASA equipment and cost about as much. The money came courtesy of one of the pieces of plastic I kept in my wallet, and if I remember correctly, I hadn't even finished paying it off before I realized the computer was already obsolete. I bought a name brand, thinking it was a safe buying decision, only to find out most name brand companies make their computers impossible to upgrade. Yep, I was looking at another two thousand dollar purchase real soon. Ah, the wonderful world of electronics and consumerism.

Despite the fact that my computer was at the end of its lifespan, it was plenty fast for my work purposes. Most of the databases and investigative programs were years old anyway, and didn't require anything too powerful to run. Games and the Internet were a completely different story. If I were the suspicious type, I would think that the game companies and the computer manufacturers were in bed with each other, because each year the minimum requirements to run the latest games jumped drastically. The problem was, once you were hooked on the games, you had no choice but to live a life of constant upgrades and endless computer purchases. Unfortunately, I was a charter member of such a group.

After waiting for my computer to boot and for Windows to load all the programs before letting me get to business, I logged onto the Internet. Because of the work I did, and more importantly, the online games I played, I had my local cable company install a cable modem in the apartment. I was one of the first in my area to get it, and the installer barely knew what the hell he was doing. But damn, the thing was fast. I really didn't understand how you could get Internet access from a cable that supplied television signals, but that really wasn't important. What was important was how much faster my connection ran when I was running through a game trying to shoot down everyone in sight. For that, the modem and its inexplicable operation were a godsend.

I really didn't know what I wanted to do on the Internet, so I just logged onto my mail server and checked to see if anyone sent me a message. The mailbox had eight new messages, six of them from addresses I didn't recognize. I knew at least half of those were porn solicitations. Those companies were getting more and more clever, titling their messages with phrases like "Don't Forget About Tomorrow" or "Urgent membership Notification." It used to be that they would be more straightforward, saying the emails were about how to get an expensive free membership so you can see college coeds having naughty fun together. I'm not sure how those companies are still in business with all of the deceptive tactics and spamming they practice. I guess once you are a certain distance past the legality line, it didn't matter what the hell you did. It would be like a bar letting a seventeen-year-old drink, but then worrying about getting in trouble for selling them a pack of cigarettes. If you're going to break the law, you might as well go for the whole enchilada.

One email struck me as interesting. It said "Investigate Anyone Online." I thought it peculiar that I, a private investigator, would be sent such a message. Out of curiosity I opened it, and clicked on the link. It was some company hawking bullshit software that promised to get the skinny on anyone. Of course, these programs did nothing more than give you the information in the phone book. I'm sure people bought them by the truckload, thinking they would be better off giving this company forty bucks instead of hiring someone legitimate, like myself. Hey, I was all for the Internet Revolution, but like almost anything else in the marketplace, you get what you pay for, or in this instance, what you don't pay for. For a little more than twice what this company was charging for a digital phone book, I could locate someone and even tell you what restaurant they frequented. For a little more than that, I could tell you where they worked, what car they drove, and how they liked their coffee. Okay, maybe I charged a bit more than that, but at least I delivered what I promised.

I deleted the suspicious emails, and then went on to the two from people I knew. One was from a friend of mine in Ohio, a fellow P.I. who often tossed me some work when he had something that needed to be done in New York. He didn't title the email, something he never did, probably because he didn't know how to. It read:

Darren:
I tried to call last night, but got the machine and didn't feel like talking to it. It's no big deal, but if you feel like putting in some hours on Saturday, I've got someone I need you to track down. Should be pretty easy. Call me.

Mike Holmes
Lead Investigators
American Investigators Co.

Mike always signed his emails professionally, as if he thought someone else might see the email and want to throw some business his way. It wasn't like he needed it; the guy ran his own investigation and security company and was probably pulling down somewhere around four hundred thousand dollars a year. Either he wanted the extra business, or he had inserted that tag at the end of his emails and couldn't figure out how to disable it. He was a great investigator and a good businessman, but he certainly wasn't the brightest star in the sky.

I didn't want to do any work that Saturday, but after realizing that I could use the money instead of lounging around the apartment feeling sorry for myself, I decided to give Mike a call. He picked up on the second ring.

"American," he said. He sounded busy, but then, he always did.

"You guys finally get phone service out in the sticks?"

"Wha? Oh, if it isn't my number one New York contact. How's the big city? Murder anyone recently?"

"I got a contract on a guy in Ohio. Real slippery gumshoe type."

"Maybe one day you'll be able to move up into the big leagues instead of taking bullshit contract kills."

"Good money in it though. How the hell are you?"

"Doing good Darren, doing good. Just wish I could find some free time. Haven't had a day off in six weeks. Starts to get to you, you know?"

"Yeah, sure, it's gotta be tough having more work than you can handle. I'll let you know what it's like when it happens to me."

"Right, from what I hear you've got more money than God," Mike said.

"Then we're all in trouble, because our Creator is piss poor."

"Guess that's why the meek inherit the earth," Mike said.

"What sort of job do you have for one us meek suckers?"

Mike exhaled, then laughed, which seemed like an odd combination at the time. Then again, Mike was a pretty odd guy. "Nothing big, nothing big. Seems some scientist worked for a university out here, came up with some major discovery, and then left with the information. You know, theft of intellectual property-type stuff. It won't be dangerous, and you can probably find the guy in an instant. The university wants to get a hold of this guy real bad. They're paying me five grand plus expenses to find him. What do you say, fifty-fifty and whatever expenses you incur?"

This seemed like a strange case for Mike to be handling. He was usually involved with deadbeat dads and finding lost loved ones. Of course, the fee was nice, and it couldn't have come at a better time. The last I had checked my account, I was down near the overdraft line. Business had slowed down, probably because everyone was buying that Internet software to find people.

"They say what sort of intellectual property he stole?" I asked.

"Nope. I didn't ask, and I doubt they would have told me."

"They want him brought back to Ohio?"

"No, nothing like that. They just want to know where he is," Mike said.

"Got any other details?"

"Hey, are you gonna take this job, or what?"

"You think I can afford to throw away a couple grand?"

"Then what's with the questions?"

"Investigative curiosity," I said. I always watched out for cases that seemed too good.

"Well, all I know is that he's a native New Yorker. Moved out to Ohio to work at the university about seven years ago. Split two months ago, and they figure he went back home."

"You the first one they contacted?"

"Think so. They seem pretty laid back about the whole thing. At least the lady that called to hire me sounded that way. I think they just want to get his location, then handle it internally, or maybe press charges or something. I could give a rat's ass. So long as they pay, which I am certain they will," Mike said. This I trusted him on. He was excellent at collecting. Probably why he made so much money in the first place.

I didn't have much experience with universities other than on a student level. If a university was willing to hire a private investigator and pay a large sum of money to have an ex-employee found, then that employee must have walked away with something real important. Either that, or they didn't have any idea what the going rate was to locate someone.

"Okay. Tell me what you've got on the guy and I'll get right on it," I said.

"Well," Mike said, exhaling again, "I don't have much. Just his name, a loose physical description, and the address he used when he lived out there seven years ago."

I grabbed a pen and a piece of paper, actually the back of an envelope. "Shoot."

"Name's Jason Caufield. Got a Merrick address. 186 Babylon Turnpike. You know where that is?"

It took a second for it to sink in. It wasn't until after I had written the information down that I recognized the name and the address.

"You sure about that information?" I asked, still thrown off a bit.

"Yeah, of course."

"I know the guy. Well, I knew the guy." I couldn't believe the coincidence. I didn't like coincidences.

"What do you mean?"

"I graduated from high school in Merrick with a Jason Caufield. I am pretty sure he lived on that street."

"Really?" Mike asked.

"Really. I wouldn't say I was pals with the guy, but when we were in junior high, we hung out a few times. He was a good kid, but he was a little too strange and nerdy for me."

"I don't give a shit what sort of guy he was, I just need to know where he has himself holed up."

"Yeah, yeah, I know. I just think it's sort of a strange coincidence," I said.

"Well, it should make it that much easier to find this guy."

"Of course. Do you know if they contacted his family? Are they still using that address?" I asked.

Mike paused for a moment, then said, "I tried that. They're living there all right, but when I asked for Jason they just hung up."

"Did you say who you were?"

Mike huffed, and said, "Of course not. Then again, I didn't get the chance."

"Weird," I said.

"I guess so. You know how these things can get. Guy gets in trouble, goes into hiding, and everyone rings the parents to see if they know where their little criminal is. For all I know, he could be hiding out there."

"Wait a minute, you didn't say anything about the guy being in trouble. What's going on?" I asked.

"It's like I said. The guy stole intellectual property. From what I understand, universities don't look too nicely upon such acts."

I got the feeling that Mike was holding back on me. Maybe it was because I was still reeling from the coincidence. I put it out of my mind, mainly because I had worked dozens of cases for Mike and he had always been on the level with me. I had no reason to believe anything would be different this time around. The one thing that bothered me was Mike's tone. He didn't seem right. I couldn't place it, couldn't get a firm grasp of what I felt, but something was up.

"It just seems odd, is all," I said, staring down at the name and address again. From what I remembered about Jason, he was afraid of his own shadow, and he didn't seem like the type who would have the balls to steal anything, let alone something as important as what he had taken from the university. People change, sure, but the thought of

Jason going from sissy to thief was too far of a stretch for me.

"Hey, I didn't ask for this case, but they gave it to me, and it looks like we'll both benefit fairly well from the whole thing. Just find this schmuck, get me an address and maybe some photos, and we'll be done with the matter, okay?" Again, Mike didn't seem like himself.

I was still looking at the name and address, my mind shooting back to high school, when I responded, "Yeah, I'll take care of it." I probably shouldn't have done that. I should have just turned down the case and gone back to my lazy Saturday afternoon.

"Great. Just call me when you've got something. If I were you, I would try dropping by the house. Use the 'We were friends in high school' bit."

"Yeah," I said, half-listening to him. My mind was elsewhere.

I hung up the phone, holding the envelope in my hand. Whatever Jason Caufield got himself into, I had the feeling it was more than what the university had let on. Jason was always into scientific stuff when we were younger, and it didn't surprise me that he had gone into the field as a career. He was too smart for his own good, I had remembered, and it had probably gotten the best of him this time. I almost felt bad for taking the job and ratting on him to his former employer, but if I didn't do it, I was sure Mike would have found someone else. Plus, I needed the money, and money certainly drives us to do things we later regret.

Before I got changed into more appropriate clothes, I remembered about the other email. It was from a friend of mine, Rich, who wanted to know if I was interested in bar hopping that night. I'm not sure why he didn't just call to ask, but I guess email is just that much easier. It doesn't require a lengthy conversation, and it's instantaneous. I replied, saying that I would probably be able to make it, and agreed to meet him at the bar he suggested. With that, I hit the shower, gearing myself for the grand search for my old high school chum, Jason Caufield.

* * *

After getting dressed, I gathered my gun, my P.I. license, and a magazine to read in the car in case I had to sit around awhile waiting for Jason. I can't say I felt confident about finding him easily, but the fact that I knew him somewhat and was familiar with where his parents lived, I figured I had a better than average shot. I could have spent some time logging on to the databases I used to see if I could find a trace of him. I realized that Mike had probably tried that already, and the fact that Jason had been on the run for less than ninety days meant that the databases wouldn't have any good information. My best bet was to do what Mike told me. Go to the house, tell his parents I was an old school friend, and hope they bought it. As I remembered, Jason's parents were nice, down to earth people made to suffer through raising a strange child. I particularly liked his father, an ex-cop who found just about any situation funny. That's probably how he dealt with the fact that his son was a nerd. As nice as they were, however, they weren't stupid. I figured the odds of them buying my story were slim.

I walked out of my apartment, and locked the deadbolt. It stuck as usual, causing me to curse it and the ridiculous red door it was housed in. I had lived there for about four years, and every time I brought someone new to the apartment, they would make a comment about the red door. I swore up and down that I had nothing to do with it, and they would snicker and say I must be running a brothel. I can say this, a lot of things went on in that apartment, but unfortunately, frivolous sex wasn't on the menu half as often as it should have been.

After jiggling the key six or seven times, I finally got the thing locked, and headed out to the street. The walls in the hallway were also a source of aesthetic frustration. They were painted an off white, with gold splotches that looked like someone dipped a sponge in paint and patted it against the wall. The cause for all of this decorator mayhem was the fact that, in the four years I had been there, we had gone through seven superintendents. Each one promised an update to the interior of the building, but none of them ever got too much accomplished. My bathroom tiles had been flaking off for about two years, and though the super would come and check it out, he never stayed on the job long enough to get past that point. I threatened the real estate company that owned the building several times, and even withheld half the rent one month, but all I got out of the deal was the money I saved on that month's rent. They had me over a barrel because I didn't want to go through the hassle of moving before I bought a house, and I couldn't see buying a house before I got married. And, well, judging by the way my love life was going, that wouldn't be happening any time soon. Every time I renewed my lease, I said it would be the last time. Wishful thinking, I suppose.

I made my way outside, keeping my head down as I passed fellow tenants in an effort to avoid senseless conversation. Most of the people who lived there were nice, but I wasn't one for idle chitchat, especially when I had work to do. Most of the people there knew what I did for a living, and they would constantly ask me if I would be able to locate someone for them. They never wanted to pay for such services, so I didn't particularly like to perform them. That's why I avoided talking to them at all costs, because it usually ended up costing me money. Maybe that's a little cold hearted, but if someone who worked in my building owned a restaurant or something, I wouldn't expect to stop by and chow down for free. Of course, I would never have such good luck that someone I lived next door to would own a restaurant, or anything useful for that matter.

It must have been about 11:30 when I got into my car. I was driving a white 1999 Ford Taurus at the time because it was the most non-descript car I could find. I didn't get a lot of surveillance jobs at the time, but they did pop up often enough that I needed a car no one would notice. I had bought it new a few years prior, thinking it was a practical, wise purchase. What I didn't realize was that the car came with an atrocity called "Daytime Running Lights," a valiant effort on the part of the Ford Motor Company to make the roads safer by keeping your headlights on all the time. They made Mustangs which had more power than anyone needed, no bad weather traction to speak of, and sold them to teenage boys looking to drag race, but hey, they were doing their part by brightening up the streets with useless headlights. What made me angry about the whole thing was that those headlights made my non-descript automobile incredibly conspicuous since the Taurus was one of the first cars on the road to have the new safety feature. I had to pay a mechanic friend of mine a couple of bucks to deactivate them, which he said was just sort of illegal. If I ever get put in jail or go to Hell, I said, it certainly wouldn't be for disabling a useless safety feature on my car. He chuckled, then took my money.

I lived in Valley Stream at the time, which was about fifteen minutes away from Merrick, where the fugitive Jason Caufield hailed from. My parents lived in Merrick as well, about three blocks away from the Caufields to be exact, so I was pretty much required to pay them a visit. I didn't mind seeing my parents, we got along great, but they enjoyed prying into my life from time to time, and I was in no mood to deal with it that day. My mother especially liked to talk about how my sister was married, and that I was the one who hadn't produced grandchildren for her. I would tell her that I probably have sired a babe or two, which would then prompt her to smack me on the shoulder. According to her, I was the last one left to carry the Camponi name, and if I didn't have kids, the name would be sentenced to oblivion. I don't know why she cared, I mean after all, she wasn't even a Camponi herself, but that's a mother for you. She meant well, but there were times when I just didn't want to hear it.

I started the car, pulled out of my cramped parking spot, and set my mind to thinking about Jason. I don't know what it was, but something didn't sit well with me. At first, I thought my doubts were stemming from Mike, but then I realized it was probably just my overly suspicious mind. I just couldn't picture Jason as a criminal, and I pretty much convinced myself that he wasn't. This seemed more like a misunderstanding than anything else, and the university would probably be pissed off that they spent over five grand to find someone that didn't do anything wrong. I enjoyed being a part of something that pissed a university off, since more than one had done the same thing to me. After thinking about it for a bit, I felt better, believing that my finding Jason would only help him clear his name and get on with his life. In retrospect, I know how wrong I was for thinking that way, but I didn't have the luxury or the gift of seeing things from the future. Well, not yet at least, but as usual, I am getting ahead of myself here.

Chapter 3

It took me about twenty minutes to get to Merrick, mainly because I had to fight the traffic on the Southern State Parkway, which was jammed with people running to the mall and the beach. I cursed them for having the money to spend at the mall and the free time to be able to lounge on the beach. Of course, if I had the time and the money, the last two places you'd find me at were the mall and the beach. The last time I had been to the beach had been for my nephew's first birthday, and even then, I spent my time inside the restaurant instead of outside working on a model tan. People who laid down on lounge chairs and fried like pork sausages made no sense to me, and people who considered a trip to the mall a recreational activity frightened me. On top of that, they pissed me off when they jammed up the parkway.

Babylon Turnpike, the street that the Caufields lived on, was just off the parkway, and for the life of me, I couldn't tell you why they called such a small street a turnpike. I don't even know what the hell a turnpike is. Every one I knew of was straight. Someone named this street a turnpike, and whoever it was probably met their end years before, so I couldn't even bitch to him or her. It was probably a he, because women didn't get the privilege of naming streets until only recently I suppose.

The Caufields lived about four blocks down the turnpike, and when I pulled up to the house, I instantly remembered it. It was a white high ranch, with black shutters and the old concrete shingles that seemingly every house on Long Island sported in the 70's. The

Caufields hadn't yet succumbed to the vinyl siding craze that swept the area, and the house looked like a relic compared to the other ones on the block. I personally preferred the shingles myself, mainly because all houses with vinyl siding looked the same, and I could understand why someone didn't want to spend thousands of dollars to make their house look like everyone else's. I did remember that Mr. Caufield was a cheapskate, so my fantasy about the family being the last bastion of good exterior taste disintegrated in a second's time.

I parked two houses away, more out of habit than anything else. I was supposed to be a long lost high school friend paying a visit, so I really didn't have to worry about the Caufields spotting my vehicular pride and joy. It wasn't a bad practice, parking out of sight, because you never know when you are going to have to tail someone. Still, I felt pretty ridiculous parking that far away.

In front of the house where I parked was an old man dressed in blue shorts, sneakers with black dress socks, and one of those cheap baseball caps with the plastic mesh on the back that said, "Captain." He was standing on his front lawn, gray-haired belly protruding for everyone to see, watering his lawn. If you ever need proof of the punishment for living a long life, this guy was it. I couldn't see myself centering my existence around the upkeep of a front lawn, but then again, I was only 34 at the time. I'm sure that when I get older, and when I can see Death approaching, I'll think that watering the lawn is one of the beauties of life.

The old man had a cigarette dangling from his mouth, and he attempted to talk to me through it.

"Excuse me?" I asked, trying to sound as polite as possible.

"Nice car you've got there," he said in a voice thick with cigarette smoke and congestion. I wanted him to cough, to clear it. He did, sending a nice ball of spit toward my general direction but not close enough that I thought he had aimed it at me.

"Oh," I said. "Thanks." Like I was really proud of my drivable refrigerator.

"What's that, one of them Tauruses?" He emphasized the second syllable a bit too much, and the throat clearing he did hadn't done much for his voice.

"Yes sir."

"Been meaning to get me one of them, but they're always changing the way it looks. You buy one, the next year it looks old."

"Never thought of it that way," I said.

"Course not. Probably leased it too. Can't afford that."

"Oh."

"You a policeman?" he asked. This seemed like an odd question.

"No."

"You look like one. Figured you were another one coming to see Laura," he said, gesturing toward the Caufield's house. I guess when all of your time is spent watering the lawn and watching the people that come and go you develop good investigative skills.

"Laura?"

"Laura Caufield. Well that's not her name anymore. She's been remarried. Poor woman, losing her husband like that. Guy works on the job for twenty years, never sees a bullet. He goes in to get some milk a couple of years ago, and catches one in the back. Never found the guy who'd done it either."

I appreciated the information this man was freely giving me, but I really wanted to go see Mrs. Caufield and hear it from her. This man's tone, his protruding belly, and his sickly voice were beginning to get the best of me.

"I see. Shame," I said.

"You're right about that. You know them?" he asked, this time gesturing with the hand he was holding the hose with, spraying water all over the beat up Oldsmobile in the driveway. He didn't seem to mind and I figured it was the first time that car had seen water in a long time.

"I was friends with Jason."

The man raised an eyebrow as if he wanted to say something about Jason. I thought about asking him if he'd seen Jason, but I decided I was better off leaving that alone.

"I don't remember that kid having too many friends. I don't remember him having any friends. Now, all of a sudden, he's got tons of them."

"What do you mean?"

"You're about the fifth guy this week coming around here to see their old buddy Jason. What, he owe you money or something like that?" the old man asked sarcastically.

I laughed, trying to make it sound as genuine as possible. "No, nothing like that. I just figured I'd stop by and see how he's doing."

"He don't live here. Hasn't in about eight years. If you were such good friends with him, I guess you would have known that."

"I haven't seen him in a long time."

"Of course. I guess you'll want to ask me next if he's been around lately."

I didn't answer because I had no idea how to.

"Well, far as I know, he hasn't. That don't mean he ain't been around, just means I haven't seen him. If you ask me, I think he got himself into some serious trouble. If you really are an old friend of his, you might want to try and find him and let him know what's going on."

"What's that?"

"Ain't you been listening? I told you, a lot of friends have been stopping by, and a few policemen have been around too. Whatever that boy's up to, I get the feeling it's no good."

I couldn't imagine why this old geezer was telling me all of this. Maybe he just liked to hear himself talk and he hadn't gotten a pair of ears to talk into in a long time. Whatever the case was, my ears had had enough, and it was time for me to move on. I started walking away, and said, "Yeah, I'll do that. Take care."

"You too, son. You too."

I walked toward the Caufield residence realizing that it would be difficult to pull off the "old friend" bit after others had tried the same thing. I wouldn't be lying to Mrs. Caufield if I told her I was an old friend and there was a chance she might even remember me, but she probably had her guard up. I needed a different angle, and nothing was coming to me. I thought about it for a moment, standing on the sidewalk right in front of her house, and came up with a plan. It was weak, and she probably would shut the door in my face, but it was worth a shot.

The front door of the Caufield house was old, with chipped white paint showing the black underneath. I didn't notice a doorbell, but there was a large brass knocker on the door. I opened the screen door, grabbed the knocker, and bashed it three times. I heard a dog bark, a large dog, and then I saw the curtains in the bay window move. I made a gesture to whoever was peering through them and waited for someone to answer the door.

After about twenty seconds, the door opened, and an older woman, dressed in sweatpants and a white t-shirt, looked up at me. She was holding a large chocolate lab by the collar. She took one look at me, made a face like she had been through this a thousand times, and opened the screen door a crack. With this, the dog started howling, and though I don't understand dog speak too well, I was pretty sure he was telling me he was going to take a bite out of my ass.

"Stop it, Rex," the woman shouted at the dog. I caught a good look at her face, and I was sure I had seen her somewhere. I knew it was Mrs. Caufield, even despite the years, but something told me I had seen her more recently. I just couldn't figure out where. "Can I help you?" She didn't look or sound like she wanted to.

"Mrs. Caufield."

Sigh. "Yes?"

"Maybe you don't remember me . . ."

"I don't, but I am sure you are another one of Jason's old friends miraculously stopping by because you were in the neighborhood, right?"

"No ma'am. Well, not really."

"He's not here, and he hasn't been around in a long time. Now if you'll excuse me." She went to close the door.

"Wait. Please, just hear me out for a second," I said, already embarrassed at how bad I was failing.

Mrs. Caufield rolled her insanely blue eyes. I was amazed that, even though she had to be somewhere in her sixties, she looked almost striking. Her hair was black, like I vaguely remembered it, cut short, and her face didn't have any visible wrinkles. I recalled that a lot of guys my age had the hots for her back when we were kids, but I couldn't remember if I was one of them. I must have been. This woman was well put together in her sixties. She had to be a real looker back in her forties.

"I'm listening, but make it quick. I don't know how long I can hold old Rex back here."

I hoped she would be able to hold the huge dog back a little longer. I didn't want to suffer the embarrassment of being chased down the street by an angry animal.

"I did go to school with Jason. My name is Darren Camponi. Jason and I were friends back in junior high, but I'll tell you right now that I was not good friends with him in high school, and that's not why I am here."

"You're Dr. Camponi's son?" she asked.

"Yes."

"How do I know that?"

"I have a driver's license, if you want to see it."

"What good will that do me?"

Again, I found myself not answering a question because I didn't know how.

"Hold on a second," she said, and closed the door. I could hear her rustling with the dog, and I guess she was putting him away somewhere. She left me standing on the porch for about five minutes, and I was just about to turn to leave when the door opened again.

"Come on in," she said, and I carefully stepped into the foyer of the house, afraid that old Rex was waiting around the corner to take a bite out of me. "Don't worry. I put Rex out back. He's really a good dog. He's just overprotective I guess."

"Nothing wrong with that," I said, silently thanking God. I don't get along with dogs too well. When I was young, we had a boxer who absolutely loved people. He never barked, was great with kids, and pretty much never bit anyone. Well, he never bit anyone but me. That dog must have bitten me in the ass half a dozen times, and he'd caught me in the hand and the leg a few times as well. That wasn't the worst of it. When I was twelve, I was playing in the backyard with Jack, the dog, and he up and bit me in the nuts. He didn't do any damage, at least none that I am acutely aware of, but it was the most frightening and painful experience I ever had, next to dating my ex-girlfriend. My father always said it must have been my bad karma, that I must have mistreated a dog in my previous life. My father wasn't spiritual or anything, he just liked to bust balls. And my dog liked to bite them.

"Come in. Have a seat." Mrs. Caufield led me up a small flight of stairs into a colonial-decorated living room. From my foggy memory, the house was exactly the same as it was when I had been there over twenty years before. The only difference was the omnipresent smell of Rex. I guess when you live with a dog, you get used to the smell. When you don't, a dog owner's house smells like old wet leaves. Everything was neat, and there wasn't a hint of dust on any of the oak furniture Mrs. Caufield had in the living room, but it stank like a kennel.

I sat down on the love seat, which was all wood with a flower-pattern cushion. The back was made of wood slats, and when I leaned back, I realized how uncomfortable it was. This was one of those living rooms that really served as a museum. My mother had the same sort of living room, complete with furniture no one ever sat on. I never understood why someone would go through the cost and the time to make a room that would never get used. One of those unsolvable mysteries that were peppered through my life.

Mrs. Caufield was holding a large book, and I realized it was Jason's high school yearbook. She must have used it to identify me, and I was instantly horrified that someone in the room had just seen that picture of me.

"With all the people stopping by recently saying they were friends of Jason, I have gotten a lot of use out of this. You're the only one who checked out." She walked over to me, opened the book to my picture, and pointed at it. "That's you."

I didn't need her to tell me that, and I certainly didn't need her to show me evidence of the ravages of adolescence. I had worn my father's blazer for that picture, and it was huge on me. I saw the Acne Mountains which had settled on my face for that picture and remembered why I hadn't had much luck with the ladies in high school. I hadn't seen the picture in years, and it was worse than I had originally thought. I should have won the "Most Likely to Never Get Laid" award, and I couldn't be sure if I didn't.

"Unfortunately," I said, rolling my eyes.

Mrs. Caufield chuckled. "Oh, it isn't that bad. Well, except for the oversized jacket."

Great. This lady had been through the harassment of police and strangers about her son, had buried her husband two years prior, but she found it possible to crack a joke about me and the ridiculous jacket I wore for Senior pictures.

"It was Dad's. My mother insisted I wear it."

"It's not terrible. I guess all kids do that."

But none looked as bad as me.

"So, Darren, if you are not here looking up Jason, why are you here?" Looking at her across the living room, it started to bother me about where I had seen her recently. It could have been anywhere, and was probably nothing important. Still, it nagged me.

"Well, I am here about Jason, but I didn't want to lie to you about being friends with him."

"Jason wasn't a popular kid in school, I am sure you know that."

"I do. I liked him, but we just ran with different crowds."

"Stop it. Jason didn't run with any crowd. He was a loner. Still is."

"Yeah, you're right."

"So, why are you here?" Laura pressed. I could tell that, though she felt comfortable knowing who I was, she really didn't want me around. Because of this, I wasn't sure if I should dive right into it with her. I had no idea what she knew about her son, and I was pretty certain she didn't want to hear bad news from me. Unfortunately for her, she really didn't have a choice if that was the case.

"I guess you know people are looking for Jason. Do you know why?"

"No," she answered bluntly, almost angrily.

"Are you sure?" I asked.

"Yes I am sure. What do you have to do with all of this?"

"Well, Mrs. Caufield, I am a private investigator. I received a call from an out of state colleague this morning, and he asked me to locate someone in New York for him. I agreed, and when he told me the name, I obviously recognized it, and I figured the best thing I could do was come and talk to you about it." While standing outside waiting to build up the courage to knock on the door, I had decided to come clean with Mrs. Caufield, hoping she would level with me and tell me everything she knew about Jason. I wasn't sure if it was going to work, but I figured I would get further with the truth. This wasn't some moralistic decision I had made. I just knew that the approach a few others had tried wasn't going to work for me.

"Someone hired you to find Jason?" she asked. Her tone didn't indicate any real surprise.

"Yes."

"Who?"

"That's really not important. It's just someone I do work for from time to time."

"Well, who hired him?" Mrs. Caufield tried to appear genuinely surprised about this whole thing. Something told me not to buy it.

"Did he work for a university out in Ohio?"

"Yes. In Cleveland. He quit about two months ago."

"Well, they are the ones who are looking for him," I said.

Mrs. Caufield looked out the window for a moment. I felt uncomfortable sitting there, even worse because I was delivering this poor lady bad news. It wasn't the first time I had to be the deliverer of bad news, but it didn't get easier each time I did it, that's for sure. Yet, I didn't feel too guilty because I had a feeling this wasn't *new* news.

"He told me people would be looking for him," she said, as if in a daze.

"When?"

"He called about three weeks ago."

"Have you seen him?" I asked.

"Not since Christmas."

"How was he then?"

"Normal. Well, normal for him. His brother said he seemed a little worried, but I didn't notice that. Jason was always a nervous boy, so I just thought he was being himself. I guess I was wrong."

"Did he say why he was leaving the university?" I asked.

"He said he had a better opportunity, but he wouldn't get into it with me. He just said that things were going to improve after a little while. He also told me that people would come looking for him, and he said to deny that he had spoken to me and to tell these people as little as possible. I thought that was strange behavior for him, but he had been working on some pretty important stuff for the university, and I had gotten used to his desire for secrecy long before this happened. What do you think he did wrong?"

"I don't know if he did anything wrong, though it sounds to me like he thought he did. The university that hired my colleague didn't get into specifics with him. They just want to know where Jason is. What did the police say?"

"What makes you think the police were here?" Mrs. Caufield asked.

"Your neighbor, the old man that lives three houses down, told me."

"You questioned Sam?"

"No, he just told me in casual conversation. He said that a few policemen had stopped by to talk to you."

"He's an old wash woman. And he's wrong. It wasn't the police that stopped by. It was men who worked for the government. They never really went into detail about why they wanted to talk to Jason, just that they needed to see him. I told them what Jason told me to tell them, and they have been back a few times since. Every once in a while, I see a strange car parked down the block or across the street. I'm pretty sure that's them."

That wasn't a good sign. If the feds were interested in finding Jason, it meant he had done something pretty bad. It didn't bode too well for me either, if they wanted to find him and couldn't. The last time I checked, the federal government had a few more resources at their disposal than I did when it came to finding someone.

"And they never said what they wanted him for?" I asked.

She shook her head. "No. They told me over and over how it was no big deal, which made me think it was a very big deal. I told Jason the last time I spoke to him, and he said not to worry, that it would all be taken care of soon. He swore he hadn't done anything wrong, and I believed him, but now I am not so sure."

"When did you last speak to him?" I asked.

"About a week ago. He gave me a number I could reach him at, but he hasn't told me where he is or when I would see him. Jesus, I think he is in a lot of trouble."

"Why don't you give me that number?" I asked, surprised at my own balls.

"No, I couldn't do that. You'll just turn him in to the university, and then God knows what will happen."

"Listen, ma'am, I'm going to find him one way or the other. It seems to me that he has to face whatever it is he has done, and I would assume the best way to do that is to turn himself in, or at least contact the university. I don't need that number to find him, but it would help, and he might even listen to me if he remembers who I am." Of course, most of this was pure, unadulterated bullshit, but it sounded nice coming out of my mouth, and it made some sort of sense. I was confident I would find Jason, only because there were only about two or three people I couldn't find out of the thousands I had located over the years.

"I don't know."

"Listen, Mrs. Caufield . . ."

"Call me Laura. I don't use that name anymore."

"Oh, right. And I am sorry to hear about Mr. Caufield. I have memories of him being a fun guy."

"Richard was a man who enjoyed life. It's always the good people who become victims of senseless violence. There are some days I still expect to see him in the kitchen cooking breakfast, but I know that's just dreams."

"I hear you've remarried. Congratulations," I said. It seemed appropriate, but I still had a hard time saying it.

"Thank you. Alan is a good man."

Boom, it finally hit me where I had seen Mrs. Caufield. She had been the woman on my ex-grandfather's arm at the restaurant the night before. I don't know how I missed it, but I guess my focus had been on Alan, the scumbag, instead of the lady he was with. I got instantly angry when she told me that was her new husband, and I wanted to tell her what I thought of him, but I figured that wouldn't gain me too much ground on getting that phone number she had. I must have had anger on my face, because Laura noticed it.

"Are you okay?"

"What? Yeah, I've just had migraines the last two days."

"Oh. You're a bit young to be getting those."

"Well, if you had the two days I've just had, then your head would be pounding too."

"I understand."

I didn't think she did. If I had told her that my best friend was the man who shot her husband, then maybe she might have had an inkling as to what I was feeling right then. I really wanted to talk, to tell her to divorce Alan immediately and save herself from an untimely death, but I really had no way to prove that to her, and she probably would have thought I was out of my mind. It also bothered me to have experienced so many coincidences in such a short time. I had read once that there are no coincidences, and I was beginning to subscribe to that theory. What I didn't realize was that the subscription card had already been mailed out in my name.

"I'm happy for you," I said. "It's nice that you got the chance to meet someone else after what happened."

"Alan was a friend I had known for years. We never ran around with each other or anything like that. To be honest, we had met at an AA meeting about six years ago, and after Richard was killed, something just happened. He'd be here today, but he had some business in Jersey."

Oh, how I was upset he wasn't home. I don't know what I would have done if I saw him right then. Probably nothing, though I dreamt of better than that. That's the beauty of the human mind. It allows you to carry out fantasies of strangling someone with their own socks without getting caught, or having to actually remove their shoes.

Laura looked at me, and I wondered if perhaps she was trying to figure out what I was thinking. Hopefully, she wasn't a mind reader.

"You know, Alan is worried about Jason as well. They never really have gotten a chance to talk, and I know Jason resents him a little bit, but Alan really wants to help. I didn't even tell Alan about the phone calls, only because Jason told me not to. I just wish there was something I could do," Laura said.

"You could help him by giving me the phone number. Listen, I'm not going to let Jason get into more trouble than he is already in, and like I said, I will find him anyway."

"I don't know. Jason will be pretty mad if I do something like that."

I realized I wasn't getting the number. I was angry, mostly because I was confronted with Alan for the second time in two days, and I really didn't want to take that anger out on this poor lady. I decided to give in, and play the nice guy role.

"I'll tell you what. I'll give you my number, and when you speak to Jason again, you tell him that I need to talk to him. Tell him I won't tell anyone about our conversation, and that all I want is to help him get through this mess." I took out a business card and wrote my cell number on the back. I handed it to Laura, who smiled, and walked toward the stairs.

"He's not a bad kid," she said.

"I know, ma'am. That's why I want to help. Just give him the number. Take care."

I walked down the stairs, opened the door, and felt the warm air hit my face. I didn't realize how high she had the air conditioning cranked up, but when the 80-degree wind hit me, I started sweating almost immediately. I made my way down the walkway and saw old Sam still standing on his lawn as if he were the king overlooking his kingdom.

Before I made it to the sidewalk, I heard Laura call out to me.

"Darren," she said, walking to meet me, "I don't know if I am doing the right thing, but I think I am." She handed me a piece of paper with a phone number written on it. "There's the number. Please don't prove me wrong and turn him in. He needs help, and maybe you can give that to him."

I took the piece of paper and put it in my jeans pocket. "I will do the best I can." That wasn't a complete lie. And when Laura said, "Thank you," I almost felt compelled to do whatever I could for Jason.

Chapter 4

When I got back to my car, old man Sam was still purveying his lawn. I can't really be sure what it was he stared at, but I was happy it wasn't me. He barely noticed me when I approached my car, and if it wasn't for the chirp of my alarm deactivating, I might have gotten away scott free.

"Told you he ain't been around," he said, lighting another cigarette. Part of me wanted to tell him to quit, yet, I knew that was a waste of time. The guy had to be in his late seventies, and if smoking was one of the few pleasures he enjoyed, who was I to ruin it for him? Plus, he had lived this long inhaling cigarette smoke.

"Well, you were right about that."

"It's a shame what that lady is going through. Cars staking out her house. Poor woman can't even go and walk the dog without someone watching."

"How often do you see cars on the block?" I asked.

"Every day, son." He gestured toward a Mercury parked down the block. "See that car there? No one on this block owns it. The guy in there thinks he's slick, but I see him pop his head up from time to time. He's watchin' her all right. If I were younger, I'd knock on his window and tell him to get the hell away from here. Just his bein' here unnerves me."

"I understand," I said.

"And I'm guessing I'll be seeing your car parked on my block from time to time."

"No, I doubt that."

"Well, I know what yours looks like, so I won't have any problems knocking on your window and saying hello," Sam said.

I couldn't tell if that was a threat, and I hoped it wasn't. Of course, I had no intentions of staking out the Caufield residence, and I certainly didn't want to get into a scuffle with a senior citizen if I had to. I did take notice of his house number, and decided to get whatever information I could on old Sam. I didn't doubt I could call him and get some information, and in my business, information is invaluable.

"I don't think that's going to happen. And I wouldn't worry about that guy parked down the street. After another week or so, they'll realize they are wasting resources having him there."

"Probably. But I'd really like to know who 'they' are."

"Like I said, I wouldn't worry about it."

"You don't have to. You don't live here," Sam said.

"Of course."

"Well, you take care. Hopefully, I won't be seeing you around."

"You won't. Take care."

I got into my car and pulled away fast, just to aggravate the old man a little bit. I don't know why, but I guess I needed to aggravate someone. With the news of Jason's problems and Alan's remarriage, my mind was racing from one direction to the next. I needed to focus on my approach to finding Jason, but my mind seemed more content on staying with Alan. It made no sense, only because there was nothing I could do about it. I couldn't tell anyone, I couldn't confront Alan, and I couldn't prove any of my far-fetched theories about him. Bottom line was, he was a piece of shit, and in this world pieces of shit end up on top.

* * *

Like I said, because I was in such close vicinity to my parents' house, I felt obliged to pay them a visit. I hadn't been by in about two weeks, which was near criminal activity. I had even missed two Sunday dinners, which certainly was criminal. My parents were both Italian, and though they were born here in the United States, they still carried on certain traditions, the most important of which being the Sunday dinner. When I had first moved out years before, my mother was depressed, and my father, who had always stayed out of my personal life, sat me down and told me that I was expected to keep the

Sunday tradition whenever possible. You could say I felt threatened about this, and for the first three years or so, I made it every Sunday. I tapered off a bit after that, mainly because my sister got away with not showing up for the lamest reasons imaginable. This didn't work for me though. My sister always got away with murder, and I couldn't even get away with petty theft. I guess that was because my father was more involved with me than he was with her, and because I wasn't married. Marriage was the escape from one life sentence, but it got you another one. My family wasn't happy unless you were serving hard time.

When I pulled up to my house, it must have been about 2 o'clock. I saw both cars in the driveway. My father's ten-year-old BMW coupe and my mother's pride and joy, a Ford Conversion van. She had it since we were kids, and even though she really didn't have much of a use for it anymore, she refused to get rid of it, stating that it was important for when she wanted to drive her grandchildren around. Most people who have met my mother couldn't picture her five-foot frame behind the wheel of such a large vehicle, but she drove that thing like an experienced trucker. That van had made appearances at several high school parties my sister and I tried to attend over the years, and it had become a common practice for friends to come and find me at such parties to warn me of her arrival. All of them feared her, mainly because she had no problems confronting them, taking beers away, and generally causing a scene. How I made it through my high school years, I have no idea.

The minute I stepped foot out of my car, the front door opened, and I saw my mother standing there. She looked at me, and then went back inside. This was her way of letting me know she was upset with me, and I felt like the wayward son she always accused me of being. I had flashbacks to when I was a teenager, coming home late, or bringing home a report card that was less than stellar. There I was, 34 years old, feeling like a kid because I couldn't make Sunday dinner. Ah, the powers of maternity.

When I got to the door, my father greeted me. He gave me the stern look of an unhappy father at first, then smiled and hugged me.

"You're alive," he said.

"Hey Dad." His embrace was firm, as it always was, and he patted me on the back.

"To what do we owe the pleasure?"

"I was in the neighborhood," I said.

"I thought you forgot how to get here."

"Come on, Dad, enough."

"Oh, you know it doesn't bother me, but you're mother, well, you know how she gets. She thinks you don't like her cooking or something." That, of course, was a total untruth. My mother could make shoe leather taste good.

"I've been busy," I said.

"Of course. Well, come on in and take your medicine," Dad said.

He opened the door, and we walked in. The entrance to the house was a large hallway with beige ceramic tiles that had been there for what seemed like centuries. My parents had decorated the house when they first moved in, and didn't see the need to update it. They really didn't have to, and I appreciated the fact that every time I was there, it all was the same as it was when I was growing up.

Dad was dressed in his usual Saturday attire: black sweatpants, sneakers, and a white t-shirt that was almost transparent from so much wear. Normally Dad was a pretty sharp dresser, but he was like me when it came to lounging. The only difference was, he would have the balls to go to the store dressed like that. He was in pretty good shape for his age, maybe about ten pounds heavier than he was when he was younger. Overall, he was a handsome man, even with the wire rim glasses that always sat on the bridge of his nose. His only problem was that he lost most of the hair atop his head, but for him, it looked okay. I just hoped on what they say about a son following in his maternal grandfather's footsteps when it came to hair. My grandfather, who had died at sixty, had bushy gray hair. I'd take that tradeoff, a massive heart attack in my sixties, for a full head of hair up until that point.

My father had threatened to shave his head completely if he lost any more hair, and I did whatever I could to sway him away from that idea. In my opinion, only young guys and black men can get away with a bald head. This isn't racism on my part. I just think that most white men look ridiculous completely bald, whereas black men actually look distinguished. The only white men that can get away with the bald head are the big, stocky sort, and it wasn't because it looked good. It was only because no one had the guts to tell such a large man the truth. My father was tall, but he was lanky, and a bald head would make him look like an idiot.

47

We made our way upstairs, toward the kitchen and past my mother's museum living room. Our furniture in there was purchased sometime in the early seventies, and it looked pretty much the same as it did when it was purchased. The only damage that had been done to it came courtesy of my good friend Jack the boxer, who decided it was his territory, and marked it accordingly. Rest in peace, Jacko.

My mother was doing something in the sink, and when I walked over, I noticed she was working on a leg of lamb, which was probably the main course for Sunday. This would remind her of my absence from the two Sundays prior, and I knew my best bet was to confront the situation as soon as possible.

"Hey Mom," I said, hugging her gently from behind. She didn't pull away, but she didn't do or say anything either. "What you got there?"

"Something you won't be eating tomorrow, I presume." Mom never pulled any punches, that's for sure.

"I'll be here tomorrow," I said, not sure if that was anywhere near the truth.

"Right. I'll hold my breath."

"No, really."

She turned around, looked me in the eyes, and then finally kissed me hello. "You know, you're life can't be so full of things to do that you can't make it here for one day out of the week. Your sister has two kids, a dog, and works part time, but she still makes it when she can." What that meant was that Debbie stopped by maybe once every two months, but she was an angel in my mother's eyes because she constantly complained about how busy she was. She had learned to work the system, and like I said before, she was married, so she was free and clear.

"I know. I've just been busy the last two weeks. Working on cases."

"Since when do you work on Sunday?"

"Since the landlord likes to get his rent on time," I said.

My mother turned back to the lamb. "You could move back home if things are that tough."

The odds of me moving back home were even worse than me getting married the next day. It wasn't that my parents were bad, they certainly weren't, but at 34, I'd have to be a complete loser to move back home. I couldn't use this argument with either my mother or my father, because they would never take it the right way.

"It's not that bad."

"But it's bad enough that you have to work on Sunday." Mom, though, a kind and loving person, was not the one you want to get into any sort of argument with. She knew how to play the guilt card like a champion, and she went for the throat whenever she needed to, even with her own children.

"It's not like that. It just turned out that the last two weeks have been that way," I insisted.

"You need money, or something?" my father asked. He had been silent for this whole exchange, and now he decided to get involved at the wrong time. Thanks Dad.

"No Dad, not at all. You know what they say about making hay when the sun shines."

"He's just been too busy to stop by, Michael, that's all. Right Darren?"

For the third time in one day, I found myself not knowing how to correctly answer a question, so I didn't.

"Well, enough of this. He's here now, and he says he'll be here tomorrow, so let's not make him uncomfortable so he doesn't want to come back." *Thanks again, Dad. Really.*

I sat down at the kitchen table, facing them. My mother stayed at the sink, and my father came down and sat next to me. He smiled, as if he understood what I was going through. He had been the recipient of my mother's guilt trips countless times over the years.

"So, what brings you into the neighborhood, a case?" Dad asked.

I normally didn't talk too much about what I was working on with anyone, even my parents. They understood this completely, and when my father asked, he really was only making conversation, not trying to get any information out of me.

"Yeah. Interesting one, too." Because this case involved someone they knew, and because I wouldn't be giving away anything confidential, I figured it would be okay to tell them what I was working on. "Remember Jason Caufield?"

"The one you went to high school with?" my mother asked, not looking up from the sink.

"That's the one."

"What about him?" my father asked.

"I'm not sure. I got a call from a fellow detective who works in

Ohio. He wanted me to find someone, and that someone turned out to be Jason."

"His mother's the one who lost her husband at the convenience store shooting a couple of years ago, right?"

"That's the one."

"Poor woman. She had to live with a cop for a husband, probably waiting up at night hoping not to get the call, and she loses him to some animal after he retires." My mother was always up on what went on in the town. She wasn't a gossip monger or anything like that, but being married to the main pediatrician in town afforded her the opportunity to come across tons of information from mothers who came into the office and needed someone to talk to.

"I treated Jason when he was a kid. He was the one who won the science contest out in California when he was in high school, right?" Dad asked.

"Yep."

"Why would anyone be looking for him?"

"I wish I knew the details, but I don't. The university he worked for wants to find him. Something about stealing intellectual property."

"Really," my father said.

"Yeah. It's strange, too. I mean, I've never worked for a university before, but my colleague said they were pretty intent on finding him."

"Did they say what he stole?" my mother asked.

"No. I guess it must have been something important."

"That's so ridiculous. How can a company or a university decide what intellectual property is? If you think of something when you work there, it automatically becomes theirs? That's not fair."

"Well, I guess that's how it works. They pay you to research, and if you discover something, they are the ones who benefit from it. You can get the Nobel Prize or anything else, but they get the cash."

"I don't remember Jason being a troublemaker," my father said. "He was a complete hypochondriac, but not a troublemaker."

"He wasn't, but I guess people change as they get older."

"That poor woman, Mrs. Caufield. She loses her husband, and now her son is on the run," my mother said. I wanted to tell her about Laura's remarriage, but that would require me to bring up my grandmother's death. The loss of my grandmother changed my mom, closing one of the several doors to her large heart. The world was a degree colder because of it, and I don't mean just my world. Bringing up such a bad experience didn't seem to make sense.

"I heard she remarried," my father said, thus bringing me closer to mentioning Alan. Did they know about it? I was pretty sure they didn't, because they undoubtedly would have said something to me about it.

"So, what? Did you go see Mrs. Caufield?" my mother asked.

"I did."

"How is she?"

"Well, remarried. Worried about her son, and confused about what's going on."

"Has she seen Jason?" Mom asked.

"She said she hasn't, and I believe her."

"So, what are you going to do next?"

"She gave me a phone number I can reach him at, but I am not sure if I should just call him. I mean, he might remember me, but we weren't what you would call great friends in high school, so he would probably be suspicious."

"You thought he was a geek," my mother said.

"I did."

"You were always so judgmental." *I was?*

"He was a strange kid, Mom. When you're young, that sort of thing is important. Maybe I was wrong for not being friends with him, but it's not like I can do anything about that now."

"That's what happens to kids who are outcast at a young age. They become troubled, and then they go and do something stupid," Mom said.

"Well, I don't know for sure if he did anything stupid, but I promised Mrs. Caufield I would do what I could to help him out. I just don't know what that is."

"You're not going to turn him in, are you?" This question came from my father, and he delivered it with an expression that told me to do the right thing, whatever that might be.

"Well, if I don't, I don't get paid, and I might piss off a colleague who has given me some good business over the years."

"Again with the money. You know Darren, your father turned away a lot of money many times. He could have been one of those doctors that milked people for every penny they had, but instead he chose to work on people for free more times than he should have.

51

You don't have to go and ruin some kid's life just because you need a few dollars."

"Hey, I'm not going to ruin his life. He made the decision to run away with someone else's property, be it intellectual, or some computer from the lab. He broke the law, according to the university. And I am not saying I will definitely turn him in. I'll try to talk to him, I guess, and if he's willing to let me help him, then maybe I will. If he won't, and I find out where he is, then I'll have to do what I have to do. I was hired for a job, and I will complete the job."

"He has no choice, Maggie. Darren's not going to do anything wrong if he doesn't have to, right?"

"Right."

I was beginning to feel uncomfortable, probably because I was really getting into more detail than I should about a case. And also because, in the back of my mind, I wanted to talk about Alan. I shouldn't have worried so much about it.

"You meet Mrs. Caufield's new husband?" my mother asked, still not looking up from the sink. I glanced over at my father, who rolled his eyes, letting me know that they knew.

"No. He wasn't home."

"Thank God," my mother said, "that piece of shit." Now, understand, curse words rarely, if ever, came from my mother's mouth, and when they did, it usually signified either intense amounts of pain, or anger. Even when we did something horribly wrong as kids, my mother rarely cursed. Most of her curse words were in Italian, like "fongul." the Italian for the "f" word, and she really didn't consider such the word a curse word. For her to refer to Alan as a piece of shit was indicative of her deep hatred for the man. They didn't get along while he was married to my grandmother, mainly because he resented the relationship between his wife and her daughter. He also thought that, because my father was a doctor and my mother didn't work, we had tons of money. He was wrong. We lived a fairly good life, but my father put in ridiculous hours, and my mother did work as a receptionist at the office when she wasn't shuttling around us kids. To this day, I don't know how much money my parents made, but whatever it was, it came the hard way.

"Yeah, I was happy I didn't see him." I wanted to mention that I had seen him the night before in the restaurant, but that would require me to explain who I went to the restaurant with and what happened.

Like I said earlier, I didn't mention Tanya to my family. Thinking about that reminded me of how bad things went at the restaurant. I hadn't even thought of it for most of the day and I was unhappy that I had to be reminded of it.

"I don't know why such a beautiful woman would be attracted to such a man," my father said. Normally, his talk of another woman's beauty would incur the wrath of my mother, but I guess he knew he could slide this one by, given the circumstances.

"He's a conniver," my mother said. "I don't know how I let my mother marry him."

"I don't remember you having a choice. Plus, despite the fact of what sort of man he was, he made her happy at the time. That was the most important thing," my father said.

"Was it Michael? Because she was dying, it was okay for me to let her marry such a piece of garbage?" Now Mom was looking up from the sink, and I sort of wished she hadn't. She had fire in her eyes, and I could see that she was hurting as well.

"Maggie, this all happened almost twenty years ago."

"Well, I remember it all like it was yesterday."

"I know, honey, I know." I thought my father was going to get up and console her right then like he always did when she got upset, but I figured he knew this wasn't one of those times. She needed to vent, and attack the leg of lamb in the sink with a passion which she was doing.

"I wouldn't be surprised if that man had something to do with this," my mother said, a bit of anger lingering on the end of that sentence.

"I doubt that," I said.

"I wouldn't. I wouldn't put anything past him."

"I'll give you that," my father said. "Anyway, let's talk about something else. Darren, did you hear your nephew hit a home run in his first baseball game last week?"

Of course I hadn't. I spoke to my sister only when we saw each other at a family function. We got along well, it's just that we were both so busy, and neither of us were phone people.

The change of topic seemed to work, because my mother was concentrating on the lamb, and she didn't say anything.

"No."

"It was great. Your sister brought over the video tape last Sunday.

53

Kid's got a good swing. Reminds me of you a little bit."

"If only he inherits my good looks as well, the kid will have it made."

"Almost makes you want to have a son of your own, doesn't it?"

Well, no, it didn't. I loved my niece and nephews to death, but I preferred giving them back to my sister when I was done. I decided not to answer Dad's question.

"He's going to take after Charlie," my mother said. Even though I was happy to change the conversation from Alan to something else, I didn't appreciate the topic turning to me and my romantic life. Uncle Charlie was my mother's brother who never got married, and died of a bad liver at forty-five. He was an unashamed alcoholic, a helpless gambler, and a convicted womanizer. Good company I was being associated with. Good company.

"He's not like Charlie."

"Look at him. He lives on his own, never brings any girls over here, and goes out with his friends all the time." That wasn't all true. Most of it was, but not all.

"He's young. He'll find someone eventually."

I really loved being talked about like I wasn't there. My parents did this often. It must be somewhere in the guidebook.

"He's never going to get married. He's going to be single the rest of his life."

"Stop it, Maggie."

"You do want to get married, don't you Darren?"

What was it with unanswerable questions?

"I don't know, Dad. I really don't think about it."

"Well, you should. You are getting older."

"Didn't you just say I was young?"

"Yeah, you are now. Probably having a great time being single and all." I was?

"It's not like that. Women are different these days. You either find someone who has been married already and has a kid, or they are completely out of their mind."

"You're too picky," my father said, which pretty much hit the nail on the head.

"He doesn't like to date," my mother added.

"I'm gay." No, I'm not, but this was my signal that I didn't want to talk about this. Of course, that signal never made it to its destination.

"Stop that."

"What if I was?"

"You're not. We didn't raise you that way." Of course, homosexuality was based on the upbringing of the individual.

"No, of course I'm not. But I'd rather talk about something else other than my love life."

"He's right Maggie, it's none of our business."

"So, what, he'll give me grandkids when I'm dying in a hospital bed?"

"Stop it Mom."

"Your sister is married and moving on with her life. You're going to have kids when you are too old to enjoy them."

I wanted to say something about how kids didn't seem all that enjoyable to me, but I knew that would take the conversation in another wrong direction. As you can see, this was really a losing battle for me.

"I'll have kids. I'll give you dozens of them. I might have already."

Luckily, my mother had nothing readily available to throw at me, because the look on her face indicated that she wanted to do exactly that.

"Don't talk like that Darren," my father said.

"I'm just kidding."

"Well, it's not funny," my mother said. My humor is always lost on my audience.

"I thought it was."

"You think everything is funny." This was true.

"Nothing wrong with having a sense of humor," my father said. "You hungry?" he asked, offering yet another successful change of topic.

"I could eat."

"Probably be the first home cooked meal he's had in weeks." Again, another hauntingly true statement from my mother.

"What've you got?" I asked.

* * *

After my goodbye kiss to my mother, my father walked me to the door and said, "Just make it here tomorrow if you can. I understand. And watch out for yourself. I didn't want to say anything in front of your mother, but this case you're working on stinks of trouble."

"I'll be alright Dad."

"I don't doubt that. Just watch your back, okay?"

"Okay."

With that, I got into my car, and headed back home to do a little investigation. My father's words stuck in the back of my mind. Even though I told him everything was fine, I did agree with his assessment of the situation. Something wasn't right with this whole thing, and though I wasn't worried for myself, I did want to get to the bottom of it all. That started with Jason Caufield and I decided I would spend a few hours investigating him. Before the afternoon was over, I intended to find out everything the guy had done since high school. My afternoons never worked out they way I intended them to.

Chapter 5

I made it back to my apartment by four, and there were a few messages on my answering machine when I got there. One of them was from Rich, the friend I was supposed to go bar-hopping with later in the evening. He had called to confirm, which made me wonder why he bothered to email me in the first place. I deleted that message, and the one after it, which was from my father. He had called before I stopped by, sternly recommending that I stop by the next day. The last one was from someone named Dave Hovelle, or something like that. He wanted to know if he had the right Darren Camponi, the investigator, and if I was that Camponi, he wanted me to call him. He didn't say what it was about, and I had no idea who it was, so I deleted the message without writing down the number. I had more important things to do than call back complete odd strangers.

I had left my computer on, so I didn't have to wait for it to boot up this time. I sat down at my desk, and went to work on one of the databases. I got charged by the minute by the companies that ran such databases, but Mike had said the university would reimburse me for all my expenses. It was a lot more fun using them on someone else's tab, and I decided I would take my time and get every little bit of information I could.

Before I actually started to accrue charges, I figured it would be a good idea to call Mike and let him know where I was at this point. I also wanted to make sure that the large bill I was about to ring up would actually be paid.

"American," he answered on the third ring.

"It's Darren."

"Found the guy already?"

"I wish. This is going to be a bit more involved than I thought."

"What, finding a science geek has become more difficult?"

"Seems that way. I don't think the university was on the level with you about this one," I said.

"Why do you say that?"

"The feds are on his tail."

Mike paused for a moment, and then said, "Yeah, that's not too unusual. The university might have contacted them first. I mean, once the guy crossed the Ohio border with whatever is in his head and in his suitcase, that becomes a federal offense, no?"

I hadn't thought of it that way, but to be honest, Mike didn't sound too convincing. Something was going on.

"Well, they have the mother's house staked out. Neighbor said he sees the cars every day, and the mother said the same thing."

"She tell you if she's seen him?"

"She said she hadn't."

"Believe her?" Mike asked.

"I have no reason not to."

"Sure you do. She's his mother. You think she's gonna give her son away?"

"Probably not, but I think I earned her trust."

"Her protective interests in her son will go far deeper than her trust in you."

"You're probably right, but I don't think she lied to me," I said.

"Okay. You get anything else?"

Now, right here is when I should have told Mike about the phone number Laura gave me. After all, the guy hired me for the job, but it was his case. He had the right to know anything I came across, but I felt the need to hold this from him, which put me in an awkward place.

"Not really. I was just about to go online and find out whatever I can about this guy. You think the university will eat that expense."

"Of course they will, but I think you should focus your efforts on the mother and try to find out where this bastard is hiding. He could have been in the attic while you were at the house for all you know."

"The neighbor told me he hadn't seen the guy at all. He's the type that would notice such things."

"I guess that might be reliable information, but I still think you're wasting your time looking for a paper trail on the guy. He hasn't been in hiding long enough."

"I'll find him."

"I know you will. Just do it as fast as you can so we can be done with this," Mike said.

"I will."

"And try not to run up the bill too much. I don't know how deep the university pockets go on this thing."

I had the feeling they went quite deep, but I didn't say that.

"Call you if I get something."

"Thanks."

I hung up the phone feeling less confident about Mike than I had before. I didn't know what exactly had my suspicions aroused, but once they were awake, there was no putting them to sleep. My father's words of watching my back echoed in my head once again.

By five o'clock, I had a pretty good amount of information on Jason. He had started college at Stonybrook University on Long Island, a well-respected state college that specialized in the sciences. Though it was a good school, I had thought that Jason would have earned a scholarship to a bigger school somewhere else in the country. Maybe he didn't want to be too far away from home, or maybe Stonybrook offered him something the others didn't. After two years, he transferred to UCLA, where he completed his bachelors, and went on for his doctorate. He received this around the time he was 26, and it looked like he stayed in California for a year or two. I knew this because he had utility bills for that time period.

Things got interesting after that. It appeared as though he moved to Washington, D.C. after leaving California, but I saw no record of employment there. The only evidence I had was a residence he was registered at in that area, and a conviction on a speeding ticket. He continually used his Merrick address as well, sending random credit card statements and other unimportant things there. From the time he was 26 until he was almost 30, Jason had no record of employment whatsoever. This didn't mean he wasn't working, but none of the credit bureaus or any other database that I consulted showed employment. In 1997, Jason took the job at the University of Ohio at Cleveland. He moved there, and his residence appeared to be on campus. He received another speeding violation in Ohio, so I guess he

59

liked to drive fast. He kept the same 1989 Toyota Celica registered, and it didn't appear that he bought any other automobile. He also didn't seem to buy much, because his credit card accounts stayed at or about zero for most of this time period. I would assume that a university researcher would get paid decent money, but perhaps I was wrong. I decided to find out.

A quick check into his financial information proved my assumption. Normally, I would need a court order, or some other legal paperwork to perform such a search, but I had connections that could do it for me without them. This wasn't totally illegal, but it certainly flirted with criminal behavior. That was my connection's problem, not mine. Jason had almost $120,000 dollars in a savings account, and almost half that in his checking. That was a lot of money for a guy his age to have, and I figured he was a penny pincher. Why that money wasn't locked up somewhere earning better interest was beyond me. Maybe Jason knew something was going to happen and he was stockpiling cash up in case he had to make a run for it. What he must not have realized was he would have a hard time getting the money without someone detecting it. He knew the feds were after him, his mother had told him that, and he must have known they would be watching his accounts.

Upon further inspection of his bank records, I noticed that he had made a small withdrawal, about six hundred bucks, the previous week. He had done it at a Washington branch, alerting me and anyone who was looking for him that he was in that area. I took out the piece of paper Laura had handed me with his phone number on it, and noticed she didn't supply an area code. It looked like a cell phone number based on Long Island. The first three digits were the same as my old cell number. He probably carried around that phone so his mother could reach him, and I figured he probably had been on Long Island recently to set up the account. This probably meant that he had gone to see his mother and that Laura had lied to me about not seeing him. I couldn't blame her, but it did make me feel less confident in my ability to read people.

I printed up all the important documents on Jason and stashed them in a blank manila folder like I did with all information I got on a case. I should have called Mike to tell him that I thought Jason was in Washington but I didn't for two reasons. One, I wasn't entirely sure that was where he was and, two, and more importantly, I didn't like the way I felt about Mike. I knew this was all without reason, but I never walked away from a bad situation wishing I had been less cautious. Mike would get his information on a need to know basis, and he didn't need to know anything until I was confident telling him. My next step was to call the number Laura gave me. If my assumptions were correct, Jason would answer the phone thinking I was his mother. I didn't think she had called him after my visit. Actually, I hoped she hadn't, because all of my plans would be shattered to pieces if she had.

I decided to call from my home line, which had Caller ID disabled. Before I did that, I called a friend of mine to help out.

"Hello?" my friend, Darlene said when she picked up the phone. Darlene worked for Sprint, the cellular phone company. I had met her a few years before when I was working on a case, and we had hit it off pretty well. She had done some work for another investigator friend of mine, the sort of work that she could lose her job for. She always said that Sprint never paid her enough, and screw them if they wanted to fire her. Both of us were helplessly single, and despite the fact that our relationship had crossed the professional/sexual barrier one night after too many margaritas, we both knew we could never date, and stayed professional friends.

"It's your dream boy," I said.

"Ricky Martin? How nice of you to call."

"The other dream boy."

"Oh, Harrison Ford. Haven't heard from you in a while."

"Stop it."

"Oh, it's you Darren. What do you want now?"

"You could try asking me how I'm doing."

"You didn't ask me. You only lied about being my dream boy, getting me all excited for nothing."

Darlene was definitely one of the most down-to-earth people I had ever encountered. When I said that we both knew a relationship between us would never work, I neglected to say that I had the hots for her, and I would have dated her in a heartbeat if she would have let me. Darlene was an overly attractive female trapped by such beauty. She had long light-brown hair and glowing green eyes that were constantly paying attention to her surroundings. She stood about 5'4" and, physically, she had what I considered a perfect body. To achieve that consideration, she had to have 34D breasts, a tight ass, and curves in all the right places, which she did. The best part about it was she was either unaware of these proportions or she didn't care. I voted the latter.

"Sorry to ruin your day. How are you doing?"

"The same. Underpaid, overworked, and under laid."

"I could fix one of those for you."

"I bet, but I'm not that desperate."

"Thanks."

"Don't mention it. What can I do for you?"

"I need a cell trace. Long Island number. I think it is located in D.C. though."

"Then what do you need me to trace it for?"

"To find out for sure?"

"Oh, of course. Ex-girlfriend on the run from you or something?"

"It's a legitimate case, Darlene."

"Like the last time?"

I won't get into that, because, well, it is embarrassing.

"This is serious."

"Okay, okay. What's the number?" Darlene asked.

I gave it to her.

"That's a Long Island number. Registered to a Laura Swenson. Who are you stalking now?" Swenson was Alan's last name. So, Jason had been to see his mother. I made a mental note of that.

"I'm not stalking anyone but you. That's the mother of the guy I am trying to find."

"Tangled web you weave."

"Shut up. If I call the number in a minute or so, you think you can trace it?"

"No problem. Just make sure the call lasts the full thirty seconds this time."

"I will. Jesus, you don't forget a thing."

"Right. You getting married yet?" Darlene asked.

"Of course not. You?"

"Dumb question."

"Hey, maybe after you get off tonight, you can meet me and a friend for drinks."

"Dumber question."

"It wouldn't kill you."

"That remains to be seen. Just make the call and then I'll call you when I have a fix on it."

She hung up, and I dialed the cell number.

"Yeah," Jason said when he answered the phone.

"Jason Caufield?"

"Who is this, and how did you get this number."

"Jason, they know. They're on to you. They're looking for you. You're in trouble."

"Who is this?"

"That's not important. People are looking for you, Jason. That's important. And they are going to find you," I said, trying to sound as serious as possible.

"Yeah? You think so? Trust me, they won't find me."

"Maybe not, but how long do you think you can run?"

"How did you get this number?"

"Also not important. What is important is that you come out of hiding and face your problems. You can't avoid them forever."

"Fuck you." He hung up.

The call lasted about thirty-two seconds, which was more than enough for the trace. Within ten seconds, my home phone rang.

"What've you got?"

"Is this Darren Camponi?" It wasn't Darlene. It was a man, and I didn't recognize the voice.

"It is, who's this?"

"My name is David Hovelle. I called you earlier. Left a message."

"Yes, I got it, but I didn't recognize the name."

"As you shouldn't."

"What can I do for you?"

"I think it is more a matter of what I can do for you." I didn't like this guy's tone of voice.

"And what's that?" I asked.

"Keep you from getting into trouble you don't need."

"How are you going to do that for me?"

"By telling you to stay away from Jason Caufield and stop investigating him," Hovelle said in quite and unfriendly tone.

"Who told you I was investigating Jason Caufield?"

"Don't play stupid, Mr. Camponi. Just heed my advice. We know you are trying to find him, and I am telling you not to bother. It's not your problem. Don't make it yours."

"Why should I listen?" I asked.

"I think you know why."

The man hung up, leaving me with the cordless phone in my hand and even more worries on my mind. My initial thought was that Mr. Hovelle was a fed, which scared me a little, but it wasn't going to stop me from doing my job.

The phone rang again, while it was still in my hand, and I jumped when it did. I hesitated answering it, but I was certain this time it was Darlene.

"Hello," I said, warily.

"Good idea to make a phone call when you knew I was trying to get you," Darlene said.

"Wasn't my idea. What've you got?"

"You were right. The phone is being used in Washington. Well, not exactly in D.C., but in a suburb called Crystal City. Ever hear of it?"

"No," I said, still thinking of Hovelle.

"Nice place. Friend of mine went to college down there, and I visited a few times. Good party town."

"Of course you would know that."

"That's how you treat me for doing you a favor?"

"You charge for favors."

"This one's on the house, because I get the feeling you were telling the truth about it being legitimate. Besides, I had nothing exciting to do today anyway."

"The people that hired me will pay."

"Don't worry about it." Darlene gave me the most detailed location she could on Jason's cell number. She had actually narrowed it down to less than a mile radius, which was pretty impressive, even for her. I jotted the information down, realizing that I would be taking a little trip.

After I hung up with her, I logged onto the Internet and booked myself a flight to Dulles International Airport in D.C. I had only been to Washington once before, on a field trip in junior high, so this would be a nice little venture, I thought. Just before I booked the flight and the return flight with my credit card, I remembered that I wouldn't be able to bring my gun on the plane, and for some reason, I didn't feel too secure going down there without it. I cancelled the order, and then logged onto Amtrak's website and booked a train. For some inexplicable reason, Amtrak didn't check passengers for weapons. Maybe because the last person that tried to hijack a train was Jesse James. Whatever the reason, I was happy they didn't, affording me to get to Washington armed.

After completing the transaction, I remembered the promise I made to my mother about coming over the next day. I was about to call her and let her know immediately, but I decided she would take the information better if I called her from Washington. At least then, I had a chance that she would believe me.

Now, it might seem odd that I had gone against my original intentions of calling Jason, telling him who I was and offering help. After speaking to Mike, my suspicions had gotten the best of me. Also, I got the feeling that Jason wouldn't have been too receptive to my help. I had promised Laura that I would do the best I could to help her son, and I intended to do that. I didn't plan on having the feds call me and offer a veiled threat, either, and Laura hadn't been totally up front with me. I was on my own with this case, and my interest was at its highest level considering what was happening. My best bet was to go to Washington, locate Jason, and then play the "old high school friend" routine. Though he was looking out for suspicious people, I didn't think he would totally shun me when I went down there.

I shut down my computer, packed a bag with two changes of clothes, one casual and one suit, and got together all of the things I would need to bring with me to Washington. I packed two guns into the bag—my .40 caliber Glock and my small Ruger .22. Packing the guns, I felt like an assassin. I thought about returning the Ruger to its place in my night table drawer, and then decided to just take it. I kept the Walther PPK at the small of my back, where it had been so long that day that I almost forgot I still was wearing it. I zipped up the bag and put it by the front door. I then changed into a long sleeve blue dress shirt, kept the jeans on, and headed out to meet my friend Rich for drinks. Luckily for me, my train didn't leave Penn Station until noon.

Chapter 6

Rich had told me to meet him at a place called Croxley's Ales, located about five minutes from me in Rockville Centre. It was one of those micro-brewery places, where you can get any beer you could possibly imagine, except for name brands like Budweiser or Coors. I didn't go to the place too often, not because I didn't like it, but instead because I usually drank too much when I went there and few women frequented the joint. It was a guy hangout, complete with a dark atmosphere, seven televisions showing all types of sports, and cute female bartenders wearing tight black pants. Croxley's boasted over seventy different beers on tap, ranging from Pet's Wicked Ale to Blackened Voodoo Obsession to German beers I couldn't pronounce, let alone spell. I didn't drink any of that crap. It was all just the same type of dark thick bitter beer that I couldn't imagine anyone getting down their throat. Despite my repulsion to these beers, guys drank them by the gallon in that place. I usually drank John Courage, a British beer I had liked when I visited London back when I had money I didn't know what to do with. John Courage was what they considered an amber bitter, whatever the hell that meant. It really wasn't amber and it certainly wasn't bitter. Rich drank those disgusting concoctions I mentioned earlier, and called me a sissy for drinking Courage.

When I got to the bar, it was about seven-thirty, and there were about eight guys at the bar, watching a football game. It was a new football league that was started by some guy who didn't seem to understand no one liked to watch football in the warm weather. Well, no one but the morons at the bar. One of morons sitting at the bar was Rich, who was passing the time hitting on the same blonde bartender he hit on every time I went there with him. From the looks of things, he was already a little drunk, and he wasn't making any more ground on the bartender.

"Hey asshole," I said, patting him on the back, "why don't you lay off my girl here?" The bartender smiled, but it wasn't one of those smiles that made me think she liked me. It was more of a smile that indicated she was happy Rich had someone else there to talk to beside her.

"You're late," Rich said.

"You never gave me an exact time."

"You know I always get here at six-thirty on a Saturday."

"I forgot the bartender's schedule. Sorry."

"Shut the fuck up and drink your beer." Next to Rich was a nice tall glass of John Courage. Despite what they said about Rich, he was a good guy in my book. We had gone to school together, from elementary all the way up to high school. He was about 6'4" and put together like a linebacker. He'd always worked out when we were kids, and he kept himself in shape. The only thing that belied his age was the grays peppered through his black hair. Rich went to the local community college and walked on to the football team, further feeding his dream of making the NFL. That dream was derailed by a Connecticut running back who made him zig when he should have zagged, tearing his left knee apart. After that, he actually focused on his studies and was now a lawyer. I'd seen him at work once or twice, and it was frightening. I never knew him to be outspoken, but when he was in the courtroom, he used his incredible size and his booming voice well to his advantage. The funny thing was, when we socialized, he didn't look like a lawyer, didn't talk like one, and rarely even mentioned he was one to strangers. He told me work was work and fun was fun. He hated people who had nothing else to talk about but their jobs, so he didn't practice that.

I sat down next to him and took a sip of my beer. It was just the right temperature, and I sighed in appreciation.

"I called you about ten minutes ago. When you didn't answer, I figured you were on your way and ordered accordingly."

"How sweet of you."

"Don't push it. What the fuck have you been doing all day?"

"Working."

"Ha. That's a line of shit if I ever heard it."

"I'm telling you the truth."

"Are you know? Working on anything exciting?" Rich asked.

"The usual crap."

Something happened in the game that Rich didn't like. I don't watch football that much, but it looked like the orange team returned an interception off the black one for a touchdown.

"Fuck," Rich said.

"Betting on the orange team, I presume?"

"Florida was favored by fifteen fucking points. They're down by three now."

"What you get for betting on other people?"

"They'll pull it out, watch."

I didn't intend to watch the game too closely, but I didn't have much of a choice since my only company was heavily involved in it.

"I hope they do."

"You could give two shits?"

"That's exactly how much I could give."

The first beer went down way too smoothly, and I called the bartender over to order another one.

"Let me get another Courage and a . . ."

"Hoegarten," Rich added.

"Whorehouses make beer now?"

"Shut up."

The bartender returned with the two beers and took away the empty glasses. With nothing much else to do, I stared at my surroundings. Croxley's was all about dark wood. The bar was dark wood, the paneling on the walls was dark wood, and the tables and chairs were dark wood. Even the floor was dark wood. The only things that weren't made of wood were the mirror behind the bar, and the seven large ceramic taps on the bar. Each tap had about ten handles, and most of them were out of the ordinary. One looked like a ladle, another was a furry tiger, and one looked like a fire engine hose. Not only did these companies make strange beers, but they insisted on giving them strange names and making strange tap handles for them. If you're going to be strange, you might as well go for the whole gambit and be fucking strange.

The game ended about fifteen minutes and two beers later, and despite all of his faith in Florida, it was obvious that Rich had lost money. He revealed this by making a vague statement about it.

"Those Florida pricks cost me two hundred today," he said, leaving me to wonder how he made out.

"Nice to know you have that sort of money to throw around."

"I won it last week on the Atlanta game." What I've noticed about gamblers is, they never actually lose money. Any losses they talked about were from previous winnings. If that was the case, then why did they get so upset when they lost? Someone had to be losing money somewhere to support the bookies, but it certainly wasn't any gambler I knew.

"That's cool."

"No it's not. They shouldn't have lost that fucking game. Their quarterback throws more passes to the other team than he does to his own."

"Maybe he should play for them," I said.

"Maybe I should get another beer. Hey, toots, get me another round," he said to the bartender, which prompted her to roll her eyes and get to pouring. I don't know how she tolerated him. The only benefit she got from his harassment was the large tip he always left her. In my eyes, that made her, well, a prostitute.

She came over with the beers, my fourth. I didn't feel drunk or anything, probably because I had drank a good amount of gin the night before. The first few beers after a hangover usually got absorbed with little effect.

"You see Tanya last night?" I forgot I had told Rich about that.

"Yeah," I said.

"You finally get the balls to tell her to get out of your life?"

"Yeah."

"That'll do a lot of good."

"I hope it will."

"Stop lying to yourself. There's only three ways out of that relationship."

I figured this ought to be interesting. "Go ahead."

"One, you marry her," Rich said, smiling.

"Not likely."

"Whatever. Two, she kills you."

"Hopefully, not likely."

"Three, you kill her."

"Not likely either, but definitely the best of the three options."

"They're all you've got," Rich said.

"Thanks for brightening my mood."

"How'd she take the news?"

"She walked out."

"You tell her before dinner?"

"Yes."

"Cool, so she saved you a couple of bucks," Rich said.

"I didn't look at it that way, but yes."

"Sure you didn't. If I know you, you planned it that way. Cheap bastard."

"I'm not like that," I said.

"What about the time you broke up with that girl the night before Valentine's Day?" Rich asked.

"I don't want to get into that."

"Of course you don't. It doesn't matter. And what you did last night doesn't matter either. It isn't over yet."

"How about we talk about something else?"

"Your ex-girlfriend isn't a good topic of conversation?"

"No."

"It used to be all you talked about. Tanya this, Tanya fucking that. No matter what we started talking about, it always ended up on Tanya."

"Well, she's out of my life now, and she's out of our conversations, okay?"

"Sure, you believe that all you want. Twenty bucks says she calls you within the week."

"I'd rather not bet on that," I said.

"Because you know you'll lose." I couldn't argue with him on that. Luckily, I'd be in Washington the next day and wouldn't be there for the call.

"Whatever."

"Exactly."

Rich took a swig of beer, and then lit a cigarette. He usually smoked like a stack, and smoked even more when drinking.

"Let me get one of those," I said.

"I thought you quit."

"I did."

"Didn't you tell me when you quit not to give you a cigarette under any circumstance whatsoever?"

"I did, but that was six months ago, and I'm just in the mood for one now."

"I only have four left," Rich said, shaking his pack.

"Yeah?"

"I don't want you to take one drag like you always do and then put it out because you realize you don't want to smoke."

"I'll make sure I get every cancerous drag I can out of it, okay?"

Reluctantly, he handed one over. I lit it with a pack of matches off the bar, and inhaled. It tasted like burning cardboard and I wanted to put the thing out, just like Rich predicted. I didn't, because the last thing I wanted was to hear him complain. What a great reason to inhale cancerous smoke, eh? I took a long drag and let out a cough.

"Jackass," Rich said through a chuckle.

"I just had the urge, you know?"

"Of course I know."

I tried to make like I was enjoying the cigarette, which I wasn't. I hadn't had one in at least four weeks, and I didn't enjoy it then either. It was just a thing with me. When I did smoke, it was usually while I was drinking, and though I had broken the smoking habit, I couldn't unassociate the two. Hanging out with Rich only made matters worse, because he was the one who got me started smoking in the first place, and every time we drank together, the urge became that much stronger.

"I just finished reading a cool book," he said.

"You read?"

Rich was certainly a smart guy, and he did have to have a way with words because he was a lawyer, but I never heard him talk about books. He was one of those functional illiterates, or dysfunctional literates, or alliterates, or whatever the hell you called someone who could read but didn't.

"Cut the shit. Can't I ever say something without you making a comment?"

"No."

"Well, anyway, I heard about the book on Howard Stern, and it was great."

"Was it, now? What was it about?"

"Time travel. It was fiction, that's the one that isn't real, right?" I nodded, wanting to say something about a book about time travel would have to be fiction, but decided to let him continue unhindered. "Yeah, fiction. It was about this guy that gets to go back in time and relive all the events in his life he wanted to change."

"Like Back to the Future?"

"Exactly. Only this book went deeper into it, and I'm telling you, this guy could write."

"If Howard Stern thought so."

"I wish I could do that."

"Write a novel?"

"No, go back in time. Be able to change shit. See how my life would end up. Don't you think that would be cool?"

"I never really thought about it much."

"Of course you did. Everyone thinks about going back and changing things," Rich insisted.

"Well, yeah, I guess there are some things I wish I could have done differently, but I never really thought about being able to actually do it."

"Neither did I, until I read this book. You gotta read it. I think you'll love it."

"Maybe I will."

"You won't. You wouldn't read anything I recommended to you."

"You never told me about a book you read, unless you want to count the biography of Hulk Hogan," I said. I'm serious, he really did read it.

"That one was good too, but this was better. It was like, real."

"I'm sure it was."

"You're patronizing me."

"Me? Course not."

"You can be such a condescending pain in the ass when you want to, do you know that?"

"Had no idea."

"Well, you've got an idea now, so cut it out."

"Okay," I said.

"There you go again."

"Sorry."

"Don't you have anything else better to do than annoy me?"

"If I don't do it, who will? Everyone else is afraid of you."

Rich chuckled because I was right. I was the only one he

wouldn't flatten when he get angry with me because I was his best friend, and because we both knew it wouldn't be a fair fight. I mean, I could handle myself pretty well, and I might even get in a shot or two on him, but he would waste me in no time. I'd seen him do some pretty good damage on big guys throughout the years, and I'd say once we were juniors, I had come to the conclusion he was one guy I didn't want to mess with.

"You remember Jason Caufield?" I asked.

"Who?"

"Jason Caufield."

"Who's he?"

"We went to high school with him."

"Don't remember him."

"Yes you do."

"If I remembered him, don't you think I would have said so?"

"He's the guy that got caught whacking off in the gym bathroom in sophomore year."

"Oh, him." Rich was one of those guys with what I would call a situational memory. When I asked him about Jason straight up, he had no idea who he was talking about, but when I threw in a little factoid or an anecdote, he followed me right away. "What about him?"

"Just wanted to know if you remembered him."

"Has to be a reason why you asked. What, you run into him or something?"

"I wish," I said, half to myself.

"Why would you wish to run into that geek?"

"Because it would make my job easier."

"That's the work you were doing this afternoon, looking for some computer nerd? What, you working for the alumni committee now?"

"No. Some guy I know in Ohio hired me for the job."

"Why you talking to me about it? I thought you never liked to discuss what you're up to."

"I don't, but this one's been bothering me, and I thought I would bounce it off you."

"What the hell does a guy in Ohio want with Jason Caufeld?"

"Caufield, and the guy in Ohio really couldn't care less. Some university hired him to find the guy, and he contracted me."

"University looking for him? What, they find out? He cheated on exams fifteen years ago?"

"They claim he stole intellectual property."

"Well, that's the guy who'd do it. Egghead."

"You familiar with that type of law?"

"On intellectual property?"

"Yeah."

"A little. Not enough that I could defend the guy or anything."

The bartender came over and I gestured for her to get us another round.

"She's got a cute ass," Rich said.

"You should know, you've stared at it enough."

"I can't crack her, though. I thought I was close last week."

"Why, she say hello to you or something?"

"No, we actually had a decent conversation. Something about law, believe it or not. She's going to law school now."

"Human race is gonna lose another one, huh?"

"Looks that way. Well, at least Hell will be well populated."

"So, what happened?"

"What do you mean?"

"You said you were close."

"Yeah, I was. Least, I thought I was. We talked, we joked. It was nice. Then, when I came in today, she acted like we never had that conversation."

"She might think you're stalking her. Maybe I should give her my card."

"Cut it out. I'm trying to talk serious here."

"About picking up a bartender you have no shot at?"

"Thanks for the vote of confidence."

"So, what do you know about that type of law?"

"Stalking law?"

"No, asshole, intellectual property law."

"Not much. Just that it's illegal."

The bartender returned with the beers. Rich smiled at her, one of those weak, "I like you" smiles. She didn't return it. As a matter of fact, she made no expression whatsoever and just went back to work. Rich had bullet holes in him again.

"She's a bitch," he said. Of course, all women who turned him down were bitches, or lesbians. According to him, 90% of the female population was either bitches or lesbians, or both.

"Do the same laws of theft apply to the stealing of intellectual property?"

"I don't know. I would guess so."

"So, if a guy were to steal intellectual property, let's say he created a better wheel, and crossed state lines, would it become a federal offense?"

"You mean if he like took that better wheel with him to another state?"

"No, let's say the ideas are in his head, or maybe he has some notes, or a disk with the information on it, and he took his head and the information across state lines. Could that be considered a federal offense?"

Rich thought about that for a moment, taking a large gulp of beer. As far as the law went, Rich knew a lot more than he let people think, probably because he hated being asked questions like I was asking him right then. He didn't mind it so much from me, only because I didn't abuse the privilege.

"I'd say that might be a federal offense. Why you asking?"

"I think the feds are looking for Jason as well."

"What makes you think that?"

I told Rich all about the government men that had stopped by Laura's house and how they were staking out her house. Reluctantly, I also told him about the phone call I received earlier in the day.

"What makes you think that guy was a fed?" Rich asked.

"He sounded like one. Besides, who else would know I was investigating Jason?"

"Anyone could know. Maybe Caufeld was involved with the mob or something. Maybe he just pissed the wrong people off."

"It's Caufield, and I don't think the mob has much to do with universities."

"The mob is involved with everything."

"You watch too much TV."

"I've seen it firsthand. They've branched out."

"What, we gonna have a Mafia University next? Teach kids bookmaking, contract killing, and all that?"

"The mob doesn't do that stuff too much anymore. Besides, I didn't say it was definitely the mob, but it could just be some shady characters Caufield got involved with."

"Maybe, but I think it's the feds."

"Then watch your ass. The feds can be worse than the mob on a

75

good day."

"Trust me, I know."

"Why are you still working on this? I would have taken that phone call as my ticket out of this one."

"I'm curious. Plus, Jason wasn't a bad kid. I want to see what he's up to," I said.

"You're out of your fucking mind."

"Probably."

"Definitely. No sense in even trying to deny it. You don't owe anything to this Caufield guy, or his mother. There's no need for you to go any further with this. Tell your P.I. friend you tried, but you just can't get anything on him."

"I can't do that."

"You had better do that."

"I'm going to Washington tomorrow to see if I can locate this guy. I've got a pretty hot trail leading to him down there, and I figured I'd give it a shot."

Rich finished the last of his beer, and basically ignored me. I wasn't used to that.

"What's the matter?" I asked.

"What's the matter? Nothing's the matter. I am just saving oxygen."

"You don't have to sit there silent."

"What should I do, give you advice that you won't pay any attention to instead? I don't know about you, but I'm not a big fan of wasting my breath."

"You don't think I should go to Washington?"

"Well, I won't tell you my opinion, cause I would be wasting my breath again, but I will point something out to you. Now, you said 'Washington' and when most people say that, they aren't talking about the state, where you get great apples, hear good grunge bands, and pal around with the biggest software guy in the world. I assume you were talking about 'Washington D.C.,' the seat of the American government. People you refer to as 'Feds' generally make their living there. Why the fuck would you go to D.C. if you think the feds are on to you?"

Rich normally didn't get genuinely mad too often. He would fake being mad to add emphasis to what he was saying, but he rarely got hot. He was fairly hot right then, and I really didn't know why this all bothered him so much. I figured it was because the bartender was giving him a hard time, and his ego was bruised. Well it wasn't just bruised, it was fucking destroyed.

"Look at it this way," I said, "Caufield knew the feds were after him and he went there. If it is safe for him, it's gotta be safe for me."

"Did you ever stop to think that this guy may be in cahoots with them?"

"The feds?" I asked.

"No, The Magnificent Seven."

"That's just a movie, Rich. They were actors."

"Again with the wisecracks. Why do I bother to help you?"

"Because you're my friend. So, you really think Caufield could be working for the feds?"

"I didn't say that. I just said it was possible. Anything's possible."

"So it's just as easily possible for him to not be working with them, and hanging out right underneath their nose undetected."

"Yes."

"So, there's no reason for me not to go and find him."

"You should be a lawyer."

"I can't. I haven't had my heart removed and my conscience deleted yet. But thanks for the offer."

"I'll go with you."

"To have my heart removed?"

"To Washington."

"Nah."

"What do you mean, nah?"

"I mean, nah. I don't need you coming along. I appreciate the offer, but I can't guarantee that we'll be back in time for you to make work on Monday."

"I'll take a sick day."

"Really, it's okay. I'll be fine."

"You're sure."

"Absolutely."

"Good, because I didn't want to go."

"I figured. Appreciate the effort though."

"Wasn't bad, right?"

"Top notch. Great performance."

"Well, if you really are crazy enough to go down there by yourself, be careful. If that guy who called you figured out you were investigating that geek so quickly, he'll pick up on the fact that you are going to Washington. You don't need any trouble on the enemy's turf."

"I'm bringing two friends along," I said.

"Guns. Great. I get the feeling the federal government might have you out-powered just a tad. I wouldn't even bring a gun if I were you."

"Have you been to Washington recently?"

"No."

"Neither have I. But I heard it can get real dangerous down there."

"Only for private dicks that rub their nose where it doesn't belong."

"Stop it. I am a public dick. Everyone knows that."

"Just be careful."

It was unusual for Rich to play the protective mother role, which made me appreciate his concern that much more. I couldn't imagine what he was so worried about. Yeah, I was pretty sure that the Hovelle guy was a fed, but he was stationed in New York. Plus, I thought the call he made was only to scare me. There was no reason for the federal government to waste resources on a guy like me. Actually, I was probably helping them out anyway. If they couldn't find Caufield, then my locating him would make their job that much easier.

And I knew I would find Jason.

We sat at the bar at Croxley's for another hour, just sipping beers and harassing the bartender. Well, I played no part in that, but I was guilty of laughing a few times at both Rich's and her expense. If I was her, I would have told him to fuck off. She decided it was best to ignore him, which only got him even hotter under the collar. Rich usually did fairly well with the ladies, better than I did, so it was nice to see him squirm.

What I didn't understand was why he felt so strongly about her. I mean, she was nice looking, but not someone worth embarrassing yourself over. She had short blonde hair, not even down to her shoulders, with a slim body and brown eyes that indicated to me her hair wasn't natural. What turned me off were her large teeth. They seemed a bit long for her mouth, making her resemble a horse a little. This is harsh criticism coming from a guy who could be labeled average at best, but I call them like I see them, and there was a good chance this chick had Mr. Ed in her bloodline.

After Rich decided his battle was lost, we decided to walk up the block to another bar called Versage. Where Croxley's was the ultimate guy hangout, Versage was the place to meet women, or at least ogle them a little. It was one of those Long Island bars that struggled to produce a New York City atmosphere. Personally, I think the only way to achieve such an atmosphere is to open the place in New York City, but I am usually considered a cynic by saying such things.

At the door was an ox of a man, complete with bald head. He didn't look too bad with it, and I wouldn't say anything derogatory to such a large man anyway. He stood about six-five, and was about as wide. His name was Archie, and Rich and I went to high school with him. He would have graduated with us, but Archie had size everywhere but in his head. Still, he was nice, and he and Rich had played football together.

"Ricki," Archie said, when he saw us coming. He didn't bother to address me, probably because he couldn't remember my name. This was despite the fact that I had located an ex-girlfriend for him for free.

"Arch. What's up man?"

The two embraced each other, slapping each other on the back so loud it sounded like gunshots.

"Why didn't you show up last night?" Archie asked. "I told you we were having that lingerie party. This place was mobbed. Chicks everywhere."

"I ended up working late. Was too tired by the time I got home."

"You missed out man."

"Next time."

"Hey," Archie said, reaching out his meat hook of a hand for me to shake it.

"What's up," I said, calmly. I really hated being around two people that knew each other really well. It wasn't that I didn't like Archie, it was just that we didn't have anything to say to each other, and I wasn't at all interested in their conversation.

Archie opened the velvet rope in front of the place and let us in.

"They're with me," he called out to the girl behind the glass window with overly large breasts that she had no qualms about showing the world. The girl nodded, and we were able to successfully skirt the ten-dollar cover charge at Versage.

Versage prided itself in playing the loudest music on the planet. It was a small place, with a steel bar along the left side, and couches in the back. It had a modern look to it, with fancy drapes hanging from the walls and expensive-looking barstools which I guess is how they tried to achieve that city atmosphere. It might have worked for some people, but the main thing getting in the way of complete success was the attitude of the people in the place. In the City, you do get all types of attitudes, but people really don't look you up and down so much. New York City might be the fashion capital of the world, I'm not sure, because I am not much into fashion, but people in the City make their observations with a little more couth than Long Island people do.

I think the issue with Long Island people comes from the fact that it is predominantly middle class. The problem with the middle class is that they are between the upper class above them, and the lower class below them. They are constantly either a good move away from getting to the top or a bad move away from hitting the cellar. Because of this, Long Island people are obsessed with money, and want to show off how much they have, even if that's not a lot. I'm no psychiatrist, but I have noticed that one of the most prevalent problems with human beings is their dislike of the middle. You've got the middle class problem, the middle child syndrome, the negative reference to being caught in the middle, and various other problems caused by middledom. I can't say this is true of everyone, only because I don't know everyone, but it seems to be pretty clear. Oh, and I came from a middle class family. Guess that means I am screwed.

We found two stools in the middle of the bar between two groups of girls that looked at everything from our shoes to our haircuts. I figured I failed on both accounts because I was wearing beat up black shoes and needed a trim. A girl told me once that you can tell almost everything about a guy from his shoes, and if that was the case, I was indicating to these women that I was a loser. That probably wasn't too far from the truth.

Another large-breasted woman was standing behind the bar. She was frighteningly attractive, with jet black hair, green eyes, perfect skin, and those huge mammary glands I mentioned. She was also tall, about six feet, which made her about three inches taller than me. Yet, another woman out of my reach.

"What can I get you?" she yelled over the techno music blaring in the background.

I looked at Rich. He said, "Heineken."

"One Heineken, and one gin and tonic."

She nodded and went to get the drinks. I noticed that almost everyone in the place was wearing black, in the middle of June no less, except Rich and me. I had on my khakis and the blue shirt, and Rich was wearing a white polo shirt and brown chinos. We weren't underdressed, but we certainly stood out. That made me uncomfortable.

The bartender returned with the drinks and I handed her a twenty-dollar bill. She came back with three dollars. Here's where Versage successfully achieved the city atmosphere. They emptied your wallet without remorse.

"Seventeen fucking bucks," I said.

"Price you gotta pay to stare at her tits the way you are," Rich said.

"For these prices, she should take her shirt off and rub them in my face."

"That's Gentleman's Quarters, down the block."

"Never been there."

"Of course not."

Chapter 7

I woke up the next morning with a booming headache. Rich and I had stayed out to about four, drinking and schmoozing with the women in Versage. Well, I didn't do too much schmoozing, but I did plenty of boozing, and I broke the cardinal drinking rule. As the saying went, "Beer before liquor, never been sicker." I made a sacrifice at the porcelain altar that night, and I vaguely remembered asking aloud why there were french fries in my upchuck when I hadn't eaten them in weeks.

Rich had made some headway with the girls to the left of us, landing himself a really hot redhead. I, of course, was introduced to her friend, the marginally attractive brunette named Tina, or Gina, or Lina, or something else that ended in "ina." She didn't have much to say, and our conversation was further hindered by Rich and his girl's constant making out. He had her pinned against the bar, and they were both so drunk that they kept sliding back and forth, knocking over drinks, and bumping into the brunette and me. My girl worked as an accountant for a large travel company, but hadn't been anywhere exciting and didn't plan to change that. She didn't go out much, she said, but she thought I was nice and gave me her number. She also said she didn't drink much, but I saw her pound four Red Devils in the course of two hours, and she was the one who was driving. Not that I should talk.

By the time the girls had left, it was near four, and Rich and I were about the only ones left in the place. He had lipstick all over his face, on his forehead even, and his shirt was out of his pants. He

82

looked like a drunken mess, which he was. I had sobered up somewhat, at least I thought I had, and I talked Rich out of going to the diner because I wanted to go home and sleep. I think he was a little mad at me because I had ignored the girl he tried to hook me up with which ruined his chances of going home with his little hussy. The hussy wanted to stay, but the brunette gave the old "I'm tired and want to go home" routine which translated into "This guy's a jerk and I am not letting you screw his friend." I didn't mean to ruin Rich's good time, and he knew that, but he still called me a "fuck-face" among other things for derailing his sexual plans for the evening. He also mentioned the fact that I wasn't about to get laid any time soon with my attitude. He had tried to convince me the girl I was talking to was hot, and though she might have been in his drunken eyes, I just didn't see it. Plus, she had one of those dull whiny voices that hit my ears like a ball-peen hammer when she spoke. That certainly didn't score her any points with me.

* * *

I got out of bed, still dressed in the clothes from the night before, and checked my clock. It was nine o'clock, a bit early to be getting out of bed after a night of drinking, but I had a train to catch. I praised myself for packing the night before, steadied myself on my feet, and headed into the bathroom. Luckily, I had good aim into the toilet the night before, and I had even cleaned up pretty well, leaving no trace of my worship. I caught a look at myself in the mirror, noticing the bloodshot eyes and the puke stain on my relatively new shirt. The ladies down at the Laundromat were going to love me that week. I took off the shirt, balled it up, and threw it into the laundry bag I kept in the bathroom. After that, I took a long hot shower, and exited, feeling almost human.

I made it out of the house at a quarter to ten, dressed in a pair of jeans and a button-down gray oxford shirt. I lived about four blocks from the Long Island Railroad train station, so I didn't have to worry about taking my car and parking it at the station. It was fairly cool compared to the day before, and I was happy I put on the long sleeve shirt. I didn't have much of a choice in the matter because it was about the only acceptable shirt that was clean.

My train left Valley Stream Station at 10:15 and arrived in New

York just before eleven. I figured that gave me enough time to get my ticket from the agent, and make it to my train in plenty of time. The train to the city was pretty much empty, with only an old man sitting a few seats away from me, and a family with two small kids who I figured were out of their minds for taking them into the city. I fought falling asleep, only because I had to change trains at Jamaica Station, and didn't want to get caught in Brooklyn by missing the transfer. I had taken a computer game magazine with me to read, but it wasn't interesting, and I put it back in my bag. All I could do was stare out the window and watch the decrepit buildings pass me by.

I stayed awake for the transfer at Jamaica, a nice little old slum that served as the LIRR's main terminal. Where you had two tracks going into each station, Jamaica had ten, and there was a large rail yard with broken down trains below the station. Looking at the trains, I wondered how, after they were built, did they get them on the tracks? I had a stupid thought for a second, reasoning that they might even build the trains on the tracks themselves, then came to my senses. They had to have some way of doing it, and though this piqued my interest, I knew I would never ask anyone, or find out on my own how it was done. I figured I would only be disappointed when I found out the secret.

Though I had successfully fought sleep on the train to Jamaica, I had no chance or intention of doing so on the train into New York. It was an express train and Penn was the last stop, so I had nothing to lose by nodding off. I think I dreamt about a beautiful female with the head of a rhinoceros during that nap, further scaring myself about my own mental health. I awoke with a jolt as the train screeched into the station, gathered my bag, and walked off the train hoping I hadn't yelled out in the middle of my dream. A few people accused me of talking in my sleep, and if I had done so during that dream, my fellow passengers would have thought I was nuts. No one made any strange faces at me as I exited the train, and I made my way up the escalator and toward the Amtrak counter. It was exactly eleven when I got there.

Where the Valley Stream and Jamaica trains had been nearly empty, Penn Station was mobbed. There were clumps of people everywhere, especially by the screens which displayed the trains and which tracks they were on. The station itself was a mixture of numerous smells, ranging from croissants to pizza to coffee, along with the unique stench that Penn always emanated. Every time I came into that station, it reminded me of the trips my family used to take into the city every Christmas to see the tree and go ice skating. I hated going back then, but looking back, I convinced myself those were the best years of my life.

The lady at the Amtrak counter, an overweight fortyish gal with bleach-black hair and pock marks on her face, frowned when I asked for my ticket.

"How did you make this reservation Mr.," she looked down at the credit card I gave her," Campeeni?"

"I made it over the Internet yesterday."

"Did you get a confirmation number?"

"I don't remember."

"Did you print the screen like the instructions told you?"

"My printer isn't working," I said, feeling like a student explaining to his teacher why he didn't hand in a book report on time.

"I see."

"Is there a problem?"

"Well, the 12:05 Metroliner with service to Washington appears to be booked."

"That's fine. One of those booked seats is mine," I said.

"Um, no it isn't."

"You're saying you don't have my reservation?" I asked, trying to stay calm.

"What I am saying is that we had a hold on your seat, Mr. Campaneeni, but that expired after twelve hours when you didn't confirm."

"It didn't say anything about confirming."

"It did. It clearly states on our website than any hold on a seat made less than a week before departure must be confirmed within twelve hours, either by the web, or over the phone with a representative."

I couldn't believe this was happening. The website had thanked me for choosing Amtrak, which I took as a confirmation that I was on the train. I didn't see anything like she was describing, but it wasn't like I had a computer I could show her with. I wanted to start screaming, demand to see a supervisor and get my seat, but that really wasn't my game. Sure, if it got any worse, there was a good chance I was going to grab her by her hair, rip off that wig, and smack her around a little bit.

"So, you have no seats available for that train."

"I didn't say that. I just said there are no reserved seats available."

Yes, she did say that. But it didn't make a difference. "What do you mean?"

"Well, you asked for a seat in reserved coach. There are no more seats available in reserve coach, but there might be a chance you can sneak on unreserved coach."

"What's the difference?"

"There is none, other than the fact that you can reserve a seat in reserve coach."

"Probably where they got the name from," I muttered.

"What?"

"Nothing."

She tapped away at her keyboard, her fingers hitting just about every button at the same time.

"Oh, I'm sorry."

"What?"

"It seems that unreserved coach is booked."

"How can it be booked if you can't make a reservation in that section?"

The lady was undaunted by my anger. She'd probably seen it a million times.

"Unreserved coach is sold on a first-come, first-served basis, and it appears we have sold the maximum amount of tickets for that section on this train."

"When is the next train?"

"Four-fifteen."

There was no way I was spending the next four hours in Penn Station. I hated the city, and didn't plan on sitting in the homeless hangout known as the waiting room for that long. I cursed myself for my own stupidity, even though I was pretty sure I hadn't done anything wrong. I wanted to choke this lady, but I figured that wasn't going to get me anywhere. My only chance was to plead with her and hope she saw it in her heart to get me a seat on that train.

"Listen, I understand that I might have made a mistake, but I really need to get on this train. I have an important meeting in Washington at five o'clock."

She looked me up and down as if to see if I looked like someone that would have an important meeting. She frowned.

"Let me take a look."

She went nuts on the keyboard again.

"Ah, I have a seat."

"Great."

"It's in first class."

"Okay," I said.

"Your original fare was $150 round trip. The first class ticket is an extra sixty dollars. I'll have to charge your card for that extra amount."

"Why did you guys charge my card if I didn't have a reservation?"

"We always put a hold on your credit card when you ask to have a seat held."

"Why didn't you guys cancel that hold when you canceled my seat?"

"It's standard procedure sir."

"Is it now?"

"Yes. Would you like the first class seat? It looks as though I only have one left."

I mumbled something about how I was getting fucked and said, "Sure."

She took my card, swiped it aggressively on her card reader, and handed it back to me. She then took the credit card printout from the computer and handed it to me, which I signed and returned. She took the credit card from my hand again, scrupulously checked the signatures, and when she seemed pleased that they matched, she handed it back, along with my ticket.

"Thank you for choosing Amtrak," she said, "Have a nice day."

"Thank you for fucking me," I half mumbled as I walked away from the counter.

I sat down in the huge waiting area on one of those hard black chairs that offer neither comfort or aesthetic beauty, still pissed off at the lady behind the counter. It wasn't her fault, but she could have at least been nice about it. People forgot how to be nice sometimes in the late seventies, and it seemed like it would be a long time before they remembered again. If she would have been pleasant, I might not have been in the bad mood I found myself in.

I thought about going to get a slice of pizza, one of those Penn

Station slices that were bigger than the plate, but I didn't want to spend the entire ride to Washington burping it up. Instead, I just sat for twenty minutes until they called the train for boarding. I expected a mad rush of people to head toward the track, but this didn't happen. About three dozen or so people made their way down the escalator with me, making me wonder about how sold out that train was.

I didn't have to wonder much longer. When I got to the train, I walked up to the first conductor I saw, showed him my ticket, and asked him where my seat was. He gestured toward the front of the train, and as I made my way towards my seat, I passed dozens and dozens of empty seats, both in the reserved and nonreserved sections. My blood was near the boiling point when I saw the next conductor in my section.

"Third row, window seat," he said when I showed him my ticket.

"This train sold out?"

"Doubt it," he said. "Although we might pick up a good crowd in Philadelphia."

"Unbelievable," I said, plopping myself down in my seat. I stashed my bag underneath my seat, mainly because I didn't want to have the guns too far away from me. I had visions of the train hitting a bump or something, the bag falling out, and the guns hitting the floor, causing mass hysteria. That really couldn't happen, though, because you need a mass of people to cause mass hysteria. There were two other people in the first class section—a middle-aged gentleman with white hair who had already fallen asleep, and the stalwart conductor. I told myself I was going to write a nasty letter to Amtrak, but I knew that wasn't going to happen. By the time I made it to Washington, I would probably forget about it all. I also realized that I wasn't the one paying for this. I just hoped that the university would pick up the fare for a first class Amtrak ticket. I mean, who the fuck rides first class on a train? Apparently, not too many people.

I got settled myself in my seat and decided to sleep the anger off. My head still ached because I had forgotten to take Advil in the morning, and my whole body had a weary feeling. I didn't think the three hours of sleep I'd catch on the way down would do me much good, but that wasn't going to stop me from giving it a shot. As the train started to move, I leaned my seat back as far as it went, which was pretty far given the vast amount of space they afford you in first class, and started to drift off, almost happy that I had a seat in this section of the train.

That happiness vanished about two hours later, when we stopped in Philadelphia. I had enjoyed a good nap, the sort when you drool, until that point, when an elderly woman plopped herself next to me. She was wearing a hat and a coat, in the middle of June mind you, and she had a large pocketbook on her lap. I took a look around the car and noticed that only four other seats were occupied. I wanted to tell the lady that she had the pick of the car to sit in. I didn't want to be impolite, but I also didn't want to be stuck sitting next to someone. Of all the luck in the world.

The car started moving, and I looked out the window. I really didn't see much and didn't care either. The only thing I wanted to see was the back of my eyelids, because I was tired, and it would make the ride seem that much shorter.

"This is my first trip to Washington," the lady said. She sounded and looked sweet, like the sort of old grandmother you see in movies and such. This made it impossible to do what I wanted to—tell her to shut up and let me sleep.

"Mine too," I replied.

"My daughter always told me to see the Capitol, and so did Harry. That's my husband. He always liked to talk about traveling to this place and that. All he talked about was when he retired we would buy one of those big vans and go all around the country, seeing the things we never saw. I used to tell him he was crazy, but he insisted we were going to do it. The Lord never gave him a chance, though. He took him from me three weeks after he retired."

"Sorry to hear that."

"They tell me Washington is nice, but that I ought to be careful. Plenty of hoodlums running around the streets at night. I won't be going out too much at night. My party days are over," she said, laughing to herself.

"You just need to watch out."

"I think I'll see the Lincoln Memorial first. My sister went there and said it was beautiful. Have you ever seen the Lincoln Memorial?"

"No, ma'am. I've never been to Washington."

"The Lincoln Memorial first, and then maybe the Smithsonian. I so love going to art museums, though with my bad back, it's tough to walk around that long. I think I'll go to the modern art museum. They have a modern art museum at the Smithsonian?"

"I'm sorry, I wouldn't know."

"I bet they do. Probably a nice one. I used to draw myself, before the arthritis set in. I would draw paintings of the sunsets, and the birds in the sky, and houses. I could never really draw people. I don't know why that is. I could draw any landscape I saw, but I couldn't draw people at all."

"I see," I said.

"I once drew a picture of a farm house upstate. Everybody loved that picture. They would all ask me to draw something for them after they had seen it. I would draw one picture a week, and I would give it to a friend that had asked for one. They all loved my paintings."

"I'm sure. That's nice."

"I want to see the Hope Diamond. Estelle told me that the Smithsonian has it on display, but I don't know which museum that is."

Realizing that this old bird wasn't listening to a word I was saying, I said, "They have it on display at the Museum of Aviation."

"The last museum I will see is the Museum of Aviation. I remember when they first started having commercial flights, and my Harry always talked about being one of the first people in our neighborhood to fly on one. We took a trip to see my grandmother, oh, around 1947. Harry was all excited to go on the plane. He had gotten a bonus that week, and we used that money to take the trip to Virginia. He told all his friends about how he was going on a plane. He thought he was a real high roller doing that. Then, when we got on the plane and it took off, he got so sick. Every two minutes he would get sick, and he never even got a chance to enjoy the flight. Poor Harry."

I really appreciated the graphic detail of this woman's life. I checked my watch, realizing we had at least 45 minutes before we would make Washington, and I wasn't sure if I could tolerate this woman any longer. I knew she meant well and she was probably lonely, only that didn't make it any easier.

"Poor Harry," I said.

The woman was silent for about two minutes, making me incorrectly think that my punishment was over. No way I could be so lucky.

"I've never gone first class on anything before, but my daughter insisted she pay for everything and arranged for me to sit in first class so I would have more room to stretch out my back. Like I would ever stretch out anything. I am too nervous when I travel. I mean, you always see on television all the train crashes and derailments. It is always the people that were leaning back in their seats that get hurt the worst."

I looked over at the woman, who was staring at the seat in front of her like she had been for the entire conversation. I thought she might have been out of her mind, but I still found myself putting my seat back in the upright position. So much for being comfortable.

"I really don't know how these trains stay on the tracks moving so fast."

I looked out the window, down at the tracks. All I saw was a blur. We were moving pretty fast. I tried to shake the image of the wheels of the train flying off the tracks, sending us into the water below. As much as I tried, I couldn't stop myself from being fixated on that water.

"We should be alright," I said, more for my benefit than hers.

"My daughter said I should be alright, that I shouldn't worry. She tells me I worry too much, and I tell her that if she lived as many years as I have, and if she saw all the things I have seen, she would worry too. She's just a child."

Glancing at the woman, I figured her to be in her eighties, maybe in her late seventies if I gave her the benefit of the doubt. Her child of a daughter had to be in her fifties at best. I hoped if I lived that long, my mother wouldn't be sitting next to some stranger on a train, saying how I was just a kid.

"You have nothing to worry about. They do this every day."

"I'm probably worrying for nothing."

Now I was convinced that this lady was either out of her mind, or damn near deaf. I decided to test the latter.

"I have two guns in the bag. First, I am going to shoot everyone on the train, then myself. After I make sure the thing derails of course." I said this to her quietly, not so she couldn't hear me, but because I didn't want the conductor, or any of the other passengers in the car to hear me. That would have been a tough one to explain.

The old lady next to me made no reply. I didn't think this was because she was frozen with fear, her grip on her bag had loosened, and she was playing with the clasp. The old bird didn't hear too well. Probably hadn't heard a word I had said to her. This was great, because she could have her own audible monologue, and I wouldn't appear rude by not answering.

She continued for the rest of the ride to Washington, talking about her other two children; they were Michael and Rosalie. Michael was a good kid who still didn't know what he wanted to do with his life, and Rosalie had been a nurse, had four children, and had moved to Tulsa for a reason the lady never gave. She also talked about her degenerative hip, her shoddy nasal passage, and the fact that she had to watch what and when she ate so as not to have any "bowel surprises" as she called them. I instantly hoped that she hadn't eaten the wrong thing before getting on the train. I didn't want to have to toss an old lady across the car.

Believe it or not, the old lady did help pass the time a little bit, after I resigned myself to that fact that she wasn't going to sit there quietly. It was like sitting down next to Miss Daisy, and I got to learn about how much different things were during her time. I heard about the transition from ice boxes to refrigerators, the advent of television, the installation of phones in the majority of houses, and how Franklin Roosevelt was the best president we ever had. I almost wished I could engage in the conversation, but that would require me to scream at the top of my lungs into her ear. I didn't feel the need to do that.

Once the train stopped, I helped her with her suitcase, which was on wheels, so I didn't have to worry about carrying it for her into Union Station. I would have felt compelled to do that, but that lady whipped that thing around like a pro. I slung my bag over my shoulder, checked my reflection in the window to see if my hair was a mess, which it wasn't, and disembarked the luxurious Amtrak Metroliner.

Union Station in Washington looked a lot like the train stations I saw in movies. It was huge, with a ceiling that had to be over twenty feet high, and it had the pew-type benches that I had remembered seeing on TV. It looked old, like it had been there since Lincoln was president, and I might have been right about that. There were many modern updates, like a Sharper Image store and a McDonald's, and I saw another modern update, transients hanging around the place. I made my move to the information counter and asked the nice lady there for a hotel recommendation. She directed me to a place across the street, and old Irish hotel complete with a pub, and it sounded like a perfect fit.

The O'Malley Inn looked to be about two hundred years old, in an attractive sort of way, and the person behind the counter seemed to be about the same age, not in an attractive sort of way. The man behind the large oak desk was tall, with bushy white hair and bushier eyebrows. He had lines in his face that looked like they were etched with a razor. They had to be about an inch deep.

"Help you?" he asked. He was reading a newspaper and didn't bother to look up from it when he asked the question. Behind him was one of those large wooden key holders they used to use in the old days, and I could see the room keys in them. Cool.

"I was wondering if you had a room for tonight and possibly tomorrow night."

He got up, consulted the key holder, and said, "Regular room or a suite?" After my Amtrak experience, I was a little wary about that.

"What's the difference?"

"Regular room's a regular room. Suite's bigger. Got a separate sitting room, along with a computer table, if that's the sort of thing you're into." I had stuffed my small laptop in my bag, just in case I needed to access any databases or contact someone other than by phone.

"The regular room doesn't have computer access?"

"Didn't say that," the old man said, his back still turned to me. "What I said was, the suite has a separate table for your computer."

"What's the price difference?"

"Regular room'll cost you sixty a night, and that includes breakfast and the paper. Suite costs ninety, and you get lunch in the pub if you want."

Even though I wasn't too keen on pumping up my expenses any more than I had to, I figured I wouldn't have been able to get a closet in one of the major hotels for ninety bucks. A suite would be nice. Whenever I did travel, which unfortunately wasn't often enough, one of the most important things to me was the room I stayed in.

"I'll take the suite."

"Good choice," the man said, grabbing a key from the holder and handing it to me. "Now, be careful with your key. It'll cost ten dollars if you lose it, and to be honest, the guy who cuts the keys doesn't come around all that often. The maid can let you in if you need to, but I really hate having to replace keys, okay?"

"Yeah, no problem."

"I'll need a credit card, if you want to use the phone."

I handed it to him.

"Maid comes at eight each morning, and then at ten if you're the type that likes to sleep late. She also turns down the bed at six, if you like. There's a minibar in the suite, and that gets checked every day at ten. Breakfast is served between six and nine, so make sure you don't miss it. If you do, the pub opens at eleven, and you can have just about anything on the menu sent up to the room. If you want to eat dinner in the pub, just show the waitress your key, and she'll charge it to your room. Any questions?"

I tried to remember everything he said, so I had no new questions for him. I shook my head.

He handed me back the credit card.

"We do an automatic hold of fifty dollars to go towards your phone bill, minibar, and network access. Computer system'll cost you two dollars an hour, but you'll like it. It's fast."

"Great."

"You've got room 717, which is on the seventh floor. Take the elevator just past those two doors over there, take it to the seventh floor, and turn left when you get out of it. Your room is at the end of the hall, on the left side."

"Thank you."

"My name's Tim, and if you need anything, I am here everyday from six until six, except Tuesday's and Thursdays, but I don't expect you'll be here till then."

"Probably not."

"Roger works nights from six to six on weekends, so if you need something later, ring him. We have toothpaste, toothbrushes, hair spray, and just about anything else you might have forgotten to pack. If you need something more complicated, there's a pharmacy down the block open 24 hours."

"Thank you again."

I picked up my bag, and headed toward the elevator, which looked as old as the building. It had one of those sliding metal doors, and it took a good deal of my strength to get it all the way open. I stepped inside, noticing that the thing could hold three people at most. I slid the door closed, which was easier than opening it, and pressed the button for the seventh floor. It took a moment, but the elevator then let out a loud creak, and made its way up. There were several bumps and jolts on the way to my top floor, and I told myself I would be taking the stairs. Lord knew I could use the exercise.

Chapter 8

After getting settled in the room and unpacking, I set my mind to thinking about finding Jason. The room was nice, a real large room with a sitting room and the computer table Tim had promised. I particularly liked the bed, which was a huge king size, and the five down pillows atop it. I figured I would get some quality shutdown on that bed, if I ever got the chance to do that. I had to stop myself from taking a nap right there. I still felt weary, and the travel probably hadn't helped any. I was truly convinced that there was something seriously wrong with me, but my father would have called me a hypochondriac, like he called anyone who thought they were sick. You could walk into his office the color of a lime, with puke spewing from your mouth, and he'd say you just had a cold or something. Quack.

Medical conditions aside, my main problem was locating one Jason Caufield. Crystal City, according to Darlene, was about ten minutes away. Neither one of us was convinced that Jason was staying in Crystal City. I had found evidence of a previous address right in the heart of D.C., so I figured he was probably taking care of something in Crystal City and living somewhere near his old address. The trick, of course, would be to find that.

My main idea was to hop into a cab, contact Darlene, then have her trace a call on the cell phone again. She wasn't at work, but she had her own computer setup at home that she said kicked the work computer's ass. I had called her before I left for Washington and told her what I had in mind. If she had told me the truth, she was waiting by the phone for my call.

I took the stairs down to street level, a cell phone in my front pocket and a gun at the small of my back. I chose the Glock .40 caliber because it fit there better and also because of Rich's sideways comment about the federal government overpowering me. Not much could beat the Glock for sheer firepower. Not that I had any intention of using the damn thing.

As I walked out the front door of the hotel, I checked my wallet. I had sixty bucks in there, plenty for a cab, but certainly not enough carry money. If I had to sit in a restaurant or bar staking out Jason, I would need a couple of bucks to do so. Also, I was from the school of thought that said you never had enough emergency money. I looked down the street and saw an ATM and decided to withdraw some funds from my already near-empty checking account.

I was able to get $150 dollars from the ATM, which politely charged me two bucks for the transaction. I wasn't the sort that kept a good eye on my checking account balance, but I figured I had somewhere around six hundred left in there. I knew that was probably way off, and I could see the two checks I had written two days before bouncing like a rubber ball. Remember, I never said I was organized.

I stuffed the money in my wallet, trying my best not to think about my financial situation. If I found Jason, my bank account would increase nicely, and I had a few accounts that owed me some money I expected to receive soon. I made my way back toward the hotel, and asked the doorman if he could hail me a cab. He gave me a funny look which made me think not too many people requested this service, and after he got one for me, I handed him a five dollar bill, which prompted him to make another face, again making me think not too many people did that either.

The cab was an old Chevy Caprice, and the driver was one of those guys you'd see on TV commercials posing as cabbies. I guess most people thought such cabbies existed in New York City, but there you were lucky to find a cabbie that spoke English and knew how to get around the city. This guy driving me around Washington was a classic one, and I half-expected him to be chomping on a stogie, which he wasn't. The cab did stink of cigar smoke, though.

"Where you headed?" the guy asked in a deep, raspy voice. I thought about that for a second. I really had no destination in mind. I thought about asking him to just drive me around the city for a little while, but I didn't get the feeling he'd be down with that.

"Crystal City."

"Gonna be fifteen bucks."

Great. "Whatever." The cabbie pulled away from the hotel and got onto the quiet street. Washington looked like a ghost town, which made me think finding Jason would be a snap. I took my cell phone out of my pocket and dialed Darlene.

"Yes bitchboy?"

"You were expecting someone else I presume."

"No, I knew it was you, hence the name."

"Bitchboy?" The cabbie overheard me and chuckled.

"Bitchboy," Darlene responded.

"Thanks. You ready?"

"Like I had nothing else to do today."

"You probably didn't. Bet I caught you on the couch watching TV and sucking down a half-gallon of ice cream."

"Bon Bons."

"Of course. I'll wait two minutes, then make the call."

"Hopefully I can nail him for you. Try to stay on as long as possible."

"I'll do my best."

I hit the End button, then hit the two digit number I had Jason's cell number programmed into. I had really thought this out more than I normally did. I was almost proud of myself. After three rings, Jason picked up.

"Who is this?"

"Hello Mr. Caufield, this is William Riley from Sprint. I was calling you about a new promotion we are offering our customers. Do you have a second?"

"I'm not interested."

"If you'll just give me a second," I said. I was trying to disguise my voice, even though this was unnecessary because Jason didn't know my voice. I guess this came from vast phony phone call experiences as a teenager. Ah, the days before Caller ID.

"I don't have a second." Jason sounded like he was outside from the interference on the phone, but I didn't hear too many ambient sounds to give away his location.

"It'll be quick. We'd like to offer you free nights and weekends, or, if you travel, free selective long distance." Don't ask. I had seen a commercial about being able to select two states you want to call to and from for a savings package.

"Selective long distance?"

"Yes. Our records indicate you make and receive long distance calls on this phone."

"I do. But I am not interested in changing my plan."

"You won't have to. It is a promotion. If the two states you want to call to and from are in our regional calling matrix, I can sign you up for the service right now, for free."

"I don't know."

"Where do you make the majority of your long distance calls to? It says here that you have the phone registered in New York."

"No. I make calls to New York," Jason said.

"Yes, I see that. Where do you make the calls from, predominantly?"

"Washington."

"I'm sorry, Washington State is not in our matrix. Perhaps you would prefer the free nights and weekends?"

"No, Washington, D.C."

"Oh, most of the D.C. area is in our matrix. There are some blackout areas, however. Do you have a residence in D.C.?"

"That's none of your business," Jason said.

"I'm sorry. I didn't mean to pry. Where do you make most of your calls from?"

"The heart of D.C. I would say. Sometimes Crystal City."

"When you say the heart of D.C., do you mean Georgetown, or more in the center, like the Lincoln Monument?"

"The center. Why is that important?"

"For the matrix, Mr. Caufield, for the matrix."

"Wait a minute. How do you know this is my phone. It isn't registered in my name?"

Uh-oh. I had forgotten Jason registered the phone in his mother's name. I had to act fast.

"I know, Mr. Caufield. I contacted Mrs. Swenson, and she said you were the decision maker on this phone."

"Oh." He didn't sound too convinced. "I'm not interested, sorry."

He hung up. I didn't care, because I had spent plenty of time on the phone with him, giving Darlene ample opportunity to trace the call. I hit the End button, then called her back.

"This is tough, but my guess is he is at the Capitol Building. He's stationary, there's no doubt about that, but I couldn't pinpoint it exactly. He could be at the Smithsonian, which is right near there, but I doubt it."

"The Capitol?"

"Think so."

"You're the best."

"I know."

I ended the call and placed the phone back in my pocket.

"I changed my mind. I want to go to the Capitol," I told the driver. He gave me a suspicious look through his rearview mirror. I imagined he had seen a lot worse than what I was doing in his cab over the years.

"That's completely in the other direction. And we're almost at Crystal City. I don't want to bang you over the head, so let's just say I turn off the meter and charge you an even twenty?"

It seemed like the best transportation deal I had received all day.

"Fine."

It took less than ten minutes to get to the Capitol building, despite the constant turning we had to do. Washington D.C., like the politicians who populated it, wasn't direct in any way or fashion. To go straight to a destination, you had to make an insane amount of turns and detours. I couldn't imagine anyone wanting to live there.

The cabbie pulled into a parking lot about five hundred yards from the beginning of the Capitol building property, and I paid him the twenty, plus an extra five as a tip. I wasn't too sure about doing that, considering he had shut off the meter and was probably pocketing most of the fare, but it seemed like the right thing to do.

"You want to go right up to the front of the building, or do you want to go to the observation area?" the cabbie asked. I thought about that for a second, and took a guess.

"Observation area."

"Take a left right there," he said, pointing to a long walkway. "That'll take you right to it."

"Great, thanks."

I got out of the cab and headed toward the walkway. The gun at my back was starting to irritate me a bit, so I tried to adjust it without making it too obvious. I felt like an idiot carrying it around right then, but I still felt like it was the best thing to do.

The walkway up to the observation area was long, and I was almost out of breath by the time I got there. I made a mental note to join a gym when I got home. I always made mental notes about doing so, thinking that one day I would actually carry it out. Fat chance. The only exercise I got was from chasing down people to hand them court summonses, climbing stairs when an elevator wasn't working or was too scary to use, or when I had to make my way up long walkways like the one I just traversed.

The observation area for the Capitol Building was vast, with park benches spotted here and there. It did offer a nice view of the building, the sort of few that tourists used as a background for the ridiculous pictures they foisted on uninterested friends and family. There were about thirty people scattered about the area, most of them elderly couples and families doing the Washington tour. All of the benches were taken up, and from my vantage point, I didn't see anyone that could be Jason.

I looked at the Capitol building for a moment, impressed with its overall size and its architecture. I wasn't a big fan of architecture or anything, but this building was impressive—made out of what looked like marble. The only time I had seen the building was on the back of a bill. In person, it was something to see. I almost wished I had a camera with me, so I could take one of those useless pictures like everyone else was doing.

I walked further into the area, trying not to be obvious, and scanned the people there. Like I said, most of them were elderly couples and families, although I did spot two separate women sitting alone on benches, seeming to stare out to nowhere. I had really hoped that I would have gotten to the Capitol building and spotted Jason immediately, but that was just wishful thinking. If Jason was there, he wasn't in plain view, so it would take a little investigating and patience to locate him. That's of course, if he was still there.

When I made it to the end of the observation area, I noticed some benches that were closer to the building and previously out of sight. They were below the main observation level, and I noticed two people sitting on different benches, alone. One of them seemed to just be relaxing, and from the distance, looked to be a middle-aged man. The other one seemed younger, and it looked like he was reading the paper. My heart jumped a second. It seemed I might have scored.

I knew I couldn't just go right up to Jason, stick my hand in his face, and say how great it was to see him after all this time. That might have worked, but I didn't want to jeopardize my chances of actually talking to him by scaring him off. He had to be a little jumpy, with the feds coming around his mother's house and all, and he would probably get up, and put as much distance between myself and him. Plus, I wasn't sure it was him. I did have a surefire way to find that out.

I reached into my pocket and pulled out my cell phone. I punched in Jason's cell number and hit the Send button. As I did so, I watched the guy sitting on the bench, waiting for him to move. The phone rang about four or five times, and from my vantage point, it seemed like the guy sitting down looked to either side of him, then reached down and put a phone to his ear. I heard Jason say "Hello" into the phone, and then I hung up. The guy below put the phone down, and I was certain I had my man. I put the phone in my pocket, and worked my way closer to where Jason sat.

As I approached, Jason put together what I now noticed to be a laptop computer, stuffed it into a bag, and got up. He moved quickly away from the Capitol Building and in my general direction. I found an empty bench and sat down without him noticing me. I pretended to be staring at the Capitol building in awe, and then bent down to tie my shoes. Just as I was finished, Jason walked by, and I recognized him. He was a little heavier than he was in high school, and he was sporting a goatee, but it was certainly him. I would notice those scared eyes anywhere. He didn't look in my direction, which was a good thing because, minus the acne, I looked almost exactly the same as I did in high school.

I watched Jason walk through the observation area and toward the long walkway. I dreaded taking that walk so soon after the first one, but it wasn't like I had a choice. This was the big moment, and I wasn't about to pass it up because my ass was out of shape. Again I promised myself that I would join a gym, the same way I had promised the night before that I would never drink again.

After I was confident there was enough distance between Jason and me that I could follow him without being detected, I got up and pursued him. He was walking fairly briskly, which made me think that he was spooked. Maybe the three unknown calls to his cell phone had made him think someone was on to him, and if that was the case, he was dead right. He definitely had no idea who it was, and I intended to keep it that way for as long as I could.

Jason made it to the street when I was two thirds down the walkway. He stopped at the corner, looked in all directions, and then crossed. I tried to walk as fast as I could without drawing unwanted attention to myself, and made it to the corner in time to see him duck into a coffee shop. This was good, because while he was there, I had a chance to catch my breath. When I smoked, it seemed as though I didn't run out of breath as quickly. This was ridiculous, of course, but that's the way it seemed.

I stopped by one of those boxes that sell newspapers, and leaned on it. I would have bought a paper to read and look less conspicuous, but, as usual, it was empty. Those boxes operated on the trust of the public, one of the stupidest things you can try and count on. Why take one paper for fifty cents when you can have seven? I mean, you're only going to read one, but they're there, right? I personally think people are scum, if you haven't already noticed.

After leaning on the empty, abused newspaper box for about two minutes, I decided to get myself out of clear view, and positioned myself behind a building, where I couldn't be seen but had sight on the coffee shop. There weren't too many patrons in there and it was difficult to see anything through the dirty windows. All I could make out were blurry silhouettes, and none of them even faintly resembled Jason. I didn't think he was smart enough to sneak out the back, although for a moment I thought about checking to make sure. It would suck if I went back to cover my bases, only to miss Jason coming out the front door. I decided to go with my hunch and watch the front. It paid off.

About five minutes later, Jason came out the door of the coffee house. He didn't seem overly aware of his surroundings like someone who was suspicious. He just walked out the door and turned left, heading down the street. I waited until he was a block down the street before I tailed him. He was walking slower this time, seeming to take in the sights as he made his way toward his next destination.

I followed Jason for about ten blocks, ducking into doorways when he stopped to look around. Even though I didn't think he was suspicious or anything, he might have learned to look over his shoulder from time to time. Following him down the street, I wondered what it was that he had gotten himself involved in. Jason was a scientist, not the sort of person you would expect to display criminal behavior. I had seen people from all walks of life committing crimes, cheating on their spouses, and generally acting like the pieces of crap that they were. Most of them did reveal their evil underpinnings rather easily, but I just couldn't see this hapless guy I was following doing anything wrong. Of course, I might have been absolutely wrong about Jason. I also realized I had pretty much done what Mike had asked of me. All I had to do was follow Jason to his current home, report it to Mike, and then be on my way back to New York. I felt if I did that, however, I would be forsaking my promise to Laura, and I would be going against what I felt was right. I felt that I should at least talk to Jason, and find out what happened. Of course, if I did this, Jason might get spooked and relocate again, knowing that someone had discovered his hiding spot. It was a chance I was willing to take.

Jason walked all the way to R Street, which is pretty far away from the Capitol. He took a left on R, and walked into an apartment building on the left hand side of the street. It was a pretty nice looking place, with a security guard at a desk by the front door, so I wouldn't be able to just walk in and surprise my old high school pal. I would have to announce my arrival, and the guard would have to let Jason know I was there to see him. I didn't want to give Jason the opportunity to think about it. I stayed outside for about five minutes, then decided to try my luck.

The inside of the lobby was plushly decorated, with two leather couches and a few paintings on the walls. It didn't look like the sort of place that came cheap, and I wondered how the hell Jason was affording it.

The guard was a portly black man, in his fifties I figured. He was watching a small black and white TV, and whistling a song I vaguely recognized. He noticed my entrance but didn't say anything immediately. After I had taken a good look at the place, he finally addressed me.

"What can I do for you?"

"That guy who just walked in, his name Jason?" I asked.

"What's it to you?"

"I think I went to school with him. Looks familiar."

"His name ain't Jason."

"You sure?"

The man nodded. I needed another approach. I reached into my pocket and pulled out my Investigator license.

"I'm a private investigator, and I was hired to find that man." The guy didn't even look at my license.

"But that man isn't Jason," the guard said.

"So he says. What name is his apartment under."

"That's not information I am allowed to give out."

"Listen, I have reason to believe he is in trouble."

"That would be his problem, not mine. I don't make it a practice of worrying about the tenants' lives."

"It's really important."

"I'm sure it is."

"Couldn't you help me out a little?"

"And what's in it for me?"

He was looking for the old grease job. I had seen it thousands of times before and practiced it frequently because nothing worked better. I pulled out a twenty dollar bill and placed it on the counter.

"Is there any information you could give me?"

"I said, 'What's in it for me?'"

I pulled out another twenty. "That better?"

He scooped up the two twenties. "Much." He then took my license from my hand. "This says you're from New York. What the hell you doing looking for someone down here?"

"That's where the trail led."

"I see." He looked at the twenties for a moment, then back at me. "I shouldn't be telling you anything."

"I know, and I won't tell anyone. This is a serious situation."

"Right."

He paused for another moment or so, like this was one of the toughest decisions he ever had to make in his life. He kept looking at the money and then at me, as if weighing his options. He put the bills in his pocket.

"That man there's named Kenobi. Ben, I think."

"Ben Kenobi?" I thought this guy was pulling a joke. "The guy that just walked in, the one with the glasses and the goatee, his name is Ben Kenobi?"

The security guard took a clipboard, looked at it, then slid it across the counter so I could read it. The last name signed was one Ben Kenobi. At least Jason had a sense of humor. I saw his apartment number was 15H.

"The apartment registered to him?"

The man shook his head.

"Mind telling me who it is registered to?"

"I do. That's confidential information." I went to reach into my pocket for some more money. "Don't bother, I don't think you have enough in there. I'd lose my job if I told you that."

"Okay. Could you tell me how long old Ben's been living here?"

"I'd say about a month."

"He come and go a lot?" I asked.

"Nope. Usually stays holed up in there, from what I see. He goes out for an hour or so in the afternoon, but most times, he stays in that apartment. He orders most of his meals in there. Strange man."

"Well, I appreciate the information."

"You gonna go up and see him?"

"Don't think so." I took out a piece of paper from the little pad in my wallet and jotted down my cell number. I slid the piece of paper, along with another twenty, across the counter toward him. "I'll tell you what. I'd really appreciate it if you call that number if Mr. Kenobi leaves anytime soon."

The man nodded. "I might be able to do that."

"Thank you."

I turned and walked out of the building. When I got outside, I looked at the writing above the door. It said "Maplecrest Apartments." I jotted that name down, along with Jason's apartment number. In essence, my official work was done, but I knew I wasn't about to leave Washington until me and Jason had ourselves a little talk.

Chapter 9

After visiting Jason's apartment building, I walked across the street and parked myself inside the small pub, which advertised itself as just "Bar." There was no other name to the place, and when I walked in, I realized that the person who named the place had done so aptly. The place consisted of a small black Formica bar, two tables on the left hand side of the place, and two bathrooms. The place was dimly lit, and there were only two other people in the place besides me. One was the bartender, a surly-looking gentleman in his late thirties, and an old man sipping a beer at the far end of the bar.

"Customer," the old man announced. The bartender made a face at him, and walked over to me as I sat down at a barstool that gave me a perfect view of the front of Jason's building.

"Hey man," the bartender said, "What you need?"

"I'll take a Coors Light."

"Man wants a Coors Light," the old man said.

"Don't pay any attention to him. He's drunk out of his mind."

"No problem," I said.

The bartender walked over to a cooler, got me a bottle of Coors Light, and placed it in front of me. I put a twenty on the bar and took a sip of the beer, shocked that I was drinking for the third day in a row. I hoped something would happen with Jason quickly, in order to save my liver.

"Name's Steve," the bartender said. He seemed genuinely happy to have someone else in the place besides the drunk old man.

"His name's Steve," the old man said.

"Quiet, Jake," Steve said.

"What the hell I gotta be quiet for. I'm payin' for my drinks."

Steve ignored this and said, "He's been drinking vodka all day. I don't even know how he's still awake. The last three drinks I gave him were mostly water. Doesn't even notice it."

"He's probably got an iron liver," I said.

"Bet you he doesn't even have one."

I took another swig of my beer, looked down at the old man who was staring at his glass, and chuckled to myself. The guy had to be in his sixties, and he was pounding drinks on a Sunday afternoon. I felt bad for him. He was probably just some lonely old man who had nothing else better to do with his life. Hell, I could have been wrong. That guy might have been a Senator for all I knew.

"You visiting?" Steve asked.

"Something like that. How'd you know."

"You don't look like you're from D.C."

"New York," I said. "This your place?"

"Unfortunately. Friend of mine talked me into going partners with him, then he got married and bailed. Left me with this place and that drunk over there."

"I ain't drunk. Hell, I ain't even gotten started yet."

We both ignored the old man and he didn't seem to mind.

"The name of this place is just 'Bar?'" I asked.

Steve chuckled. "Yeah, when we bought this place, it had been closed down for a year or so. We tossed around about fifteen different names, and then one night, when we were both drunk, we came up with the idea to just call it that. Thought it was funny."

"It is."

"I guess so. Been thinking about changing the name, but I haven't come up with anything yet. Gotta come up with something that would make the college kids want to come here."

"Can't help you with that. College was a long time ago."

"I hear you, but that's where the money is, you know?"

I nodded, like I had any idea what made a bar money. I just knew how to give a bar my money.

"What hotel you at?" Steve asked.

"O'Malley's."

"By the train station, right?"

"Yep."

"What brings you all the way down here?"

"Looking for an old friend." I thought about asking Steve if he had seen Jason, but I highly doubted Jason would ever walk into a bar, let alone this one.

"Gotcha."

Steve gave me an empty look like he didn't know what else to talk about. That made two of us because the only thing I cared about was finding Jason. Steve seemed like a nice guy, the sort you could toss a few beers back with and tell a few jokes, but I wasn't in the mood for either. I took a long swig of my beer and was about to make some idle chat when my cell phone rang. I took it out of my pocket and looked at the number. It was my parents, and I instantly remembered that I had forgotten to call them and let them know about my trip. This wasn't going to be good, I figured.

"Yeah," I said, trying to sound harried.

"Darren?" It was my father, thank God.

"Hey Dad."

"You okay?"

"Yeah, just in the middle of something."

"Your mother's a little upset that you didn't show up today, as you can guess."

"I know. I'm sorry. I had to go out of town on a moment's notice."

"Out of town? Where are you?"

"Washington."

"The state?" *Why does everyone ask this?*

"D.C."

"What are you doing there?" Dad asked.

"Working, believe it or not. I meant to call to let you guys know but this all happened so quickly that I really didn't get the chance."

"Hey, no problem. I'm sorry to bother you. Just wanted to know what was going on is all."

"No big deal."

"Everything alright?"

"Yeah, fine," I said.

"You sure? You sound bothered about something."

"No, everything's good. I should be able to wrap this up sometime today, and be home by tomorrow."

"This is about Jason?"

"Yep."

"In Washington?"

"Yep."

"I told you this case was strange. Be careful, okay?"

"I will."

"Oh, and someone called here looking for you."

"Who?" I couldn't imagine anyone calling my parents' house looking for me. I hadn't lived there in years. "They leave a name or message?"

"No. When I said you didn't live here, they hung up."

"Male or female?"

"Female."

"How long ago?"

"About ten minutes ago, I'd say."

"Strange." The old man at the end of the bar started singing "People Are Strange," a tune I was surprised he knew.

"Shut up Jake," Steve said. Of course, Jake kept going on.

"Maybe an old friend or something," my father said.

"I don't have any of those."

"Well, I'll let you go. If this person calls back, should I tell them anything?"

"If I don't know who it is, probably wouldn't make any sense."

"This is true. You take care of yourself, alright?"

"Yeah, of course."

"I mean it."

"I know, Dad. Tell Mom I'm sorry, and I'll stop by during the week."

"You got it."

I ended the call and placed the phone on the bar. I finished my beer, and Steve replaced it without asking. I didn't want it, and was thinking about getting out of there and watching the building from somewhere else. The bar was depressing. I mean, it wasn't ugly or anything, but just sitting there with Steve and the old man drinking beers I didn't even want wasn't my idea of a good time. Still, I had nothing else better to do, and the place did have a good view of Jason's building.

After about ten minutes of sitting and being quiet, my bladder decided it was time to be emptied. I picked my phone up, and told Steve to keep an eye on the building for me while I was answering nature's call. He gave me a strange look, and I explained to him that I was waiting for an old friend and wanted to surprise them when they came out of the building. He mentioned something about surprising the old friend by knocking on their door, but I ignored it and went to the head.

The bathroom was as plain as the rest of the place, if you are one who cares about what public bathrooms look like. There was a toilet and a urinal, and both looked as old as the drunk man at the bar. It wasn't very clean in there either, which made me a little wary. I used to laugh at the people who refused to touch a toilet handle, or who insisted on using the aerial method when taking a dump in a public bathroom. After thinking about it once for an extended period of time, I realized that though such people might be a little touched, they were onto something, and at least they wouldn't have to worry about contracting some disease from a public bathroom. Since that epiphany, I made sure not to touch handles in the bathroom. Yes, I am one of those idiots that always leave a urinal unflushed. So, I am basically more concerned with my own health than anyone else, and whoever used a urinal after I did either had to touch the handle I refused to, or risk splashing my piss all over their pants. I know, I'm too nice a guy.

I finished my business, zipped up, and left yet another urinal unsanitary. Actually, my urine might have improved the sanitary condition of that bathroom. I walked out the door, and noticed the old man was staring at the door as if he had been waiting for me.

"Come here," he said when I walked out of the bathroom.

"Excuse me?"

"Come over here for a second."

Out of curiosity, I walked over. "Yeah?"

He extended a large hand. "What's your name?" he asked, squeezing my hand like a vise. This man might have seemed drunk and feeble, but his grip was formidable.

"Darren."

"What?" he asked, pulling my hand down lower and squeezing harder. It hurt.

"Darren," I repeated, hoping this guy would leave me alone.

"Darren. What sort of name is that?"

"One that begins with a 'D,'" I said.

"Wise guy, huh?"

"Me? No sir."

"What sort of name is Darren? You Irish?"

"No." The man still hadn't let go of my hand despite my subtle efforts to get it free.

"What are you?"

"Italian."

"Wise guy Italian."

"No, sir."

"My name's Jake. Jake the Sailor, they used to call me, 'cause I kicked the shit out of everyone in the place years ago."

"I bet," I said.

"What you say?"

"Leave him alone," Steve said.

"He's a grown man, he can speak for himself. Right, you Wop bastard?"

This guy was genuinely amusing. "What's a wop?" I asked.

"You're a Wop."

"I figured that, but what does it mean?"

"It means Wop, Ginny."

"I thought it meant 'Without Papers,' which would refer to immigration papers, that I don't have, only because I never needed them. So, although I might be a Wop, as you say, I am not the type you are thinking of."

The old man's face contorted a bit as if this was just too much information for his marinated brain to handle at one time. I got a sick enjoyment out of this. He looked out the window, gathered his thoughts, then turned to me.

"How would you like it if I punched you in the nose?" he asked. The amazing thing was how polite he was about it.

"I probably wouldn't like that very much, to be honest."

"I thought you were a tough guy."

"Enough, Jake," Steve said, coming over to our side of the bar.

"Relax, I'm just talking to this tough guy over here," Jake said, finally releasing my hand. I put it in my pocket, wanting to rub it but not wanting to look like a sissy.

"Leave him alone, I told you."

"It's okay," I told Steve.

"He does this to everyone."

"It's alright."

"You see? He's a tough guy. Don't worry about him."

Steve shook his head and went back to the other side of the bar. I wondered why he didn't just throw Jake out, and figured it was because he was afraid of him. That grip could instill fear in anyone, despite how weak this man looked.

"So, whaddya say I punch you in the face."

"I don't think that would be such a good idea."

"I do." Jake balled his fist in his lap. I thought about what would happen if he took a swing at me. I didn't see myself hitting him, even if he did piss me off. I figured the best thing to do was duck if the old geezer decided he wanted to box. He'd miss, and probably fall flat on his face. I almost wanted him to try, for the fun of it. I was bored.

While I was running it all through my mind, old Jake seized his opportunity and let go a quick left hook, which caught me on the side of the head. I caught the blow midway, which was too late, but I was able to grab his arm and pull him off his stool. I was falling backward, and he was about to come right on top of me. I sidestepped, and had my right hand ready to strike. I thought the better of hitting an AARP member, and just watched him stumble to the floor. He hit his head on the paneled wall with a crack, and was instantly unconscious. I stood over him, not sure whether to laugh or just get the hell out of there in case he got up.

"That was nice," Steve said.

"What should I do with him?"

"Leave him there. It's the best thing for him anyway. He does this about once a week. Usually, he knocks the other guy out with him."

"He almost did that to me too," I said, feeling the side of my head where a nice-sized knot had already started to form. I was happy he missed his target, my nose, because if he had been accurate, I would be bleeding all over the floor. That would have been embarrassing. "You sure he'll be okay?"

"He's not okay, and probably never will be. For right now, he's better off on the floor over there than he is sitting at the bar."

"You want me to move him?"

"I wouldn't."

"Okay."

My cell phone rang. I fished through my pocket, found the phone and answered it.

"Yeah."

"This is Walt, over at Maplecrest. Mr. Kenobi is still in his apartment, but I figured you'd like to know that he's getting a pizza delivery."

"A pizza delivery?"

"Yes sir. I'm going off duty now, but I thought you might want to know."

"Thank you," I said.

"No problem."

I ended the call, went over to where I was sitting, took the change I had on the bar, which was about eight bucks, and slid it over toward Steve.

"Nah, you don't have to do that."

"Take it. Don't worry about it. Good luck with the place."

"Yeah, thanks."

Chapter 10

I walked out the front door and waited for the pizza delivery guy to show up. I could have opted not to do what I had planned, and wait for another opportunity to meet face to face with Jason, but I learned a long time ago to seize the first opportunity you had. This way, I wouldn't be cursing myself later. Nothing worse than that.

The delivery guy showed up in a battered Honda Civic, parking in the "No Parking" zone in front of the building. I walked across the street and caught him as he was taking the pie out of the hatch. He was a twenty-something kid, dressed in jeans and a white t-shirt. I was happy to see he wasn't from one of the large chains like Dominos, or Pizza Hut, because one of those guys might have given me a problem with what I was about to try.

"Excuse me," I said, walking up to him.

"I'll move the car in a second," he said, not looking at me.

"No, I don't care about that. Is that pizza for 15H?"

He looked at the yellow receipt on the box. "Yeah."

"Thanks," I said, putting a twenty in the kid's hand.

"But I was told to deliver it directly to the apartment."

"I changed my mind."

He hesitated a second, then looked at the twenty.

"You need change?"

"Nope."

"Have a nice night," he said, getting back into the car and driving away. It had gone easier than I had thought. I can't remember that happening too many times.

I walked into the lobby of the Maplecrest, and this time there was a middle-aged bald guy there, with bifocal glasses. He was organizing his work station, or trying to look busy. He came across as one of those guys that took a job like his a bit too seriously. I just hoped he wouldn't give me a problem. Before I walked up to him, I glanced at the receipt on the box. Luck was going my way, because the name of the place was on the receipt. Okay, so I looked a bit old to be delivering pizzas, but I had seen some real losers holding a job like that.

"Delivery for 15H," I said, not making eye contact with the guard.

"15H?" he asked, in a voice that sounded way too high for him. "Where from?"

"Romanelli's. I've got a half-sausage here."

The guard checked a clipboard, then looked at me. I tried to look innocent, if that was at all possible. He gave me the expert once-over, or at least he thought he did, and then nodded.

"Go ahead up. Fifteenth floor, second door on your right."

"Thanks," I said, and made my way to the elevator at the end of the room.

On the ride up to the fifteenth floor, which was one from the top by the way, I tried to run the scenario through my mind. I was fairly confident that Jason wouldn't recognize me, even if I hadn't changed a bit from high school. I figured him to be wary of any stranger, but he seemed wiling to risk ordering out for a pizza. Think about it. Who would ever suspect someone to carry out the plan I just started? I complimented myself for my genius and waited for the elevator door to open.

The hallways in the Maplecrest were narrow, and there seemed to be only ten or twelve apartments on each floor, leading me to believe they were large. I walked straight down the hallway to the second door on my right, which was Jason's apartment, and rang the bell. At first, nothing happened, then I heard Jason say, "Hold on a minute." I heard footsteps coming to the door, and I figured he was looking through the peephole. I resisted waving at him.

"Who are you?" he asked through the door.

I leaned closer to the door and talked into the jamb. "Romanelli's"

"Where's Tim? Doesn't he usually work tonight?" Jason was

wary, much more so than I had thought.

"Sick. At least he called in sick."

Jason paused for a moment, then I heard the unlatching of about two deadbolts. He opened the door and looked me over. He did look considerably different from high school. He had put on about twenty pounds, and he was sporting the goatee I had mentioned earlier. He was dressed in shorts that looked to once be full sweatpants and a tank top. Certainly not the attire I would expect of someone of his stature.

"How much?"

"Eleven-fifty."

Jason eyed me again, then opened the door all the way. "Come on in," he said, and then walked into another room.

The apartment was huge. I could see a big screen TV in the right corner of the room, a black leather couch with matching love seat, and a Persian rug on the hardwood floors. Directly ahead of me was the sliding door to the balcony, and from where I was standing, I was treated to a nice view of the city below. This apartment cost a bundle, no doubt, and I wanted to know who actually owned it. That information wasn't pertinent. I was just curious. Maybe I could talk the guy into lending it to me for a little while.

Jason came back into the room with a twenty-dollar bill in his hand. He handed it to me, then took the pizza from my hand. He took it to a coffee table in front of the TV. There were papers scattered all over that coffee table, and a big brown briefcase on the floor next to it. Jason scooped up the papers and stuffed them into the briefcase. I pretended like I was fishing through my pockets for change, and then decided to end the charade.

"What are you working on there?" I asked, then closed the door.

"Nothing. Hey, what are you doing?"

"My job, Jason."

The look on Jason's face turned from irritation to absolute fear. In all my years on this planet, I had never seen someone so genuinely afraid before. "I knew it." His hand went into the briefcase and produced a snub-nosed .38. He lifted the gun toward me, his hand shaking visibly.

"Hey, put that fucking thing away," I said. Incredibly, I didn't even feel like someone was pointing a gun at me. I guess that was because I didn't think he could have come within a hundred feet of hitting me with a shot from that gun.

"Who are you?"

"You don't remember me?" I asked, casually reaching behind my back and getting my hand on my gun. I wasn't going to shoot Jason, or even take out the gun unless I absolutely had to. I just wanted to have all my bases covered.

"No, I don't fucking remember you."

"It's me, Darren. Darren Camponi."

Jason eyed me, keeping the gun pointed in my direction. "From Merrick?"

"Yep."

"What the fuck are you doing here?"

"Put the gun away and we'll talk about it."

"How do I know you're who you say you are?"

"Because I remember when you got caught whacking off in the gym bathroom in tenth grade. That prove it to you enough?"

Jason winced when I reminded him of the incident, but he didn't put the gun away.

"I should shoot you just for bringing that up," he said.

"You're not going to shoot me."

"What makes you say that?"

"Because you can't. And you'd get into a lot of trouble for shooting someone without provocation."

"You're in my apartment," Jason said.

"You invited me in, and this isn't your apartment."

"How did you know that?"

"Just put the fucking gun away, and we'll talk all about it."

Jason thought about this for a second, but he didn't seem convinced. I had to make some sort of move here. Even though I was sure he had horrible aim, I had become aware of the fact that he might accidentally pull the trigger with the way his hand was shaking. On an unintended shot, I figured he might have a chance of hitting me. I didn't feel like having my lead intake increased that day.

"Jason, put the gun away. I didn't come here to do you any harm. I just want to talk to you. Is that okay?"

"About what?"

"About a lot of things."

Finally, Jason laid the gun down on the coffee table. He put his head in his hands, and exhaled loudly. I walked a little closer to him and sat down in the love seat which was across from the couch he was sitting on.

"I can't take this anymore," he said.

"I can imagine."

He looked at me, again with a look of fear. This poor guy must have been through Hell. "How could you imagine? I'm a fugitive for no reason, and every day I have to worry about getting killed. What would you know about that?"

Nothing, I figured. "It's a figure of speech."

"Why are you here?"

"To help you out."

"How the hell are you going to do that?"

"I don't know," I said.

"Then why am I even talking to you?"

I thought about telling Jason the whole truth, about how I was hired to find him, and then how I was battling with the idea of not giving away his location in an effort to help him, but I figured he wouldn't buy that.

"I'm a private investigator."

"You're the one that followed me today."

I wondered how Jason had detected this, and why he had let a stranger into his apartment when he knew he had been followed. Maybe he had more trust in his firing aim than I did.

"That was me."

"Why?"

"Listen, Jason, word gets around in my business real fast. I found out that people have been hired to find you, and being that I knew you from high school, I figured maybe I would let you know what's going on."

"We weren't friends. Why would you do that?" I saw his hand inching toward the gun.

"Let's just say I became curious, and I needed something to do."

"You're one of the ones that was hired to find me, right?"

"I was approached about it, but I declined."

"So, you came here anyway, to help me out. I don't buy it."

"You don't have to. Listen, if I can find you, anyone can find you. People probably already have. You're in trouble, and I bet you didn't need me to tell you that."

Jason didn't say anything at first. He just stared out the sliding door. His hand hadn't gotten any further away from the gun.

"You're the first one I noticed around here. Either you are bad at what you do, or you are telling the truth."

I didn't like the criticism of my tradecraft, but I wasn't going to argue with him. Better to let him think I sucked at my job than think I was really after him. Besides, I had thought I did a pretty good job of getting to him undetected. He might have just been trying to provoke me, for whatever reason he had to do so.

"If I was really working on finding you, you wouldn't have noticed me. I wanted to try and talk to you back by the Capitol, but I figured you would just get spooked and run off," I said.

"Well, put yourself in my shoes. Wouldn't you be suspicious of everyone you met?"

"I don't know, Jason, only because I have sketchy details about what's going on with you. Why don't you tell me what you are going through?"

"I should trust you?"

"Let me put it to you this way. If I was hired to find you, I would have just located your address, staked out your place to confirm that, and then I would report to whoever hired me. I wouldn't come into your apartment and sit down with you, only because I would know you'd get the hell out of here right after I left."

"I might just do that anyway," Jason said.

"What, leave these accommodations?" I asked.

"My uncle owns this place. He isn't a blood uncle, and only someone close to my family would know we are even friends with him. That's why I chose to come here. It's pretty much untraceable. At least, I thought it was until you showed up. How did you find me here, anyway?"

"Long story," I said, "but I liked your alias. Real slick."

"I'm a big Star Wars fan. I've never had to go under a different name before and couldn't think of anything else. I wanted to use Han Solo, but I thought that no one would ever buy that name."

"Good point."

"These last few months have been hell."

"I'm sure."

Jason stood up, and went toward the kitchen. "Hey, I'm gonna get a soda. You want anything?" How nice of Jason to play the good host. I thought for a second that he might go into the kitchen and come back with a shotgun or something, but I had gotten the feeling that he trusted me. I am a trustable sort of guy, or at least that is what people tell me. Whether this is true or not is a completely different story.

"Got any diet soda?"

"It's all I drink."

"I'll take one."

Jason went into the kitchen, and when he did, I took his gun and put it back into his briefcase. When I opened the case, I saw about ten folders, all labeled "Continuum" which meant nothing to me. I thought about rifling through the papers, but I figured Jason wouldn't be too happy if he caught me doing that. I just placed the gun in the briefcase and waited for him to come back.

Jason brought me over a tall glass of soda with ice, and placed it on a coaster in front of me. I saw him notice that the gun was missing, and he looked at me funny, so I pointed to his briefcase. He got the message.

"I didn't think you needed that anymore. Take a look if you want. It's there."

"No, that's alright. Sorry about pulling that on you, but I have had death threats constantly. I figure if someone's gonna come and try to kill me, they'll leave with a few bullet holes themselves." Jason had tried to sound like Dirty Harry when he said that, but he came off more like a scared little scientist trying to protect himself. I doubted he would ever get a shot off if someone did come for him, and if he did manage to squeeze the trigger, he would probably damage one of the watercolor paintings on the walls instead of his target.

"You should be careful with that thing. Is it registered?"

Jason sat down on the couch. "No. A friend got it for me."

"You could get in a lot of trouble with that."

"I could get killed without it." I wanted to mention to him that he would get killed either way, but I didn't want to offend him.

"Just be careful."

"So, you became a private investigator after high school? I would never have picked that for you."

"Neither would I. It just happened." I told Jason the story of my college experience, along with my attempt at police work.

"That sucks. So, you became a private investigator instead of a policeman. I guess that's close enough."

"Yeah, I only don't get medical, I don't get to wear a uniform, and I don't get a pension. Other than that, it's pretty much the same thing. What are you doing with your life?"

Jason told me about how he went to Stonybrook because he was uncomfortable being away from home. He commuted to the school for two years, and he said because he was always working so late at the lab, it didn't make sense to commute anymore. After deciding that paying to live on campus at Stonybrook made no sense, he took an offer from UCLA. He had always wanted to see California. It turned out he didn't like it as much as he thought, but stayed there for his masters and doctorate. After that, he accepted an offer from the government to work as a researcher in Washington because the girl he fell in love with was moving there. I figured that's why I couldn't find any evidence of a residence in Washington. Maybe he had lived in that same apartment back then. He told me that the relationship broke off after he moved to D.C., and I said the girl probably got spooked, thinking aloud.

"She said she wasn't ready for a real commitment," Jason said.

Of course, this was the token reason given when you break up with someone. She was probably banging someone else on the side the whole time they were at UCLA, and used poor old Jason to help her with her studies or something. I couldn't remember Jason ever having a girlfriend in high school and I couldn't picture him ever having a girlfriend. Not that I thought he was gay or anything, he just seemed too nerdy to be interested in girls. Of course, the nerds are probably the most sex-obsessed group of men on the planet, if you can really divide us into groups that way. We're all sex-obsessed.

I wanted to ask Jason for more information about his job with the federal government, but I didn't want to make this seem like an interrogation. He was talking freely, and I figured I'd let him talk about whatever he wanted, and stick questions in here and there when I thought I could get away with them.

He told me about his leaving the job at the federal government, which I figured wasn't an easy task. He said he wanted out of Washington after the breakup, but he couldn't find a job he wanted so quickly. He said he had a few offers, and accepted the one in Cleveland because they had offered him the best research opportunity.

"What sort of science do you research?"

"Quantum Physics," he said. I had no idea what that was. He

must have noticed this, because he said, "That's the area of science that studies sub-atomic particles and how they affect the rules we have associated to common physics. Most people know it as the study of time travel, but that's not what it is all about."

"Sounds interesting."

"It is. I mean, even Einstein was confused when it came to Quantum Physics, and all he basically said was that we couldn't disprove its existence. I've followed it from when I was in junior high, and I always wanted to prove the existence of sub-atomic anomalies. That's what I won the Intel Science Award in high school for."

"I remember you winning that."

"All the colleges had started to heavily recruit me after that, but, like I said, I didn't want to be too far away from home. It was pretty stupid, actually, because Stonybrook really didn't have the facilities to handle what I wanted to study. I basically wasted two years there."

"Well, it seems things turned out okay for you. How did things go in Ohio?"

"Things went great. They gave me my own lab to supervise, and the students and I were getting into some real serious stuff. I was on the verge of making a major discovery before I left."

"Why did you leave?"

"Long story."

"That's what I came here for."

"You really want to hear all of this?" Jason asked.

"I came here to help, Jason."

He gave me a look like I must be crazy. In fact, I wasn't crazy. I was just curious. And, I was a liar as well. As much as I felt bad for him, I couldn't turn down the two grand for locating him.

"Well, after I was at Cleveland for about two years, I started getting phone calls from my former employer."

"The government."

"Right. You see, much of what I was doing at Cleveland was a continuation of my work for the government. A lot of people don't realize how heavily into science the government is. Many of the programs they are engaged in are top secret, and though most of them are harmless, the government guards their programs. They were worried about me divulging classified information."

"Was that what you were doing?"

"No." He paused for a second, looked at the pizza box, then back at me. "You wanna eat?"

"Sure, why not?" I was hungry. Jason opened the box, took a slice, and then slid the box my way. Even though I am Italian, I hate sausage, so I took a cheese slice.

"Their pizza is the closest to New York's," he said with a full mouth.

I took a bite. It wasn't even close to what they serve at the worst places in New York. I know what they say about New York water being the best for bread, bagels, and pizza, but this pizza wasn't bad because of the crust. The sauce tasted like tomato soup, and the cheese was stiff.

"Not bad," I said.

"Better than what I used to get in Cleveland, and I won't even talk about the crap they pushed as pizza in California."

"So, were you really taking the information you got from the government and using it at the university in Cleveland?"

"No. You see, there is pretty much a common pool of information in the science community about Quantum Physics. Of course, each scientist working on it comes up with his or her own theories, but the facts, if you want to call them that, are the facts. I was working on a parallel project at the university, but I didn't take any of the information I gathered at the government job with me to Cleveland."

"Well, some of that stuff had to be in your head."

"That's the catch. They didn't want me to leave at first. They tried to sweeten the pot and all that, but I just couldn't stay here after breaking up with Diana. Everything here reminded me of her. They said that they would transfer me to another part of the country, and I thought about that for a while, but the truth is, I took the government job because of her. I would never have gone to work for them if it wasn't for her. It took about a year for them to let me leave, and in that time, I noticed that they had removed me from the main projects and had me doing unimportant stuff. I figured they didn't trust me anymore, and that was fine with me, because I was leaving."

"Sounds like working for the government is like working for the mob."

"It's not much different, I'll tell you that. I bet the mob pays better though."

"The higher the risk, the better the pay."

"Yeah. Well, like I said, after I had been at the university for two years or so, my old supervisor called me a couple of times. At first, he called just to see how I was doing. Then he started to ask questions about my research and all that. I answered him, mainly because I didn't think he was prying. We had gotten along pretty well when we worked together, and I thought he was just being friendly. At worst, I figured he would try and apply some of what I was doing to his work. I didn't care about that because, if he made a discovery, it wasn't like he was going to win the Nobel Prize for it. His name would never make it into the papers."

"All work, no fame," I said.

"Pretty much. Then he started calling and telling me I should be careful. I asked him what I should be careful about, and he told me I should know. I told him I had no idea what he was talking about, and he told me to think about it. These calls went on for a year or so, and I even spoke to someone at the university about it, and they told me not to worry. So I didn't. I went about my business. I didn't hear from my supervisor after that, and I thought everything was fine until one day when I got a visit from some guy claiming to be from the FBI. His name was Hoven, or something like that." That was Dave Hovelle, I figured, solidifying my belief that the man who called me at home did work for the government. That didn't make me feel too confident. "He said he was doing a routine checkup on me because I was a former employee of the government. He asked to see some of my work, and when I initially refused, he went to one of the higher-ups at the university. I was told to put together a file for this guy, which I did. I didn't hear anything from him for a while, but then he showed up again, saying he needed more information. Again, I refused. I didn't want the government to steal everything I was working on, and I'll tell you this, that file I put together for him contained very little information. It wasn't that I was afraid of getting into trouble, I just didn't think they needed to see all of that."

"The government needs to see whatever it wants."

"I guess so. When I told this fed guy that I wasn't going to give him any more information, he threatened me. Well, he didn't necessarily come out and say something, but he hinted at the fact that I could be in a lot of trouble if I didn't give him what he wanted. I tried calling my supervisor from Washington, but he wouldn't take my call. I talked to the people at the university, and they started acting strange. I mean, they were always so concerned about leaking out research information. They had told me a story about how one of the researchers at the university had published some of his work on the web, and how someone had taken that information and made the discovery he was working on before he did. Universities make a lot of money when they come up with a scientific breakthrough, and they are very protective of their work. For the university to want to willingly hand over information to the government didn't sit with me right. I told them this, and they said that they recommended I comply with the government but that ultimately the decision was up to me. I called the fed guy and told him that, as far as I understood it, I owed them nothing. He disagreed, but didn't threaten me again. Everything went along smoothly until I noticed I was being followed from work to home. I would hear strange sounds on my phone, which led me to believe it was tapped. And one time I saw that the lab had been broken into. They wouldn't have found any of my paperwork there. I took that home with me every night. But the computers were acting funny. This was a lot for me to handle, and I didn't know what to do."

Jason reached for another slice of pizza, and so did I. Even though it wasn't good, I was starving. Jason took a large bite, dropping crumbs on the floor. He didn't seem to mind.

"So, what did you do?" I asked.

Jason swallowed the large chunk of pizza in his mouth. "Nothing. What could I do? It's the government, for Christ's sake. I guess I should have just given them what they wanted, but I didn't think that was the right thing to do. I deleted any information on my computer at work, and I made sure there were no files lying around the lab. The students weren't directly involved with my research so I didn't have to worry about them giving anything away. Again things calmed down a bit, but one day a female student came into my office crying about how someone was harassing her for information on what I was working on. She told me that someone offered to pay her to steal something. That's when I knew I was in trouble. I mean, if the government wanted my information so bad, couldn't they have just gotten a court order or something?"

"I would think so. They are the government, right?"

"That's what I thought. I told myself that things were happening that didn't make sense. Someone wanted the information I was working on, and it seemed like they would do anything to get it."

"That's pretty much how it works, I suppose. What did you do?"

"What could I do? I wanted to find this guy and threaten him somehow, but how would someone like me be able to do that? Instead, I made up phony research documents and stored them in my office and on my computer. It took a little over a week, and while I was doing that, the fed guy called again and I told him I was preparing what he wanted. He kept pressuring me, and I did my best to stay composed."

I watched Jason as he spoke, checking his body language for any hints that he might be making this all up. I was pretty sure he trusted me, and that he was telling me the truth, but you never know when someone is going to give you a line of shit. As a matter of fact, everyone in this case had lied to me so far. Jason's mother lied about seeing him, that I was sure of. Mike had lied too, most likely, about the details of the case. I couldn't really be mad at him, because he told me what I needed to know. He just wanted Jason found. He probably couldn't have given a shit about anything else. From what I saw in Jason's body language, I decided he was telling the truth. I thought he might have been exaggerating a little bit here and there, but I appreciated that. It made things more interesting.

"It must have been tough," I said, finishing the last of my soda. I placed the glass on the coffee table, and Jason gave me a look. I found the coaster, which I had inadvertently knocked on the floor, and put the glass on that. Some people are just too touchy.

"It was tough. I worked day and night, both on the dummy papers, and on my real research. I had to close off all the students from the real work, only because I didn't know if that fed guy would go after another one of them, one that would break under pressure. None of them came to me and said that they had been questioned, but that didn't mean they hadn't. I started suspecting all of them of working with that guy, and I distanced myself from all the students. They noticed, and a few of them asked me about it. You know, they'd roundabout mention it, asking me if I was okay and all that. What bothered me is that some students that I never talked to asked me if I was okay. Why would they care? I figured they were definitely working for the other team, and I knew it was time to end the game."

"How did you plan on doing that?"

Jason eyed the pizza box, and went for his third slice. I didn't have trouble figuring out how he gained the weight. Sucking down a half a sausage pie doesn't exactly do wonders for the waistline. I had the feeling he would have eaten the whole pie if I wasn't there. I did all I could to get through two slices.

"I didn't have many choices. What bothered me the most was that I was so close to a breakthrough. I was right on top of it. All the work I had been doing since the beginning was about to pay off, and someone wanted to take that away from me. What gave them the right?"

"They are the government. They don't need rights."

"Yeah, well, I outsmarted them."

"You did?" I asked, a tinge of disbelief in my voice.

"Absolutely. You see, I shipped off that phony paperwork to the feds, and I stored it all on my computer. I had a program that scrubs a hard drive to the point where no deleted files are retrievable in part or whole. All my old information, the real paperwork and files, I saved those on a laptop and put it in a safe deposit box under another name, a member of the family. And then, one day while I was sitting in my office, I decided it was time to leave. I walked into the Dean of Science office and quit. They asked me a million questions, all of which I refused to answer, and I walked out the door. Then I went to New York for a week, but realized it wasn't safe there so I came down here. That's when the shit hit the fan. The university realized the paperwork I left behind was bogus, and they wanted the real information. It was valuable to them, even if the government got hold of it. It's Nobel Prize-winning research, that I can tell you. The government starting poking around my mother's house, and that's when I realized I was in trouble."

"So, you did steal intellectual property," I said, watching him scarf down the last of his third slice. He eyed the box again, and took a fourth slice, to my amazement.

"This pizza is so good." Yeah Jason, of course it was. "Well, if you go strictly by the letter of the law, I am guilty on two counts. I did happen to lift a little information from the government, and I certainly walked away with everything from the university."

"You signed an agreement with them?"

Jason nodded.

"Do you think they would just drop this whole thing if you returned the information to them? I mean, just pass it on to them and get on with your life."

"It's too late for that."

"Why?"

"Because the government is involved. It's out of the university's hands now."

"Is it?"

"Yes."

"I don't think so," I said.

"What do you mean?"

"Exactly what I just said. I don't think they are out of this at all. I think they have some sort of interest."

"What makes you say that?"

"Because they are willing to pay over five grand to find you."

Jason's eyes opened wide and he put the slice of pizza back into the box. He looked angry, and scared. I would say more scared than angry.

"You were hired to find me."

"I didn't say that."

"But you just told me how much you are getting paid to find me."

"I told you how much the university is paying someone I know. I never said I was the one getting paid for it." Well, that wasn't a total lie.

"You helping him?"

"I told him I'd think about it."

"Are you going to help him?"

"Doubt it. I'm not in the business of helping out the federal government. They don't pay well."

Jason went back to his slice of pizza, dripping sauce on his shirt. He didn't seem to mind, or he didn't notice. I don't know which. He didn't say anything for a while, he just sat there eating his pizza and thinking about whatever was on his mind. We were both sitting there in near silence, the only sound coming from Jason's cow-like chewing. How some people are raised without proper table manners is beyond me. Why does eating have to be an aural experience? Why can't people just close their fucking mouths and eat like human beings?

As you can see, loud eaters bother me.

"Five thousand. That's all they offered?" Jason said, breaking the disturbing silence. I welcomed his voice in place of his chewing.

"From what I heard."

"That's not a lot."

What, did Jason think he was worth more than that? "It is by the industry's standards. Usually finding someone costs one tenth of what they are paying."

"It's still a pittance," Jason said.

"What do you mean?"

"I am much more valuable to them. I am worth millions. It's foolish of them to pay so little in order to find me."

"Maybe they didn't want to draw too much attention to you."

"This guy that is on the case . . . Wow, that sounds weird. I never thought I would be the center of a 'case' or anything like that. This is like the movies, only I don't know the end of the plot. I'm afraid to know, if you want the truth."

"What did you want to ask?"

"Oh, this guy that was hired to find me. Is he any good?"

I thought about that for a moment, along with Jason's criticism of my tradecraft. "The best," I said. "Only, he doesn't have many resources in the New York area, where he thinks you are."

"That's why he called you."

"Exactly."

"Wow. Small world."

"Tell me about it."

"I hope I can stay on the run long enough. I am almost at the breakthrough point. Once I do that, things will change."

"How?"

"I'll have a bargaining chip. Because I took all the real research with me, no one has the accurate figures they need to continue the research. As far as I know, I'm the only one who is this close. If I'm successful, the President himself will order me protected, in the name of national security."

"What sort of breakthrough?"

"I need to test it. I need a volunteer to test my project with me."

"No, I mean, what are you working on?"

Jason didn't hear this question. "You want to be my volunteer?"

"For what?"

"A time travel experiment."

It took a while to set in. When I realized what Jason was talking about, I understood why the government was so anxious to get a hold of his research. This definitely pertained to the security of the country, and if the wrong person who got hold of it, it could be disastrous. It always turned out that the wrong person does get a hold of such information. Without this, the plot of the world would be boring at best. I wondered if perhaps Jason was the wrong person. I couldn't imagine him doing anything evil, but then again, one never knows.

"What do you mean, time travel?"

"I mean exactly what I said. I am offering you the ability to travel back in time."

I remembered the conversation I had with Rich the night before, about exactly the same thing. Yet another coincidence. I didn't like it. "Why me?" I asked.

Jason forced a chuckle. "It's not like I have anyone else."

"I don't know. I kind of think time should be left as is. I don't want to be a part of screwing around with it."

"Well, I am going to screw around with it. You might as well be a member of the team."

"It's not my bag."

"What, you don't want to go back and change things from the past?" Jason asked. I thought about that for a moment.

"If I wanted to change something from the past, it would be everything. I don't think that's possible. Plus, in the first turn with time, I made it to 34 alive. Who's to say that I would be so successful this time around? I had a lot of close calls that could have gone either way."

"I understand, and that's what's so fascinating about the time continuum." Now I understood the labeling on the folders in his briefcase. "Anything is possible. But my question goes deeper than that."

"How so?"

"Well, not one scientist in the history of the world has been able to disprove the possibility of time travel. That is a given. It is just a matter of time, so to speak, to reach the breakthrough. In actuality, I'm not even trying to answer the question of time travel, I'm trying to answer an even bigger question."

Jason started to get excited, but he was talking almost as if he was giving a speech on a podium. I didn't appreciate that sort of thing, but I sat and listened to him. I waited for him to continue, but I think he was waiting for me to ask the question. So I did. "What bigger question?" Jason's eyes opened wider and he went back to "Speech" mode.

"The question about what governs us all."

"What are you talking about?" Truly, I had no idea.

"I'm talking about whether there is a big honcho sitting up there, looking down on us."

"What does that have to do with time travel?" I asked, not completely following him.

"Nothing, really. You see, time travel and its discovery will be major. More important that the cure of AIDS or cancer. That's because you could conceivably go back to before those diseases came and prevent them from happening, I suppose. Well, that would be easier with AIDS, I guess, but you know what I mean. So, I make the discovery, the breakthrough. Man is now able to travel back in time . . ."

"Only backwards?" I asked, cutting him off.

"Well, it appears that way. At least, in my research, I have only been able to theorize time travel through the lifespan of the volunteer."

"You've had other volunteers?" I asked. "How did they fare?"

"No, they were theoretical. It's all theoretical, but I am almost one hundred percent sure it will work. It has to work. The government was working on a similar project, and I saw how close they were getting. Only they were making a big mistake. They altered the prototype too much. There was too much of a deviance in their machine."

"What machine? A time machine?"

"Not really, not in the sense you are thinking. It's not like *Back to the Future*, or H.G. Wells, though he was pretty close. There is no 'machine' that you sit into and get launched back in time by. Instead, it is done through computers and your brain. The computers latch onto the waves in your brain and pinpoint your entry back in time through your memories. It's quite fascinating."

"I'm sure."

"But that's not my point."

"Right, you were talking about the big question."

"Well, let me put it to you this way. If you were able to go back in time, and let's say you live your life quite similarly to the way you did, but you accidentally kill someone in a car accident, or something like that. That wasn't originally in the cards, so not only have you changed your immediate fate by going back in time in the first place, but you ended someone's life who wasn't supposed to die. You altered the 'Master Plan,' something we are taught from a young age we cannot do. From as early as the Ancient Greeks we were taught that anyone who tries to usurp the power of the gods ends up destroyed. That's what happened to Patroclus. Even thought he didn't usurp the power of the gods directly, he tried to take on the role of a hero by wearing Achilles' armor in battle, and he died for it. Look what happened to the men who built the Tower of Babel, if you want to take a Judeo-Christian example. All around, you've got references to the negative consequences of trying to play god. If you go back in time and kill someone, you are usurping God's power, and you must then be destroyed according to the teachings."

I thought about this for a second. I wasn't too up on literature or religion, but I was familiar with what Jason was talking about. It made sense, what he was saying. We are always taught to honor our god, and not to try and be too much like him or her. But, then again, there were genetic scientists who were on the verge of cloning human beings, the most god-like action you could carry out. Nothing was happening to them. Hell, it could be argued that God was at fault because he let the technology be discovered. Maybe time travel, like cloning, was just a tool that God allowed us to create and do with what we please, the same way he let the Tree of Knowledge grow right in the middle of the Garden of Eden. He either had a grander plan that we could imagine, or he was a sick and sadistic god who enjoyed tempting us with our own destruction.

"What if time travel is just an extension of God in us? I mean, he created us, if you believe that, and anything we create is just a by-product of his creation. Nothing we do can be God-like, because he created us, not the other way around."

"I never thought of it that way," Jason said. "Maybe you're right, but I think the discovery of time travel will prove it either way. There has to be some governing factor in our lives, something that makes us breathe one day and then stop the next. That something either lives within us, or it resides up above us, looking down in Judgment." He said the word judgment with conviction.

"Which one do you think it is?"

"It resides within us."

"So, you're doing this to disprove the existence of God?"

"The atom bomb did that. Millions of innocent people were killed for no reason."

"I don't remember being given a contract when I came to this planet. I think you get what you can make out of it. Unfortunately, those people were in the wrong place when the wrong thing was dropped on their country."

Jason smiled. "That's a unique outlook on it. Most people are too consumed in either religion or the debasing of it to try and see a thread of truth that runs through everything in our existence."

"You think you know what that thread is?"

"I don't know for sure, but I think time has something to do with it. I want to try and tear that thread and see what happens. And I want to see if the God we all talk about does exist, and see if he tries to get in my way."

"Well, good luck."

"You sure you don't want to volunteer?"

"With all your talk about the destruction of usurpers?"

"Well, yeah."

"No thanks. And my advice is, if you find another candidate, tone that part down a little bit. The whole Greek/Tower of Babel thing can get a little frightening."

I stood up, stretched out a bit, and decided it was time to leave.

"You gonna turn me in?"

"To who?"

"Come on, you can tell me if you were hired to find me. I didn't buy the whole thing about some out of state P.I. being given the job. The university contacted you, right?"

"Nope." Again, not a lie. A distortion of truth perhaps, but not a lie.

"I don't know. I can't imagine why you came all this way."

"I promised your mother I would try and help you."

"How is she?" Jason asked.

"Worried. The feds have her staked out every day."

"I knew it. I have to end this soon. I need to get this thing proven."

It was interesting how Jason was talking so casually about proving time travel. This was a major breakthrough, and he was talking about it like he was talking about the creation of a better toilet seat. Although, the new toilet seat would be welcomed. Still, we were talking about the dreams of scientists for years. Yeah, we realized many of their dreams, doing things they thought impossible, but this one seemed to be the granddaddy of them all. And here I was, being offered the opportunity to be a part of it all, only to turn it down. I guess I was scared. Okay, I was shitting my pants at the idea of going back in time.

"You leaving?" Jason asked.

"Yeah. I heard what I wanted. I'll head back up to New York, and tell your mother you're doing fine."

"You promised her you'd help me?"

"I did."

"And how did you do that?"

"I tried to get you to call it quits. You don't want to do that. I didn't promise your mother that I would make everything better, just that I would try to help."

"I can't just turn this stuff back to them, I think you can see that."

"I can, and that's why I decided to leave. There's nothing I can do to help you."

"You could be my volunteer."

"Not gonna happen. Sorry."

"Well, I gave it my best shot," Jason said, shrugging.

"You gave it your best three shots."

"Take care of yourself, Darren. It was good seeing you again. Oh, and thanks for the pizza."

"Yeah, thanks for pulling a gun on me. Be careful with that thing, okay?"

Jason looked down at the coffee table like a kid who had just been scolded. "I will."

"Good boy. Take care."

Chapter 11

I left Jason's building and went back to my hotel. The whole taxi ride there, I thought about what Jason told me. He really did make a major discovery, if everything he said was true, and I didn't have a hard time imagining the university and the government sparing no cost to get a hold of it. That explained the university's willingness to pay five grand to find him, and it also put that guy Hovelle's actions into perspective. The fewer witnesses the better, and I figured that Hovelle's job, among other things, was to make sure I didn't get to Jason and find out what he had to say. Well, it was too late for that, and I couldn't have given a shit. I found out what I needed to know. All I had to do was decide whether or not to report my discovery to Mike. I didn't think I had a chance of making him see the importance of not turning in Jason. Mike looked at things in black and white. In his mind, I gathered, Jason's location was worth money. What happened after he delivered that information wasn't something Mike would ever concern himself with. That made him a good businessman, I'm sure, but it didn't do too much for his reputation as a good man. Most P.I.'s that I knew didn't want to deal with him. They thought he was too much of a hardass, and he was accused of underpaying. I never had a problem with him, and couldn't imagine him to be the scumbag he was being accused of. I just wouldn't trust him to do the human thing if there ever was a chance for him to have to.

With Jason's situation, Mike could have had the opportunity to prove his humanity. I wasn't sure how he would handle the situation, so I decided to delay telling him anything until I got back to New York. I would give it some thought, and hopefully come up with a solution I could live with. I knew that wasn't going to be easy. I either had to protect someone that I hadn't seen in over a dozen years and lose a substantial sum of money, or I could take that money and pay off some bills that were collecting dust. Or, if I was really creative, I could find a way to get the money and protect Jason.

The catch to the whole situation, the thing that made it hard to decide, was the involvement of the government. They seemed to be the evil ones, the ones who I wanted to work against. If I gave Mike the information about Jason's whereabouts, the federal government would have that information almost instantaneously. I'm not anti-government, or anything like that, but they spend a good deal of time, and a good deal of our money, to cover up their shady practices. They are constantly deceiving the public, albeit many times for our own good, and I figured it was about time they got a taste of their own medicine. My desire to help out Jason had nothing to do with the fact that I felt sorry for him, or that I thought he was innocent, but because I wanted to cheer him on against the government. I knew this was foolish, as well as just plain wrong, but I enjoyed the idea of helping the rebel out. Now, all I had to do was find out how I was going to do that.

It was 9pm when I got back to my hotel room, and I wasn't sure what to do. I thought about getting on the phone with Amtrak to see if there was a late train to New York. That way, I could go back to the daily routine. Realizing my daily routine sucked, I figured one night in Washington wouldn't be too bad for me. Plus, who wants to arrive in Penn Station after midnight?

I called the front desk and asked what time the pub closed. The man informed me they were open late, until about 2am. I hung up the phone, changed into my suit, and decided to hit Washington with class. One never knew when the next female encounter lurked around the corner, and I had a funny feeling that night would be lucky for me. I even fixed my hair for the second time in a day, and threw on some cologne I had bought four years before. I was ready to go, and no one was getting in my way.

Idiot.

The bar downstairs in O'Malley's was called the Artful Dodger. It must have been the fifth place I had encountered in my life with the

137

same name. I don't know who thought that the old Artful Dodger was a good name to base a bar on, but it seemed like the idea caught on. This one was older than most I had been in, and judging from the oak bar and the signage behind it, I figured it was built sometime around the turn of the century. I liked the feeling of the place, just the essence of old furnishings and no nonsense decoration. Maybe I have an old soul. Or maybe, my soul is 34 years old and I just happen to like old stuff.

I sat down at the bar, took a look around at the forty or so patrons about the place, and waited for the bartender, a young guy with dyed white hair, to take my order. He was busy talking to a couple of guys at the end of the bar who appeared to be the same age as him. Sitting there, waiting, I thought about what Jason had offered me. Sure, he could have been some wacko thinking he had the next great scientific invention, but what if he wasn't? What if he was really offering me the chance to go back in time and change the past? I didn't know what I would change and what I would keep the same, but my mind instantly ran to a few key moments in my life. I thought of Tanya first, only because someone at the bar looked remotely like her, and I realized I was afraid of never talking to her again. What I once had been so sure of was now a major dilemma in my life. Sure, I would have loved to go back and repair that relationship. I also would have tried to prevent my jackass knee injury, and see what it was like to work on the force. I can't say it was what I always wanted to do, but it was close. Actually, I wanted to work as a cop, then be able to write about it.

College was another dilemma. If I really wanted to be a policeman, then did I need to go back and fix my college mistakes? I was proud of my degree, but I couldn't see myself going through four years of that again. And that brought me to another question. How long was Jason able to send me back? I wondered if he had the ability to send me back for an infinite period of time, or if there were intervals, or something. He did mention the act of killing someone in the past, which you would need a certain amount of time to do. Then again, he mentioned theories a lot, and he might have just been theoretical with me about that.

I couldn't think of too many things I wanted to change, but the prospect of going back to high school and taking advantage of all the things I passed up did sound nice. I mean, I did have a few obstacles in my way in high school, but I figured I could talk my way around acne and whatever else prevented me from getting laid during that time period. Actually, there were a lot of things that prevented me from getting laid over all the time periods of my life, which brought me to the present moment and my thinking it was my lucky night.

The bartender came over. "What'll it be?" he asked. He had a thick Irish accent, like the sort the rural people of Ireland had.

I looked around the bar, unable to decide what I wanted. Hell, I was in an Irish bar with an Irish bartender, I might as well do as the Irish do.

"Let me have a Guinness," I said, proud I was acting like one of the boys.

Now, I didn't drink Guinness too often, mainly because it was too thick and bitter for my tastes. My sister one time referred to it as soy sauce, and I can't say she was too far off the mark. I thought it had more of an engine oil consistency, but then again, I hadn't ever drank motor oil. On the bright side of Guinness, I had a Jamaican friend who insisted that Guinness was like a brewed Viagra. "It keeps ya goin' all night, mon," he said to me one time when I asked why he was drinking it. I didn't have problems with the hydraulics, but the idea that the stuff the bartender was pouring and letting settle for me would lube those hydraulics was welcomed. Like I said, this was supposed to be my lucky night.

After about three minutes, yes I timed it, the bartender was finished with the process of pouring the Guinness and brought it over to me. He had even made the shamrock within the head of the beer, and I appreciated his artistry. Something about an Irishman pouring my beer made me feel all that more authentic.

I reached into my pocket and pulled out a twenty, realizing that bill only had two others to keep it company. That guy at Jason's building had milked me pretty good. I put the bill on the bar, but the bartender waved me off.

"Yer drink is with the lady," he said, gesturing toward a brunette six stools away from me. She looked to be in her late thirties, and though I didn't get a look at her body, something told me she was well put together. She just gave off a sexual vibe. I looked at the Guinness, raised my glass to her, and took a long sip of the sexual elixir. Work your magic Guinness, I said to myself.

I wasn't sure if I should walk over to the woman, or stay where I was. I wasn't too schooled on the etiquette of the bought drink, and I wasn't the type to send drinks to a woman. I did it a few times when I was wasted, and most of those experiences ended unsatisfactorily, to say the least. I tried to think of what I would expect if I had bought this woman a drink. Well, that wasn't too hard to figure out. I would have expected her to come over, say hello, and come up to my room with me to check out the springs on the bed. Fantasies aside, I felt like a jackass sitting there not knowing what to do. I wished I had someone there that I knew, someone who could give me advice. No such luck.

The bar was crowded, making a walk over to her part of the bar even more difficult. Plus, if I screwed up, I'd have an audience. Not cool. So, I ruled that possibility out. The next option was to shoot for eye contact. I could try and get her to come my way, if I was lucky.

I looked at her, and she smiled at me. She had a seductive smile. I raised my eyebrows, as if this was some sort of international message for her to get her hot little self over to my part of the bar. She raised hers in return, finished her drink, and got up. God, I was good.

"Well hello," she said. She had a deep voice. Not a manly voice, but sort of like Madeline Kahn. I always thought Madeline Kahn was hot. I couldn't remember if she was still alive at the time, and felt guilty for thinking sexually about someone who might be dead.

"Hi," I replied. To me, my voice sounded weak.

"What are you doing here all by yourself?"

"I was about to ask you the same question."

"Cute." By stroke of pure luck, there was an empty seat next to me. She looked at it, and said, "Do you mind?"

"Yes."

She chuckled, then sat down. "You're funny."

"I guess that's a compliment."

"Of course." She had deep green eyes, and I caught a look at them. They were emerald. She seemed extremely well manicured. Her hair was perfect, and her skin was smooth, with just a touch of makeup, enough to accent her already striking looks. Yeah, she was turning me on.

"Thanks for the drink," I said, raising the glass. I took a sip. The worst part about Guinness, other than the thickness of it, was the head. It always managed to get on your upper lip. I took a napkin and wiped it off. I felt like an idiot.

"I saw you walk in, and I said to myself that you needed company. Sorry if that was too forward of me." She didn't seem like she cared about offending me. I wondered for a second if maybe she was a prostitute, and quickly dismissed it. I was a good looking guy. This woman was genuinely interested in me. At least, that's what I told myself.

"Not at all."

"What are you all dressed up for?"

"Someone told me this place required a jacket."

She laughed, one of those laughs that made me think she was trying to impress me. "No, really."

"I just felt like getting dressed."

"Nothing wrong with that." Going for another sip of my beer, I realized this woman was sitting there without a drink. How slick I was.

"What are you drinking?"

"Seven and seven."

I got the bartender's attention by waving my hand, but he didn't come over. Instead, he just went and poured her another drink. He brought it over and took the twenty I had tried to give him before.

"Where are you from?" she asked.

"Guess I don't look like a D.C. boy?"

"Nope."

"New York. Long Island, actually."

"That's what I figured. Heard the accent." Speaking of which, I couldn't place hers. Actually, she didn't have any accent whatsoever. She spoke clearly, something my New York ears weren't accustomed to. "What brings you to D.C.?"

"Just visiting a friend."

"Female friend?"

I shook my head. "Old high school friend."

"That's nice. What do you do?"

"Private Investigator."

"You here on business?" she asked.

"Not exactly." I didn't like the direction this conversation was headed. "You originally from here?"

She took a sip of her drink and shook her head. "No. I was born in Nebraska. Raised on a farm and the whole thing. After college, I realized I couldn't do much out there."

141

"What do you do?" I asked.

"Political consultant." I had no idea what that meant, but I didn't want to seem like an idiot for asking.

"Interesting. Guess you fit right in here."

"You could say that. The funny thing is, I miss home. The people there are just so much more genuine. I don't know how to describe it, but the people here strike me as phony. They don't look directly at you when they talk to you."

I could imagine several places someone would look at when talking to her, most notably her ample chest. "I know what you mean."

"People in New York the same way?"

"No. They look directly into your eyes when they tell you off," I said.

"You're so refreshing," she said. That's one thing I had never been called. "What's your name?"

"Darren."

"I'm Suzette, but you can call me Suzy. Everyone does."

"Okay, Suzy," I said, extending my hand. She shook it. Her hand was soft, yet her handshake was firm. She had it going on, you could say. "Nice to meet you."

"You too," she said.

Here's where things get uncomfortable, I thought. We had gone through the obligatory questions and statements, and I had even made a few attempts at humor, but I didn't know what to say next. I mean, I had an idea she had something in mind when she bought me the drink, but I didn't know how to cultivate that. I could have been wrong, of course. She might have just wanted someone to talk to. That's the problem with meeting people in bars; you never knew when to go for the gold and when to sit tight and let things happen. Being the coward I was, I chose the latter.

"Been here long?" I asked.

"You mean in Washington, or the bar?"

"Both," I said, figuring this would extend the conversation a bit.

"I've been in Washington for ten years, and in the bar for about an hour." Well, so much for extending the talk.

"Okay."

"You don't do this too often, do you?"

"What?"

"Meet women in bars." Now, how was I supposed to answer that? If I said I didn't, I sounded like a gentleman but also a schmuck who didn't score with women. If I said I did, I would come across as a womanizer, which, depending on her intentions, was either a good or bad thing.

"From time to time," I said, going for the middle ground.

She laughed again. "You seem uncomfortable."

"I'm not." I took a sip of my beer, actually tasting it this time. It was good, with a nutty sort of flavor. I could see myself liking it.

"Well, you seem that way to me, and I'm pretty good at that sort of thing."

"Do you buy drinks for guys often?" *Good one, Darren.*

Another laugh. "No. You just seemed like a nice, approachable guy. And you were alone, so I seized the moment. Plus, I didn't see a ring on your finger, which I know means nothing these days."

"I'm not married."

"Who is in a bar?"

"True. But I mean it, I'm not married."

"Neither am I. I'm not ready to serve that sentence yet."

"Same here."

"No girlfriend? Jesus, listen to me. Like you'd tell me either way. Forget I asked."

"I'm between girlfriends, if you want the truth."

"What does that mean, that you broke off with one and about to start with another?"

My turn to laugh. "No, I broke off with one, but haven't gotten close to signing a new contract yet. You?"

"Do you care?"

"Guess not."

"Then leave it at that."

"Done."

I finished my beer, and the bartender, without a word, took it to refill it. Nothing better than good service. You don't find that too often anymore. I looked over at the woman next to me. She wasn't exactly my type, as if I really could define my type. She was wearing a black miniskirt and dark stockings, and the best part about her was her legs. She had well-defined ones. Not muscular, but toned. I'd say she had a dancer's legs, the sort where you could see the outline of the muscles, but the muscles weren't ripped. I liked that. I could picture my hands running all over them. Now, all I had to do was find a way to make that happen.

"You want another drink?" I asked. After doing so, I noticed hers was half full.

"I'm okay. What, you trying to get me drunk?"

"Of course not."

"You don't have to," she said, sliding one of those beautiful legs against mine. I didn't know what to say, so I stayed silent. "You staying at the hotel?"

"I am."

"Interesting," she said.

"You think so?"

She slid her leg against me again. "I do."

Okay, so she was flashing me signs like an interpreter for the deaf. The only thing left for her to do was to grab me, and drag me to my room.

"Tell me about this friend you came to see."

"Not much to tell." The bartender brought me my beer and I sipped from it.

"There's always something to tell. The question is whether or not it is interesting."

"Then, like I said, there's nothing to tell."

"Why'd you come here to see him if he's not interesting?"

"Good point. He had some answers to questions I had."

"And, did you get those answers?"

"I did."

"Were you happy with them?"

"I guess so. He told me some things I might not have wanted to hear, but that's what you get for asking questions, I presume."

"Do you not want to talk about this? I mean, the only reason why I am bringing it up is to make you feel more comfortable." She smiled at me, making herself even more attractive, if that was possible.

"It's no big deal. He's a scientist, and he told me about some experiments he's working on."

"Oh, are you into science?"

"No."

"Then what were the questions you wanted answered?"

"I needed to know if he was okay," I said.

"That's nice of you. Is he?"

"I'm not sure, but I guess that's not my problem. He's on the verge of something major, and he got himself into a bit of trouble because of it. I'd tell you more, but it's really complicated and I don't feel like getting into it."

"No problem. It must be great to know people like him."

I took another sip of beer and shook my head. "I don't know him that well. I was doing a favor for someone by checking up on him." I don't know why I was sitting there telling her all of this, but she was right. I was uncomfortable, and having something to talk about eased that.

"But you got the information you needed," Suzy said.

"I did."

Suzy looked around the bar for a moment, then she looked at me with eyes that had something almost tangible behind them. If I had been in a better frame of mind, meaning if I wasn't thinking with the mind below the waist, I might have been suspicious. But, of course, I wasn't. "I have to use the bathroom. Don't you go anywhere, alright?"

"I wouldn't even think of it," I said.

She got up, and treated me to a nicely shaped rear-end. I am a big fan of a woman's behind. It ranks right up there with the breasts, the legs, the face, and the hands. She had a sensual walk to her, accented by the high heels she was wearing. There's something about high heels that just does it for me. I'm sure some psychologist would have something to say about that, probably something referring to my mother, but psychologists are sick bastards. That's why they have the word "psycho" in the beginning of their title.

Suzy was in the bathroom a good ten minutes, and the time passed slowly. I had another beer in that time, and the Guinness was doing good work on my brain. I wasn't drunk, but I was relaxed, and fully confident that my Casanova skills were finely tuned. I finished that beer, and the good bartender took it and refilled it again. By the time he brought it back to me, Suzy was sitting next to me.

"Had trouble powdering the nose?"

She laughed. "No, silly, I had to call my roommate and tell her I might not be home tonight." She made this last statement matter-of-factly, as if it was assumed from the minute she bought me the drink. This woman thought I was that easily purchased, and she was damn right. Hell, she didn't have to buy me the drink.

"What makes you think you won't be home tonight?" I asked.

"Oh, I don't know. I thought I might have something else better to do," Suzy answered, rubbing that blasted leg of hers against mine. The old third leg decided it was time to wake up. *Not now boy*, I thought. *Give me a minute.*

Now, there are a few things I need to clear up. First, I'm not an ugly guy. Second, I have decent luck with the ladies. I'm no expert in the field, as I am sure is already blatantly obvious, but I could hold my own. Third, and more importantly, under most circumstances I can weed the good women from the bad women. What I mean is, if someone is coming on to me for a reason other than the fact that they find me the most attractive man on the planet, I can figure it out. I had studied Suzy in this light, and I had come up with the fact that she was genuinely interested, and she wanted nothing more than to press that beautiful body of hers against mine. Could I blame her?

"And what else did you have in mind?" I asked, gulping from my beer this time. I got that nervous feeling in the pit of my stomach, the sort that makes you feel a bit weak.

"Well, I was thinking. I've never seen what the rooms in this hotel are like. Perhaps you could show me yours?"

I was about to say yes, when I realized I was missing one key ingredient to this night of pure hedonism. I didn't have any condoms. Though I had thrown the old Johnson on the crap table many times in my younger days, I didn't want the thing to fall off. My mind flashed to the desk clerk's comments about how they had anything that one forgot to pack, and that the pharmacy down the block had anything else. I had assumed that meant condoms and the like, and I hoped I was wrong.

"I'll tell you what, now it's my turn to use the facilities. When I come back, I'll give you the O'Malley tour."

"Sounds wonderful. Don't be long."

"Oh, I won't," I said, already moving away from the bar and toward the bathroom.

Luckily for me, the bathroom was right by the entrance to the hotel lobby. I could make it look like I was on my way to the john when I was really going to see the clerk. I briskly walked in that direction, and took the necessary turn toward the lobby.

Behind the desk was a younger man than the one who had been there in the afternoon. I'd say he was about my age, with close-cropped blonde hair, and a large earring in his right ear. When I was growing up, an earring in that ear meant you were gay, but these were different times. I think, if I understood the current culture, that you were gay only if you slept with the same sex. Earrings didn't mean anything anymore.

"What's up?" the guy said to me.

"Got a question," I said.

"Go ahead."

"You got, um, toiletries back there?"

"I do."

"You know the type I'm talking about?" Yes, even at 34, I felt uncomfortable asking for condoms.

"I don't. We've got toothbrushes, hair spray, combs . . ."

"Nope. I'm talking about the late-night sort."

"Oh," he said, eyeing me. "No, I don't have rubbers." Thanks for the subtlety, pal.

"Well, I am in a bit of a bind here."

"I bet you are."

I fished into my pocket, finding two twenties. I put one on the desk. "You think you could find someone who could get one for me?"

"I think I might."

"You think you could get that person to go get one, and place it discreetly in room 717?"

"I could."

"Great. How long do you need?"

"Five minutes. And so you know for the future, the pharmacy delivers at all hours. But thanks for the tip."

Bastard. Actually, I couldn't have cared less. It was worth the twenty bucks. "Yeah, no problem."

"Look in your night table drawer."

"Thanks."

I walked back into the bar, finding Suzy staring into the mirror behind the bar. She looked bored. I couldn't have been gone too long. I walked up, touched her shoulder, and sat down next to her.

"I thought you just left," she said.

"Now, why would I go and do a thing like that?" I said, picking up my beer and drinking from it.

"You never know. I've seen guys do stranger things."

"Then you must be meeting some pretty strange men."

"You don't know the half of it."

"I bet I don't want to."

"You're right." She looked at me in the eyes, and said, "You ready to give me that tour?"

I tried to take a sideways look at my watch. I needed about another two or three minutes. The last thing I wanted was to have the person delivering me my latex goods as I was going to my room with Suzy. "Just let me finish my beer and then consider me your tour guide."

After I was sure my delivery had been made, we headed upstairs. We used the creaky elevator, and I had visions of the thing crashing right before I scored. That would be my luck, I thought, but it didn't happen. Suzy had stood close to me in the elevator, letting her body touch mind, and brushing her hand across my leg. I looked into her eyes and I knew she wanted me to kiss her, but I felt uncomfortable doing it in the elevator. I had seen many movies where two people had sex in an elevator, but I didn't trust the one I was in to hold up. I mean, what a way to go, but I wasn't ready to go just yet.

I must admit I wasn't a good tour guide. I had barely even shown her the sitting room when she shucked off her jacket, let her miniskirt slip down to the floor, and wrapped her arms around me. I gave in, kissing her deeply. She was a good kisser, a major prerequisite for me. Passionate kissing is so important to good sex, and we nailed that part down perfectly. The whole time, I couldn't believe I had gotten so lucky.

We had sex on the couch in the sitting room, we had sex in the bedroom, and we even had sex in the shower. Throughout every step, she led the way, choosing positions and directing me as if I was an amateur porno star. I felt like one. I'd never had such involved sex before, and it felt good. As much as I didn't like to admit it, it had been too long.

I woke the next morning with a body that felt as if it had gone to battle. If a winner had to be declared, Suzy got the nod. I could feel abrasions from her nails on my back, irritation on my neck from her teeth, and sore spots in other areas I'd prefer not to mention. I stretched, reached my hand over to her side of the bed, and touched a piece of paper resting on the pillow. I flipped over onto my back and read it:

Thanks for last night. I needed that. Suzi.

I admired her terse writing, leaving nothing to the imagination. I half-expected her to leave her phone number, but alas, there was none on the paper. I guess it was better that way. Like I would have called her anyway. Maybe I wanted the number so I would have evidence of the evening, something to brag to Rich about. Childish, I know, but I never walked around claiming maturity.

I spotted my wallet on the nightstand. I didn't remember putting it there, and out of fear, I grabbed it and opened it. Everything was there. I never kept money in my wallet, only because it's an invitation to have your money stolen. Still, I had my P.I. license, drivers license, credit cards, and several important business cards in there. The most important part of my wallet, the little notepad attached to it, seemed to be in place as well. My thoughts of Suzy stealing anything from me dissipated.

Beside my wallet was my cell phone, and I remembered that Mike had called somewhere in between the sitting room couch and the shower. I didn't know what I told him word for word, but I recalled telling him I was indisposed and that I would call him back in the morning. A glance at the clock told me it was 9:30, but I didn't feel like calling Mike just then. I also figured he wouldn't be in his office just yet. The one good thing about being up so early was the fact that I could catch a breakfast that my tired body desperately needed. The last thing I had eaten was the crappy pizza at Jason's.

I got dressed in the other outfit I brought with me from New York, a denim shirt and a pair of black slacks. Being that I had showered with Suzy only hours before, I didn't feel the need to do so again. The hotel shower would have just felt empty without her anyway. I packed the suit and other clothes into my bag, gathered my wallet and cell phone, and took the stairway to the lobby. Tim, the old man from the day before, was sitting behind the desk. He gestured toward the pub, and I assumed that was where breakfast was being served. I was right.

I dug into a plate of scrambled eggs, bacon, and hash browns. I normally didn't eat much for breakfast, but the food felt like it was rushing to supply energy to my overworked body. It seemed as though Suzy had sucked the life out of me, and I almost wanted to look in the mirror to see if I had teeth marks on my neck. I hadn't felt so tired in a long time, but it was a satisfying tired, the sort that comes after a long nights work.

While sitting at the small table in the corner of the pub, I thought about everything that had happened. I was fairly confident that I wasn't going to sell Jason out, but I had to formulate some sort of story to tell Mike. He had hired me to do a job, and I felt guilty not delivering. Mike was a source of income from time to time, and I needed that. I figured I might be able to screw this assignment up and still be alright with him, but I wasn't sure. I knew he had a lot more information on Jason than he led on, and I used that to rationalize my screwing him. If you're going to put the screws to someone, it's always nice to have something to rationalize it with.

I looked around the pub and noticed several other people eating breakfast. Most were dressed in suits, and I figured they had come to Washington on business. There were few women, quite unlike the night before, and I found myself looking toward where Suzy had sat. Of course, the bar was empty, but in my mind I saw her sitting there, beckoning me. Thinking about a woman in this light made me think of Tanya, someone I didn't want to think about at all, and I quickly tried to think of something else. My mind fell to Dave Hovelle.

I really couldn't figure out why I was thinking of Hovelle, other than because he seemed to be the link in Jason's mess I didn't understand. His initial involvement made sense. He worked for the government, and had an interest in Jason's work. What didn't fit was his manner of doing things. Hovelle operated with veiled threats. Veiled threats are worse than open threats because they involve the imagination. If someone were to tell me that they were going to punch me in the nose, the way that old Jake had at the bar, I'd be prepared to either block the blow or suffer the pain of a busted nose. If someone threatened to inflict pain on me, then it is completely open to interpretation. They could punch me in the nose, or worse, punch me in the nuts.

Hovelle liked to instill fear in people. Though it didn't work on me, it had succeeded with Jason. The poor guy had gone out and found a gun, something he certainly didn't need. He was a scientist for Christ's sake, not the sort of person who should have to worry about being armed. Hovelle was the cause for that. I wanted to meet him, stare him in the face, and see if he could return the stare with any sort of intensity. I pictured him to be a weasel of a guy, the sort I knew was just a coward in hiding. He hid behind the shield of the federal government, but that didn't stop me from thinking I could get to him.

I finished the breakfast, which was decent despite the watery eggs. I hated watery eggs. Some people prefer them that way, but to me they are undercooked. The hash browns, on the other hand, were the way I liked them, burnt. Why this particular chef chose to undercook the eggs and overcook the browns was beyond me.

It was time for me to return to New York. Though I enjoyed the little bit of time away, I longed to be in my apartment, and back to work. I had a few background searches I needed to conduct for a home care agency I worked for, and I figured I would have a call or a message at home relating to new work. I figured that, once I got home and finished what needed to be done, I'd drop by Jason's mother's house and let her know that her son was okay. If she hadn't lied to me about seeing him, she probably would have wanted to hear that.

When I had booked the train to Washington, I had also reserved myself a seat on a return train for Monday at 2pm. I envisioned another episode at Union Station like the one I experienced with the lady at Penn, but that didn't happen. The guy at the Amtrak counter in Union Station was friendly, and he even had my reservation in his computer. He noticed that I had upgraded to first class on the train to Washington, and asked me if I wanted to do the same for the return trip.

"That was involuntary," I said, and then explained to him, in little detail, what had happened in New York. He raised his eyebrows as I spoke.

"You want to file a complaint."

I thought about that. Even though that lady had gotten me pretty riled up, and I was certain she had screwed up, I didn't want to make a bigger deal out of it than it was. Yeah, on the way to Washington, I had dreams of getting her fired, but standing there in Union Station, I realized that was just mean. Plus, this guy's attitude made it tough for me to take vengeance on Amtrak.

"I don't think that's necessary," I said.

He smiled. "I'll tell you what. Why don't you give me the credit card you used for the upgrade in New York, and I will refund you that money. I don't think it was fair. Maybe the agent in New York had a reason for what she did, but I just don't see it."

I handed him my card, and he swiped it through the card reader in front of him, then handed it back to me. He then printed my ticket, and handed it to me as well.

"Thank you," I said, taking the ticket.

"No problem. Sorry about what happened, and thank you for using Amtrak."

"You're welcome."

With about an hour and a half to kill at the station, I decided to browse through some of the shops. There really wasn't much of interest there. I walked in and out of a coffee bean store, a Sharper Image, and the gift shop. In the gift shop, I found a collector's spoon with "Washington D.C." on it, which I bought for my mother because she collected them. I think she had one for almost every state. Not wanting to leave him out, I bought my father a set of golf balls with the White House printed on them. He'd never use them, mainly because he was one of the few doctors who didn't golf often, but I knew he would appreciate the thought. Mom's gift was certainly a bribe. Dad's was a just a gesture. What a good son I was.

By the track, I showed the conductor my ticket, asking him where I was seated.

"First class is in the second car, all the way up that way," he said. Angry, I looked at my ticket, thinking the courteous agent was just another Amtrak asshole. It did say that it was a first-class ticket, but I saw that the price of the ticket was the same amount I had agreed to when I made the reservation. He had upgraded my ticket for free. Maybe there were some nice people left in the world.

I made my way to the first class car and found my seat in the second row by the window. I was still tired from the night before, and looked forward to catching some sleep on the ride home. I knew I was in for a somewhat late night, only because I needed to get those background checks done before the next day, or they'd be late. I stowed my bag under my seat, sat down, reclined the chair as far back as it would go, and closed my eyes.

I was just about to fall asleep when the train starting moving. My thoughts drifted, my body relaxed, and I was thankful that no one was sitting next to me. Right before I faded off completely, my cell phone rang. I debated about answering it, but figured I would regret not taking the call.

"Yeah," I said, wearily.

"You fucking son of a bitch." It was Jason.

"What's the matter?"

"You know what's the matter," he said. He sounded as though he was outdoors. I could hear cars passing by.

"If I knew what was wrong, I wouldn't ask."

"You turned me in."

"What are you talking about?"

"Oh, come on man, you know. You left here telling me that you wouldn't tell anyone where I was, and I believed you. Then, this morning as I was coming back from getting the paper, my apartment building is being staked out by the feds."

None of this made sense to me. I knew I hadn't told anyone about where Jason was, and I couldn't figure out how he spotted feds. He seemed sure, and he seemed scared shitless.

"Jason, calm down. I swear to God I didn't tell anyone where you are. If I was going to do that, I would have called to warn you. I have no desire to turn you in to the feds."

"Bullshit."

"Think about it, Jason. Do you really think I tipped you off?"

"I do."

"Well, I didn't. Now, how do you know the feds were staking your place?"

"I'm no idiot."

"You need my help?" I couldn't picture myself being able to, but figured I'd ask anyway.

"Why would I want your help? You're the one who got me into this."

"No, Jason, I'm not. I told you yesterday that if I could find you, anyone could." Of course, this didn't say much for my skills, but I was just trying to calm him down. I really had no idea how someone found Jason so fast, but I was beginning to figure it out. While cradling the phone on my shoulder, I reached into my back pocket and pulled out my wallet. On the first page of the notepad were Jason's building name and apartment number. I didn't want to believe it, but I had a nagging feeling Suzy had a motive other than pure attraction the night before. Her advances were nothing more than a tool to get whatever information I had, and me being the jackass I was, I fell for it hook, line, and sinker.

"Well, they did," Jason said.

"What are you going to do?"

"Well, whatever I am doing, I'm sure not going to tell you about it."

"What about your briefcase?"

"I always carry that with me when I leave the apartment. I'm not stupid."

"Do you have a place to stay?"

"I have an option or two. I might just pack up and . . ."

"Don't say it over this line. I can't be sure it's clean."

I think this might have convinced him I had nothing to do with his current troubles because his tone had calmed when he said, "Oh, right."

"I'll tell you what. Call me in about four hours at this number. I'll give you instructions on how to reach me on a clean line. Make sure you call from a pay phone."

Jason chuckled, which made me feel better. "I know. I've seen the movies."

"And be careful with that fucking gun."

I ended the call, and threw the phone on the seat next to me. I was pissed. I mean, how could I have been so stupid? Suzy had hit on me from the minute she saw me, and even though I had no idea how she knew I would be at the bar, there had to be a reason for her to be so forward. She was a professional, and I figured she worked for the government. This made me feel uneasy, because all of a sudden, I didn't feel so safe. I would have to be careful from that moment on.

Book II- Down the Rabbit Hole

Chapter 12

By the time I made it to my apartment, I was weary from travel. I never really understood what makes you so weary from going place to place, but I felt as though I would pass out when I opened the door to my apartment. That feeling faded quickly, however, when I stepped in. Something didn't seem right. I didn't know what it was right away, but the place seemed wrong. It wasn't a mess, and that was the problem. Everything seemed neater than it had been when I left the day before.

Someone had been in my apartment.

I didn't need to be a crack detective to figure it out. The feds had decided to toss my place to see if I knew more than I was letting on. I guessed I had been followed from the minute I showed up at Jason's mother's house, and they waited for me to leave for Washington to conduct the search. I felt violated, standing there with my travel bag at my feet. Someone had gotten a look at everything I owned, and though I didn't own much, I didn't appreciate people rifling through my possessions. If I had Dave Hovelle's phone number, I would have called him right there and let him know how I felt.

Before I had time to go through my stuff to see if everything was still there, the phone rang. I answered it quickly, thinking it was Hovelle.

"What," I said when I picked up the receiver.

"Is that any way to answer the phone?" Mike Holmes asked.

"What do you want?"

"Jesus, what's the matter with you? That little fuckfest last night not work out the way you planned?"

"How do you know about that?"

"Hmm, well, let me think. I call the investigator I hired for a job, and he tells me to fuck off while I hear a woman moaning in the background. I know you don't think much of my investigative skills, but I know a fuckfest when I hear one." In my anger about what had happened at my apartment, I had forgotten Mike had called the night before.

"You really screwed me, Mike."

"What do you mean?"

"You fucking hired me for this job, just so I could be your lackey. I don't like getting mixed up with this sort of shit. You could have had someone else do your dirty work."

"Christ, Darren, calm down. I don't know what you're talking about."

"Like hell, you don't. You knew right from the beginning the feds were involved in this. You try to sell me on the fact that this was just a simple locate, when you knew all along it was a disaster," I said, realizing that my fists were clenched at my sides. I tried to calm down but to no avail. If Mike had been standing right in front of me, I would have strangled him.

"I told you everything I knew, seriously. The university hired me to find this schmuck. I knew nothing about the feds, or anything else for that matter."

"You really expect me to believe that? You think I'm that stupid?" I realized right then that I was.

"Darren, I've known you for a fairly long time. I only hired you because I knew you could find this guy, not to get you mixed up in some cloak and dagger shit. If I knew this was that bad, I wouldn't have taken the job in the first place, you know that."

"No, I don't. And let me tell you one other thing. When you speak to that piece of shit Hovelle, you tell him he had better not come within a thousand yards of me, or I'll beat the crap out of him. Fed or no fed."

"Who the fuck is Hovelle?" Even though I had convinced myself that Mike knew about everything, he did sound pretty convincing. Perhaps he was telling the truth, and was just as much a victim of the whole thing as I was. I didn't want to believe that, only because I needed someone to release my anger on, and at the moment, he was the only one I had.

"Stop playing stupid," I said.

"What's got you so upset? I mean, I understand that finding out the feds are involved spooks you, so what? It's not like you have anything to worry about from it. It just complicates things is all."

"Only complicates things? They tossed my fucking apartment. They've probably been following me around all weekend, and God knows what else."

"Jesus Darren. I'm sorry. I really had no idea . . ."

"Of course you had no idea."

"I didn't, really. So, I guess you didn't find the guy."

The last thing I had in mind was to tell Mike I had found Jason. I didn't want to give him any information. Then I realized I could tell him about where Jason was, because Jason wasn't there anymore. If I told Mike what I found, nothing would happen. The feds had already found Jason and I couldn't picture the university making matters worse.

"I never said I didn't find him."

"Where is he?"

"Am I gonna get paid?"

"As soon as the university pays me." I didn't trust that, and if I was going to divulge information, I was going to be compensated.

"No. Fuck that. I want a guarantee from you that I get paid for my work, and for the expenses I incurred to find this guy."

Mike thought about this for a moment. "What sort of expenses?"

Thinking about getting paid lightened my mood. "I charged a room at the fucking Plaza Hotel and a few bottles of champagne. Not to mention the whore I paid a few grand for a good time."

"Oh, no problem. Anything else?"

"Concorde flight to London," I said.

"Shame it didn't crash. Now, you want to tell me about how much in expenses you incurred?"

"Hundred and fifty for train fare, and about another hundred-ten for the room."

"Where'd you go?"

"Washington."

"The state?" *Jesus.*

"D.C."

157

"What made you go there?"

"I figured the President might know something."

"Seriously."

"That's where the trail led."

"You saw the guy?" Mike asked.

"Even better. Talked to him."

Mike sighed. It seemed like he was trying not to let me hear the sigh, but I heard it. "You talked to him?"

"I did."

"Do you think that was a good idea?"

"Why not?"

"Don't you think he might have been suspicious?"

"He didn't know who I was," I said, lying.

"He say anything?"

"Hello."

"You talk to him about what's going on?"

"Why would I do that? And why do you care?"

"Just curious," Mike said.

"Well, he didn't. So, you gonna pay me, or what?"

Another sigh. "Yeah, being as how you had to do so much work. What have you got for me?"

I told Mike where Jason was living, but left out the name he was registered under, in case he was stupid enough to use it again. Mike seemed genuinely happy, and told me he would contact the university, then call me back. I was happy I was able to get paid and not actually have to sell out Jason to do so.

After I hung up with Mike, I just sat down on my couch and relaxed. Too much was happening too fast, and I didn't like not being in control. I still didn't know what Hovelle would do, or whether or not he would pay me a visit, looking for Jason's new hideout. I wanted him to come for me, and I wanted to make him regret doing so. What I didn't want was to be followed, but I knew that the possibility of that happening was pretty good. I had no problems losing a tail, but I hated having to constantly look over my shoulder.

I sat on the couch for about ten minutes, which was ten minutes too long. Sitting there made me more tired than I already was, and I had a ton of work to do. Most of it was easy, but I also wanted to see what else I could find out about Jason's situation. I really should have just let it all rest, because after I delivered the information to Mike, my involvement was officially over. Yet, it wasn't unofficially over. The feds probably had no intentions of leaving me alone, and because of my stupidity with Suzy, I had put Jason in even more danger. I blew his cover, and I figured I owed him something for that. Maybe I could offer him some sort of help for that.

I forced myself up from the couch and made my way over to the answering machine. I had five messages, none of which were prospects for work. One of them bothered me, however. It was from Darlene, and though she didn't say anything other than, "Call me back." She sounded distressed. I'd known her for a long time, and I never knew her to be someone who got that way.

I picked up the phone and dialed her home number. She answered on the third ring.

"Yeah," she said. She sounded as if she was crying.

"Hey," I said.

"Darren, where have you been? I called like five times, but you didn't answer, and I couldn't get through on your cell phone."

"I was in Washington."

"I know. I'm the one that sent you there, remember?"

"Right."

"Why didn't you answer your phone this morning?"

I didn't want to tell her I turned it off because I was getting laid. And fucked.

"Battery died, and I forgot to bring my charger."

"I was fired today," Darlene said bluntly.

"What?"

"You heard me."

"Why?"

"I think you know why. What are you involved in?"

"I wish I knew the details."

"Don't hold out on me, Darren. I've been doing this for years without ever getting caught, and I do this job for you and the next day I'm out of a job."

"I never told anyone," I said, not knowing what else to say.

"I know that, but I want to know what sort of case you are working on."

"One that the federal government has taken a vested interest in."

"That would make sense."

"What did your job tell you?" I asked.

159

"Not much. They just told me to pack up and leave. They told me I should know why they were firing me, and that I should be happy that they won't press charges."

"Jesus."

"Tell me about it. I mean, they underpaid me anyway, and I'll find a job soon enough. I guess I should be happy. I didn't like working there in the first place, and I've wanted to move out to California for a long time. I guess now I have the opportunity."

The thought of Darlene leaving New York didn't make me happy, because I always envisioned myself finally talking her into dating me. Also, I felt guilty that I had caught yet another person in the web I found myself in. The fact that someone bothered to rat Darlene out made me believe this whole thing ran deeper than I had expected. On top of that, it meant anyone was fair game, including me.

"You're just going to up and leave me?" I asked.

"I don't think it would be wise to stick around here anymore. I think I was followed home."

"Great. That seems to be going around. Someone rummaged through my apartment while I was gone."

"Wow. Who the hell is this guy you were trying to find?"

"Listen, I'd love to tell you all about it, but I don't trust this line. You have a computer where you are?"

"I'm home, yes."

"Register yourself for a Hotmail account and create an address with the name of the restaurant we went to on that one date we had. Remember it?"

"I do."

"Okay, good. I'll register one with a name you'll recognize, and I'll email you with a place to meet me at. I want to talk to you."

"Darren, I don't know."

"Do it, please. I need to go over a few things with you. I know I'm in no position to ask for a favor . . ."

"You're not, but I'll spot you this one. You're gonna owe me big time." Owing Darlene was no small thing, I knew.

"I know. And thank you. I'll email you in about an hour, and we'll meet in two, okay?"

"Alright."

"Darlene?"

"Yes?"

"I'm sorry."

"Oh, don't worry about it. I'm sure a year from now I'll think this was the best thing that could have ever happened to me."

"I hope so."

I ran through the background checks I had to do in record time. It really wasn't much work, but it was tedious having to enter in all the information to the database. It didn't help matters that the person who had faxed me the information had horrible writing, and I had to sit there and decipher names and addresses. If I wasn't a doctor's son, I might not have been able to figure some of it out.

After I finished playing data entry, I returned to the answering machine, because Darlene's was the third out of five messages, and I had stopped after hearing hers. I pressed the button to play my messages, and was greeted with my mother's voice telling me to call when I got the chance. She didn't sound angry, and I silently thanked my father for playing the negotiator. The next message was from Tanya, and it bothered me to hear her voice.

"Darren, listen, I know you told me I would do this, that I would call, but I just couldn't help myself. I don't want to cause trouble for you. I don't want to be a problem in your life. I just can't see myself without you in my life, you know? Every time something important has happened in my life, you have been there to share it. I can't change the past. I don't want to, but I also don't want to lose you. I know you won't, but I want you to call me. No strings."

She was right. I wasn't going to call her. I felt like a mean bastard by doing that, but I couldn't bring myself to do it. I was scared. Scared I would say something to lead her on, scared I might say something that would cause me to lose her forever. I knew calling her would only make me feel like shit, and I knew that not calling her wouldn't make me feel better. I just didn't know which would make me feel worse.

I deleted the message, debating about it beforehand, and went into the kitchen. I hadn't gone through my apartment yet to see if anything was missing. I didn't want to. I felt pretty confident the feds wouldn't have found anything important. The only thing I left behind was the scribbling I had done on a notepad next to the computer, and they knew anything written there already. I thought they might have put a virus on my computer just to be pricks, but it ran fine. They certainly put something on there to track me, or at least recorded my IP address, the identification number assigned to a computer that identified it on the Internet. I knew how to navigate through such a thing, so that was no big deal. When I felt like it, I would format my hard drive so their little programs would be gone.

I went into the kitchen actually thinking I'd find something to eat or drink in the refrigerator. All I had was a three-month-old bottle of Beck's, and for lack of anything else, I drank it. The last thing I wanted was a beer, but it was all I had, and I didn't feel like drinking water. I had an aftertaste in my mouth, and wanted to wash it out with something that had flavor. I slugged the beer in about three gulps and threw the bottle into the recycle bin.

I was about to go take a shower when the phone rang again. I tensed, expecting it to be someone I didn't want to hear from.

"Yeah," I said.

"It's been four hours, like you said." It was Jason. I'd forgotten I told him to call. I had to make this quick so no one could trace the call and find out where he was calling from. I gave him the number to the payphone in the restaurant across the street and told him to call me in a half an hour. He agreed, and I went to take a shower. When I got out, I fought the urge to fall asleep on the bed and got dressed in a t-shirt and a pair of jeans. I threw a red button-down shirt over the t-shirt because I was going to meet Darlene later, and I knew she liked the color red. Pathetic, I know.

* * *

Antonio's Restaurant had been there for over twenty years, from what I had been told. The same person that informed me of this also told me that there had been a mob hit there in the early eighties. Some guy got whacked sitting at a table by the big window in front. Now, if you know you might be the target of a hit, is it really a good idea to be sitting by the window? The owners of Antonio's were actually proud of this occurrence at their restaurant, and had the area marked off with velvet ropes. People would actually come in and want to just sit down at that table, to be where someone had been killed. Sick.

The restaurant was quiet. Antonio's had never been open on Mondays, but about a year ago, they decided to give it a shot. From what I could tell, it wasn't working. Maybe four or five of the twenty or so tables they had were occupied, and two people were sitting at

162

the large black Formica bar on the left. The bartender, Tony, nodded when I came in. I used that payphone a lot, and I ate there from time to time. Somehow, Tony knew when I was coming to eat, and when I wanted to use the phone.

The phone was by the back door, next to the ladies room, and when I got there, it rang.

"Yeah," I said.

"It's me," Jason replied.

"Okay, I'm sure this phone is clean, so let me know everything."

"There isn't much to tell. I was able to sneak into my apartment by using the service entrance, and I got any papers I thought I might need, along with a few changes of clothes. Luckily, I didn't bring too much to the apartment in the first place."

"Are you nuts, going in there? They could have gotten you."

"No, these guys they had staking out my place were stupid. I caught one of them sleeping in the car. I felt like knocking on the window and giving him the finger, you know, like DeNiro did in *Goodfellas*."

I wanted to tell Jason that DeNiro never gave them the finger, he just waved them on to follow him, but I didn't want to ruin his moment. Instead, I said, "That would have been pretty fucking stupid."

"That's why I didn't do it."

"So, what do you have planned?"

"Well, I look at it this way. They know I'm in Washington, and it probably wouldn't take them too long to find me here. So, I think I'm gonna catch a flight to New York, and spend some time with a friend up there. I figure it's the last place they'd look for me, plus, the city is so huge I can get lost in the crowd."

I couldn't argue with his idea completely. "Don't take a plane. They probably are looking out for your name on a reservation. I assume you don't have any false ID or anything."

"No, I don't." I would have laughed my ass off if he told me he had a Ben Kenobi false ID.

"Take a train."

"I hate trains."

"Yeah, well, do you like being taken in by the feds any better?"

"Well, no.

"Then take a train. Take a fucking bus if you don't like trains.

Pay with cash, and they won't ask you for ID. This way you can travel anonymously."

"This is like a movie," Jason said, sounding excited.

"Yeah, well, the bullets are real."

"You don't think they'd shoot me?" Jason said.

"Lose that gun of yours and you won't have to worry about it."

"It's already in the river." God, this kid actually did think this was all some movie plot. I knew he was genuinely scared, but he needed be get more realistic.

"Good."

"I think I'll take the train. It'll give me some time to catch up on research."

"Where's your equipment?"

"Equipment?"

"The machine you were talking about."

"Oh, that. It's in a safe place. I don't feel like telling anyone where. Unless, of course, you are volunteering to help me."

"Forget it."

"You don't know what you're missing."

"I can't get Patroclus out of my mind."

"You think too much." He was right about that.

"Just be careful when you get to the train station. I don't think they'll have it staked out, but you never know."

"Maybe I shouldn't have thrown the gun away."

"Yeah, go ahead and scuba dive in the river for it."

"You think?"

"Just get to the station and be careful, alright?"

"Okay."

"Call me on this phone tomorrow at noon. I'll be waiting."

"You got it. And thanks."

"No problem. Least I could do for getting you into this mess."

"What?"

"Forget it."

I hung up, pissed off at myself for letting that slip. I didn't want him thinking it really was me that was responsible for him getting found. I don't know why I felt this need to help Jason out, but I did, and I had to follow the instinct. Unfortunately, my instincts never led me in the right direction.

While standing in Antonio's, I wished I had told Darlene to meet me there. It wouldn't have been safe, I knew that, but I didn't feel like getting into my car and schlepping up to the North Shore. I hated the North Shore. I hated the snooty people, the fact that the North Shore was considered the Gold Coast, and, above all else, I hated driving there. There was no parkway that took you up far enough, and the drive always seemed endless. Like most circumstances in my life at the time, I didn't have a choice.

* * *

I found Darlene sitting at a small table in the corner of Jonathan's Restaurant, an upscale eatery that blended Friday's atmosphere with overpriced food. I had only chosen the place because I knew she liked it, and I was sure it would be busy enough so that we could be anonymous. She had gotten my email and replied, so my little undercover plan worked.

"Jacknut?" she asked, sitting at the table wearing a cobalt blue silk shirt buttoned down just enough to show a hint of cleavage. I knew she was probably unaware of this.

"You knew it was me, right?" I said, sitting down across from her. She had a martini in front of her. I didn't remember her ever drinking martinis, so I figured this whole situation was getting to her more than she let on.

"It's not even a word. Only, you think it is."

Rich and I had come up with the word. It was sort of like a super-jackass, someone who was so asinine, "jackass" just wasn't strong enough. We overused it of course, and people who weren't in the inner circle of understanding resented it.

"It was the first thing I thought of when I registered the address. Thanks for coming."

"Who am I kidding? The last thing I wanted to do was sit all alone at home and wonder what's going to happen to me next." She sipped her martini, finishing it. "You want a drink?"

"Seltzer." Her eyebrows raised. "I've been drinking a little too much lately."

"Give me a fucking break. Don't sit there like some pussy-footed little priss drinking seltzer. I'm drinking, you're drinking. Simple as that."

"I'll get a beer then, okay?"

"Fine." She signaled to the waiter and told him to bring me a Coors Light and another martini for herself. Then she looked at me in a way that made me think there was something else on her mind. She might have caught me probing her, because she shook her head and smiled. "So, I'm finally free of my servitude to Sprint."

"I'm really sorry."

"I told you not to worry about it. It's the best thing that could have happened to me. Don't get me wrong, I would have preferred it to happen on my own terms, but how many times does that happen? Things happen for a reason, and I think the reason I got fired was so I could finally go to California and do what I really want."

"What's that?"

"Write."

"California? What, the air is better out there for writing?"

"No. I want to write and I want to live in California. The two aren't necessarily related."

"You'll be back in six months. You'll miss New York."

"I might. Hell, I might go out there and absolutely hate it, but I want to give it a chance. I've always told myself that was where I wanted to be, and I think this is my last chance to go for it. Plus, I don't feel too comfortable around here. Not now."

"Did something else happen?"

"No. I told you everything."

"You sure?"

"Hey, don't start getting all protective now. Nothing happened other than what I told you. I got fired, which was a great start to my day. Then, I noticed I was being followed after I left work, and I'm pretty sure someone was watching my apartment in the afternoon. I'm not sure of that. I could have just been spooked, but it seemed that way. Other than that, nothing."

"Okay. I just wanted to make sure. I mean, a lot of things are going on right now, and I feel really guilty about having you involved. The people surrounding this thing will do anything to get what they want. That much I know." I didn't want to tell Darlene about Hovelle, or how I thought things could get more dangerous that what they already were. She was more shaken up than she wanted me to know. No sense in making it any worse.

"What exactly are you dealing with here?"

"I told you the feds are involved."

"I know, and I know they are the ones responsible for my losing my job. And to think I voted for the bastard that's in office now. I never used to vote, but I vote this one time in the last presidential election, and it's his administration that gets me fired."

"I don't think it's his fault."

"You know what I mean. Now, are you going to give me the details you promised?"

"Of course. Where do you want me to start?"

"How about with the guy you went to go see?"

I told Darlene how I got the case from Mike, and how the guy turned out to be an old high school classmate. I then told her about the visit I made to Laura, Jason's mother, and how I got the feeling I needed to help Jason instead of just locating him and turning him in. She thought it was weird that the feds would be staking out Jason's house, and I told her to hold onto that thought, that I was getting there. I then told her about my trip to Washington, even including the Amtrak disaster.

"Well, it was nice of the guy in Washington to help you out. Maybe he liked you. Was he cute?"

"A little big in the ass," I said.

"You don't like big backyards?"

"Well, let's just say he wasn't my type. He has a dick."

"That's the only obstacle?"

"Stop it."

"Well, then tell me the good stuff. I really don't care about your travel arrangements, or what hotel you stayed in. I want to know why this guy is so important, and why he cost me my job."

"He's a scientist."

"That sounds like a big deal. What, he find a miracle cure or something? Please tell me that my life was inconvenienced for a good cause. I don't want to hear that this guy developed new video game technology or something." This was why I was nuts about this girl. She never pulled any punches, and I really never walked away not sure how she felt about something.

"He thinks he's developed the ability to travel back in time."

Darlene's eyebrows raised. "He thinks?"

"Well, he seems pretty sure. I guess it's me that's skeptical."

"Time travel, really? Now that is a worthwhile cause. And the government is involved because?"

"He used to work for them. He was researching the same basic idea while he was there."

"So they think he stole their information."

I shook my head. The waiter came over with the drinks, and I didn't touch my beer. I really didn't want it. Darlene took a gulp from her martini. "I don't think this has to do with Jason taking anything from the government. I think the government just wants to have sole possession of the technology."

"Why would they want to do that?"

I shrugged. "Well, I'm sure they'd say because it would be safer for the general public and the rest of the world if they could monitor it. They'd give that 'We don't want it to fall into the wrong hands' speech. I think they know there's a lot of money and power associated with this technology."

Darlene sat quiet for a moment. I didn't say anything, because it looked like she was working on something. I didn't want to disturb that. She had one of the best analytical minds I had ever come across.

"Do you realize the ramifications of all this?" she asked. I was somewhat disappointed that she hadn't come up with anything better than that.

"Of course."

"But you don't think he really has the ability to do this?"

"I didn't say that. I'm just not sure. Let me tell you this, though. If anyone could come up with such technology, I'd put Jason pretty high up on the list. He is an exceptionally bright person."

"Is he single?"

"What, you want to latch on so you can ride to glory and riches with him?"

"Doesn't seem like a bad idea."

"I doubt he's your type."

"I could make him my type."

"That's not your style."

"I know. But can't I just fantasize a little?"

"Do whatever you want."

"So, this little science nerd says he's got the ability to travel back in time. Does he know that he could wreak havoc with such technology?"

"I think, in some way, he wants to do just that. He wants to test the limits of man's abilities. He told me he is more interested in using time travel as a way to prove or disprove the existence of God, or some other governing factor."

"He's a religious nut?"

"I don't think so. He didn't really say whether or not he believed in God. He just wants to know if there is one."

"What about you?" Darlene asked, finishing another martini. The girl could drink, that I had seen evidence of before. If I had polished off two martinis in the time she did, I'd be wasted.

"What about me?"

"What do you believe?"

"About God?"

"Yes. Do you think He exists?"

"I'm on the fence. I don't really see evidence of His existence, but that doesn't mean he isn't there. What bothers me is, in the Old Testament, God was all over the place. He was in the burning bush, on the mountaintop making the tablets for the Ten Commandments, and in Egypt wreaking havoc. Acts of God were commonplace, it seemed. Nowadays, or more correctly, in the last 2000 years, we haven't heard word one from him."

"Did you ever think that things we take for granted are acts of God?"

"What, like the sound of children laughing and all that shit? I think those are evidence of life. Maybe someone created the world, or maybe the world created itself. Voltaire said it best when he said, "'God created man, then man returned the favor.'"

"So, you don't believe in God?"

"Actively, no. But I am afraid that he might exist, and therefore I worry that my atheism will get me a lifetime in Hell."

"That's a pretty sideways way of looking at it."

"How do you look at it, I asked."

"Well, I was born Catholic, which is pretty much a doomed existence to begin with. I don't believe in the church so much, because it is manmade and subject to the deficiencies of that. But, I do believe there is some higher being involved."

"Why not a lower being?"

"What? Satan?"

"No, nothing like that. It's just, whenever we talk about something we don't know about, like aliens or God, we always attach a higher intelligence to them. Maybe the being that created the earth is nothing more than some run of the mill being."

"You're out of your mind."

"True."

"I think there is a higher being. You should too."

"I'll try."

"What else did Jason tell you?"

"That he's been confronted by the feds, and that he needs a volunteer for his research."

"A volunteer who would go back in time?"

I nodded.

"He asked you?"

"He did."

"What did you do?"

"I agreed. I went back in time and made you lose your job. I also set it up so that you would fall madly in love with me and marry me in two years."

"You'd need more than a time machine to do that."

"True."

"So, did you agree to volunteer?"

"No."

Darlene's eyes opened wide. "Are you crazy?"

"I don't see how that's relevant."

"This is an opportunity of a lifetime."

"I'm sure it is. I just don't know if I want to be caught in the middle of it. You said just before that there would be ramifications involved."

"So what? You'd have to be out of your mind to not jump on that opportunity. Plus, if the government gets a hold of whatever he has, no one will ever find out about this discovery. If you help him, you'll be helping all of the world, indirectly."

"I'm no hero."

"Then I'll do it."

"I don't think he'd go for it." I wasn't sure about that, but I didn't want someone I knew to take the opportunity Jason had offered me. I didn't want to deal with someone else experiencing it, and then telling me all about what I missed. Also, secretly, I was afraid that someone close to me could screw up in the past and make my life miserable somehow. If anyone was going to fuck up my life, it was going to be me.

"Then you have to do it. You have no choice."

"It could be real dangerous."

"What are you, a sissy? Grow some balls. You're always talking about how unexciting your life is. This is your chance to really do something."

"It might be, but I guess I am scared."

"Well, that's natural. Listen Darren, I know you don't think this, but I really do care about you."

"I knew that," I said, lying.

"Yeah, well, maybe I care about you more than I let on."

"Enough not to go to California?"

"No. It's just not that way. You are pretty much all I could ask for in a guy, but I'm not asking for anything right now. I just want to get my life together." Darlene shook her head. "Jesus, I didn't want to get into this right now."

"Now's as good a time as any."

"I doubt that. What I'm trying to say is that I do care for you, and I think I know what's good for you and what isn't. I think you should volunteer. I think you need something new in your life, something that can change you."

"Didn't you just say I was all you could ask for in a man? Now you're saying I need to change?"

"You don't need to change anything about you, so to speak, but you could use an attitude adjustment. You've been miserable lately." I couldn't argue with that, so I didn't. "You're a smart guy who could do anything he wanted, but you're stuck in some sort of rut, and maybe doing something as fantastic as time travel might help you get out of it."

I really didn't totally understand her logic, but I got the general idea. I'm not sure I agreed, and I didn't have any intentions of changing my mind. And I didn't really know what I was so afraid of.

"Yeah, well, it just doesn't seem too enticing to me."

"You're full of shit. It's enticing as hell. You're just scared."

"I already admitted that."

"Well, I figured it had to be said again. You'll do this. Once you think about it and realize what sort of opportunity you have here, you'll agree. Just think, you'll be the first person to do it. You'll be remembered like Alexander Graham Bell's assistant."

"Yeah, and no one remembers his name."

"You'll live forever in history and science books."

"That's if it works." Even though I was disagreeing with her, her ideas were penetrating. Yeah, I would be famous. Then again, there was a chance I could be dead, or worse. That God that may or may not exist would have good reason to be pissed off at me.

"You're so negative."

"I try not to be."

"Sure you do."

"Well, anyway, that's what Jason told me. You lost your job because the government wants this information badly, and I have to tell you, they'll do anything to get a hold of it. Don't let anyone know you have a clue about any of this."

"I know, I know. I won't post it on the web or anything."

"Good idea."

Chapter 13

I stayed at Jonathan's with Darlene for about two hours, most of the time listening to her trying to convince me to volunteer. She seemed overly interested in my doing this, and I did my best to not argue with her completely. I thought that by doing so she would stop, but she didn't. I left, telling her I would think about it, and let her know what decision I had come to. She told me she was leaving for California in two days. I said I thought that was quick, but she said she didn't have too many possessions, and she had a place she could stay at in Santa Monica. I wished her good luck, and walked out of the restaurant wondering whether or not I would ever see Darlene again, and whether or not I was terribly upset about the possibility of her being out of my life forever.

I took the nightmare drive home from the North Shore, passing by houses the size of hotels, and cars that cost more than a house. It amazed me the amount of resentment I had toward those people. I knew most of it came from jealousy, but I rationalized it by telling myself I had all I wanted monetarily, and having the sort of bucks most people on the North Shore had wouldn't make me any happier. I believed that to an extent, but generally I was bullshitting myself. I did that often.

Because the drive home was long, I had plenty of time to think about what Darlene had said. She was right, I knew that, but I just didn't want to get involved. I would be famous if Jason succeeded, and I might even get that fortune I told myself I didn't need. I didn't have a huge desire to be famous, but I don't think anyone wouldn't be tempted by the charms of fame. My main stumbling block was the danger of it all. I had to worry about any ramifications of the changes in the time continuum, along with the dangers of a failed experiment. Jason had mentioned the machine would latch onto my brain waves, so what if something went wrong and I ended up a vegetable because he fried my brain? Thinking about it all, I realized I was just trying to find reasons not to do it.

When I got home, I was tired, and all I could think about was getting some sleep. As I pulled into my designated parking space in the apartment lot, I knew I wouldn't be sleeping anytime soon. Parked next to me was a non-descript Mercury sedan, much like the one I saw in front of Jason's mother's house. I felt my hands get hot, and I took a deep breath to calm myself, then stepped out of the car.

As I did, the passenger door to the Mercury opened, and a short, stocky man exited. He stood about four inches shorter than me, with dark brown hair that had turned gray on the sides. He looked to be about fifty, and he had a commanding presence about him, despite his lack of height. I knew immediately that it was Dave Hovelle.

"Mr. Camponi," he said, in a southern accent. It wasn't thick, but I detected it.

"Mr. Hovelle," I replied, trying to stay calm. A second man got out of the driver's side of the car. He has huge, say about six-four and two hundred-twenty pounds. His being there calmed me down quite a bit.

"You don't take suggestions too well, do you?" Hovelle asked.

"Depends on where they come from. I personally don't put too much stock into what assholes say. All that comes out is usually gas and stink."

"Watch it Camponi."

"Why, you gonna go through my apartment again?"

Hovelle's expression didn't change. "I don't know what you are talking about."

"Of course not. What do you want?"

"Just to talk."

"I have nothing to say."

"I think you do."

"You see, right there, it proves this conversation isn't going to go anywhere. We can't even agree on the simplest of things."

"You might think this is a joke, Camponi, but it's not. This is a serious federal matter, and you could be brought up on charges of tampering with evidence and getting in the way of a federal investigation." I knew those were empty threats.

"I would have to do something to get brought up on those charges, unless you want to go after an innocent man."

"You're not innocent, we both know that, so cut the crap. You're not helping Caufield anyway. You're just making things worse for him."

"And you're terrorizing everyone, even people close to me. I don't appreciate that."

"I'm doing what needs to be done. Caufield is a dangerous man. Did you get the chance to find out what this is all about?"

"I told you, I don't know anything."

"You spoke to him. We know that much. What did he tell you?"

"He told me you are a prick. I tend to think he was right about that."

"Enough with the wisecracks. I'm going to find Caufield, and when I do, I am going to get what I need. He might have told you some sob story about how we are after him unjustly, but that isn't the case. He stole things from the federal government, and from his former employer. He is a thief, and he thinks he is going to get away with it. He's wrong."

"How nice of you to play the role of judge, jury, and executioner."

"That's not how it is, Camponi. I'm just doing my job. I'm only asking that you not get in the way of that."

"And how can I do that for you?" The whole time we were talking, the other guy just stood behind Hovelle, arms folded, not saying a word. He looked like an ex-military guy, with crew-cut blonde hair and thick neck muscles. If it wasn't for him, I might have tried my hand at giving Hovelle a beating.

"You can start by ending your investigation."

"I don't have an investigation." I wasn't lying.

"Well, you stop whatever it is you are doing that pertains to Jason Caufield. That means you tell your investigator friend in Ohio that you couldn't find Caufield, and that you have no intentions of trying any further. I know you received information from Caufield, and I am pretty sure you intend to continue keeping contact with him. I advise against this, because it will only get you into trouble. I also think he told you about what he is researching, and what he stole from the government." It was too late for me to not tell Mike anything, but I figured the information I gave him was harmless.

"If he did, I don't remember."

"Maybe you need us to jog your memory a little bit?"

"Are you threatening me?" I reached toward the back of my pants, forgetting that I had left my gun in my apartment.

"No, I was just offering help with your memory."

"I don't know anything. I was hired to find someone, I did so, and now my involvement is over. If you don't want me to tell my contact about this, then fine. But otherwise, leave me the fuck alone."

I turned to walk away, and Hovelle said, "Be careful, Camponi. It would be a shame if more people around you started having bad luck."

I rushed up to Hovelle and grabbed him by the collar. The big guy stood still for a second. "You piece of shit. You stay away from anyone I know. I hear that you came within a thousand yards of anyone, and, whether you work for the government or not, I'll fucking beat the shit out of you."

The big guy grabbed my arm and effortlessly pulled me from Hovelle. Hovelle adjusted the collar on his shirt and glared at me. "Watch yourself Camponi. You don't know who you are fucking with."

"I don't care."

"You will."

"Go fuck yourself," I said.

"I'm going to be keeping an eye on you Camponi."

"You do that."

I walked away, and heard them get into their car and pull away. I knew what I had done was stupid, but Hovelle was just the sort of guy that got under my skin easily. I couldn't control myself.

* * *

By the time I got into my apartment, I was no longer tired. I mean, my body was weak and I needed sleep, but I was still hot over my confrontation with Hovelle. I never really had any dealings with the feds, unless you count the asshole who dated my sister years before, and I didn't like the idea that I was tangled with them then. It didn't help matters that Hovelle came across as the worst a fed could be—a man who thought his status allowed him to do whatever he wanted. I thought about the repercussions of my argument with him, and felt pretty confident he couldn't do anything to hurt me other than physically hurt me. If he had wanted to do that, he would have right there in the parking lot. I gave him enough reason to. No, Hovelle's main purpose was to frighten me, and keep me away from Jason. I couldn't blame him for that, but his determination made me all the more curious about the situation. I had no doubt in my mind that I would get to the bottom of Jason's situation.

I couldn't fall asleep, so I parked myself on the couch with a half-empty bag of Doritos and did some channel surfing. If network television spoke volumes of the pathetic state of society, then late night TV represented the underbelly. When I first got the apartment, cable TV was still hooked up, and I had gotten a free ride for about a year. Then, when it was time to get my cable modem, I had been worried they would discover my free hookup and not be pleased, so I ordered a package which cost me about sixty bucks a month. They called it the "Rainbow Package," which brought to mind a virtual spectrum of channels covering every taste imaginable. I had fourteen movie channels, various documentary stations, and the requisite sport channels. At midnight, you'd expect a potpourri of shows and movies to watch, but this wasn't the case. Three of the movie channels were showing the same movie, and the others displayed straight-to-cable atrocities. I found one movie, which looked to be an action mystery of some sort, and I stayed with it because the first scene I caught involved a rather large-breasted woman bathing naked in a pool. Unfortunately, she didn't last long, falling victim to the mysterious strangler.

I watched the movie for a while, amazed that, one, something so terribly written and acted could actually make it to production, and two, that I was still watching. I just sat there, watching my intelligence get sucked from my head, and munching on my Cool Ranch Doritos. The main character of the movie was a private detective, and I found it amusing how he operated. Not once did he do any investigating. Instead, his job consisted of cracking skulls, and he was pretty adept at that, knowing karate or kung-fu. I knew plenty of P.I.'s, and though some were probably good fighters, they didn't go around roundhouse-kicking informants or even bad guys. I wish my work were that exciting.

I'd had enough when the main character had a showdown in a mansion. He was going after a corporate exec who he figured had something to do with the murders, and, without even thinking twice about it, he broke into the house in search of the man. This, in and of itself, was ridiculous, but it was a movie, and I could suspend my disbelief enough to buy this. What did it for me was when a woman came busting out of a room in a red karate outfit, launching over a banister and drop kicking our stalwart hero. Who the fuck ran around in a karate outfit? The fighting was good, even though it seemed fake, but I just couldn't get over the ridiculousness of it all.

The movie did serve one purpose. I fell asleep on the couch in the middle of it. I would have preferred to sleep in my bed instead of the stiff couch, but I needed sleep and my body didn't seem to care where I got it.

* * *

I woke about eight in the morning, with a stiff back and some Shirley MacClaine movie on the television. Having enough of my intelligence sucked from me the night before, I quickly flipped the TV off and got up.

I had dreamed of an event very close to what had happened over the previous few days, and I hate that. I knew I dreamt of my confrontation with Hovelle, and my dream even included things I did the next day. I did this a lot, and even had showed up to work late sometimes because I had dreamt I already went in. When my dreams got like that, I often ended up confused about what I did in real life and what I had dreamt about. I didn't have that problem this time, only because in the dream I had sex with Darlene and she told me she changed her mind about California because she couldn't live without me.

I walked into the kitchen, made myself another Diet Coke breakfast, and took a shower. I felt less tired and ready to start my day, only I wasn't sure where I was going to start. I would have the results for the background checks from the day before, but processing those would take all of about fifteen minutes. There wasn't much I could do about Jason. I had to wait for him to get to New York. There were countless chores I could do to kill time, like laundry, grocery shopping, and the like, but I had no head for it. I slapped on semi-clean clothes, and because my supply of socks and underwear hadn't reached the danger zone yet, I figured I could get by for a little while longer.

I decided, after I processed my little bit of work for the day, I would visit Laura and tell her what I learned about her son. I wanted to let her know that I was aware she lied but dismissed the thought. Jason was her son, for Christ's sake, and I knew my mother would have done the same thing for me. Hell, my mother would kill someone for me, but only if I made myself a regular for Sunday dinner. If I didn't start showing up, she'd kill me. That's just how Italian mothers are.

I walked over to the answering machine and noticed I had a new message. The phone must have rung while I was in the shower. I hit the play button. It was Mike, and he didn't sound happy.

"Darren, it's Mike. Listen, we have to talk. I need you to call me at your earliest convenience. Please get to me as soon as you can." Mike's voice was distressed, and I figured he was upset because I gave him information that was useless to him. I didn't feel like getting into an argument with him, so I deleted the message and figured I would call him later in the day.

* * *

I was halfway through my work, which was taking longer than I thought because my computer was acting up, when the phone rang. I didn't want to answer it at first, but I checked the Caller ID and saw it was my father on his old office line.

"Hey Dad," I said.

"Darren," he said, in a voice that was thick with either anger or disappointment, I couldn't tell which. I tried to think if I had forgotten about something but came up empty. That didn't mean that I hadn't forgotten something.

"You alright?" I asked, almost afraid to hear the answer.

"I don't know."

"What's up?"

My father exhaled loudly, and for a second I thought he was smoking a cigarette, which he hadn't done in about twenty years. "What sort of mess are you involved in?" he asked.

"Nothing terrible."

"Level with me, Darren. Someone came by yesterday, asking questions about you. I'm pretty sure they did that just to scare us, but I didn't like their tone."

Hovelle. "A short stocky guy?"

"That's the one. Who is he?"

"Some federal agent who thinks he can do whatever he pleases."

"He's trouble."

"I know, Dad."

"Don't give me that. You're up to your neck in something here, and it seems that it's going to involve everyone else. If you're in some sort of trouble, or if you did something wrong, I need you to tell me." This wasn't the sort of conversation my father and I had. He hadn't talked to me in that tone of voice in years, and though I didn't like it, I found myself feeling more guilty than angry.

"Something else going on, Dad?"

"Remember Michael Bromwell?"

"Vaguely, but I can't place it."

"About fifteen years ago? He's the one whose parents claimed I misdiagnosed him with a stomach ailment, and he nearly died in the hospital. The Bromwell's sued me for malpractice, remember?"

Of course I did. In all the years my father practiced medicine, he never once had any trouble, except for Michael Bromwell. If I remembered correctly, the family didn't have insurance, and my father did most of the work gratis, only to be sued for malpractice because the kid never mentioned that he swallowed a ton of vitamins. The case had been dropped, as I remembered, and my father's record remained clean.

"I remember. Everything worked out fine with that. They never really had a case."

"Well, it seems Michael Bromwell is coming back to haunt me. I just got a letter in the mail from Medicare, stating that I am under investigation for insurance fraud, and Bromwell's case is one of the seven mentioned."

"Holy shit."

"Yeah, exactly. I don't know, I keep getting the feeling that the man that came to visit yesterday and this case are related. What do you think?"

Of course I thought it did. I just didn't know how to explain it all to my father, who was now in danger of losing whatever money he had because I pissed Hovelle off. When I had thought Hovelle could do nothing to me, I never considered my family, and even if I would have, I'd never have suspected Hovelle would do something like this.

"I don't know, Dad. It could be. The guy's a real prick."

"Have you spoken with him?"

"He was at my apartment when I got home last night."

"And what did he say?"

"He told me to stay away from Jason Caufield."

"Did you agree?"

"Well, no, not exactly."

"Darren, did you piss this guy off?"

"Maybe. But he threatened me, and I didn't react to that too well. Jesus, Dad, I'm sorry. You know I would never do something to get you or Mom involved. This whole thing is ridiculous, but I guess I didn't realize how important Jason is to the government."

"Calm down, Darren."

"I just can't believe this."

"Well, believe it. And don't worry. Medicaid has nothing on me. I didn't do anything wrong. This guy you spoke to last night is just trying to scare you off, and he's using me because he probably realized going after you directly won't do anything."

"You sure you have nothing to worry about with this?"

"Positive. Well, as positive as I can be. If they want, they can misconstrue anything I did to make me look guilty."

"Damn it. Does Mom know?"

"Of course not. Your mother would have everyone's head. She'd march right into the Medicaid office and threaten them all. You know how she gets. I didn't tell her, and I don't intend to, unless I have no choice. I'm going to call Uncle Steve, and see if he can handle the case for me. At least, that way, I won't have to pay too much for a lawyer, if it gets that far."

"Well, that's a relief at least."

"Didn't I warn you to be careful the other day?"

"You did."

"And you didn't listen," my father said.

"I tried. It wasn't like I intended to piss anyone off. When I got involved in this, I had no idea it would get this crazy. I only intended to find Jason, see if he was okay, then back out of it. There's a lot more going on than I originally expected."

"Like what?"

"I can't get into it now, this line is sort of staticy, if you know what I mean."

"Of course."

"Listen Dad, I'll get to the bottom of this all, and I'll make sure that everything will be okay. Don't worry, alright?"

"You just watch your back. Obviously, whoever wants to find Jason doesn't care about crushing people along the way, and there's no need for you to be one of them. I'll take care of this Medicare bullshit. You just make sure you don't create any more problems for yourself."

"Okay Dad, I will."

"And your mother finds out about none of this. Your sister too."

"Got ya."

"Call me when you can and let me know that you're okay. You've got me worried about you now."

"No problem. I will."

I flung my cordless phone across the room, and it landed on the couch, luckily not breaking. I knew Hovelle was a scumbag, but I didn't expect him to go after my family. It might not have been Hovelle that started that Medicare investigation, but I had a hard time thinking it was anyone else but him. It was another coincidence, and I was getting sick and tired of them. If Hovelle could go after my family like that, what would he do next? I wondered if maybe I should just drop the whole thing, but I thought the better of it. Even if I did back away, Hovelle would never believe me. He would just keep pushing and pushing, trying to find out whatever it was I knew. If he was going to do that, then I was going to gather as much information as possible. I wanted to stick it to him good. I just needed a place to start. It didn't take long to figure out.

Chapter 14

Before leaving for Ohio, there were a few things to sort out. I wasn't happy about having to travel again, but I knew that most of the answers I needed could be found at the university. If Jason had told me the truth, then I knew that the people at the university really were working with Hovelle and the government, and I figured I could get some sort of information out of them. It was risky, but worth a shot. In order to make sure that I stayed on top of everything, I called the phone company and had them forward all of the calls to the number Jason had for me to my cell phone. I knew this would guarantee me a large cell phone bill, but I had no choice. I needed to stay in contact with Jason, and there was no way I could reach him before he got to New York. Luckily, I had been suckered into one of those long distance cell phone plans, where a call anywhere in the country cost about the same as a local call. I hadn't really tested this feature out, and I hoped I wasn't going to get banged over the head for it.

I also called my bank, to see what sort of funds I was working with. I had seven hundred dollars in my checking account, a bit more than I had expected. That was the best news of the day. I went to the branch and withdrew four hundred, for pocket money in Ohio. I didn't worry about someone noticing the withdrawal if they were watching my account. I was safe making the withdrawal in New York instead of out of state, and I had no intention of using the account until I returned home.

A few years back, I had created a false identity. I really didn't have a need for it, but I figured, since a friend of mine at DMV was

183

able to set it up, I might as well take advantage. I had a phony driver's license and a credit card which was attached to another friend's account. This way, I didn't have to worry about applying for a card under the false name and all that. With the extra card on the friend's account, I could reserve hotels, flights, and anything else I needed. It was a pretty slick setup, and I was proud of myself for setting it up. It was now going to be put to good use.

After going to the bank, I called the airline and found a flight leaving JFK for Cleveland at four in the afternoon. I then called the Holiday Inn, and set myself up with a room not far from the university. The whole thing was going to cost me about six hundred dollars, but I knew my friend, whose credit account I was using, would let me pay it off. With no clean clothes to speak of, I made a quick run to the mall and picked up two outfits that I stuffed into my overnight bag when I got home.

The only problem I saw was the fact I wouldn't be able to carry a gun to Ohio. I didn't worry about this too much because I really didn't think I needed one, and if it turned out I did, I could always drop by Mike's. Mike had more guns than the NRA. I thought about giving him a call to tell him I'd be in the neighborhood, but I changed my mind. I didn't want anyone to know Darren Camponi was headed out of state. Warren Combs was the only one going to Ohio, and no one needed to know any different. Plus, I really didn't feel like getting into an argument with him over the information I provided about Jason. In my eyes, he had been the one to screw me over, and I had delivered what he asked for. The best thing to do was let him sit a little while, and then talk to him about it face to face if I had the time.

* * *

It was eleven-thirty when I got back to my apartment. I knew that, if Hovelle discovered I wasn't around, he might decide to toss my apartment once again. There was no way for me to prevent this, so I figured I might send him on a wild goose chase. I took out my notepad and jotted down bullshit comments, leading anyone who read it to believe Jason was headed to North Carolina, and that I would be going down there to meet him later in the week. I also wrote stuff like, "Dave Hovelle is a short prick-bastard," and the like, just to steam him if he decided to invade my privacy once again. If I had any mousetraps lying around, I would have placed them strategically around the apartment, but alas, I didn't.

Even though there was nothing important on my computer, I installed a password program that would prompt anyone using it for a security code when they tried to access any file or program. The program was a bitch to install, but I figured I might as well make things as difficult as possible for the good men who worked for the federal government. Once I was certain everything was working properly, I shut down the computer and disconnected the keyboard and mouse. I pictured the idiots sitting there for an hour trying to figure that difficult problem out.

With a few hours to kill before I had to be at the airport, I went across the street to Antonio's for lunch. I took my overnight bag with me, and planned to leave directly from the restaurant. The owner, Nick, greeted me when I walked in.

"Long time, no see, Darren," he said. Nick was a great guy, but he always made me feel guilty if I didn't come into his restaurant often. He was about 5'7" with curly black and gray hair and a mustache the same color. In a lot of ways, he reminded me of Mario, from the Nintendo games. He was dressed in chef's whites, except for the colorful silk shirt he wore underneath. The pattern of the shirt looked Hawaiian, and it seemed ridiculous in comparison to the chef's outfit. Yet, Mike dressed like this all the time when he worked afternoons.

"I know. I've been busy."

"How are things going for you?"

"Involved."

"I understand. You want to sit at a table, or the bar?"

The last thing I wanted was to be near alcohol. "Table. The one by the window over there is fine." The place was empty, which wasn't too surprising. Antonio's didn't do much of an afternoon business. I liked it that way. it gave me time to gather my thoughts before I went to the university.

I sat down at the table, and Mike asked, "You know what you want?"

"I'll tell you what, why don't you surprise me?" I said. When Nick did the cooking, which wasn't too often, he always liked to make things that weren't on the menu. It was almost like going to an uncle's house and enjoying a good Italian meal.

"You got it."

He went to the back, and immediately came back with Parmesan cheese and pepperoni on a platter, along with a carafe of red wine. I shook my hand at the wine, but he said, "You want me to make you a good meal, you wash it down with wine. Capisce?"

Again, someone was forcing alcohol on me. I didn't have a hard time imagining how some alcoholics never get cured. The people around them just wouldn't allow it.

"Alright, but only a glass or two. I have a long trip ahead of me."

"Where you going?"

I remembered how I didn't want anyone to know where I was going, and though it was a long shot that someone would ask Nick, and even longer shot that he'd say something, I didn't want to take the chance.

"I have to drive out east to do some investigating."

"Someone cheating on their wife again?"

You'd think all I did was follow around adulterers, with the questions people asked me. A very small percentage of my work had anything to do with that, but I think this aspect of my work fascinated people. Probably because many of them were guilty of it, and wanted to know how good I was at finding out.

"No, it's a corporate thing. Boring stuff."

"It can't all be exciting. So, you want fish, or meat?"

I thought about that for a second, breaking off a piece of the cheese and enjoying it. I ate meat all the time, and I couldn't remember the last time I had fish.

"What sort of fish you got?"

"Monkfish, Mahi Mahi, Chilean sea bass, and red snapper."

"I'll try the snapper."

"Good, I'll blacken it the way I did for you last time."

"You're the boss."

He walked back into the kitchen and I poured myself a glass of wine. It was cold, which is either the right way to serve it or the wrong way, considering your idea of what room temperature is. I had argued with Nick about this one time after drinking a bottle or so, and he said that room temperature for wine really is meant to gauge the temperature of a wine cellar, which was about ten degrees colder than the 68 degrees we all associate with room temperature. I said that wine tasted better when it was warmer, at least red wine did, and he told me I should be shot for such blasphemy. He turned out to be right, but I still liked my wine warm. God forbid he ever serve it to me that way.

The wine was good, despite it being cold. I recognized it as his own house wine that he made himself but never served to customers because I think there was a law against it. It was a bit stronger than regular wine, but it was exceptionally smooth, and I told myself to watch what I drank, so I didn't end up passed out at the table.

Mike brought out a Caesar salad, and I went to work on that while thinking about my plan for Ohio. I had come up with this idea quickly, and didn't have the time to properly set it up. My initial idea was to just go to the university and talk to anyone who would listen. I figured the Dean of Science that Jason mentioned would know the most, but would probably talk the least. The students Jason worked with would still be there, if they stayed on for the summer. I had called the Dean of Science's office to see if he was on campus, and he was, but the students would be another matter. I didn't even have any names. Like most of my life, I would have to fly this one by the seat of my pants.

Nick had made one of the best snapper meals I ever had, not counting some blonde I had picked up one time at a bar in the city, but that's a different story. It was tender, with just the right amount of seasoning. I washed it down with another glass of wine, but stopped at that, which didn't necessarily make Nick happy. I already felt a little tipsy from those two glasses, and if I had anymore, I would have never made it to the airport.

Nick only charged me twenty dollars for the whole meal, and I decided to charge it on my own credit card, to show normal activity, in case someone was watching my accounts. I left, telling Nick I would see him soon, and made my way to the airport, which was only a short ride from there.

On my way, I dialed Laura's house, realizing I wasn't going to get the chance to stop by anytime soon. A man answered, and I knew it was Alan. *Great.*

"Hello," he said, and I fought my urge to call him a shithead.

"Can I speak to Laura please?"

"Who's calling?" He wasn't pleasant over the phone. At least he was consistent.

I thought about who I should say I was. I knew he would

recognize my name, and I didn't want to walk down that path. I assumed that Laura had told him of my visit, and I wondered what his reaction was.

"Mike Holmes," I said, for lack of a better name.

"What is this regarding?"

I had to think fast. "It's a personal matter, sir."

"Well, I'm her husband."

"I understand, sir, but I need to speak with Mrs. Swenson," I said, proud of myself for remembering to use the correct last name.

Alan huffed, but said, "One moment."

Laura picked up another extension, and said, "Hello, this is Mrs. Swenson." I waited until I heard Alan hang up the other extension before I started speaking.

"It's Darren Camponi," I said.

"Oh, hello." I could tell by the sound of her voice that she knew not to say my name out loud so that Alan could hear it. She must have told him, and he must not have been happy to hear my name.

"I just wanted to call to let you know about your son."

"Great, he hasn't called in a while."

I didn't know if this was true or not. "He's doing fine."

"Are you sure?" Of course I wasn't sure, but I didn't know what else to tell her.

"Yeah, I saw him and spoke with him."

"What did he say?"

"I can't get into that right now. Are you still being watched?"

"Sometimes. I don't see the car as often as I used to."

"Trust me, they're still there. Be careful."

"What's going on?"

"A lot. That's all I can say. I just figured you'd want to know that your son is okay, and that I am going to do what I can to help him."

"Did he tell you what this is all about, how he got himself into this mess in the first place?"

"It's a long story, ma'am. And there's probably more to it than I know."

"And you're going to help him?"

"I am."

"Oh, thank you so much. If you speak to him, tell him to call me. I need to hear his voice and know that he's okay."

"I'm not so sure he's going to be able to do that easily. I can

188

guarantee your phone is tapped, and they might be able to locate him if he calls."

"Where is he?"

I decided to add more credibility to my bullshit story. "I think he's going south. I'm not going to say any more than that for obvious reasons."

Laura didn't say anything at first, but then asked, "Are you sure? That doesn't sound like Jason."

"He's trying to not act like Jason, so he will be that much harder to find."

"My phone isn't tapped, I would know if it was. Why don't you tell me where he is?"

"That's up to him to tell. I'll relay your message if I speak to him, and let him decide from there, okay?"

Another pause. "Okay. I appreciate everything you're doing."

"No problem. I told you I'd help him, and that's exactly what I am going to do."

"Take care."

"You too."

I ended the call, feeling strange about Laura. I figured half of her weirdness over the phone could be attributed to her not wanting Alan to know she was talking to me. But, there was something else in her voice. Maybe she had already talked to Jason and didn't want to tell me, and from that she knew Jason was on his way to New York. I cursed Jason for being so stupid, but there wasn't anything I could do about that right then, so I dismissed it, and set my mind on Ohio.

Chapter 15

The flight to Ohio was short, and I had gotten through airport security with the phony ID easily. For all the talk about strict airport security, it was real easy to beat if you knew how, and if you had the right connections of course. The Warren Combs ID was as valid as my own, and there wasn't any way for someone to verify it anyway. All they did at the check-in counter was make sure that the picture on the license matched the face they were looking at. After that, I was in the clear.

I stayed awake throughout the flight, thinking about what I planned to do once I landed. I would arrive at 7pm, too late to go to the university. I decided to pay Mike Holmes a visit, being that his house was on the way to my hotel anyway. He probably wouldn't be too happy to see me, and I was taking a chance by letting someone know I was in Ohio, but I didn't think Mike was that much of a scumbag. Plus, I had to deal with him sometime, and there was no better time than as soon as possible. Unless, of course, you are talking about paying bills or making an appointment with the dentist.

I rented the smallest car they had at the Budget counter in the airport. Again, the license and the credit card worked without a hitch. I was a little worried because the car rental company had access to DMV records and all that, but they took it without a problem, and within ten minutes, I drove out of the airport in the beautiful piece of machinery known as a Chevy Metro. I thought it was a bargain for twenty bucks a day, until I hit the gas pedal and realized that I could run faster. I hoped I wouldn't be involved in any car chases or vehicular escapes in that thing, because I didn't stand a chance.

* * *

Mike lived in a suburb of Cleveland, even though his address listed him inside the city itself. The person behind the counter at Budget had supplied me with a computer printout which mapped the route from the airport to Mike's exact address. It was about a twenty-minute drive, and along the way I realized I would never want to live in Cleveland. I always pictured myself moving out of New York someday, maybe the same day that I became a world-renowned writer or something like that, which basically meant I was stuck in New York for the rest of my life. New Yorkers are a strange breed, and I was the epitome of that. On any given day on the streets of New York, you could find some car with a "Move Out of New York State" bumper sticker. New Yorkers were just as proud of their state as anyone else across the country, but we did have a good amount of disgruntled people. What I didn't understand was, if someone took the time to plaster such a bumper sticker on their car, why didn't they move out themselves? Maybe they just wanted New York to have less New Yorkers in it, and decided to shoo away as many as possible with such a sticker on their car. I never said New Yorkers were normal. As a matter of fact, I don't think anyone ever said such a thing.

Mike lived on a cul-de-sac, the last house on the left side. It's really tough to describe it that way, because a cul-de-sac is circular, so there is no last house on any side, but I mean that his house was the one to the left of the center house, if that makes sense. It was a white colonial, and rather large with a huge front yard and a nice big bay window out front. There was a late model Mercedes sedan in the driveway, along with a black Toyota RAV4, a small sport utility vehicle. I parked in front of the center house and made my way up to the door, which was a nice solid oak job with white-frosted windows. I found the doorbell and rang it.

It took a few seconds for someone to answer, then the door opened up revealing a quite attractive blonde who looked to be in her late thirties. It was Ellen, Mike's wife, who I had met the one time when Mike visited New York a year before. She was striking, and she looked at me as if she had no idea who I was.

191

"Is Mike around?" I asked.

"No, he stepped out. Can I help you?"

"I wouldn't expect you to remember me," I said, "but we met in New York a little over a year ago. I think it was your anniversary. My name is Darren," I said, extending my hand. She didn't take it.

"Oh, yes, the private investigator. I remember you. You're working on a case for Mike right now, aren't you?"

"Well, sort of."

"He mentioned it. He actually told me to expect your call. He had a message he wanted me to give you."

"Okay, well, I guess you now have the opportunity to give it to me personally."

"Yeah. Actually, he shouldn't be long. He just ran out to get something from the store. He should be back any minute. You want to come inside and wait?"

"Sure, why not?"

She led me into the hallway, which was tiled with ceramic, or marble, I couldn't tell which. There were five stairs made of the same material that led up to a large living room, furnished in a Santa Fe style. I saw Indian feather headdresses and other stuff along those lines, and figured them to be her personal touch. Mike didn't strike me as the sort that was into that. We went upstairs, and I sat down on a couch that had cacti and a picture of a sunset on it.

"Can I get you something to drink?"

"Water would be fine."

"Sparkling or no?" she asked. *Classy.*

"Regular is fine."

I looked around the room as she turned to go to the kitchen, only because I didn't want to stare at her ass. I knew she had a nice one, but I was totally against drooling over an acquaintance's wife. Just a general rule I followed, and yes, I really wanted to look. She was that well put together. There was nothing in the room of interest, except maybe the bear skin hanging from the wall, complete with its head. I wondered if maybe Mike had killed it himself. He was an avid hunter. He always invited me out to Ohio for hunting, and I always turned him down, telling him I'd rather shoot people than animals. I never saw hunting as a sport, mainly because Bambi usually doesn't walk around with a shotgun. If you wanted to call hunting a sport, which would require it to be somewhat fair, then go after a bear with a

Bowie knife. Then I would respect the hunter. Staring at that bearskin on the wall, I found it funny picturing Mike doing exactly that.

Ellen returned with a tall glass of water and ice, and I took a sip. She sat across from me, and I avoided making eye contact with her. I didn't want my eyes to give away what my head, the lower one, was thinking. She was probably used to that sort of thing from men.

"So, what brings you to Cleveland?" she asked.

"Just a little business trip."

"For Mike?" she asked. "Well, probably not. If you needed something done on his case out here, I guess you would ask him to do it."

"Yeah, I'm working on something else. The trip came out of nowhere, and I figured I would drop by, considering I have never come to see him before. Maybe I should have called first."

"Oh, it's no big deal. Like I said, he should be home soon."

"How's he been?"

"Busy, as usual. I keep telling him to take on a partner, but he likes working for himself and having no one to answer to. It's really too much work for him."

"I can imagine."

"Yeah, well, you should know, you do the same thing." I wanted to tell her that I would have no idea what Mike was going through, because I didn't have that good of a business, but I didn't want to seem like a complete schmuck in front of her. She was the sort of woman who seemed to enjoy money, and judging from the diamond-studded necklace and large rock on her finger, I figured I knew why Mike was working so hard.

"Yes, I do."

"I'll tell you, it's not like a regular job. He keeps all sorts of hours, even though he doesn't work directly on cases the way he used to. It's like living with a police officer."

"The two aren't so different."

"If I didn't have my job at the boutique a couple of days a week, I would go completely out of my mind all alone here."

"I'm sure."

"You want something to eat or anything?" she asked.

"No, that's alright. I had some of United Airlines' fine cuisine on the flight over."

She chuckled. "Okay, just let me know. If you don't mind, I just want to finish in the kitchen." She got up. "Mike likes to have his dinner at a specific time every night."

"No problem. I'll just sit here and read the . . ." I noticed a magazine, *People*, sitting on the coffee table. "I'll be reading the magazine."

"Just let me know if you need anything."

"I'll be fine, but thanks." Ellen got up, and again I found myself staring at the bearskin so not to stare at her behind. It was awkward, but like I said, it was a golden rule of mine.

I flipped open the magazine and read about the latest Hollywood marriage that was on the verge of collapse. What Hollywood marriage wasn't? I think the media was responsible for more breakups than anything else. They would report a rumor of a troubled marriage, and then, maybe, one of the two involved would say to themselves, "Yeah, I should leave him. He doesn't treat me right, and his last movie tanked. I should leave him, I have to leave him, in order to save my career." Well, maybe it didn't work quite that way, but I wouldn't have been surprised if I was on the money with that.

Ellen was in the kitchen for about ten minutes, and I was already done with the magazine when she walked back into the living room.

"That's funny," she said, staring out the bay window, "I would have thought he'd be back by now."

"Maybe he knew I was coming," I said.

"No, seriously. Well, don't get me wrong, he does this all the time. He'll tell me that he'll be back in five minutes, then three hours later he shows up. It's okay for him to be late, but God forbid I don't have dinner out at the preset time."

"You sure everything's okay?"

"Positive." She seemed pretty sure of herself. I knew one thing, Mike wasn't out somewhere banging someone else. Not with this beauty sitting at home. Then again, I had read in the newspaper once that men who cheated always did so with someone less attractive than their wife. This made no sense to me. Why risk the filet mignon for chopped steak?

"You want me to go look for him or something?" That sounded stupid when it came out of my mouth, but it was too late to take it back.

"No, like I said, he does this all the time. He probably just got caught up doing something he didn't want to do. I'm sure he'll be along."

I didn't want to sit there waiting. The boredom, not to mention the sexual temptation, was just too much for me to stand. I needed to make an exit.

"Tell you what, why don't you just tell him I stopped by. I have to check into my hotel and all that, so, I guess I should get going."

"Sure, no problem. Um, he wanted me to tell you something."

I had forgotten about that. "Yeah, what was it?"

Ellen gave me a blank stare, further proving my belief that all beautiful women are stupid. "Hold on," she said. "I wrote it down. I'll go get it."

This time, when she turned to walk out of the room, I decided to sneak a peek. She had a tight curvy butt that wasn't too small and wasn't too big. It was just right. I shook my head at my own sinfulness, and went back to admiring the bearskin. Ellen came back into the room with a piece of paper in her hand.

"He said to tell you that he's sorry, that you were right. He needs to talk to you about a federal plan, and a man named Dave. Any of that make sense to you?"

"Too much," I mumbled.

"What?"

"Yeah, I understand what he meant. You tell him to call me at this number," I said, handing her my business card with my cell number written on the back, "You tell him to do it as soon as possible. If he calls before he comes home, tell him to call me on the road. We really need to talk."

"Is everything okay?"

I didn't know how much Mike told his wife, and if he told her anything, I had no idea how much she retained. I figured it would be best to tell her nothing. "Everything is fine. I just need to speak to him about something before I move forward, okay?"

She nodded.

"Thank you for everything." I walked out of the house and into my sparkling Chevy Metro, trying to figure out what the hell was going on with Mike. It wasn't like him to apologize for anything, and he even bothered to send the apology through his wife. What did he find out that made him change his tune so fast? I thought maybe he came into contact with Hovelle, but then again, I had figured him to be in cahoots with Hovelle from the very beginning. Maybe I was wrong, and Mike had only been doing his job up to that point. If that was the case, then something changed, and I needed to speak to Mike as soon as possible. I started the car and headed toward my hotel.

Traffic was horrible on the way to the Holiday Inn, caused by the most frustrating thing on the road—rubbernecking. People always have to get a look at a tragedy. I was stuck in bumper-to-bumper traffic because everyone had to get a glimpse of the BMW Z3 coupe that was in flames on the other side of the highway. When it came time for me to pass it, I took a good look myself. I got the chills, because I realized whoever was in that car got burned real good. Whoever it was, they were an idiot. They must have been going real fast, because the car was facing the wrong direction. Flames were everywhere, tearing through the convertible top, and melting anything that wasn't metal. What a way to go, I thought, and then prayed to whatever was in control that I wouldn't die that way. Give me a heart attack, an aneurysm, anything other than a fiery death like the guy in the BMW suffered.

The fire department had arrived about two minutes before I passed the car, and they really couldn't do much until the car had been eaten completely by the fire. There were three fire trucks taking up that whole side of the highway, and I felt better knowing that I was headed in the right direction. Even though my commute was delayed, it was a hell of a lot better than the fate the people on the other side suffered. Those people wouldn't be getting home for hours.

I made it back to the hotel, checked in with the desk clerk, and went to my room. I had requested a room on the first floor, though I really don't know why, and the clerk gave me a room that faced the parking lot. I parked right in front of my room, took the overnight bag out of the hatch, and settled in. The room was small, but I really didn't care. I was only going to use it for sleeping, and sleep was exactly what I had on my mind. I made sure my cell phone was powered on and lying on the nightstand, just in case Jason tried to call. Then, I unpacked my bag, got undressed, and shut the eyelids.

I must have been asleep for about four hours when the phone rang. At first, I had a dream that a phone was ringing and I answered it, then I woke with a jolt, not sure if I was still asleep, and answered the phone that was really ringing.

"Yeah," I said, though it probably only sounded like a groan.

"Darren?" It was Jason.

"Yes."

"Jesus, it didn't sound like you."

"Probably because it's three in the morning, and I'm only dreaming that this conversation is really happening."

"Sorry. I figured this time would be the safest to call. Besides, it's only two."

"It's 3AM here."

"Where are you?"

"Cleveland."

"What are you doing there?"

"Decided it was time I saw the place. What do you think? I'm investigating."

"Oh." Jason paused for a moment. "You think that's a good idea?"

"Why, you don't?"

"I don't know."

"What's the problem?"

"You gonna tell them you spoke to me?"

"Now, why would I do that?"

"I dunno. I mean, the guy who is looking for me is from Ohio, right? The university hired him."

"They did. But that's not why I came here."

"What are you going to do?"

"I want answers, Jason. A lot of things are happening to people around me, and they are all related. I figured some of my answers might come from here."

"You gonna speak to the people at the university?"

"I intend to."

"Be careful. I don't think those people are going to be too friendly."

"Is there something you haven't told me, Jason? Something about all this you might have forgotten to mention?"

Jason sighed. "No, I told you everything. Understand, though, this is serious stuff we are dealing with here, and if the wrong people think you know where I am, it could get dangerous."

"It already has gotten dangerous. The feds have decided they want to make my life miserable."

"They're good at that."

"Who should I speak to down at the university?"

"Well, Dean Wilkins would be the best place to start. That's the Dean of Science, the one who was basically my supervisor. He's not a bad guy, but I really don't trust him."

"What about students?"

"None of them really knew what was going on."

"They probably know more than you think. Wasn't there one that was confronted by the feds, the girl who came to you crying?"

"Yeah, Aileen."

"You know her last name?"

"Hmm, let me think. Uh, Turner, yeah that's it. Aileen Turner."

"You think she'd still be around? You know, it is summer."

"She should be there. She's doing an internship, so I think she is there year-round. She's a nice girl, but I don't know if she'll talk to you. She was really frightened about the whole thing."

"Don't worry about that. Anyone else I should talk to?"

"You could try getting a hold of Manny. He was my head assistant, but I'm not sure if he'll be around. He's a strange guy." Coming from Jason, I knew this Manny would be some character.

"Okay, got a last name for him?"

"Hirsch."

"Hirsch? You sure about that?"

Jason chuckled. "Yeah. He's half Spanish and half Jewish. He used to joke about that all the time, how his mother used to put matzo balls in his chicken and rice."

"I see. Oh, by the way, I spoke to your mother. I told her you were doing okay, but I didn't say where you were going. I couldn't be sure her line was clear."

"Yeah, I should call her. Last time I tried, I got her husband. Don't like that guy."

I wanted to tell Jason I felt the same way, but I didn't feel like explaining that. "I haven't had the pleasure of meeting him."

"Yeah, whatever."

"You in a safe spot?"

"Yes. I'm somewhere that no one would expect to find me."

"That's good. Listen, I want to get some sleep. I have a long day ahead of me."

"Just be careful at the university. I have no idea what's really going on over there, and I don't want you to get into any more trouble."

"It's too late for that, Jason, but thank you. I'll be careful."

"I'll call you from time to time, to let you know I'm okay. Have you given my offer any more consideration?"

"A little."

"I'm going to be setting everything up in the next day or so. I'd rather use you as a volunteer instead of some junkie on the streets of . . ."

"Don't say it."

"Oh, yeah, forgot. Well, you know what I mean."

"I'll think about it."

"Take care."

I ended the call, but as soon as I hit the button, the phone rang again.

"Yeah."

"Darren Camponi?" It was a female.

"This is he."

"It's Ellen Holmes." She sounded like she was crying.

"Is everything okay?"

"Mike died in a car accident this afternoon, on I-46."

I-46 was the highway I had taken from Mike's house to the hotel.

"Jesus Christ." I wanted to ask her if Mike drove a BMW, but then I would have to explain that I had seen the accident. I didn't want her asking me for details or anything. Whatever she knew, she knew, and I wasn't going to tell her anything else.

"It's horrible, Darren. He was on his way home from the store. His car went out of control, hit the embankment, and just blew up."

The coincidence was too much to ignore. That had to be Mike's car that I saw on the highway. "I'm so sorry, Ellen. Is there anything I can do?"

"What could you do?"

Nothing, I figured, but it was just something you said. "I know. Really, I am sorry. Listen, I have to ask you a question, if you are able to answer it."

"What?"

"Do you have any idea who that guy Dave was, the one Mike told you to tell me about?"

"No."

"Have you noticed anything strange with Mike lately? Did anyone come around the house?"

"Not that I remember? What are you getting at?"

"Listen. Ellen, you need to be careful. I think Mike got himself involved in something."

"You think he was murdered? Oh my God," Ellen said, her voice breaking up. I didn't know if mentioning what I did was a good idea. I just wanted answers. But I really had no doubt that Mike's death was no accident.

"I don't know. I mean, the case we were working on together has been nothing but trouble from Day One."

"Well, the police will look into all of this, won't they?"

I doubted that. "Maybe. It all depends. Have they told you anything?"

"Just that Mike was in an accident. I am at the hospital now. Jesus, I can't believe he's gone. Are you going to look into this yourself?"

"I'll do what I can." I didn't know if that was true, but it sounded good.

"I just can't believe this. I can't."

"I know, Ellen. You try and hold yourself together, okay?"

"I'll try."

I ended the call with Ellen and sat up in bed. There wasn't any doubt in my mind that Mike had gotten into some sort of trouble over the Caufield case. Hovelle's warning about my telling Mike what I knew rang in my head. I felt guilty, even though I had told Mike before Hovelle warned me. All my thoughts about how Hovelle couldn't do anything to me seemed so ridiculous right then. What had I been thinking? I guess I hadn't realized how important Jason's research was to the government, and whoever else was involved in all of this. I knew right then I wasn't safe, and no one around me was safe either.

I thought about Mike. I always liked the guy, and he was the sort that enjoyed having a good time. I pictured him laughing over the phone, telling jokes, and the like. I felt guilty again, not only because I might have indirectly caused his death, but also because he had been a friend, and I never spent the sort of time with him I should have. He had always been asking me to come to Ohio to visit, and the only time I did so was to prove that he was lying to me. I had never experienced the death of a friend, and even though I wasn't that close to him, I went through the series of "What if's?" that people do when they experience death close up. Mike had two kids and a wife, and now they were left alone because Mike probably went digging where he shouldn't have. I wanted to have a look at Mike's records, to see if he had really gone to do some investigating instead of to the store like he told his wife. I knew she probably wasn't ready for me to go rifling through his papers. The poor woman had just lost her husband, and I knew it wasn't a good idea to fill her head with conspiracy theories and all that. I would have to settle for answers from the university, and maybe from a few other sources as well, if I had the balls to go hunting after Hovelle.

Chapter 16

I didn't sleep much at all that night, constantly waking up, out of fear that the phone was going to ring with bad news. It didn't, thank God, but I still couldn't get any rest. I woke up about eight, feeling worse than I did when I went to sleep. I had almost forgotten Mike was dead when I woke up. I thought about going to his house to talk to him. Realizing he was gone made me feel even worse, and I didn't feel any better when I got out of the shower. I tried to tell myself it wasn't my fault, that Mike was the one who got me into this mess to begin with, but I kept going back to feeling as though I could have prevented Mike's problem. After all, Mike had called before I left for Ohio, and I hadn't returned the call. He sounded troubled on the answering machine, and I had attributed that to his being mad at me. Maybe he wanted to tell me something, and I might have been able to prevent him from doing whatever he did to get himself killed. Such thoughts get you nowhere, though, because I surely didn't feel any better after thinking that way.

I got dressed, and felt naked when I didn't have a gun on me. When I left New York, I hadn't seen a need for a gun, but right then, I wanted a gun more than anything. No one knew I was in Ohio, but that didn't stop me from thinking someone could have figured it out. I hoped no one stopped to see Ellen, and I wanted to call her to tell her to make sure not to say anything, but the last thing I wanted to do was bother her. I would just have to be careful.

* * *

The University of Ohio at Cleveland was about fifteen miles from my hotel, and the hotel clerk had given me good directions. I had to travel on I-46 again, which made me think of Mike's untimely departure, so I tried to keep my mind occupied on who I had to speak to, and what I thought I could discover. I had to travel through a more rural area, but mostly, I saw factories and such, which made me dislike Cleveland more than before. There was nothing to see in the town, and it had already caused me enough grief and anger to last a lifetime.

* * *

Dean Wilkins' office was on the north side of campus. The campus itself was huge, and I felt like a freshman having to ask students for directions. There weren't too many students around, probably because it was summer, and most of the ones I asked for directions had no idea where they were going either. Finally, an older man who I figured was a professor, led me down the right path.

I entered the building, a large rustic looking one, and found my way to where Wilkins' office was. There was an empty secretary desk, and I decided to poke my head into the door with Wilkins' name on it.

"Anybody here?" I asked. The office seemed empty, but there were papers on the desk and the computer was on. A door on the left side opened, and Wilkins walked out of the bathroom and into his office. He was a tall thin man with nearly shoulder-length gray hair and a barely noticeable goatee.

"Can I help you?" he asked, taking a seat behind his desk.

"I hope so."

"Have a seat," he said, gesturing to a book-filled chair on the left side of his desk. I walked over, and picked up the books. There must have been about ten of them. I looked around and noticed clutter all over the place.

"You can just put them on the floor for now," Wilkins said. He seemed like a friendly guy, but it looked as though he didn't know what to make of me. I put the books on the floor and sat down. I felt like I should cross my legs or something, to make myself look more professional, but decided against it because I thought it would make

203

me look like a fag. "You need help with a schedule or something?"

"No," I said, "I'm not a student."

Wilkins' facial expression changed from helpful to concerned. "Then what is it I can help you with?"

"I wanted to talk to you about Jason Caufield."

Wilkins took on an aggravated look, as if he had been asked this more times than he wanted. "Who are you?"

"A concerned party."

"That doesn't tell me much."

"I wish I could tell you more than that, sir, but for reasons of confidentiality, I can tell you no more."

"Jason Caufield is no longer employed here, and there really isn't much else I can tell you, for reasons of confidentiality. If that's all . . ."

"Wait. I only want to ask you a few general questions. It is really important that I have answers to these questions, and I think you can provide them."

"What sort of questions?"

"Things that are probably common knowledge, but I'd like to hear the answers from you."

"Go ahead. If you start asking questions that I think inappropriate, I won't answer, and I will ask you to leave. Deal?"

"Deal." I could tell that Wilkins wasn't a bad guy, but I had a feeling he knew he was caught up in something more serious than he desired. "While Jason Caufield was employed here, were you his direct supervisor?"

"Yes, if you could call it that. He was pretty much his own boss, but he did report to me from time to time. If he needed authority on something, he had to come to me for it. So yes, I was his supervisor."

"How was his work? I mean, was he a good employee?"

"The best. Jason went about his work and bothered no one. He is a genius, and he translated that into some fine work."

"How did he get along with the students?"

"He didn't have too many dealings with them. When he started out, we had him teaching a beginner science course, but that wasn't his thing. It was too simple for him. He had a good rapport with his students, many of them gave him compliments, but he really didn't want to teach. He was a researcher and a scientist first and foremost, so teaching only took him away from that. After two semesters of teaching, we moved him permanently to the lab so he could dedicate all of his time to his research."

"But he worked with students in the lab, right?"

"Most of the students in the lab didn't work directly with him. He acted more as a supervisor, to make sure that the students treated the equipment properly and all that. If they had questions, they could ask him, but they really weren't involved in what he was doing."

"Okay, are you familiar with what he was working on? I know you can't talk about that directly, but I need to know if you were aware of what he was researching."

Wilkins raised his eyebrows, then eyed me over a bit. "Of course I knew what he was working on. It was no secret that he was studying Quantum Physics."

"What did you think of his research?"

"Like I said before, Jason was a genius. His work was excellent, if a little far-fetched."

"So, you didn't agree with the course he was taking."

"All Quantum physicists end up going down that path at least once in their careers, but it is a dead end. Time travel just isn't possible."

"But isn't it that exact research that got the university interested in Jason in the first place?"

Wilkins laughed. "Don't be foolish, of course the work he was doing interested the university. To have one of your staff researchers make a major discovery in that field, even if it is to disprove the possibility of time travel, it is fantastic. I think the current administration thought Jason could make headway, but I doubt if anyone thought he was going to prove time travel. It's science fiction. It sells movies and draws attention in the media, but it really just isn't feasible."

"I wouldn't know anything about that."

"I understand." Wilkins reached into his desk and pulled out a pipe. "I'm not supposed to do this in here, but I doubt you'll mind," he said, lighting the pipe.

"Of course not. So, can you tell me anything about Jason's departure from this university?"

"Jason wasn't happy here. He had told me on many occasions that he felt constricted. He didn't like the politics, and he didn't like the fact that no one in the science department wholeheartedly supported his research. He was a loner, and most people thought he was a little too eccentric. I guess all scientists are eccentric to one degree or another, but Jason was exceptionally so."

"So, he left because he was unhappy with the conditions?"

"I believe so."

"He didn't leave because he was being told to supply information to the federal government?"

Wilkins' eyes lit up, and he took a long draw from the pipe. He exhaled, and I could smell the cherry tobacco he was smoking. It smelled nice, actually, reminding me of a great uncle who smoked a pipe all the time.

"I would appreciate if you kept the questions reality-based," Wilkins said.

"So, you're saying that there is no truth to that?"

"That's exactly what I am saying."

"Have you ever heard of David Hovelle?"

"I think maybe it is time for you to leave."

"So, you admit you have heard of him."

"I have no idea who you are talking about."

"Dr. Wilkins, I want you to know that people's lives are at stake here. If you know anything, I need you to tell me. One man has already died because of Jason's situation."

"That's Jason's problem. I wouldn't concern myself with it if I were you."

"Did you know that the university is searching for Jason, that they claim he stole intellectual property?"

"Nonsense."

"Stop lying to me. I know you know something about this. Maybe you want to protect your own ass, and I understand that, but if there's something you could tell me, it might help matters."

Wilkins slammed his hand on his desk. "Dammit, what's the matter with you? What makes you think I want to get involved?"

"So you do know?"

"Of course I know, and there's no way I am telling you anything. I don't even know who you are."

"That's not important."

"It's very important. You think I asked to get in the middle of this?" Wilkins stood up and stared out of his window. He took a few draws from his pipe to calm himself down, and then turned to look at me. "Alright, I'll tell you this, and then you leave."

"Fine."

"A little while after Jason started working here, the president of the university paid me a visit, telling me to keep an eye on Jason. He said that there were some stick issues they had to worry about, but they never told me what that was. The administration here had suffered a few bad circumstances where researchers took all of their information with them to another university and claimed all the credit. I figured they didn't want that to happen again. So, I kept an eye on him, and noticed he was doing nothing wrong. Then, about a year later, I got another visit. This time, it was the president of the university, and another man who never said who he was. The president told me there was a problem with Jason's former employer. Maybe he didn't know that Jason told me that his former employer was the government. I assumed the man in the office with the president was with the government, and I realized that things were more serious than I originally thought. I wanted to talk to Jason about it, but I figured the best thing to do was stay our of it. So, that's what I did.

Then, one day, I was told to make Jason create a file with all of his research. Jason came to me and told me he didn't want to do that. He didn't tell me why, but I figured it had something to do with the government again. I told him the best thing to do was just comply, and he did. I never looked at the file. They made him seal it. But I could tell he didn't give them everything they wanted. I knew this was true when they told me to have him create another file. He refused, and a few weeks later he came into my office and told me he was leaving. I tried to talk him out of it, but I think he figured I was just working with them. I never said I wasn't, because I didn't want to get into all of that. I just told him to think about what he was doing. He seemed scared, and he walked out of my office telling me that he would give the administration the file they wanted."

"Did he?"

Wilkins laughed. "Well, he did give them a file, but I don't think they were too happy with it because after he left they ran through his office and the lab. They were pissed, and that guy who was in my office paid me a visit, asking if I had spoken to Jason. I told him no, but he didn't seem happy with that."

"A short stocky guy?"

Wilkins nodded. "That's him. You said his name was Hovelle?"

"I think so."

"Well, I wouldn't know because he didn't give a name. He just dropped a hint or two that he worked for the government and I left it at that. Jason called about two weeks after that, yelling at me for selling him out. I told him that wasn't the case, but he didn't believe me."

"He said you were a decent guy," I said.

"You've spoken with him?"

"On the record? Of course not. But I might have come into contact with him once or twice."

"Has he done it?"

"What?"

"Proved his theory?"

"I don't know."

"I think he will. I know I told you before that all that stuff is science fiction, but I was lying. I really believed in his research, even if I never showed it."

"He wants a volunteer."

"Then he's done it."

"What makes you think so?"

"Jason would never have someone volunteer, never tell anyone about his research, unless he has already theoretically proven it. My God, I never thought this day would come. He's in trouble, isn't he? That's why you are here."

"Exactly."

"What do you intend to do?"

"I don't know. I want to find out why he is in so much danger."

"Because what he has is immeasurably valuable. It doesn't take too much to figure that out."

"Yes, but would the government kill for this information?"

"What do you think?"

"Then what can I do to help him?"

"Whatever you can to make him prove his research true. Once he does that, he'll have garnered too much attention for someone to do something to him."

"I don't know about that."

"Well, it's his best chance."

"You're probably right."

Wilkins sat back down again. "Listen, you be careful as well. I don't want to get into specifics, but let's just say that I have been threatened. I haven't done anything either way, but that doesn't seem to matter. I probably shouldn't have even talked to you, but I felt like I had to. Sorry about the attitude earlier, but I am sure you understand."

"I do, and I'll be careful. You do the same."

"I will."

I stood up to leave. "You know someone named Manny?"

"Hirsch?"

"That's the one."

"Yes, I know him."

"He around?"

Wilkins shook his head. "You don't want to talk to him."

"So, he is around."

"Listen to me on this one. Anything you say to him will get right back to the people you want to steer clear of. Got it?"

"Yes. What about Aileen Turner?"

Wilkins sighed. "Don't ask."

"Why?"

"Well, she would have spoken to you, but she can't."

"What are you talking about?"

"Aileen had been working late one night about three weeks ago. I don't know what Jason told you, but she was directly involved in all of this whether she knew something or not. She and Jason had something going, I think, but that's not important. Her body was found behind one of the buildings in a dumpster." Wilkins looked completely stressed about this.

"Murdered?"

"There were two murders here last semester. The police attributed it to a gang that had formed on campus, but I didn't know Aileen to be someone who got involved in that sort of thing. I could be wrong about that, but I doubt it."

"You think this is related."

"Don't you?" Of course I did. It made me angry to think that people would go so far as to kill an innocent girl over some research.

"I guess I see the logic in that."

"That's why I am telling you to watch out, and that's why I think speaking to Manny Hirsch is a bad idea."

"Let's say I might get in the mood to do something stupid. Where might I find this Manny if I wanted to?"

Wilkins rolled his eyes. "If you're crazy, you might find him in the science lab. He is always working on something. If you want my opinion, he's trying to complete Jason's research before Jason does."

"Okay, thanks for the help."

"If that's what you want to call it."

I left Wilkins' office, and located the science lab, but it was empty. I did find a student hanging about, and they told me that Manny would be around in an hour or so. He was in charge of the lab for the summer, and I found out that he closed it sometime around nine. I decided to go have some lunch, and do whatever I could to kill time until Manny closed the lab. I wanted Jason to call, but he didn't, and I found myself sitting around the hotel doing nothing. I could have stopped by Mike's house, but I figured I would only bother Ellen for information I already had. If it wasn't Hovelle that had something to do with Mike's death, then it was the tooth fairy. I watched a movie, the latest one from Harrison Ford, and took a nap, making sure that the hotel gave me a wakeup call around six-thirty. I needed the sleep, and though it was fitful I felt a little better when I woke up. Before I went to sleep, I booked a morning flight back to New York, and made arrangements to return the rental car. This way, I had everything taken care of. I even called my friend, the one whose credit account I was using, and told him of the charges. He wasn't particularly thrilled, but he understood.

* * *

The science lab was in a huge building not too far away from Wilkins' office. The building was empty, and the hallway was fairly dark. I had stolen a peek into the lab, and saw a tall dark-haired guy in his twenties working on a computer. I knew it was Manny, and I waited to the side of the door for him to finish and exit.

About fifteen minutes later, somewhere just after eight, I saw the lights go off in the lab. The door opened, Manny came out, turned, and locked the door, never seeing me. I grabbed him by his free arm and yanked him into the stairwell, throwing him against the wall. He fell onto his stomach, and I got right on top of him, twisting his arm behind his back so he wouldn't move.

"What the fuck," he said.

"Just lay still."

"I don't have any money on me, I swear."

"This isn't about money. It's about what you have been up to, Manny."

"What are you talking about?"

"You know exactly what I'm talking about."

"Mr. Hovelle?"

"No, I'm not Hovelle, but thanks for proving to me that you know what I'm talking about."

"What do you want?"

"I want to know what you think you are doing."

"I'm not doing anything."

I twisted Manny's arm a bit more, and he moaned. "Alright, alright. What do you want to know?"

"Who told you to sell out Jason Caufield?"

"If you're here, and you're asking that question, then you know."

"I want to hear it from you."

"Hovelle."

"How long you been working with him?"

"Six months. He came to me. Jesus, I shouldn't be telling you this."

"Why? You afraid you're going to end up like Aileen Turner?"

"I had nothing to do with that."

"But you let it happen."

"She knew too much. I tried to tell her to stay away, to get a transfer if she had to, but she wouldn't listen. She started asking questions."

"So, you had her murdered."

"Fuck no."

"You told Hovelle who she was."

"He knew that already."

"How do I know you didn't kill her yourself, for Hovelle?"

"I never would do that." Manny started wiggling, like he was going to try and break free.

"Don't even think about it, or I'll put a bullet in the back of your head."

Manny stopped cold. "Please, don't. I didn't do anything wrong."

"Two people died because of this, and you have something to do with that."

"Who else? That private investigator?"

"How did you know?"

"He came around here asking questions yesterday. I told Hovelle, because he told me to tell him everything. He said he'd take care of it."

"And you just let it happen?"

"What was I supposed to do?"

"Call the police perhaps?"

"You think they aren't involved in all of this? They're the ones that said Aileen's murder was gang related. Jesus, they are in this just as deep as I am."

"What are you working on in there?"

"I can't tell you that."

"I think you should," I said, twisting the arm again. I'm pretty sure I tore a ligament or something because Manny screamed as if I was tearing his arm off. "Shut up, or I'll have to kill you."

Manny didn't say anything, like a good boy. Of course, unless I planned to snap his neck, something I wasn't necessarily experienced in, there was no way I was going to kill him. I just wanted him to shut up so I wouldn't have to deal with campus security. I hated those bastards when I went to college, and I didn't think I would like them now.

"I know you're working on Jason's research. Who told you to do that?"

"The university."

"Bullshit. Hovelle told you to do it."

"No, he didn't. You have no idea what's going on here. You might think you can trust Wilkins and the rest of the people here, but you're wrong. Everyone's obsessed with getting this research done, and they are trying to do it themselves. But Jason didn't leave enough information here to finish his work. Plus, I don't even have the prototype he had to work with. I tried telling them that, but they didn't want to hear it."

"So, you're trying to tell me that you are just an innocent student caught up in all of this."

"Yes. Hovelle came to me six months ago and wanted me to report directly to him and the president of the university. They wanted me to give them any information I could find on Jason's research. I didn't come up with much because Jason figured out what was going on. He had no idea it was me, but he knew someone was doing it."

"And you see Hovelle often?"

"No, not really. He hasn't been around in a while. He calls from time to time, but I mainly deal with the people here."

"I want you to fuck up your research. Do it any way you can without being caught."

"What do you think I've been doing? They keep telling me that I'll end up in serious trouble if I don't make some headway. I don't know who they think I am, but I try to make it look like I'm doing something. If I don't, I'll end up dead."

I didn't doubt that, but I didn't care either. Manny had sold Jason out, and was now trying to complete his research. Maybe he didn't have a choice, but he did know what sort of problems he and Hovelle were causing, and he really didn't convince me that he gave a shit about that.

"What's going to happen next?"

"What do you mean?"

"I want you to tell me what you know."

"I don't know anything."

"Bullshit."

"All I know is that they think they're going to find Jason."

"What are they going to do when they find him?"

"I don't know. I think they just want his research."

"They're going to kill him, aren't they?"

"I don't think so. He's too valuable to them. All these killings are his fault. If he would have just turned himself in, none of this would have happened."

"Of course not."

"They know about you," Manny said.

"What are you talking about?"

"You're the guy from New York, the one that found him, aren't you."

"I never said that."

"They told me you might come here. And they told me to let them know you came."

If that was true, then they probably already knew I had spoken to Wilkins, which meant I had to watch my back. I didn't want to end up like Mike Holmes.

"You're not going to tell them a fucking thing. If I find out you did, I'll come back here and kill you, you got that."

"Yes, yes. Listen, I don't want to be a part of this. I want to run somewhere, but I know they are watching me, and I know they'll find me."

"You're a smart kid. You just keep on pretending everything is normal. This will all be over soon."

"I don't know about that."

"Trust me." I thought that was funny, that I was asking someone I had just thrown around to trust me.

"Yeah," Manny said, sounding like he was just saying anything he thought I wanted to hear.

"I'm gonna let you go now, but I'll have a gun pointed at you until I leave. You turn around, I shoot you. Just stay on the ground for two minutes. And don't get any ideas about calling security or I'll . . ."

"Or you'll come back and kill me. Got it."

I got off of Manny, who did as he was told and stayed on the ground, and I ran out of the building toward the parking lot. I half-expected someone to come after me, or someone waiting by my car, but that wasn't the case. I got into my car, started it, and got off the campus as fast as that little piece of shit could take me.

Chapter 17

When I got back to the hotel, I called the airline to see if I could change my reservation to an earlier flight. They had a 2AM flight, and I made the change. I didn't feel like sticking around Ohio any longer, for fear that Hovelle and his boys would be on to me. I couldn't trust that Manny wouldn't say I had been around, and though they would have a hard time linking me to my false identity, I didn't want to take the chance. What made matters worse was that I didn't have a gun to protect myself. Even though I had never fired my gun in defense, there was a certain security that came with carrying it. I packed everything quickly, returned the rental car, and got myself home, where at least I felt a bit safer.

* * *

When my flight landed, it was nearly six o'clock New York time, and I was exhausted. I had spent the entire flight awake, thinking about Mike Holmes and Aileen Turner, and how there might be new members added to their group. It pissed me off that someone like Hovelle felt he could get away with what he was doing. I had heard about corruption in the government and federal agencies, just like anyone else who saw movies and documentaries about such things, but I never expected to witness it myself firsthand. I felt powerless, knowing I couldn't personally stop Hovelle, but I knew I could help out by volunteering for Jason's experiment. I hadn't totally convinced myself to do it, but I was close. I didn't see any other way I could help. And yeah, I was curious about whether or not it would work. If all these people had died for something that was nothing more than a stupid idea in Jason's head, then I figured I might just strangle Jason.

I walked off the plane and remembered that my father had his own troubles to worry about. I found a pay phone and gave him a call.

"Hello," he said. I knew it was early, but my father always got up around five. He sounded exhausted.

"It's me," I said.

"Where the hell have you been?"

"I had to go out of state for a while."

"I've been trying to reach you all night."

"Did you try my second office line?" That was the one that was forwarding the calls to my cell phone.

"No. I tried home and your main work number. I tried your cell phone but couldn't get through."

"Is everything okay?"

"No."

"What's wrong?"

"It's your mother. She had an accident last night." *For Christ's sake*, I thought. What was going to happen next?

"Jesus, is she okay?"

"She's fine. She took a good bump on the head, and the hospital wanted to keep her overnight, but she's fine. No concussion or anything."

"Oh, my God."

"Don't worry about it. I just got nervous when I couldn't reach you."

"What happened?"

"She was on the Southern State, coming back from her sister's house, and someone cut her off. Lucky for her she was driving the van, because God knows what would have happened if she were in my car. The van's totaled, but she's going to be fine."

"Where is she?"

"South Nassau. It was the closest. It's not my favorite hospital, but this isn't anything serious, so I figured she'd be okay there. Besides, I know one of the head doctors, and I made sure he's watching over her as best he can."

"I can't believe this, Dad."

"You think this is related to what you are working on?"

"I don't know, Dad."

"Stop it. You're letting your imagination get to you. Some asshole just cut her off. She's going to be fine."

"You heading over there soon?"

"I'll be there at seven-thirty."

"I'll meet you there. There are a few things I want to go over with you."

"Okay, I'll see you there."

I hung up the phone, then decided to call Rich. I knew he sometimes took off on Wednesdays, and I hoped that was the case then.

"What?" Rich said, in a voice thick with sleep.

"It's Darren. You working today?"

"What the fuck? No. I mean, I was going to go in for a little while, but that isn't until late in the afternoon. I was planning on getting some sleep."

"Forget about it."

"What's wrong?"

"My mother was in a car accident. She's okay, but I want you to come down to the hospital. I need to talk to you about some things."

"What time?"

"Can you get there for seven-thirty?"

"Yeah, no problem. You sure she's okay?"

"She's fine. And thanks."

"Don't mention it."

* * *

My mother was sitting upright in the hospital bed, a small bandage over her right eye. She seemed fine, but it still hurt me to think that it was my fault she was there in the first place. My father was sitting in a chair next to her, checking her over.

"Leave me alone, I'm fine."

"I know honey. I just want to make sure they did everything they're supposed to."

"They did more than that."

"But still . . ."

"Enough. Sit down, so I can talk to the son I never see anymore."

"Stop it Mom. Are you sure you're okay?"

"I told you, for the tenth time, I'm alright. My head hurts, but what do you expect?"

"You remember what happened?"

"Someone cut me off, I turned the steering wheel, lost control, and ended up hitting the side of the bridge. I'm just lucky I didn't hit it any harder."

"Dad says you hit it hard enough."

"Your father exaggerates."

"Did you get a look at the car that cut you off?"

"Of course I did. It was a big car. I don't know much about cars, but it almost looked like a limousine." That made me think it was a car like the one Hovelle drove. The Mercury he used and a Lincoln Town car, a car often used as a limousine, were very similar.

"What color?"

"Dark gray, I think."

"Did you see anything else?"

"Other than the bridge I hit, no. Why are you asking all of these questions?"

"You know me, Mom. Just the investigator in me."

"Well, you leave your investigating to your work. This was just an accident. I doubt if the guy in the car even realized what happened."

"He still ran away from the scene," my father said.

"Enough of that. The insurance company will pay for a new van."

"It is a crime, Mom."

"I said, enough. I don't want anyone bothering with any of that. Like I said, the guy probably had no idea what happened." I thought the exact opposite of that. I figured the person who cut my mother off knew exactly what they were doing, and had gotten the desired result. I wondered if maybe I was just being paranoid, like my father had suggested, but I knew better. My father had no idea what I knew, and it was about time I told him. I saw Rich walk into the room. He was carrying a bouquet of flowers, which he probably bought from the gift shop.

"Hey," he said, handing the flowers to my mother.

"Oh, thank you Richard. You didn't have to do that."

"You okay, Mom?" Rich had known my mother since we were grade-schoolers, and had called her "Mom" since high school because he had gotten tired of "Mrs. Camponi." Plus, he said, she was more a mother to him than his own.

"I'm fine. If you listened to these two over here, you'd think I was dying."

"Don't even say that," I said.

"You look fine," Rich said. "Had a big scare, huh?"

My mother told the story again, downplaying the whole thing even more this time. When she was finished, the nurse walked in with her breakfast.

"Time for your gourmet meal," I said. "Listen, why don't you eat? There are a few things I need to talk to Dad and Rich about, so we'll be right back."

"Go, go ahead. I'll be fine here. It'll be nice to be left alone for a little while." I knew the last thing my mother wanted was to be left alone, but she was the classic mother, not wanting to bother anyone.

My father, Rich, and I walked out of the room and into a general waiting area which was empty. We all sat down, and my father got a cup of coffee from the machine. When he was done, I told them both what I had learned. I told them what Jason had to say, about his research and all of that, and I told them what I thought about Hovelle and the university. They just sat there and listened, their eyes opening wide during some parts. When I was finished, Rich spoke first.

"You have to do it, you have to volunteer," he said. "It's the only way you're going to get anything done."

My father just sat there silent. "What do you think, Dad?"

"I don't know. As your father, I would tell you to just drop everything, but that's just the protective side of me. As a doctor, and therefore somewhat a scientist, I would agree with Rich. As a human being, I would have to tell you that I would do it in a heartbeat. This is a once in a lifetime opportunity."

"So, you'd go back in time if given the chance?"

"Without question."

"I would too," Rich added.

"Well, Dad, let me put it to you this way. You lived your life once, and you've gotten this far, you know, without falling victim to any mishaps. Also, you successfully married a woman you love and had two kids that I will assume you care about."

"Don't stretch it," my father said, causing Rich to laugh out loud.

"You know what I mean."

"Of course I do."

219

"Well, if you were to go back in time, let's say before you got married, you'd be risking never marrying Mom, and never having us."

My father thought about that for a moment, then shook his head. "I never thought about it that way, and though I understand where you are coming from, I think you are wrong."

"How so?"

"It's crazy, what you are saying, Darren," Rich chimed in.

"Well, it's not crazy," my father said, "but Darren is forgetting something. All of us have some sort of destiny, and I believe my destiny was to be a doctor, to marry my wife, and to have my children. Going back in time might put a few simple things at risk, but I don't think it would affect the important things in my life. It's just not possible."

"You believe in destiny?"

"Of course."

"I don't," I said.

"Why would you? You're too young to accept something like that. Now, I am not a religious man, but I do accept certain truths about religion and such. I've seen the horrors of life, and I have seen some of the most beautiful things life has to offer, and I'll tell you something has to be controlling all of that."

"I don't know. What about you?" I asked Rich.

"I don't know about destiny and all of that, but I agree with what your father is saying. There has to be something. Maybe it is God, or maybe something we haven't even thought of yet. Besides, what do you have to worry about? It's not like you have kids like your dad here. You have nothing to lose."

"Yeah, you're right about that, but part of what Jason is trying to do is prove the existence of a supreme being, or disprove it."

"How does he want to do that?"

"By sending someone back in time, and seeing if their actions affect the overall scheme of things in the present. He never really said exactly how he was going to do it, but he said something about murdering someone in the past, someone who lived to the present, and see what sort of effect that has."

"He wants you to murder someone?" Rich asked.

"He was talking theoretically, I think. And no, I'm not going to kill anyone."

"Well, I have to admit, he has an interesting concept there," my father said.

"That's what I thought."

"But I still think you have to take the chance. You're being offered something truly amazing here. Hey, maybe he's a quack and he doesn't know what he's talking about. Maybe he can't send someone back in time, but I think you have to try it anyway."

"Your dad's right, man."

"I know. I guess I have been trying to find reasons not to do it, you know?"

"Of course," my father said, "you're uneasy about it. I would be too, but you can't let that stop you."

"You can't."

"I know."

"And this Hovelle guy, you think he's responsible for everything that's going on?" Rich asked.

"I don't doubt it. He's a scumbag, that I know for sure."

"He didn't seem like too friendly a guy when he stopped by the house."

"What did he want from you?"

"Just wanted to know if I had heard from you, and if I knew where you were. I didn't, so I couldn't tell him too much. He mentioned something about how you were involved with a case that could get you in trouble, but I dismissed that as him being overly dramatic. Obviously, I was wrong about that."

"You were."

"And you think the federal government is running around threatening and killing people because of Jason's research?"

"I can't see it any other way."

"What about the university guy, the president?" Rich asked.

"Didn't meet him. I had called, but his secretary said he was off-campus for the summer."

"I think he might have had some answers for you."

"I don't know. I think he's just tangled up in this because of Hovelle."

"Could be," my father said, "but I wouldn't keep him out of your mind completely. It seems that the people that are directly connected to the university are having worse luck than anyone else."

I hadn't thought of it that way, and it did make sense. Mike was hired by the university and was killed, and Aileen had been a student there. Sure, Darlene lost her job, my father was being investigated for something from years before, and my mother had just been in a suspicious accident, but the hard evidence pointed to the university.

"Alright. Well, if I'm going to do this thing with Jason, I won't be able to do any real investigating." I looked at Rich. "You up for a little something?"

"Of course."

"You think you could get someone to find out all they can about this president?"

"I have a few people that could look into it for me for a favor." Rich pulled out a pen and a piece of paper. "What's his name?"

"William Lowenstein."

"Got it. I'll have someone on it before the end of the afternoon."

"Alright, just be careful. Tell whoever it is you're gonna get to do this to be careful. I don't know what's being watched and who is being protected, but if you guys are right and this president is involved, I'm pretty sure they'll be looking out for him."

"Of course. My guy knows how to handle these things."

"Your guy? You deal with another P.I. besides me?"

Rich laughed. "Of course, man. I don't want you to get involved with some of the seedy shit I deal with."

"That's the stuff that pays."

"Shut up. You do this thing with Jason and it pays off, you'll have more money than you'll know what to do with."

"And if it doesn't work, I'll be dead, broke, or worse."

"Don't worry about it," my father said. "You just be careful and do what you have to do. I'll keep an eye on your mother and do anything else I can."

"Thanks, both of you."

"No problem," they both said together.

* * *

I went home and waited for Jason to call. There wasn't anything else I could do, because I had no way of contacting him myself. While I was waiting, I decided to do a little research of my own. Rich's guy would be working on it, but I wanted to find some information myself. I did a search on William Lowenstein, but didn't

222

come up with anything too solid. There were several that lived in Ohio, and the one I was looking for could have been any of them. Changing gears, I decided to search on Hovelle, even though I figured I wouldn't find much. I was right in the middle of the search when the phone rang. It was the secure line I had given Jason.

"Yeah," I said.

"It's me," Jason said.

"I figured. How's everything going?"

"I think I'm in the clear right now. Just wanted to let you know I was okay."

"Appreciate it. Say, you still need that volunteer?"

"Of course."

"Count me in."

"Great."

"Oh, and by the way, I have some news for you."

"Like what?"

I was about to tell him about Aileen, then remembered that Wilkins told me Jason and Aileen were an item. I didn't want to give him such bad news over the phone. "I spoke to your buddy Manny."

"You did?"

"Yep. Real nice guy."

"Right. A little strange, but nice."

"You really think so, don't you?"

"What do you mean?"

"He's the one that sold you out in the first place."

"No way."

"It's true. The way I figure it is, Hovelle approached him, and he agreed to steal your research and give it to Hovelle. That's how they figured out you were further off with your research than you let them know. That's how things have gotten as bad as they are."

"That's impossible. I don't believe it."

"Believe it. He's trying to complete your research himself now, under Hovelle's supervision."

"Jesus."

"Exactly. Also, I need to know what you think about William Lowenstein."

"The president of the university?"

"That's the one."

"He's alright. I mean, I know he was helping out Hovelle and the government, but I think that's it. Why do you ask?"

"Just curious. So, you don't think he could be behind any of this."

"Wow, I don't know. I never even thought of him that way. It's possible, but I doubt it. This is all Hovelle's doing, I would presume."

"You sure?"

"As sure as I can be."

"Okay. I'm having someone look into it. I want to make sure I have all our bases covered. When can we meet? When will you be ready to do this?"

Jason thought for a moment. "Later tonight?"

"That's fine. Where?"

Jason gave me an address in New York City, in the sixties.

"That where you're staying?" I asked.

"No, that's where we'll meet. That's where I have the prototype."

"Okay. I'll see you at eight?"

"Perfect."

"Anything I need to bring. Anything I need to do to be ready?"

"Just bring yourself. And, between now and then, I need you to think of a specific event that you remember really well from your past. It can be anything, but try not to make it something really important, or tragic, or anything like that. Just a day that you remember well. Understand?"

"Not really."

"Well, I don't want you to go back to a time where you're gonna feel like you have to change something. I want you to go back to a safe time, a time where not much happens, so you can get yourself acquainted with your surroundings."

"You don't want me to change anything?"

"That's not what I said. I don't want you to feel compelled to. You can change whatever you want, but I need you to be as unemotional about the time period as possible. Think you can do that?"

"Sure. You think this is going to work?"

"Would I be doing it if I didn't?"

He had a point. "I'll see you at eight."

"Got it."

I hung up the phone, still not fully comprehending the fact that I was going to be traveling back in time. I went back to the search on Hovelle, and found some results. Because his name wasn't too common, I found him, and what I saw amazed me. Though he had the FBI listed as his employment, that information was no longer current. As a matter of fact, he didn't have anything for current employment. That didn't mean he wasn't employed by the government anymore. It could have meant there had been a mistake in the credit report, or that the government no longer had him on official record. I wasn't experienced enough in this field to know anything else, but I decided to call another detective friend of mine to dig a little deeper.

"JPD Investigations," Joe said when he answered the phone. I had known Joe for about two years. He was a small-time investigator like me, and he was a good guy.

"How are you Joe," I said.

"Darren, long time."

"Yeah, I've been busy."

"What can I do for you?"

"I need you to take a look at someone for me. I'm going to be out of town for a little bit, and I need this done while I'm away."

"Yeah, no problem. What sort of thing you working on?"

I thought of Mike Holmes, and how sticking his nose where it didn't belong had gotten him killed. I didn't want anything happening to Joe. "Hairy stuff, that's all I can say. You'll be investigating someone who I think works for the government, so put the protective gloves on, alright?"

"Yeah, no problem."

"No, I mean it. This has gotten more dangerous than I could have imagined. Listen, I didn't even want to get you involved, but I really don't have a choice right now."

"I got ya, I got ya. I'll watch my ass."

I gave Joe the name, again telling him to be careful.

"Jesus, what do you think, I'm deaf? I know how to tiptoe around this sort of shit. What do you need to know about him?"

"Everything."

"Starting with?"

"Well, I need to know if he still works for the government, and I need to know in what sort of capacity, if that's possible."

"That could be tricky."

"I know. Just see what you can find out."

"No problemo. Anything else?"

"Well, I guess it all hinges on whether or not he still works for the government. If he doesn't, get me everything you can on him. I won't be around, so you can deliver the information to a friend of mine." I gave him Rich's name and number. "You can call him if you have any questions or problems."

"You working with lawyers?"

"No, he's just a friend."

"Didn't know lawyers were capable of that."

"Not many of them."

"Hey, before you go, got a joke for you."

"Shoot." Joe told jokes more than anyone I knew, and most of them were pretty bad.

"How does a guy know his wife is dead?"

"How?"

"The sex is the same, and the dishes are piling up in the kitchen." Joe laughed uncontrollably.

I forced a chuckle. "Not bad, not bad." Yeah, I know, it sucked.

"Lawyer told me that one."

"I thought you said lawyers couldn't be friends."

"True, but they pay well."

"Call my friend if you find anything."

"I will. You take care, okay? I get the feeling you're mixed up in some shit here."

"You're not too far off."

"I'll get on this as soon as I can."

"Thanks Joe."

"Don't mention it."

* * *

I made it to the designated spot a little before eight. It was a large building, with mirrored glass windows, and revolving doors leading to the lobby. I didn't know why Jason wanted to meet there, and felt stupid sitting outside on a brick planter, staring off into space. Jason arrived a few minutes later, with two large briefcases in his hands and a large notebook tucked under his left arm.

"Been waiting long?" he asked.

"No. But long enough to think I'm out of my mind for doing this."

"What are you worried about?"

"Want a list?"

He gestured for me to grab one of his briefcases. I took the one from his left hand, and it felt like he had a body stashed in it. "Why don't you talk to me about it on the way up?" he said.

"Okay." We walked into the building through one of the revolving doors, and Jason flashed a security badge to the man behind the counter. The tiles on the floor were shiny granite, along with the walls. The lobby reminded me of the one in The Matrix, where the acting-challenged Keanu Reeves entered with an arsenal of guns and proceeded to tear the place up.

"Thirtieth floor," Jason said.

"Take the third elevator on your right. It'll take you directly to it." The security guard tapped a few keys on his keyboard, and by the time we got to the elevator doors, they opened for us.

"So, what are you worried about?" Jason asked. He was dressed in a pair of khaki pants and a denim shirt, and he looked more like a scientist than he had at his apartment.

"Well, I'm worried about you frying my brain."

"That won't happen."

"How do I know that?"

"Just trust me."

"That doesn't sound too convincing."

"Don't worry about it. What else?"

"How far back am I going to go?"

"I would suggest not going back too far. Just far enough so that you'll know everything is different. Have you come up with a day and date?"

I nodded. While sitting in my apartment waiting to leave, I had run several time periods of my life through my head. Jason had said not to pick anything overly emotional, so I had remembered a baseball game from my senior year in high school. The opposing pitcher had thrown me a curveball when I expected a fastball, and I struck out, so I figured I wouldn't mind doing that one over again. I didn't really care about that, but I figured it would be cool to see if I could have changed the outcome of the game.

"I can go back to something minor to change, right?"

"How minor?"

"Baseball game."

"You want to change the outcome of a pro game?"

227

I shook my head. "Nothing like that. I just want to get a hit instead of striking out. It was a high school game. Nothing important, nothing I really care about, but I figured it was a day I could remember vividly."

Jason smiled. "Then it's perfect."

"Okay. Any other concerns?"

"I'm still worried about the Iliad."

"I really spooked you with that, didn't I?"

"You could say that. I guess what I want to know is if you have some ulterior motive with this. Am I some test subject for your other theory?"

Jason made a sound with his mouth like he was sucking in his cheek. "Not exactly."

"Don't give me that shit. Am I or aren't I?"

"Well, you are, but not like you think."

"I'm not going to do your bidding. I won't be your fucking guinea pig."

"Relax. You might prove my other theory, but only if you act on your own. I won't tell you to do anything, other than give you guidelines on how to act, what to expect, and that sort of thing. Think of this like a computer game, where you are free to roam around the game world as much as you want, but there are certain restrictions and rules you have to abide by."

"You mind telling me what they are?" The elevator doors opened, and we stepped into a carpeted hallway. I saw only one oak door, and Jason went up to it, slid his card through the slot on the wall, and the door clicked open. It seemed there was no one in the place. "How did you manage this setup?"

"Long story."

"I'd like to know."

"Let's just say that no one knows I am here, and they might not be too happy if they find out."

"What are you talking about?"

"This isn't my lab."

"I knew that. Who's is it?"

"Scitech's."

"Who the hell is that?"

"More like, what the hell. They are the largest independent research company in New York. They've been around for about forty years, and they were the ones who came up with the first prototypical quantum computer. I think they did that back in '79, but I am not sure."

I didn't like where this was heading. It was bad enough that I was actually going to volunteer. To know that we would be doing this illegally, or at least covertly, didn't make me feel too comfortable.

Jason plopped his briefcase and notebook on the counter in the center of the room, then turned on the lights. The room was large, with doorways on the left and right leading to other, smaller rooms. There were about four computers in the main room, but none of them looked special, like the quantum computer Jason mentioned. Then again, I wouldn't have known a quantum computer from a typewriter.

"You can put that briefcase up there," Jason said, gesturing toward the counter. He went to one of the computers and powered it on. "Scitech is aware of my research, but they haven't made the strides I have. They've tried to get me to come into their fold, so to speak, and it would probably be a good alliance, but of course, I haven't had the opportunity. A friend in the company got me the security clearance, under a different name of course. He's the only one that knows who I am, but he only thinks I am coming here to get a look at the prototype. He doesn't know I am going to actually try and use the thing."

"Try?"

"Okay, use it. You know what I mean."

I sat down on a stool next to the counter. "So no one knows what we are about to do?"

"Nope."

"You think that's a good idea?"

"It's the only way." Jason started frantically typing on the computer. "If anyone knew, people would be swarming all over the place. I don't want that."

I understood, but I would have preferred there to be someone with Jason, to help out if something went wrong. I had no idea what could go wrong, but that didn't stop me from having images flash through my mind of Jason trying to revive me. I flushed that thought from my mind the minute the idea of mouth-to-mouth resuscitation came.

"What are you doing?"

"Just setting up the primary temporal matrix."

"The what?"

"Don't worry about it. It's just technical mumbo-jumbo to explain how I will tell the computer where you want to go."

That made enough sense, so I didn't question it any further. I started to get a knot in my stomach, realizing what I was about to do. Despite all the worrying I had been doing, I had never really considered the wonder I was about to experience, if the experiment worked. I was going back in time, for Christ's sake, and as far as I knew, I had the ability to change things and experience parts of my life I only fantasized about doing. I would be living a dream, so to speak. I had seen the movies and TV shows, and images flashed through my mind of reliving the past, correcting the wrongs, and making decisions I had brushed off when I was younger. I really didn't know what sort of effect I could have on my present and future if I went back to the past, and I doubted Jason had more than theoretical answers to such questions, so I didn't bother to ask.

"I'm almost done," Jason said, never taking his eyes off the computer screen.

"Take your time. Anything I should be doing right now?"

"You can try and relax. And keep thinking of that situation you want to go back to. The more solid your memory of that period is, the better chance we will have at success."

"You don't sound too confident."

"You really need to take a deep breath. Wow, you come across as a tough guy, and here you are like a kid in the doctor's office waiting to get poked with a needle."

I resented what he said, but appreciated how accurate his analogy was. I hated needles when I was a kid, like every other kid I guess, and would get so worked up when my father was ready to needle me that I had to be held down by my mother and my father's assistant. I didn't think Jason would have to restrain me, but I had that same nervous feeling running through my body. To get my mind off it, I tried to remember details of that baseball game. My jersey was green. The other team's were blue and yellow. The pitcher had long, light brown hair falling out of the back of his baseball cap. Tommy Coles was on first base, Charles Rubin at third. It was about five-thirty at night, and the sky was beginning to darken. The date was March 31, 1984. I was pretty sure my parents were in the stands. Tanya had stopped by to see the game. We hadn't been dating yet. We were just friends, but looking back I knew we both wanted more than that. We just thought the other wasn't interested.

Rich was there. He was on deck. He told me before I got up to the plate to watch out for the curveball. Of course I didn't listen, that time. My coach, Mr. Stanford, was a short pudgy man who insisted on wearing a uniform that didn't fit. We played the game at Baldwin High School, the opposing team's home field. There were stands on the first-base side, but none on the other, so people were sitting on a hill along the foul line.

I was in the middle of trying to conjure up some more detailed memories when Jason turned to face me and said, "Just about ready. When was the last time you ate?"

"What?"

"For the anesthesia. I need to know if we need to wait a little longer, or if you are ready to go."

"Anesthesia?"

"Yes. You need to be sedated for the computer to latch onto your brainwaves. If you're conscious, you'll have too many active thoughts and it would complicate the process unnecessarily."

"Why didn't you tell me about this before?"

"Because I knew you would stress about it."

"Good point."

"So, when was the last time you ate?"

"About five hours ago, I'd say. I had something to drink . . ."

"That doesn't matter, unless you slugged a six pack in the last two hours."

"Of course not, though I wouldn't mind being drunk right now."

"You'll be better than that in a little while. Let's go into the other room."

Jason got up, and I followed him through the door on the right. The room was small, with bright white paint on the walls, and a contraption sitting in the far corner. It looked like an MRI machine, with a padded table and a huge round white tunnel on top. Looking at the thing made me claustrophobic.

"There she is," Jason said.

"That's the computer?"

"Not exactly. The computer, or at least the brain of the computer, is incorporated into this machine. The other terminal in the room we were just in runs the program, and this machine translates it, incorporates your brain waves, and the connection is made. From

231

there, you are set on your way."

"It looks like an MRI machine," I said.

"It does, doesn't it? Scitech originally used the housing from an MRI machine, but they needed something that received instead of just transmitted. They perfected the prototype, but they didn't have the proper software, or the correct hardware to make the thing work. I made a few modifications to this machine yesterday, and I installed the software on both computers as well. I was amazed at how easy it was. They were closer than they thought."

"And no one knows about their research?"

"Only a select few, and most people think they are just off the wall. No one really thinks this sort of thing could work."

"And you're sure it will?"

"As sure as I can be. At worst, you'll get treated to a nice nap, then wake up and find out that nothing happened."

"You just saying that to make me feel better?"

"No. Nothing horrible can go wrong. The worst that could happen is that the computer gets overloaded, but it would break the connection with your brain before that happened. I have at least five different fail-safes installed. You've got nothing to worry about."

"You keep saying that, but I still don't feel any better."

"You got that memory nailed down."

"To some intricate details."

"Perfect. I know this will be tough, but try to think about nothing but that day. Try to get into the situation you are going back to. Just keep running it through your mind. I'll be giving you instructions, but try not to lose that image, okay?"

I nodded.

"Good. Now, sit down on that padded table on the machine, and give me your right arm."

I sat down. The cushion was exceptionally soft, and I sunk in a little bit. I pulled back my sleeve, and reached my arm out to Jason, who produced a hypodermic needle. Now I was doubly frightened, from the machine and the needle.

"You know what you're doing with that thing?" I asked.

"Of course. Just relax. And don't say anything. Just keep your mind focused." Jason searched my arm for a vein, and when he found one, he prepared to put the needle in. "This should take about a minute or two to set in, so you're not going to be awake while I set up the machine and all that. Have you ever been under before?"

I nodded.

"Have you ever had any adverse reactions?"

I shrugged as if to say I didn't know of any.

"Well, your dad's a doctor, so you'd know, I am sure."

I nodded in agreement.

"This is a special anesthetic, unlike anything you've ever been given before. It's going to make you immobile, and you are going to be unconscious. You'll feel like you are dreaming, yet you might be aware of some things I am doing. Try and stay focused, and understand what is real and what is induced by the medication."

I nodded again.

"The machine monitors all of your vitals, so if there is any sort of problem, I will be able to interrupt if I have to. You're going to be back in time for what will seem like a day or two, maybe longer. It's really hard to explain the passage of time, but when you wake up, you'll feel like only minutes passed. I should be able to get some feedback on what you are experiencing, so if there is any sort of problem, I should be able to detect it."

"You mean, like if I am in mortal danger," I said, speaking when I wasn't supposed to.

"Exactly."

"And I can do whatever I want?"

"Events will flow somewhat beyond your control, but yes. There is a lot of gray area to cover, and I hope your actions will give me greater insight to that. I wish I could give you more information, but as you surely understand, this is the first time."

I nodded. I felt the image of the day I was going back to slip my mind, so I grasped onto it again. The last thing I wanted to do was screw this whole thing up.

"Just remember that this is an exercise, but also remember that anything you do might have repercussions in the future, or, well, the present. You're probably going to feel like you are dreaming for the beginning part of this experiment, but remember, you'll be conscious. Have you ever experienced lucid dreaming?"

I had no idea what he was talking about, and made a face to convey that.

"Have you ever felt that you were conscious in your dreams, that you could make active decisions, and maybe even change your surroundings? For example, if you were having a nightmare, you could change the dream to your liking?"

I nodded, having remembered doing exactly that once or twice.

"Good, that will help. It's going to feel like that until you get accustomed to your surroundings." Jason looked at his watch, then back at me. "We're ready to go. Close your eyes and try not to think about the needle. Try and remove any fear you might be experiencing now."

I didn't know how to do that, but I took several deep breaths and told myself that everything was okay. It worked, to a degree. Jason plunged the needle into my arm, and I felt immediate pain. I tried to block it, instead focusing my mind on that pitch I missed. My mind felt like it was slipping from me, and the last thing I remembered was Jason putting something on my head, and then leaving the room. Then, everything went black, or dark gray at least.

Book III-Wide Awake In Dreamland

Chapter 18

I woke with a jolt, back in bed in my apartment. My mind was foggy, with only vague recollections of my experience with Jason. It all felt like a dream, the meeting at the lab, the machine, the needle. I shook my head, but my mind still stayed focused somewhere else. I felt as if I was dreaming right then, but I could feel the sheets on my bed underneath me, and everything in my room was the same as I had left it. I thought maybe this was some side effect from the medication, but even that didn't make sense. I was tired, so I laid back down and closed my eyes, falling instantly asleep.

"Just keep your mind focused," I heard Jason say, and I couldn't be certain if he had just said it, or if I was remembering his words from earlier.

* * *

I heard people cheering all around me. I opened my eyes, and there I was, standing on the on-deck circle at Baldwin High School. I turned to look at the field, and saw Tommy Coles running toward first base. Charles Rubin was rounding second, and slid safely into third. The shortstop had the ball, and he held it, unable to make a play at either first or third. The pitcher slapped his glove on his thigh in frustration. I felt the rubber from the aluminum bat in my hands, and though it felt fairly real, it seemed as if I wasn't really there. Everything was as I remembered it, but something didn't feel right. I felt detached, as if I were watching myself instead of actually being inside my body. It was strange, and wasn't too unlike how Jason had said it would be.

I felt someone walk up behind me.

"This guy is going to lead you in with a fastball, but watch the curve," Rich said in my ear. His voice sounded the same, but when I turned to look at him, it was the teenage Rich that looked back at me, not the adult Rich I was accustomed to. I was taken aback, and didn't respond right away.

After a second, I found myself saying, "I know the guy. He tried that last time up," I said, remembering I had said the same exact thing the first time.

"Just be careful, Darren. We win this, we make the playoffs."

I nodded, and made my way to the batters box, thoughts both past and present swirling through my mind. My legs felt as if they were someone else's. I looked down at my hands and looked for the scar on my right forefinger, one that I had gotten in a fight when I was 22. It wasn't there. My hand started to shake.

I stepped into the batter's box, and looked around the field. There they were, all the people who I remembered, and some indistinct faces I didn't remember. They were almost faceless, both unrecognizable and indistinguishable. I held my hand up to the umpire to give me a second, and dug in.

I looked at the pitcher, who made a face of disdain as he watched for the sign from the catcher. With all the thoughts I had running through my head, I worked hard to concentrate only on what was coming. The pitcher was known for having an exceptional fastball, and though I had been a decent hitter when I was in high school, I knew the best I could do with a fastball was foul it off, which I had done the first time this confrontation occurred. I closed out all other distractions, the crowd, the other team's taunts and cheers, even the sounds of my own mind.

The pitcher went into his windup. I didn't remember it this way, but he had a windup quite similar to Nolan Ryan, with the high leg kick Ryan had been famous for. He strode toward the plate, slinging a knee-high fastball in my direction. I took a cut, feeling as though I hadn't swung a bat in ten years, and missed the ball completely. That hadn't happened the last time, and I wondered what sort of effect this would have on his pitch selection.

I stepped out of the box to catch the signs from the third-base coach. It was Mr. Stanford, wearing the tight uniform I remembered him in. I knew he wasn't going to call any plays. Though Tommy was fast at first, there were two outs, and we were down by a run. To lose the game on an attempted stolen base didn't make sense. Stanford gave me a stern look, probably because I had forgotten to check the signs when I first stepped up to the plate. I watched him flash meaningless signs, realizing all of his signs would be meaningless. I couldn't remember any of our signs, and if he called a steal or a hit and run, I would never have caught it.

I stepped back into the box and dug myself in. The pitcher took the sign, nodded, and went into his motion. I knew another fastball was coming, so I prepared myself. There really wasn't much I could do, especially since I felt so rusty, but I tried to get ready to take a swing. The pitch came, a little high and outside, so I didn't swing, but the umpire called it a strike.

"What the fuck?" I asked to myself, realizing I had vocalized that thought.

"Watch your mouth, son," I heard the umpire say from behind me.

"Sorry." I stepped out of the batter's box.

"Come on Darren," I heard my father say from the stands. "You can hit this guy."

I looked up in the stands, and saw my father, my mother, and my grandmother sitting together about three rows up. Then, it hit me. With all the time I had to think about what date I wanted to be sent back to, I picked one the day before my grandmother passed away. I wondered if maybe fate had something to do with that. That I was sent back to this time to prevent her death. I was consumed with this thought, running through my mind the possibilities of what I could do, and the ramifications of those possibilities. Jason had wanted to prove the existence or non-existence of a supreme being through affecting lives, and this was the prime example. I wanted to drop the bat and run over to where they were sitting to somehow prevent the horrible chain of events that would occur the next day. I knew I couldn't do that, not right then.

"Let's go, son," the umpire said, and I stepped into the batter's box.

I no longer was concerned with the pitcher, with the game, or the situation I had previously wanted to change. The only reason I wanted to change it was to see if I could. If I could change the outcome of a baseball game, then, maybe, I could change other things as well. I tried to concentrate, remembering that I had struck out on a curveball right over the plate, because I had been expecting another fastball.

The pitcher shook off the first sign. I tried to remember if that was how it happened the first time, but couldn't. He shook off another sign, and I figured this was meant to confuse me. The guy was coming with a curveball, and I was going to do my best to deposit it somewhere deep in leftfield.

The pitcher finally got a pitch he liked, checked Tommy at first, and started his motion. I gripped the bat tighter in my hands, trying to focus on nothing else but the white sphere he was about to send in my direction. I reminded myself not to start my swing too early, or I'd be way ahead of the curveball that was coming. The pitcher strode toward the plate. I hitched the bat once in my hands, a method I used to slow myself down, and watched as the ball came toward me.

Twice as fast as I had expected.

Caught off guard, I tried to catch up to the pitch in vain, hearing it hit the glove.

"Strike three, batter out!" the umpire exclaimed. I just stood there, bat in my hands, amazed at what just had happened. Obviously, the first time around, I had done a better job of convincing the pitcher I could handle his fastball. I really didn't remember clearly how the at-bat went, but he had thrown me a fastball this time because I had been so far off the first two. Despite the fact that the pitch selection was different, the outcome was exactly the same. I sat in the batter's box for a full minute, wondering if it was because I couldn't change the past or because I had too much on my mind that caused the result to be the same.

"That was fucking strange," Rich said as he came to greet me at the batter's box. "You looked like you had never seen a fastball before."

"Tell me about it," I said, taking the bat off my shoulder and walking toward the dugout with him.

"Don't worry about it," he said, patting me on the back. "I wanted to go out Friday night instead of playing in a playoff game."

I made my way to the dugout, and received the obligatory pats on the back to try and make me feel better. Actually, I could have cared less about the game. I just wanted to know why the result hadn't changed at all. Minor details had been different, but those details had no effect on the outcome. My teammates must have seen the look of concern on my face, because they all came up to me, one at a time, telling me it wasn't my fault and not to worry about it.

But, of course, I did.

I wanted Jason to be there, so I could ask him his opinion on the matter. I wanted to be taken back to the present, so I could better prepare myself for a return. I knew this was impossible, so I would have to come to my own conclusions and answers on my own. That didn't give me too much hope, but it was all I had at the moment.

I threw the bat in the rack, ignored all of the people around me, and just stood there and looked out onto the field, watching everyone pack up and get ready to go home. I felt a little excited about reliving my past, but that excitement was dampened by what I knew was coming, and the knowledge that I might not be able to do anything about it. I wanted to run up to my grandmother and warn her of what her fate would be, but I couldn't think of a way to do that without seeming out of my mind. I wanted to warn her about Alan, but again, I had no way to do that, and no evidence to prove my claims.

"Hey," my father said from behind me. "You okay?"

I turned, and saw a younger version of my father. In the present, I never really thought he had changed at all, except maybe his hair had gone from really thin to nothing on the top. Looking at him right then, I realized how much he had changed. He had fewer wrinkles, was thinner, and his hair was much thicker than I remembered it. It was like an old photograph of him had come to life. Spooky.

"I'm okay."

"You thought he was going curveball, didn't you?" I remembered my father and I had the same conversation the first time, only it was about my guessing fastball. It all seemed so strange.

"Yeah," I said, trying to sound dejected from the outcome of the game.

"You'll get 'em next time. Come on, let's go see your mother and grandmother." He put his arm around me, and I scooped up my baseball glove and walked toward the parking lot with him.

Standing next to my father's Cadillac were my mother and grandmother, the two arm-in-arm like I always remembered them. I felt as though I was going to cry when I saw the two of them together.

Looking at my mother, she looked more like a child than an adult. She had always seemed that way around my grandmother, and I had forgotten what that looked like. I took a deep breath to hold back tears.

"Darren, I'm so sorry," my mother said. "I know you really wanted to get to the playoffs this year."

I remembered that all I had talked about before the game was how important it was, and how I wanted to at least make the playoffs my senior year. Our team had come so close the two years before, and I had complained at how unfair it was that I played for three years on a team that couldn't make it to the playoffs. Standing there, looking at a woman I knew would die within 24 hours made me think how childish I had been. Sure, I was a child back then, but thinking that didn't make it any easier. Nothing would.

"It's okay, Mom," I said, doing the best I could to avoid eye contact with my grandmother. The only thing I could be happy about was the fact that Alan wasn't there. He was the last person I wanted to see.

"He gave it his best shot, Maggie," my grandmother said. "You can't ask for anything more than that." Oh, could I. "Come here, give me a hug," she said, opening her arms. I hesitated at first, then gave her a strong embrace. I had always gotten along great with my grandmother, and it was no secret within the family that I was her favorite. Feeling the tight embrace, my grandmother said, "Whoa, what brought this on?"

"I love you, Nan," I said in a low voice that only she could hear. She patted me on the back.

"Well, do you now? I love you too Darren."

I stepped back from the embrace and looked at her. She seemed fine, but I really didn't have much of a frame of reference for that. "How are you feeling?" I asked, which brought raised eyebrows from both her and my mother.

"I'm fine, why?"

"No reason. Just wanted to know how you are." I couldn't believe I was having a conversation with my grandmother right then. She had been gone for seventeen years, and it took all I had to keep my mind from running loose on me. If nothing else, Jason had succeeded in letting me speak to someone who was no longer alive in the present. That, in and of itself, was a wonderful achievement.

"Are you okay?" my mother asked.

"Yeah Mom, fine." I turned to regard her. She too looked younger, and her hair was died darker than it was in the present. She seemed happy, a light in her eyes that I had gotten used to not seeing. This was all too much for my mind to handle.

"We getting out of here, or what?" Rich said from behind me. I turned and saw him standing next to a black Camaro Z28. It took me awhile to realize the car was mine. I had gotten it the month before as a birthday/graduation present. My father told me that my acceptance to Hofstra University had really pushed him over the top about getting the car for me. Now, even though my father was a doctor and my family was considered well off, I was never the sort of kid that would be considered spoiled. I had worked at a restaurant as a busboy and had been saving up for a car when my parents sprang the Camaro on me. It was a rare treat, and though I hadn't realized it when I was younger, the best thing my parents could have done was make me work hard for what I received. All that bullshit about character building and the value of a dollar really paid off, despite the fact that I hate to admit it.

"One minute," I said.

"Why don't you get going," my father said. He reached out to shake my hand. When I shook his, he slipped a bill in my hand. I stuffed it into the back of my baseball pants.

"I need to talk to you later," I said to him softly.

"Everything okay?"

"Yeah, I just need to talk, okay?"

My father seemed genuinely amazed that his teenage son wanted to sit down and talk to him. He half-smiled, and said, "Of course. We'll talk when you get home."

I kissed my mother and grandmother goodbye, trying hard to fight back the emotions that were swelling up within me. I wanted to do something right there, something to prevent the tragedy I knew was coming. Helplessness overwhelmed me, and it was all I could do to turn and walk toward the car.

As I approached it, a blonde girl wearing dark sunglasses stopped me. It took me a second to realize it was Tanya. Now, even more emotions were bubbling up, and I was caught between running from her because of our present, and embracing her because of our past. Because I would appear an idiot to do either, I just stood there.

"Tough break," she said. She didn't look directly at me when she spoke, but instead above me as to avoid me seeing what was behind the glasses. I remembered her boyfriend had hit her the day before, but that was something I had learned years later.

"Yeah," I said, trying to look her in the eye. She moved her head away from me casually.

"You should have known he was going to go with the fastball."

"I would have bet a million bucks he was going curve," I said, still trying to get her to look me in the eye.

"Then you'd be out a million bucks."

I reached out and touched her chin, turning it toward mine. She resisted, then backed away. It was hard for me to realize that intimacy was a step we hadn't taken yet. We were just platonic friends who held a candle for each other. We never did anymore than hold hands once, and we did sometimes send signals through our eyes, but intimacy was certainly not an area we had arrived at yet. On top of that, her boyfriend went to the same school, and he didn't appreciate our friendship. If he had seen me touch her face, he would have gone ballistic.

"What are you doing?"

"I want you to look at me when I'm talking to you," I said, more sternly than I intended because I was frustrated with the situation.

"Who are you, my father?"

"Listen, what's wrong?" I asked, foolishly thinking she'd tell me right then. The Tanya I was talking to wouldn't be ready to say something about that for another six years.

"Nothing. Jesus, what the hell has gotten into you? I came here to watch you play, not get the fucking third degree."

"What's with the shades?" I was pressing, and I knew that, but I couldn't help it. I really needed evidence that I could alter something about the past, or my hopes for my grandmother were done.

"I told you in class today, my cat scratched my eye."

"Really?"

"Why the fuck are you bothering me about this?"

"I don't think it was your cat."

I couldn't see her eyes, but I imagined they were red with fire. "Why don't you go fuck yourself, Darren? How about that?"

She turned and ran off toward her car. I wanted to run after her, but I figured I had done enough damage already. Plus, I saw my father glance at me, wondering what had just happened. He knew we were friends, and he had warned me that the friendship was based on other things. I didn't need to add more evidence to his theory right then.

"What the fuck was that all about?" Rich asked.

"Nothing."

"When are you going to just plant one on her? I mean, Jesus Christ, she hangs all over you all the time, and you don't see it."

"Leave it alone, man," I said, walking toward the car.

"I don't know what you see in her anyway. She's got a great ass, don't get me wrong, but she doesn't have much else going on in the head."

"Leave it!" I yelled, and Rich put up his hands.

"Alright, alright. Let's just get out of here."

I walked up to the door of the car, but had no keys. I searched the pocket of the baseball pants, and found them, along with the twenty-dollar bill my father handed me.

"Food money," Rich said. "Cool."

I got into the car, remembering the smell of the new leather and how I had adored that car. I looked over at Rich, started the car and revved the engine, and pulled away wondering how we had ever stayed friends.

I really had no desire to go anywhere but home, but I wanted to show some degree of normalcy. We drove around in the car, and I had trouble handling it, being used to tighter, smaller import cars for so many years. The large V8 engine lurched the car forward at even the slightest tap of the accelerator. Rich sat in the passenger seat, egging me on to go even faster, enjoying the wild ride I was giving him. I wasn't really concentrating on the road. My mind was more interested in helping my grandmother and trying to figure out what was happening in the present. If Hovelle had gotten wind of the experiment, which I doubted, what would he do? Was I in danger of Jason having to hastily bring me back? Would I be trapped in the past? None of it made sense to me, but my worried mind easily found bad consequences from even the simplest of actions. I recalled what Jason had said about a random death of someone who wasn't supposed to die, so I slowed the car down considerably, for fear of getting into an accident, or worse. I tried to remember exactly where I had gone after the baseball game, and remembered the pool hall in

Valley Stream. We had gone there after the baseball game to shoot a few racks of eight ball and drown ourselves in our own self-pity.

"Guys and Dolls okay?" I asked Rich.

"Yeah, cool. Might catch a few babes there."

I drove along Merrick road, cautiously aware of every move I made. It was certainly no fun driving like that. It amazed me. There I was, back as a teenager, driving the car I adored, reliving what were arguably the best years of my life. The difference was I knew things I hadn't known back then. I know the old saying goes, "If I only knew then what I know now," but the knowledge I had only prevented me from enjoying myself. Not only was I aware of my grandmother's fate, I also had to watch everything I did, for fear of dying in an accident I had successfully avoided the first time. You can't enjoy life like that. It becomes more of a procedure than a life, and the simple things I had enjoyed as a teenager were nothing more than distractions from my goal.

We made it to the pool hall, and parked in front. It was already dark, and the clouds overhead threatened rain. I felt like an idiot walking into the place with a baseball uniform on. Originally, I had thought I looked cool. I stepped out of the car, overly conscious of how I looked, and walked toward the door.

"You got anything on you besides the twenty?" Rich asked. I remembered that, though Rich had a better job than I did and made more money, he never carried it around with him. He always claimed that his mother took it from him to put in the bank, but I never believed it. My doubts had turned out to be true, because Rich had admitted years later that he was just a cheap bastard as a kid. Plus, he said, he had me to support him. Nice guy.

"No," I said.

"Shit. Twenty ain't gonna get us too far, Lamarr."

"Maybe if you brought some of your own money out with you, we'd do better."

"You know my mom's always taking it from me. Bitch never let's me spend a cent, Kent."

"What's with the rhymes?" I asked.

"What you mean, Dean?"

"Exactly what I said."

"Come on, man, we've been doing this for weeks, ever since that flick, Nick."

I didn't remember that. Standing in front of the door with Rich, I felt an odd sense of displacement, like this past life I was living out wasn't the same as it previously had been. Memories are tricky, of course, and I attributed my confusion to that. I figured the best thing to do was go with the flow, Joe.

"Time for me to tan your hide, Clyde," I said as we walked in.

"Good one, good one. Nice to have you back."

Guys and Dolls was a pool hall that had been in Valley Stream for thirty years. Unlike the upscale "Entertainment Centers" that sprung up in the late nineties, the place was all about pool, and it was authentic. The tables were some of the best ever made, and the owner watched over the place like it was his child. To the left of us, as we walked in, behind a large wood counter, was said owner. He was middle-aged, with curly brown hair and a thick moustache. If I had been told the truth, he was an ex-cop, and I believed that because he ran the place like one. I think that's why most people enjoyed coming there, because they knew it would be a peaceful experience.

"Hey John," Rich said, proud that he knew the owner's name. John just looked at him, as if Rich had talked out of turn.

"What can I do for you?" John asked, eyeing us over. The baseball uniforms must have made us look ridiculous.

"A table. Table one, maybe?" Rich asked, still undaunted by his first mistake. Table one was considered a house table, nestled in the corner across from the counter. John used that table himself when he played, and most of the big money games that ever went on in the place were played on that table. There were eighteen other tables in the place, and all but two of them were empty, and Rich had to go and choose Table one.

"That's for house players only," John said in a stern but somewhat friendly tone.

"Ain't no big deal, Neal. We're good enough."

"Tell you what, we play some nine-ball, twenty bucks a rack. You beat me, you can play on Table one anytime you want. Deal?"

"Table nine is good," Rich said.

"That's what I thought." John reached under the counter and handed us a set of balls, along with a white index card which indicated the table we were on, what time we started, and how many players we had. Rich took the balls, and I stole a peek into the game room behind us, where classic games like Pole Position, Gauntlet, and

Punch Out! were hiding. Being a video game freak, I wanted to run right in and play the games I grew up on.

"Come on," Rich said, walking toward the table. John turned to a large computer behind him and pressed the button for the lights on Table Nine. The large row of fluorescent lights came to life above the table, and Rich spilled the balls onto the table.

"Don't do that," John said from behind the counter.

"Sorry, Maury," Rich said as he selected a cue from the rack.

The walls of the place were painted orange, with dark wood paneling running up halfway. The building was about 90 feet deep and about forty feet wide. The tables were in the middle of the room, arranged in clumps going long ways and short ways. Eight-feet benches sat against the wall around the perimeter. It was wide open, and comfortable. That was why we drove four towns over instead of going to the places in between.

Rich racked the balls, and I selected a cue from the wall rack.

"Being that I am paying, I break," I said, lining myself up at the head of the table.

"Do what you gotta do, Drew."

"Enough with the rhymes, they're getting old," I said.

"What's with you?"

"Nothing. I'm just a little pissed off about the game."

"Forget about it, man. I would have been guessing curveball too." I wanted to tell him that I was upset because, although I changed some minor details about the game, I hadn't affected the outcome and that bothered me, but I knew he would think I had gone nuts. Maybe I had.

"Yeah, I know. But still, I should have been able to do something."

"Fuck it, man. We're here to play pool, not cry about the game. Stanford's probably crying in his office right now, the bastard."

"Probably," I said.

I bent down and lined up the break. When I was confident I had it right, I smashed the cue into the cue ball, blasting the rack and pocketing three balls, two solids and one stripe.

"Nice break," Rich said.

I never played much pool in high school, except for the times Rich and I made a run out to Valley Stream. When I got older, and moved to Valley Stream, I played more often and became fairly good at the game. I didn't play eight ball, mainly because it was too simple a game for me.

I lined up my next shot, the six-ball banked in the side, and made it easily. I then cut the seven into the corner, a tough cut, but one I had practiced many times. The four was next, banked across the entire table, into the far right corner.

"What the fuck?" Rich said. "Maybe you should have played John for twenty a rack." I had already played John, when I was at the top of my game, and he had removed me of my pride and my money.

"I'm just getting lucky," I said, sinking the one in the right side.

"Lucky my ass. When you been practicing?"

"Never," I replied, lining up my three-ball shot.

"Now you're screwed. The eight is buried."

Rich was right, the eight was stuck behind the eleven, but I saw a way out. I cut the three into the opposite corner, and hit the ball with enough English to follow the cut and bump the eleven out of my way, leaving a clear easy shot on the eight. I sunk that, and Rich dropped his cue to the ground.

"Someone get this guy on the pro tour," he said, loud enough for everyone to hear. John just looked at us as if he regretted letting us in in the first place.

We played pool for about an hour, and though I shouldn't have, I killed Rich in every game. He couldn't get over it, but he didn't dwell on it either. He was used to beating me in every sport we played, so I guess he could concede a loss easy enough. We then went into the game room and I played all the games I remembered so well. Funny thing was, they weren't as fun as I had recalled.

When we walked out of the game room, John called me over to the counter.

"You got a good stroke, kid," he said. "I was watching you."

"Thanks," I said.

"How long you been playing?" he asked.

I almost told him I had been playing for twenty years, but stopped myself. "A year or so," I said.

"You've got a natural eye. Keep practicing," John said, giving me a wink.

"Okay, I will." I didn't know what else to say. I walked away from the counter, laughing to myself about the irony of it all.

"What did he want?" Rich asked.

"He just wanted to tell me you're a jackass," I said.

"No, really."

"Really."

"Damn, I thought he liked me."

"Of course."

We got back into the car sometime around nine. I wanted to go directly home, but Rich had other plans. It was so strange sitting next to someone I knew was Rich, but wasn't the Rich I knew. We had shared so many experiences that the teenager next to me knew nothing about, and I had to concentrate on what he knew and what he didn't. I avoided any problems by saying as little as possible.

"Let's go to Nathan's," Rich said.

"I don't feel like it," I replied.

"Come on, man. Melissa might be there, and I want to talk to her." Melissa was a girl Rich obsessed over all throughout high school, but never had the guts to ask out. Rich was popular in high school, one of the most popular, yet he had problems with the ladies. His main problem was picking the wrong girls, and Melissa was a charter member of that group. Rich would attempt to ask her to the prom sometime in April, and she would accept, only to let him know she was going with someone else two weeks before the prom. I hated the girl, for that and for her arrogant personality. She was the type that was attractive, but thought she was a model. Rich never knew this, but sometime in college, she came on to me at a party, and I took her into a bedroom. Once things started to get going, I got up and told her I wouldn't ever have sex with a bitch like her. I was drunk when I did it, but I was happy I got revenge for my friend.

"What do you want to see that bitch for?"

"What are you talking about? Just yesterday you told me I should ask her to the prom."

"Well, I thought about it, and I think you shouldn't."

"Why not?"

"Because she's a bitch."

"What's up with that? I thought you said she seemed like a nice girl?" Was I that stupid as a teenager? Looking back, I was fairly certain I always knew the girl was a moron, but Rich was telling me otherwise. It amazed me how the mind changes your memories to your liking.

"I changed my mind."

248

"You're fucking weird, man. Really weird."

"But I'm right."

"Whatever. Let's just go to Nathan's and I'll see for myself."

Nathan's, the famous hot dog place, was in Oceanside. Thursday night was car night there, when everyone with classic and new cars parked and drove around the parking lot showing off their machines. When I had gotten the Camaro, I went there religiously, proud of my car. I couldn't have cared less this time around, but Rich was insistent. Also, I wanted to speak to my father when my mother was asleep, so I had time to kill.

Nathan's parking lot was jammed with cars from the 50's and 60's, along with a slew of new cars like mine. In total, there must have been over a hundred cars there, and twice that many people gawking at them. Guys would park their cars, open their hoods, and let people look at them. It was pretty much a car show, with no admission. I think people had been going to Nathan's on Thursday nights for thirty years at least. It was a Long Island tradition.

I pulled into a spot about 100 yards from Nathan's because there was nothing open anywhere closer. I shut off the engine and started to get out of the car.

"What are you doing?" Rich asked.

"Getting out?"

"Dude, what the hell is wrong with you tonight? Don't you want to cruise the lot first?"

"No."

"What?"

"Let's just go inside."

"We gotta cruise the lot, Scott," Rich said. "See if there are any ladies lurking."

"Won't we have a better chance of talking to them if we walk up to them?" I asked.

"And waste the beauty of this fine automobile, Lucille?"

"I don't want to waste all the gas in my tank, Frank."

"You're a deadbeat tonight. You sure you're okay, Ray?"

"I'm great, Nate. Come on, let's go."

Rich reluctantly got out of the car, and made a face at me like I was some schmuck. I had parked nowhere near where the crowd was, and I was pretty sure Rich wanted to be seen pulling up in my car to impress Melissa, or anyone else that saw us. I guess when I was seventeen I would have wanted to do the same thing. I was older, even if the body I occupied said otherwise.

We walked inside Nathan's, which consisted of a large fast food restaurant, and a tremendous arcade. We entered from the arcade side, and I gawked at the hundred or so classic games it housed. There were some games I didn't even remember at first, but they came to me after a while. I wanted to sit there and play them all, but I was low on money and time.

"You wanna get something to eat?" I asked.

"Yeah, dude. Let's go."

We walked out of the noisy game room and into the restaurant. There were about fifty people in there, and the place still looked empty. I wondered if the owners of the place really benefited from the car show outside, or if all they got out of it was a filled lot. We walked up to the counter and ordered two hot dogs and an order of fries each.

Rich tapped me on the shoulder. "There she is, man," he said. I turned to look, and by the window, I saw Melissa with two other girls from my school. I couldn't remember their names, but vaguely recalled their faces. They weren't eating, instead just chatting, probably waiting for some guys to come over and throw them a rap. They seemed so self-conscious, constantly looking at their reflection in the window and checking their hair.

"I see her," I said.

"Let's go sit near them."

"If that's what you want," I said, not wanting to resist anymore.

We walked over to a booth across from them, and Rich sat down without even making eye contact with Melissa. He just started eating, looking at me, or out the window. It was funny seeing him like that.

"You gonna say something?" I asked.

"Like what?"

"Like Hello?"

"Are you out of your mind? There's three of them. I go over there and crash and burn, I'll never live it down."

"And if you don't, you'll never stop kicking yourself in the ass for it."

"Sure, easy for you to say."

"What, you want me to ask her out for you?"

"Could you?"

"Give me a break. Grow some balls. I'm not going over there like some idiot and ask her out for you. That's so high school." The words had come out before I could stop them. This whole exercise was much more difficult than I had imagined.

"Huh?"

"Just forget it. I'm not doing it."

"I need a plan, Stan. You gotta help me."

"Why don't you just go over there and ask her out? What's the worst she could do? Say no?"

"Yeah," Rich said, whispering now. "And keep it down."

"You're such a pussy."

"Like you're any better. Just last week you stuttered like a retard when you tried to ask Allison to the prom."

Allison Quigley. I had forgotten all about her. Despite my secret crush on Tanya, which I thought was never going anywhere, I did have a thing for Allison. She sat next to me in Biology, and all throughout the year, I dreamt about going to the prom with her. Rich was right, I had made a fool of myself when I tried to ask her out. She had just looked at me, laughed, and walked away. Talk about teenage humiliation.

"Well, screw that, " I said. "That was the old me. Now, things are different."

"Are they now?"

"Yep. If Allison walks in that door tonight, I'll go right up to her and tell her I didn't want to go to the prom with her anyway. I can do better than her."

"Since when did you become homecoming king?"

"Since tonight."

"Yeah, we'll see how long you stick with that, Pat."

"Maybe if you put the same effort into asking out Melissa as you do making those rhymes, you just might get somewhere."

Rich didn't say anything, he just gave me a look of disgust and continued on his fries. I looked around the restaurant, basking in my memories. I had spent countless days in that place, and it was exactly how I remembered it. My eye fell upon two guys sitting at a table across the restaurant. I squinted to focus, and noticed Dan Havliceck, Tanya's boyfriend. Immediately, my hands got hot, and I balled them into fists, tapping my right on the table.

"What's up with you?" Rich asked.

"There's Havliceck, " I said, loud enough for a few people around me to hear.

"Yeah, so?"

"He hit Tanya yesterday."

"How do you know that?"

"She has a mark above her eye. That's why she was wearing sunglasses."

"She told you that?"

"No, she said her cat did it."

"So, then, her cat did it."

"No, he did it. I know if for a fact."

"How the hell do you know that?"

"I just do." I kept my eye fixed on Havliceck, whose back was facing me. I knew it wasn't a good idea, but I wanted to go over there and punch him clean in the face. He was bigger than me, outweighing me by about thirty pounds, all of it muscle. No one messed with him, yet I was thinking about it.

"Dude, relax. You don't want to get involved with him. Besides, that whole thing is between him and her. That girl's trouble, I told you that. You wanna take an ass-kicking for her?"

"You saying you don't have my back?"

"Of course I got your back, Jack. You really want to make this happen?"

"I do."

I really don't know what came over me. The minute I saw him, all of my hatred and anger over my broken relationship with Tanya came to the surface. He had been one of the guys who caused her so much pain in high school, and led her to the path of destruction she followed. At that moment, I figured I could change something. I felt that if I could bust the living daylights out of Havliceck, it might alter the course of his relationship with Tanya, thus making her future that much easier. I didn't know if it could repair my relationship with her, but all I really wanted was to make her life better. I didn't think our relationship had a chance of being saved.

"You're sure about this? You want to do this right here?" Rich said, looking into my eyes. "You know I'm here for you bro, but I want to know that this is what you need to do."

"It is, Rich. I'm positive."

Rich exhaled and said, "Led the way, Jay."

I stood up, my fists tight by my side, my heart racing from the adrenaline. The most amazing part about this was that I wasn't scared. At seventeen, I would never have even thought about going up against someone like Havliceck. This time, I figured, I had an advantage. I wasn't much of a fighter, but I knew how to win. I'd gotten into plenty of scuffles in my twenties, as well as a few while working as an investigator, and I had taken a few self-defense classes. I didn't think Havliceck had a chance, despite his weight advantage. He had gotten a reputation of being crazy, and that's why no one messed with him, but I remembered a beating he took in a bar after high school, and I hadn't been impressed with his fighting. He was just a goon. All I had to do was incite him to throw the first punch.

"You just keep his friend off me," I said to Rich as we made our way toward Havliceck's table.

"Scott? I don't think he'll be a problem. You sure you can handle Havliceck all by yourself?"

"Positive."

I didn't see the reaction on Rich's face, but I knew it must have been one of amazement. I had never been the type to fight, and to pick one with someone like Havliceck must have meant I was either insane, or just plain stupid. I knew Rich wouldn't let me get hurt too badly, but I was also afraid that his presence might prevent the fight from happening in the first place. If people were afraid of Havliceck, they were scared stiff of Rich, who was a few inches taller and a bit wider.

I walked up to the table, and tried to relax. I didn't want to just pounce on Havliceck. I wanted him to know why I was doing it. He noticed me standing there and looked up at me.

"What the fuck do you want?"

"You piece of shit," I said, mad at myself for not coming up with something more creative.

"What did you say Camponi?"

"You heard me."

"I think you better go back down and finish your fries. Tanya ain't here to cover your ass this time."

"But I'm here to cover hers. What's the matter, you too much of a pussy to fight someone other than her?"

Havliceck slammed his hand down on the counter and stood up, grabbing me by my jersey.

"What the fuck did that bitch tell you?"

"She didn't tell me anything," I said, eyeing up my openings. Havliceck had my jersey in both his hands, making him vulnerable in several spots. "I know what sort of guy you are. Fucking bully with no balls."

"Oh yeah?" Havliceck asked, rearing his right hand back. "We'll see how big my balls are."

Before Havliceck had the chance to bring that right hand down on me, I drove the heel of my hand up into his chin, knocking him back and freeing me of his grasp. He stood there stunned for a moment, but he shook it off, and came at me again. He swung his right hand out wide, and attempted a right cross. I sidestepped and he missed. I brought all of my weight down with an elbow to the back, knocking him down. I jumped right on top of him, turning him over.

The workers at Nathan's now noticed what was going on, and scrambled toward us. Rich tried to hold them back.

I threw a hard right into Havliceck's nose, spurting blood all over his face.

"You ever lay a hand on her again, I'll kill you, you got that?" I asked, bringing another right to his head.

"Get the fuck off me," Havliceck said, spitting blood as he did so.

"I guess I didn't get my point across." I grabbed him by his hair and slammed his head into the ground. "You don't lay a fucking hand on her, you understand?"

"Okay, okay," Havliceck said, trying to pry my hands off his head. I was so full of rage, I could have killed him right there. Before I had the chance to slam his head again, Rich pulled me off of him and dragged me out of the place. The last thing I saw before we got out was Havliceck with tears in his eyes.

"What the fuck got into you?" Rich asked.

"I told you, he hit Tanya."

"No, I know why you did what you did. I just don't know how."

"Anger can make you do things you never thought possible."

"Guess so. You looked like Chuck Norris there for a moment."

* * *

I dropped Rich off at home, who was still in amazement over what happened. I knew the story would be all over school the next day, and I figured I would have to watch out for retaliation. I had never been part of any of that in high school, but I figured I would learn all about it when I went to school the next morning.

I walked into my house, rubbing my right hand, which had started to swell. My father greeted me at the door, took one look at me, and said, "Jesus Darren, you just come back from a war?"

"You could say that," I said.

"Come here, let me see your hand." He grabbed me by my wrist and took me over to a light. "Is this your blood?" he asked.

"Nope."

"You wanna talk about this?"

"Not really."

"This have something to do with the game?"

"No."

"Tanya?" Kudos to Dad for having the insight.

"Maybe."

"Fighting over a girl is never worth it, son," my father said, leading me to the kitchen sink.

"Don't worry about it, Dad. This fucking guy had it coming to him."

"Whoa, watch your mouth," he said. I never cursed in front of my father until I turned thirty. By then, I figured I had the right.

"Sorry."

"What's got into you? You don't look right. What's wrong?"

"Long story Dad, and it's not important."

My father grabbed me by my chin. "I'm your father, and whatever I say is important, is. You got that?"

Something else I had to get used to—being treated like a kid by my father again.

"Okay."

"Now tell me what happened."

I explained to my father how Havliceck had hit Tanya, and how I felt I should do something about it. I embellished the story a little bit, saying that I found out what happened from Havliceck's bragging. He didn't seem too happy with me, but he went to work on washing and examining my hand.

"Well, it's not broken. It might be a slight sprain, but I doubt it. Just ice it and you'll be fine."

"Thanks, Dad."

"Now, I just want to tell you that I'm not happy about what you did tonight. I know you were trying to do something right, that you were helping Tanya out, but that wasn't your place, and you know how I feel about fighting. I never raised you that way, and I don't want you to turn out that way. Fighting is a dead end," my father said.

"I know Dad. I just couldn't control myself. You know I'm not a fighter."

"Seems to me like you learned how real fast. I know Dan Havliceck. I treated him when he was a kid. He's no small guy."

"I just got lucky, that's all. I was pissed."

"Again with the language."

"I only said pissed."

"And I don't like that sort of talk."

"Alright, sorry."

"Now, what was it you wanted to talk about?"

I walked over to the refrigerator, opened the freezer side, grabbed an ice pack my father always kept in there, and put it on my hand. I then opened the refrigerator door, and saw a six pack of Budweiser in there.

"Want a beer?" I asked, reaching for one myself. I needed a beer, but stopped myself from grabbing one, realizing the ramifications of such an action.

"What?"

"Just kidding." I reached for a can of Pepsi, marveling at the old design on the can. "You want something to drink?"

"No, I'm fine. Come here and sit down."

I moved to the table and sat down across from my father.

"Now, what was it you wanted to talk about? Everything going okay at school?"

I nodded. "Yeah, everything's fine. It's something else I want to talk about."

"Go ahead." I noticed my father's stare. It looked as though he was waiting for bad news. In a sense, that was what I was going to deliver him. I had to be careful about what I said, but I also had to make sure I got my point across.

"I wanted to talk about Nan," I said, taking a sip of the soda.

"What about her?"

"How is she doing?"

My father looked at me, a confused and somewhat annoyed look on his face.

"Who have you been talking to?"

"No one." I knew what my father was driving at. A few years after her death, my father sat my sister and me down and told us that they had hidden my grandmother's illness from us. Her cancer had been accelerating, and he said he saw no need in worrying us. We were too young, he had said, and he figured we wouldn't be able to handle it.

"Then why the questions?"

I thought about that. I needed an angle. "She hasn't looked too good lately."

"She has cancer, Darren. She has good days and bad days."

I decided a different angle. "I had a dream last night, a dream that something happened to her. It scared me."

My father sighed, but I noticed that the look on his face was softer. "Okay, Darren, that's normal. You know in the back of your mind that your grandmother is sick, and because of that, your subconscious tries to create scenarios about the situation. Dreams aren't real. They are just our minds' way of dealing with something stressful. But they're not real."

I wanted to argue that point. I wanted to say how I felt like I was living a real dream right then, but of course, I couldn't do that. Maybe I could convince my father to look into the situation a bit. After all, I had the idea of Alan doing something to my grandmother in the front of my mind, and though I had zero evidence to prove that, I was personally convinced. I needed to find a way to prevent that.

"I know they're not, Dad, but it seemed so real. It was like an accident, something that shouldn't have happened. I don't remember the details."

"It's okay, Darren. I know this has you shaken up a little, but your grandmother is doing fine right now. She's sick, and she knows that, and she is doing everything she can."

"What do you think of Alan?" I asked.

"Why do you ask?"

"Just curious."

"He's Nan's husband, Darren. I really don't have an opinion one way or the other."

"Yes you do. I know you do. You don't like him, the same way Mom doesn't."

"Watch what you say, Darren. I never said I didn't like Alan, so don't put words into my mouth. Your mother doesn't dislike him, either. I don't know where you're getting this from, but I don't like it."

"You're lying to me, Dad. I know how you feel about him. Don't you think you should do something about that?"

My father's face turned red. I hadn't seen him angry in a long time. "Stop this Darren. I'm not going to sit here and listen to you talk this way. I know what I feel, and I don't need you to tell me different. I really don't know what makes you think all of this, but you had better let it rest, you got that?"

I knew I was heading down a dead-end street. I knew pushing wasn't going to get me anywhere, but I had to try something. "In the dream, it was Alan who did something to Nan," I said, hoping this would explain my irrational behavior.

"A dream? You are going to sit here and accuse someone of something because you dreamt it? What is wrong with you?"

"It scared me Dad, and I don't like the guy."

"Since when? You never said anything before."

"I didn't want to upset you guys."

"You're upsetting me now."

"I know. But I felt I had to say something."

"Maybe you should keep your dreams to yourself."

"Could you at least take a look at her, see if she's okay? It would make me feel better."

"And what? I'm supposed to get everyone all upset over a dream?"

My mother came downstairs into the kitchen. "What's going on here?"

"Nothing, Maggie. Don't worry about it."

"I heard arguing. Darren, what's the matter?"

"Nothing, Mom." Although I wanted to let her know what was going on as well, I knew my father wouldn't let me, and I knew it would only upset her. This whole thing was going nowhere, and I was mad that I couldn't change a thing.

"Go back to sleep, Maggie. Darren and I are just talking. Everything is alright."

My mother looked at the both of us, searching for the lies written on our faces, and said, "Okay. You're sure?"

"Yes. Go to sleep. I'll be right up."

My mother sighed, then went back upstairs. My father looked at me, trying to figure out what was going on with his son.

"I really don't like the way you are talking Darren. I want to know what is going on with you. You don't seem right."

"I'm fine Dad, and I would really appreciate if you could take a look at Nan, just to be sure. I know it was a dream and all, but I can't stop thinking about it."

"It's going to get everyone worried."

"You can do it quietly, Dad."

"I'm a pediatrician, Darren. I really don't know enough about her condition."

"Maybe you could talk her into going for a checkup?"

"She was just at the doctor last week."

"What did the doctor say?"

"Everything's fine," my father said, and I knew he was lying. I wanted to call it on him, but I knew that would get me nowhere.

"Could you just try, Dad? I wouldn't ask if it wasn't bothering me so much."

My father looked up at the ceiling, then back at me. "This is going to cause a problem, you know that?"

"I do, Dad. And because I know that, you have to realize that I feel strongly about this."

"I'll do the best I can. I can't promise anything, but I'll try, okay? Maybe Saturday, alright?"

Saturday would be too late. "No, tomorrow."

"Why the rush?"

"Please?"

"Alright. I hope you are wrong about this. But you don't say a thing to anyone, all right? It's bad enough your grandmother is sick. There is no need to make things worse for everyone."

"I know, Dad. I won't."

"And I don't want to hear any more talk about Alan. Your grandmother needs someone around her, and whether you like him or not, he provides companionship for her."

"I understand."

"Good." He stood up and put a hand on my shoulder. "And you keep yourself out of fights. I don't want you coming home like this again. If your mother knew, she would go nuts."

"I know. I won't."

"Okay. I'll see you tomorrow morning," he said, patting my shoulder.

"Yeah, Dad, see you tomorrow."

I didn't want to go to sleep, afraid my time in the past would be cut short. I hadn't really accomplished anything yet, and I didn't think Jason had gotten enough information for his experiment, unless the experiment was just to see if I could be sent back in time. I figured Jason wanted more than that. That he wanted to test his other theory. As far-fetched as his theory appeared, I was counting on it to give me some time to do what I had to do. I knew this went against Jason's theory in whole, but I just had the feeling I could make it work, that I could prevent my grandmother's untimely death, and find out what really happened. It had bothered me for seventeen years, and I wanted to make sure it wouldn't bother me any longer.

Instead of going to sleep, I walked out to the backyard to just sit and look up at the stars, taking in everything about this experience. I had learned in Astronomy class that the position of the stars can show the passage of time, but I hadn't paid enough attention to that class to have any idea how to do that. The stars seemed the same to me. The Big Dipper was where I remembered it, and the North Star shined brightly in its usual position. Maybe the passage of time had to be great to notice a difference, or perhaps my limited knowledge prevented me from seeing anything.

I walked around the side of the house, noticing the old air conditioning unit that would be replaced two years later. It was somewhat the way I remembered it, but something didn't seem right. I didn't pay that much attention to it, but it did linger in the back of my mind.

I opened the gate, and walked to the front lawn, noticing the neighbors' houses and cars as they used to be. The old Cadillac my next-door neighbor had was parked in the driveway, still battered like it had been. The front of my house was the same, white shingles and blue shutters in place of the vinyl siding my father would invest in a few years later. I liked the house better this way, but I knew it was a long shot convincing Dad to stick with it the way it was. He hated the shutters but wouldn't get aluminum siding, but the advent of vinyl would make him a sold customer.

Staring out the house, thinking about how seemingly only hours ago I had been in another place and another time, I found myself overwhelmed. Part of me wanted to enjoy this time, to relish in the experience of being seventeen again. The other part, the stronger one, didn't care about frivolous enjoyment, but instead, about the important events I could possibly alter. I thought about telling my father to invest in certain stocks at certain times. I thought about warning my sister to stay away from her current boyfriend, who would tie her up in a relationship for six years before he decided he didn't want to get married. Considering it all, the power I possibly possessed, made my head hurt. It was too much, too infinite, for my brain to fully comprehend. Maybe I was better off pretending this was all just a game, that none of it mattered, and nothing could be changed. I would enjoy it more that way, but I guess I could say I felt as if this was meant to be, that I had unknowingly sent myself back to a time where I could prevent the most severe tragedy my family ever experienced. There were no answers to my questions, no cut and dry explanations. All I had were questions, and threadbare theories to back up my belief. The funniest part about it was that I actually believed in something. I actually felt as though there was a God, and he wanted me to do what I felt was best. I don't know if you could call this an epiphany, or "finding God," but it sure felt that way.

From behind me, I heard a car pull up, and recognized it as Matt, my sister Debbie's current boyfriend, the one who I had liked when I was younger but learned to hate for what he had done to my sister. The car stopped, the lights went out, and both he and my sister exited the car.

"What are you doing, Darren?" my sister asked. She seemed so happy, so innocent. The worry that I had gotten used to seeing on her face was replaced with contentment, as if her life would end up the way she planned. This never really happens for anyone, I knew, but I still thought that maybe I could prevent her some pain along the way. How to do that didn't come to me easily.

"Just hanging out," I said, not making eye contact with Matt.

"Hey chief," he said, extending his hand. I didn't shake it. He seemed bothered by this, but just said, "How'd the game go?"

"We lost again," I said.

"Sorry to hear that, man."

"I'm sorry Darren," Debbie said, rubbing my arm.

"It's no big deal. It was only a game."

261

"That doesn't sound like the Darren I know," Matt said.

"Well, maybe you don't know me as well as you think," I said nastily.

"Whoa, you must be really upset."

"I might be upset, but it doesn't have anything to do with the game."

"What's irking you, man?"

"Like you give a shit. Just let it rest."

"Darren, what's the matter with you?" Debbie asked.

"Nothing. I just came to realize a few things about certain people," I said, looking directly at Matt when I did so. He returned the look with one of bewilderment. We had actually been like brothers when I was younger, and for him to hear me speak this way must have rattled his tiny brain.

"I do something?" Matt asked.

"Not yet, but you will."

"What?"

"Darren, stop playing games," Debbie said. "I'm not in the mood."

"Of course, you think it's just games, but you'll see. You'll wish you listened to me." I turned away from them and walked toward the house. I heard Debbie say, "I don't know what's gotten into him. I'm sorry," as I opened the door and walked into the house.

* * *

I slept fitfully that night, my dreams filled with anger and violence. I didn't recall them specifically, but I knew they had something to do with me fighting with everyone—all the people who had done me wrong in the past. On top of that, I distinctly remembered dreaming that I had awakened in the room with Jason again. He had told me to calm down, and had given me another injection, which put me back to sleep. There was someone else in the room, someone I knew I had recognized, but I couldn't picture the face when I woke up in the morning.

I turned off the radio that had awakened me, cutting short an old Van Halen song. Getting out of bed, I realized I had a major problem on my hands. Though I had a good memory when it came to the past, there was no way I could figure out what classes I needed to go to for each period. I remembered that I only had four, but I had to figure out a way to find out which one was where and when, and my mind was blank. My room was a complete disaster, so I knew the possibility of finding my schedule somewhere there would be impossible. I hoped Rich was familiar with my schedule. If he wasn't, I'd have to go to the guidance office to get my schedule, and they might think I needed some sort of mental help.

After opening my closet, I found myself wondering what made me think my wardrobe at that time was anything near acceptable. I had Izod shirts, tight Levi jeans, and nothing but sneakers for footwear. I didn't like to wear sneakers, but I had loved them when I was a teenager. I tried to get together an outfit that was somewhat acceptable, finding a pair of black pants that I had probably never worn before, and an old pair of black loafers. Finding black socks was almost impossible, but I discovered a pair sitting at the bottom of my sock drawer, underneath a porno tape I had borrowed from Rich. Because my room was right next to my sister's, I remembered that I hadn't known porno tapes had sound until I moved into my apartment. Not like I ever watched those sort of tapes. Not me. Never.

I put on a button down white shirt I found in my closet, and laid the clothes on my bed, somewhat happy with the outfit I had created out of the fashion disaster in my closet. Noticing that my sister hadn't gotten into the shower yet, I seized my opportunity.

I got out of the shower, and wiped the steam from the mirror. The face that stared back at me nearly knocked me off my feet. I looked the same, but just a bit younger. It wasn't quite the way I remembered looking as a teenager, and not too far from the way I looked as an adult. None of this made sense to me, but I figured my mind was playing tricks on me, unable to make heads or tails out of the situation I was in. The worst part of it was the hair, which was a lot longer than I was used to, and I couldn't remember how I ever styled it.

I made my best attempt to make it look acceptable, using a ton of my sister's hair spray and gel to get the hair matted down enough to be manageable. I thought I had done a pretty good job.

"Hurry up in there, Darren," I heard my sister say from the other side of the door.

"One minute," I replied, cringing at the thought I would have to face her after what I had said the night before. I had meant everything, but I had felt the way I normally did the morning after going on a drunken tirade. Sure, the things I said the night before needed to be said, but that didn't make me not regret saying them.

I opened the bathroom door, my sister staring me straight in the face when I did so.

"Asshole," she said, walking past me into the bathroom.

"I'm sorry," I said, but she didn't hear me or didn't care.

"Nice hair," was all she said as she closed the door in my face. I was really doing well.

My mother was waiting for me at the bottom of the steps when I got ready to leave. She seemed unhappy about something, but I couldn't tell what. When she saw the way I was dressed, she raised her eyebrows.

"What, is it some sort of formal day at school or something?" she asked.

"No. I just felt like dressing this way."

"Well, you look handsome. I'm not used to seeing you this way."

I thought about telling her to get used to it, but decided against that.

"Thanks," I said.

"I overheard what you and your father were talking about last night," my mother said.

"Sorry about that. I didn't want you to know."

"Tell me about the dream."

I didn't want to do that. This situation obviously upset her enough as it was.

"It was nothing."

"Don't lie to me, Darren. For you to talk to your father about it, it had to be more than nothing. Why didn't you tell me?"

When I was younger, like I said before, my father and I really didn't see eye to eye. We lived in the same house and ate dinner together, but rarely had any in-depth conversations. If there was ever something on my mind, I went to my mother with it. The fact that I had chosen my father this time must have gotten her thinking.

"I didn't want to upset you, Mom. I didn't want you to get all worried over nothing."

"What was the dream about?"

"Exactly what you overheard."

"Nanny?"

I nodded.

"What about her?"

"I don't know, Mom. It was really vague. Nothing was clear. I just got worried about her is all. I wouldn't put too much thought into it."

"Has anyone told you anything? Did your father say anything to you?" I knew what my mother was driving at, and I wanted to avoid it at all costs. They had been hiding my grandmother's condition from us, and each one thought the other spilled the beans.

"No, Mom. It was just a dream. Dad said it was my mind working the whole situation out, and he was probably right."

"Then why do you want him to check on her?" My mother must have listened to the whole conversation from the stairs.

"I just thought it couldn't hurt, you know? I'm sorry to have upset you, Mom. I didn't want that to happen."

I could tell my mother was near tears, but she took a deep breath to fight them off and smiled, showing me her inner strength. I knew the mere thought of her mother getting worse upset her deeply, but there she was, fighting it off to make it seem like everything was okay. I knew otherwise, but there was nothing I could do about that.

"It's okay, Darren," my mother said, hugging me. "I know you are upset about her, and I think it is nice that you think about her. But everything's fine, don't worry, okay?"

"Okay, Mom," I said, hugging her tight for a moment, coming to tears myself because I knew the pain she was about to go through. I had precious hours to try and prevent the tragedy, and most of them would be wasted in school. I could only hope that my father would find something when he examined my grandmother, if she let him, and he would be able to delay her death. Whether or not this would prevent my mother from going through the pain she experienced the first time, I had no idea. I doubted I could find a way to make my grandmother live a lot longer. My main concern was Alan, and I wanted to keep my grandmother away from him for the entire night. That was the plan I had to work on.

* * *

I picked up Rich at his house, almost forgetting where he lived. His parents had moved when we were in high school, from one part of Merrick to the other, and I had to remember which house he was currently in. Luckily, I had made the correct guess.

"Good morning, Joe Frazier," he said, laughing as he got in the car. He took a look at me. "What, you think today was senior pictures?"

"Nah, just felt like dressing this way," I said, realizing my wardrobe choice had been a bad idea.

"What's with the do?"

"Had a fight with the hair this morning."

"Looks like the hair won, son."

"Tell me about it," I said, looking at my hair in the rearview mirror. "It look that bad?"

"You look like a fucking nerd, if you want the truth, Ruth."

"Nothing I can do about it now."

"Gonna be a long day for you, Stu." He had no idea.

I pulled into the school parking lot, finding a space near the gym. I settled in the spot and turned off the car.

"What are you doing?" Rich asked.

"Parking?"

"You swipe a teacher parking permit, Kermit?"

"No."

"Feel like getting a suspension?"

"No," I said, starting the car again and moving to a spot in the student parking area. It seemed like it was miles from the school.

"You take a shot on the head, Ted?" I really wanted him to stop the rhyming, but I knew doing that would only draw more attention to my unusual behavior.

"What makes you say that, Pat?"

"You're acting real strange, dude. Real strange."

"I'm fine, really."

"If you say so. If you ask me, I say you ain't yourself."

"You're crazy."

"That might be right, Dwight, but at least I'm the same crazy I was yesterday morning. Can't say the same for you."

"You're just imagining things. I'm the way I was, Cuz."

"Well, unless we want to be late for Dawson's class, I think we had better get moving," Rich said as he got out of the car. "Meet you at your locker?"

Great, I was saved because Rich was in my first class with me. Math with Mr. Dawson. But I had no idea where my locker was, or how to open the damn thing even if I found it.

"How about we go to yours first, then mine?"

"If that's how you want it," Rich said, shrugging.

We walked toward the school, several people staring at me on our way. I wasn't sure if they were staring because of the way I was dressed, or if word about what I had done to Havliceck had gotten around already. I figured it was the former. It was too early for people to know about the fight already.

"You're the main event, Trent," Rich said. "Must be them threads you're sporting."

"Bad choice, I know."

"You can say that again."

"My lock isn't working," I said to Rich, when we got to my locker.

"What you talking about?"

"It won't open."

"That's because that ain't your locker. The one to the left is. You sure you're alright?"

"Yeah, I'm fine."

I fumbled with the combination lock, trying to make it look like I knew how to open it, but it just wasn't working. Rich watched me, probably wondering if I was out of my mind.

"Let me," he said, turning the dial quickly and opening it. "Dressed like a nerd, and acting the part as well. You worried about Havliceck or something?"

"A little," I said, finding solace in a good excuse for my behavior, "but I think I'll be alright."

"You'll know as soon as we walk into class."

"He's in math with us?" I muttered to myself.

"Damn right he is. I'll watch your back, Jack. Your best bet is to pretend nothing happened. You walk in like you're king of the world and he'll have to do something."

"Good idea," I said.

"I got lots of them."

Chapter 19

I walked into the classroom with Rich, a knot forming in my stomach when I did so. I really didn't think Havliceck would try anything, at least not in school, yet I still feared the confrontation. My biggest concern was what would happen after I returned to the present. As an adult living my teenage years again, I had the advantages of extra experience. Once I returned, I figured I would go back to being myself, and the original seventeen-year-old Darren would have to live with the consequences of all I had done. Trying to sort it all out confused me. I didn't know what the specifics were as far as memory and all that. Had my seventeen-year-old mind been put on hold so my adult mind could run my body? Would I wake up, wondering why Havliceck wanted to kill me? It made no sense, and I told myself just to be careful not to write checks my past self wouldn't be able to cash.

I didn't see Havliceck in the classroom when I walked in, so I moved to a seat near the front.

"What are you doing?" Rich asked, "That's not your seat."

"Oh, right," I said, hoping Rich would point me in the right direction. He sat in the back, and I sat next to him.

"Wrong again, Jen. I think you should lay off the pills, Bill."

"Where do I sit again?"

Rich rolled his eyes and pointed to a seat two rows away from his. I sat down there, and smiled at him as if to say I was just screwing around. I opened my notebook, and glanced through it, barely recognizing the handwriting in it. It looked like chicken scratch. I flipped the pages until I found the most recent notes, and saw that there was a homework assignment due that day.

"You got the homework?" I whispered loudly to Rich.

"Oh yeah," he said, flipping through his own notebook and handing a piece of paper to me. "Thanks, dude."

I took the sheet from him and realized it was my work. Through some stroke of luck, I had done the homework before the baseball game and had given it to Rich. I wondered if I had done the same for all my classes.

"I give you anything else?"

"Why would you?"

"Just asking. I can't remember what I did with the other work."

"You didn't give it to me. Probably in your other book."

"Okay."

I looked toward the door, and saw Havliceck walk in. He had a bandage over his nose, and one of his eyes was black. He looked at me as he walked in, then looked away. He was scared, that much I could see. That didn't make him any less dangerous, that much I knew. He had a reputation to defend.

"He's pissing his pants," Rich called over.

I didn't say anything, or even look in Rich's direction. I knew the best thing to do was lay low, and pretend like nothing happened.

Havliceck took a seat a row away from me and two seats ahead, so at least I didn't have to worry about him sitting behind me. I could keep my eye on him without him even noticing.

Mr. Dawson walked in, a middle-aged man with thick brown hair and thicker glasses, and put his briefcase down on his desk at the front of the class. He stared at Havliceck for a moment, but didn't say anything to him. He looked around the room, noticing the empty seats, then glanced at his watch.

"Please pass your homework forward," he said with a sigh, and I handed my paper to the redhead in front of me. I knew she had sat in front of me all year, but I couldn't remember her name for the life of me.

"Hi Darren," she said when she turned to take my paper. She was cute, in a teenage sort of way, and I remembered that she turned out to be quite a looker when she hit her twenties. That's the thing about high school. The people that suffer with average or worse looks during that time are usually rewarded when they get older.

"Hey," I said.

"You think about what I asked you the other day?"

Now, what the hell did she ask me? I vaguely remembered that she had a crush on me, or at least I thought she had, but I had blown her off back then because, well, I was a dumb teenager, and she wasn't good-looking enough for me. I felt so ashamed of myself, realizing that I was as two-dimensional as the people I criticized. I thought about how I should answer her question, and came up with nothing.

"Yeah," I said, hoping a semi-positive answer would hold her off. No such luck.

"So, can you go?"

Not knowing where it was she wanted to go, I didn't have an answer for her. My mind was blank, so I figured I'd try and find out in a roundabout way.

"When is it again?" I asked.

"Tea Dance is the Wednesday before Gamenight. April 13th."

That was fortunate. Now I remembered. Gamenight was a big thing for the girls in the school. It was like a dance and gymnastics contest, and the preparations lasted for like three months. My older sister had been into it when she was in high school, and when her team lost senior year, she was depressed for the rest of the school year. I thought it was stupid, that it did nothing more than distract the participants from school, but the whole town supported it. I recalled that this girl, Lorie was her name, had asked me to the Tea Dance, and I had made some excuse about having something else to do. She had been heartbroken, if I remembered correctly. I sat there and wondered what harm could come from agreeing to go. Besides, it wouldn't be me that would have to endure it, but my past self.

"Yeah, I can make it," I said, and she beamed.

"Great. Thanks. I'll call you over the weekend and give you the details?"

"That's fine," I said. I looked over at Rich, who was staring at me trying to figure out what was going on. I winked at him and he rolled his eyes.

Class ended, and we all filed out of the room. I walked out with Rich, Havliceck in front of us. He looked back once or twice, but didn't say anything. I kept quiet, not saying a word, figuring I was better off that way. We stopped outside the classroom.

"I'll see you at lunch," Rich said, and I hoped I would know when that was and where to meet him.

"By the car?"

"Unless you want to eat in the cafeteria."

Made sense. "Yeah, right," I said, and walked away from Rich, not having any idea where I was going. The luck I had finding my first class wasn't going to come through for the second. I stood in the hallway, watching the crowd of kids walk past, all knowing where they were going and none of them even remotely in the same situation I was. My mind turned to the idea of leaving school, claiming to be sick or something, when I felt a tap on my shoulder. I turned, and faced Havliceck.

"Camponi, come with me," he said, walking toward the bathroom. I worried that an ambush was waiting for me in there, but I figured I had to deal with this problem as soon as possible. I followed Havliceck through the bathroom door, relieved that it was only he and me.

"What do you want?" I asked.

"You listen to me," he said, more calm than angry.

"Okay."

"Who did you tell?"

"About what?"

"About Tanya," he said.

"No one."

"Not even Rich?"

"Well, yeah, he knew."

"Anyone else?"

"No."

"Well, this is how I look at it. I owe you for what you did last night. I should kick the shit out of you right now. There's no doubt it would end differently," he said, now taking on the arrogant tone I was familiar with. "But, I'm going to let you slide. I know you're friends with her, and I'm not stupid. I know everything, but Tanya's my girl, you got that?"

I wanted to argue this, to tell him they wouldn't make it through the year, but then again, I didn't know what changed from my actions the night before. I had set a new series of consequences into motion, and anything was possible.

"Okay," I answered.

"I don't want you hanging around her. I don't want you giving her trouble."

I tried to remember what sort of trouble I could ever have caused her.

"And I don't want you to call her," Havliceck said.

"Why shouldn't I do that? We're friends."

"Cut the shit, Camponi. I know you're after her. I know you got the hots for her. Everyone knows about it. You leave her alone."

"You talk to her about this?" I asked. I knew that his threats meant nothing to me right then, but I still had my teenage self to worry about.

"No, I didn't talk to her about this. I'm sure she knows what happened last night. Fucking everybody knows. That's why I owe you one. People hear I got my ass kicked by you, they think I'm soft."

"Nothing I can do about that," I said.

"There's a lot you can do about that."

"Well, maybe, but let's just leave everything as it is. I don't want any trouble from you, and trust me, you don't want any trouble from me. You might think I got lucky last night, and maybe I did. But what you have to think about, what you really need to focus on, is the possibility that I didn't get lucky. Don't get me wrong, I don't want to fight. I want this to end right here."

"You do, do you?" Havliceck's threatening tone sounded feeble. I almost laughed.

"I do. But here's how it's going to go. Anyone asks me about last night, I'll say nothing. I'm not going to go around bragging, if that's what you're worried about. And I'm not going to tell anyone else what happened between you and Tanya, because that's your business. But, I'll tell you something. You touch her again, in any way, I'll come for you."

"You're threatening me?"

I moved closer to him, staring him in the eye. He had all he could do to hold the stare.

"You're damn right I am. Maybe you think it's cool laying your hands on a girl . . ."

"I never said I did that."

"You know you did it, so stop fucking lying. And if I have to come for you, it's going to be a lot worse than it was last night, that I promise."

Havliceck started to say something, but I put my hand up.

"Just shut up and listen. I'll stay clear of you if nothing happens. You can tell everyone anything you want. That you threatened me and I cowered, that you told me to stay away from her. I could care less about that. You just keep your hands off her, got that?"

"I never hit her man, I swear."

"Well, if that's the case, then you have nothing to worry about." I put my hand out for him to shake it. He stood there for a second, thinking about it, then shook my hand. "We got a deal, I presume?"

"You just stay away from her, and we're fine," Havliceck said, feeling that he had to save his masculinity somehow. I let him.

"Deal."

Havliceck actually put his arm around me. "You're alright Camponi. Where'd you learn to fight like that?" he asked.

"Judo," I said, figuring that a karate background might make him afraid of me.

"Cool. Now, don't forget, when you see Tanya in class now, this conversation never happened. You act like everything's the same."

Right. Tanya and I had Sociology together with Ms. Folson. I even remembered where the class was. It was where we first met. How could I have forgotten that?

We walked out of the bathroom separately, the pact a secret between the two of us. I figured I had succeeded in saving my former self, and might have even prevented any future problems for Tanya as well. I was happy I knew where my next class was, and planned on skipping the rest of the day. I wanted to skip the class with her as well, but I needed to tie up any loose ends with her first.

I walked into the classroom, and saw Tanya sitting in a seat by the window, still wearing her sunglasses. She looked ridiculous, and I wondered what it was I ever saw in her. She was a girl looking for male attention, that's what had gotten her into trouble in the first place. Teenagers don't know how to notice such things, or sort them out, and I probably had just fallen for her, overlooking all the warning signs that told me to keep away. I was really growing tired of witnessing the mistakes of youth firsthand.

"Hey," I said, sitting down next to her. She looked me up and down, as if she didn't recognize the person sitting next to her.

"Nice hair," she quipped. Man, you make one minor change about your look, and no one can leave you alone about it.

"Thanks."

"What's with the outfit? You gotta go to court after school or something?" Couldn't people just let it rest?

"It was just what I felt like wearing."

"Well, you look nice," Tanya said, and it sounded like she meant it. At least someone I knew had taste in clothes.

She looked at me again, and it was a look I could best describe as interest. I could tell she wanted to mention something about what happened the night before with Havliceck, but she didn't know how. My machismo made her want to get close to me, that much I could tell. I looked at her, and she smiled. I smiled back.

Ms. Folson walked in to start the class. She was an attractive woman, in her own way. All the guys in school lusted after her, and I had been one of them, but looking at her right then, I realized she wore about an inch too much makeup. She had a sexy look about her, wearing a miniskirt and a shirt that highlighted her chest. I don't know how the school administration let her walk around like that, but I was certain no one complained, at least not the male students and teachers.

"Okay," she said, "let's start with last night's assignment. I wanted you to write a paragraph or two about an issue in today's society that you think is important." I rifled through my notebook, finding no such paragraph written. As if through psychic guidance, Ms. Folson looked at me. "Darren, why don't you start?"

"Um," I said, pretending to look for my work. "I can't find it."

Ms. Folson gave me a look of disappointment and said, "Well, why don't you just tell us about what you wrote?"

Now, I knew the class was about sociology, which meant I needed to talk about some social issue facing the world at that time. I tried to place myself firmly in that time period, but my memories of events passed got all mixed together, and I wouldn't have been able to tell the difference between something that happened in the early eighties and something that happened years later. I felt my face flush with embarrassment, and latched onto the first thing that came to mind.

"I decided to discuss the AIDS epidemic."

"The what?"

Good one, Darren. Though it was happening in that time period, the general public really didn't find out about AIDS until 1985, if I remembered correctly. On top of that, when it first became public, it was known as a homosexual disease. I couldn't switch gears right then, so I just decided to go with it.

"The AIDS epidemic." I tried to remember what AIDS actually stood for, so I fudged it. It wasn't like someone was going to correct me. "Autonomic Immune Deficiency Syndrome."

"I'm sorry Darren, but I don't know what you are talking about," Ms. Folson said.

"It's a very serious illness which is about to reach epidemic proportions around the world."

"What sort of disease is this?"

"It's a sexually transmitted disease."

Ms. Folson nodded, as if she now was following me. "Go ahead. How do you think this relates to today's society?"

"I think it speaks directly to today's society. We are living in what will probably be known as the decade of excess."

"The decade of excess?"

"Yes. Everyone is making money these days, with the stock market and all that. Business is booming, and during such times, people tend to get careless and not worry about what's important. Because of this, recreational drug use is at an all time high. Among those drugs, cocaine and heroin are being used more frequently. These drugs can be injected, and in the drug community, needle sharing is common. AIDS can be transmitted this way, through the passage of blood and bodily fluids. Because of this carelessness, along with promiscuous sex, AIDS will flourish. I'm sure that the Surgeon General, as well as other noted doctors and scientists, will come out and warn people about these dangers, but no one will listen until the epidemic spreads out of control. Women with the disease will give birth to children who are born with it. Prominent people in sports or Hollywood will come out and admit they have it."

"Hold on a second, Darren. Are you making this up? Is this a real disease?"

"Absolutely."

"Then why don't I know about it?"

"Well, you can search the Internet . . . um . . . no . . . you can do some research and find information on it. No one really understands this disease, and I'm sure it will be years before the medical community gets a firm grasp of it."

I noticed that everyone in the classroom was staring at me, most notably Tanya. None of them had any clue what I was talking about.

"And why did you pick this, this AIDS as you call it, for your assignment?"

"Well, I think it really speaks to our society."

"Speaks to our society?" I figured maybe I was talking a bit too maturely.

"Yeah, you know, it shows us what assholes we can be."

Everyone in the class laughed, except for Folson. It wasn't that she minded the curse word, she used them herself in class from time to time, but I guess she just couldn't understand me right then. Or, maybe she was amazed at how intellectual I had sounded in the beginning.

"Okay, so you're saying that this disease, one which you think will get out of hand, is a direct comment on how our society doesn't pay attention to its medical needs."

"In a sense, yeah. It just shows that, even when something evil looms over us, we don't pay any attention to what can help us. We need to be taken to the brink of disaster before we do anything about it. It's like church."

"Church?"

"Yeah. No one goes to church when times are good. It's only during tragic times that people go to church, hoping that God will help them in their time of need. No one goes to church to thank God when something good happens. They only want to blame him, then ask for his help, when something bad happens."

"You wrote all of this in your assignment?"

"Yes, but I can't find it right now."

"Well, you type it up tonight and give it to me Monday, okay?"

I doubted I would be around long enough to do that. I couldn't imagine what sort of situation I set my past self up for, but it wasn't something I could worry about. I had other, more pressing concerns.

"Yeah, sure," I replied.

When class ended, Tanya pulled me aside in the hallway.

"I need to talk to you," she said.

"What about?"

"You know."

"No, I don't."

"About yesterday."

"What about it?"

"How did you know? How did you know that it wasn't my cat who did this to my eye?"

"It was just a hunch."

"It had to be more than that. I mean, for you to do what you did to Dan."

"I don't know what came over me."

She moved closer to me, touching me on my arm. Maybe when I was really seventeen that might have meant something. Now, she just seemed like a pathetic girl looking for attention. I wanted nothing to do with it. I didn't have ill feelings toward her, but I also couldn't imagine seeing myself dating her.

"I really appreciate what you did," she said, whispering in my ear. "And I know why you did it."

"You do?"

"Yes," she whispered, her lips just barely touching my ear.

"Okay," I said, moving away from her slightly.

"I'm breaking up with him," she said.

"If that's what you want to do." I realized what I had done. I had found a way to replace Havliceck with myself. If I didn't prevent something from happening between the two of us right then, I would doom my past self to nothing but turmoil.

"It's what both of us want," she said.

"I never said that. Listen Tanya, you know that there are feelings between the two of us, but I don't want to destroy our friendship. It means too much to me."

"And it means a lot to me, too. I know that it's special, but it's only special because of what we both feel for each other."

"Don't break up with Dan just for me," I said, looking her in the eyes. "You'd just be doing it because of what happened last night. I did what I did, there's no taking that away, but I didn't do that for any other reason than the fact that he had done something wrong to you. I don't want to be responsible for any decision you make, and I didn't do it so you would break up with him."

"You don't have to lie to me, Darren."

"I'm not lying."

Tanya looked at me, puzzled. Maybe she had already created a scenario in her mind about how we would date, and how I would be her savior. I had tried to play that role when we were in our twenties, and it ended in disaster. Maybe I could prevent her from going through half the troubles she did, but I didn't want my past self to pay the price for the decisions I was making and the actions I was taking.

"So, what do you want me to do?"

"I don't want you to do anything. You do whatever you think is right. I'll always be here for you as your friend."

The look on her face told me she wasn't satisfied with that, but she said, "Okay." She seemed so controllable, so willing to please whatever man was in her life. She wanted me to be in her life, but there was no way I was going to let that happen. I just hoped that my past self wouldn't see the opportunity I had always dreamed of and seize it. Remember, I was originally a stupid teenager in love with her.

I walked away from her, wondering what I would have to face when I made it back to the present. I was happy about one thing; I had made a change to the past that would undoubtedly affect the future. I might not have been thrilled about the change, but it gave me hope for what I had to do with my grandmother.

I didn't go to my next class. Instead, I went to the payphone and called home, to see if my father had done something with my grandmother yet. My mother answered the phone.

"Hi Mom," I said.

"Darren? What's the matter?"

"Nothing. I'm not feeling too well. I think I'm going to come home. Is that okay?" I figured this would get me out of school, and my mother would vouch for me so I didn't have any cuts on my record.

"What's wrong?"

"I feel a little light-headed."

"Okay. Come home then." I never tried to fake illness when I was younger, so my mother didn't doubt that I was sick.

"Anything with Nan yet?"

"Well . . ."

"What is it, Mom?"

"Your father had her in for an examination. She went to the hospital for tests. I was about to head over there now."

"Should I meet you there?"

"No, Darren. Don't do that. Everything is fine. Your father just felt it was best if someone with more experience with her condition had a look at her."

Though this was relatively bad news, I was happy. My grandmother had been rushed to the hospital later that night originally, and I figured she had a better chance if she was at the hospital earlier. I wondered what this meant about my theory with Alan.

"Tell them to check for poisoning," I said.

"What?"

"It was part of the dream. I don't remember it exactly, but I think she ate the wrong thing. Maybe it was an allergy, I don't know."

"Where are you getting this from?" my mother asked.

"I told you, the dream."

"Are you sure?"

"Yes. Is Alan with her?"

"Of course. I spoke with him before. She told him about going to see Dad, and he made her breakfast this morning, and came with her. He took off from work."

That got my mind going. If I had really thought Alan had something to do with this, my theory relied on some sort of poisoning. Nothing would work better than something in the food.

"What did he make her?"

"What?"

"Mom, she ate something in the dream. What did he make her for breakfast?"

"Nan loves pancakes. I would guess that's what he made her."

"I don't remember what she ate," I said, knowing it didn't matter. I would find out for myself soon enough.

"Well, you're worrying me, Darren," my mother said.

"I'm sorry Mom. I guess if you had the same dream, you'd probably do the same thing."

"You're right Darren. You just make sure you come straight home and get into bed, okay? As soon as we get home, Dad will take a look at you."

I really had no intention of going home, but I said, "I will Mom. I promise."

I hung up the phone and knew exactly what I had to do. I needed to go to my grandmother's house and do some detective work. Before I did that, however, I needed some scientific advice.

I found Jason in the cafeteria, sitting at a table all by himself with a stack of books in front of him. He saw me approach, and curled himself closer to his notebook. I sat down next to him.

"What?"

"I just want to ask you something, Jason," I said. Jason was exactly how I remembered him, wearing a Star Trek shirt and jeans, with the large glasses he always wore, resting on his nose. I had no trouble remembering why he wasn't popular in high school.

"Leave me alone, Darren, I'm studying."

"I'll only bother you for a second."

"I'm not in the mood for one of your pranks," Jason said, reminding me that I had played a few on him in high school. What sort of asshole had I been?

"It's not prank, I swear. It has to do with how you won that science contest."

"Won?"

"Yeah."

"What are you talking about? They don't announce the winners until May."

"Well, you know, when you win it."

"Why do you care about that?"

"I saw this movie the other night, about time travel."

"You did? What movie?"

"I don't remember, but it got me thinking. Let's say a guy goes back in time and possesses his old body, you know, his younger body."

"Impossible."

"What?" I took a look around the cafeteria and noticed several people I knew watching us. Maybe they were preparing for one of my pranks, or perhaps they were just wondering what I was doing talking to Jason. No one talked to him back then.

"It would be impossible for someone to inhabit their former self. The laws of physics wouldn't allow it."

"Well, let's just say that it happened."

"It wouldn't."

"Let's just say it could," I said, in a stern tone.

"Okay, if you want to talk foolishness."

"I do. If this person were to go back and do this, let's say for a day or two, would his actions affect the future?"

"Maybe. But I told you that is impossible."

"I know you said that, but if it was possible, what would the outcome be?"

"Disaster."

"Why?"

"Well, for one, if he were to occupy his former body, what would happen to the essence that was already occupying it? Would it disappear? Would it be put on hold?"

"I don't know."

"What happened in the movie?"

"I fell asleep, that's why I'm asking."

"Well, there are a lot of things to consider. If we can put aside the thoughts of the mental aspect of this all, you know, what happens to the man's past mind. If we look past that, then we have to decide what we think about the time continuum."

"I don't have any thoughts about that. I want to know what you think."

"Well, I think time controls everything. I don't think that someone can go back into the past and change events that would affect the future. He might think he is changing the future, but he really can't."

"So, if someone had died in the past, this guy can't go back and prevent that?"

Jason pondered this for a moment. "You know, that's exactly what I have been trying to figure out with my research. There is no real fact to base all of this in, so I'm having a hard time with it."

"Why don't you give me your best guess?"

Again, Jason paused. "Hmm, well, I guess someone could prevent the death of someone in the past, if they ever found a way to travel in time. But, I wouldn't think he'd want to do that."

"Why is that?"

"Because the ramifications of it would be tremendous."

Chapter 20

Nothing but bad news, that's all I was getting. I had hoped Jason would help me out and tell me what I wanted to do was possible. Instead, all he did was make me worry. I didn't bother to ask what he meant by "tremendous" because I realized I didn't want to know. He was just a punk kid with some far-fetched theories. The Jason in the present hadn't said anything about ramifications, or at least he didn't specify such a thing. He had warned me, but not to the extent that the teenage Jason did. I assumed the older Jason knew better, and wouldn't put me in such danger. Then again, he did tell me to pick a time period where I wouldn't feel compelled to change anything.

I raced over to my grandmother's house, intent on finding evidence to prove Alan guilty. Driving there, I thought I was out of my mind for doing such a thing, but I needed to know. I didn't even know what I was looking for, but that didn't matter. If I didn't make an attempt, I would wonder about it for the rest of my life.

My grandmother and Alan lived in Baldwin, a few towns over from Merrick. Their house was an old ranch, with an open porch out front. I walked up to the house, and looked under the mat for the spare key they always left there. Well, almost always. When I looked, there was no key. Maybe I should have turned around and gone home, but of course, I didn't do that. Instead, I walked around back, to the basement window. By stroke of luck, it was cracked open, and I was able to slide it all the way open and successfully break into my grandmother's house.

The basement had a dirt floor, and when I landed, I got dirt all over my pants. I brushed it off, looking around the room, remembering the times I had played down there when I was little. My grandmother still had the toys we played with down there—a drawing desk, some blocks, a few board games, and a rocking horse that hadn't seen use in over a decade. Why she didn't just throw them out, I have no idea. I figured she was probably sentimental, and that letting go of those toys signaled the end of her grandchildren's childhood. I wondered for a moment if maybe she hoped to live long enough to see our kids. Well, not mine. She'd have to live to 150 before I had kids, but my sister's at least. How fragile life was, and how horrible it was to look at life with the gift/curse of foresight. So far, my trip back did nothing but make me regret past actions and reflect on the bad things. If I had been depressed in my present life, then living this past one brought me to near suicide.

I made my way up the stairs from the basement, hearing the creaks and hoping they wouldn't break. Alan had an accident on those steps, and I stood there for a moment, wishing the fall had killed him. Evil thoughts, I know.

Luckily, the door leading from the basement to the main floor was open. I walked down the hallway, noticing pictures I hadn't seen in years, and made my way to the kitchen. There, I hoped to find the evidence I so desperately sought. If Alan had made my grandmother breakfast and poisoned her, which was what I was convinced happened, then I would be able to find the utensils and bowl he used. I didn't know what I would do with such evidence, but I wanted it in my possession. If my mother had told the doctors at the hospital to check my grandmother for poisoning and they found evidence pointing to that, then the bowl and utensils would go a long way to establish Alan's guilt.

In the sink, soaking in soap and water, was the bowl I was looking for. My heart raced as I realized exactly what it was I was doing. I was, if nothing else, solving a mystery that had bothered me for nearly twenty years. The answer to that mystery might have been nothing but what I had created in my head. Alan very well could have been innocent. I thought about that, while staring at the bowl in the sink, and laughed to myself. There were endless possibilities in life, countless scenarios and truths that are played out. Without a doubt I knew, however, that Alan's innocence was not one of them.

I picked up the bowl, a plastic Tupperware job that must have been as old as the company itself, and looked at it, wondering whether or not to spill the water out of it. I figured Alan was either stupid or confident for not scrubbing that bowl clean. Or, I was just plain out of my mind.

The telephone rang, and I almost dropped the bowl right there. Hearing it reminded me that I was in someone else's house. I had done a few break and enter jobs while working on cases, but this was different. This was a relative's house, and though eventually everyone would thank me for what I had done, it would be pretty hard to explain if I got caught before that.

I rushed from my grandmother's house to my house, constantly glancing at the empty but wet bowl sitting on the passenger seat. I had decided to empty it, figuring it would be almost impossible to transport the bowl with water in it. I hadn't figured out exactly what I was going to do with the bowl, and it was secondary. The most important thing was my grandmother's condition. I knew she was in able hands, safer at the hospital hours early than at home, where anything could happen. All I could do was pray that the doctors could intervene in time to save her. I did feel a sense of urgency about the whole thing, but I had relaxed quite a bit as well. My grandmother was destined to die on that day. Though I was doing everything in my power to prevent that, I knew in the back of my mind that it might be impossible.

What had caused such a sudden acceptance?

I wondered if maybe I had found God or something, then shrugged that idea off. Sure, my father had admitted a belief in a supreme being, and I always toyed with that notion, but it was my nature to question instead of accept. I knew most of that questioning was just out of habit—that I felt if I just accepted something, I would be shortchanging myself. We are asked to accept a lot of things at face value in this life. Our closest friends and family, politicians, clergymen, teachers, doctors, and especially our parents who all ask us to trust them, to put aside our doubts and blindly accept their position. Most of this is done on pure faith. We see nothing to aid our belief. We are told the eyes are the greatest deceivers, yet we always want to see. This is the way I always looked at life. That you must question before you accept, even from the people closest to you. Not a fantastic way to live, but it was the life I chose.

Driving home from my grandmother's house, I realized I had

accepted defeat. In my attempts to fight destiny and question accepted truth, I had let defeat take hold of me. It didn't do it blatantly, but instead crept up from the back of my mind to the front. I looked in my rear view mirror and told myself it wouldn't be that way. I was going to save my grandmother. No one was going to stop that. Otherwise, the whole trip back in time was a waste.

No one was home when I got there and I was thankful for that. I took the bowl, and brought it to my room. I stowed it in my closet for the time being, figuring it would be safe there until I decided what I was going to do with it. With the evidence in a good place, all I could do right then was wait. Running to the hospital wasn't a good idea for several reasons. Alan would be there, and there was a good chance I would confront him about what I suspected him of. On top of that, my mother would notice that I didn't look sick, and I didn't want to incur her wrath. Home was the safest place to be, so I sat down on the couch, flipped on the television, and waited.

Much to my disappointment, I had fallen asleep. In the middle of my most important mission, I had snoozed on the job. The phone woke me up.

"Hello," I said, in a groggy voice.

"Darren, you sound like hell," my father said. At least I succeeded in sounding sick.

"I just fell asleep is all," I said.

"I called about Nan." Dad didn't sound good.

"How is she?"

"We don't know, Darren. She's had an adverse reaction to something. The doctors are running tests, but her condition is worsening."

"Is she going to be okay?"

"It's tough to tell. What I want to know is, how did you do it?"

"What Dad?"

"Darren, you pretty much pinpointed the whole situation. How did you know?"

"I told you, it was a dream."

"Sure it was."

"I'm not lying. It was a dream." Okay, so I lied to my father. It wasn't like I could tell him the truth. He would have me committed in seconds.

"Well, that must have been one hell of a dream, kid. Like I said, we're not sure what's going to happen, but if she pulls through this, it will be because of you."

"She'll be fine," I said, not knowing why those words came out of my mouth. My instincts told me the exact opposite.

"Darren," my father said.

"Yeah?"

"I'm sorry."

"For what?"

"For giving you such a hard time last night. You were right all along."

"Are you ready to believe me about the whole thing?"

"What are you talking about? There's something else?"

"Alan."

"Don't start that again, Darren."

"Dad, in the dream, it was Alan that caused the whole thing. How is he acting?"

"He's nervous. His wife is dying."

"Dying?"

"Alright. Nan's not doing well at all Darren. I didn't want to upset you, especially after you tried so hard to prevent what is happening."

"Dad, he has something to do with it. I know it for a fact."

"Son, I don't know why you think that. I just don't see it as possible."

"And if I had evidence?"

"What sort of evidence?"

Could I tell my father about it? Could I put my cards on the table and play out the hand? That I wasn't sure of, so I decided to play it right down the middle.

"There'll be something in your closet, something I want you to send to a lab. Have it checked for whatever it is that is affecting Nan right now."

"Darren, what are you talking about?"

"Just remember what I said. I might not."

"What?"

"Your closet. The thing that doesn't belong there. That's all you need to know."

"Okay."

"Now, tell me the truth Dad, I can handle it. Does Nan have a chance?"

My father sighed. "No, I doubt it. I'm sorry, Darren." I could hear that my father was crying, but he did his best to hide it. I didn't cry. I didn't feel a thing. I felt no different than if someone had just said a complete stranger had passed away. I had been through this pain before, the pain of losing my grandmother and watching my mother go through a guilt-laden grief that changed her forever. Sure, it was nice to be back in the past, but someone was sending me a message that I didn't belong there. I couldn't change the baseball game, I couldn't prevent my sister from dating the asshole she loved, and though I had done everything in my power, I couldn't prevent the death of my grandmother. She had gotten to the hospital almost twelve hours earlier than she originally had, but it didn't make a difference. She was going to die. And I needed to go home.

"I'm sorry too, Dad. How's Mom?"

"Angry, confused, shocked. I really don't think she knows what she is feeling now. We knew this day would come, but it isn't like you can really prepare for it. Your mother's strong, stronger than anyone I know . . ."

"I understand Dad. Should I come there?"

"No, your mother would kill me if she knew I told you the truth. She doesn't want to say anything until we know something for sure." I knew that meant my mother didn't want to say anything until my grandmother passed away. I belonged at the hospital, but I hadn't been there the first time around. We were left in the dark until the very end.

"Okay."

"Just stay there and wait for us to call, okay?"

"Sure Dad."

I hung up the phone and just stared off into space. This whole trip back was nothing but a futile exercise. I don't think there was a person in the world who wouldn't have seized the opportunity, but I had regretted it. I couldn't relate to my friends, I couldn't prevent tragedies, and all the things I had previously enjoyed did nothing for me. The problem was, although I was living in a seventeen-year-old body, I had an adult mind. To get the most out of youth, you have to have a young mind. I don't mean that you have to think young, but rather, that experiences have to be new to you. It's like replaying a computer game. Sure, you might do better the second time around, avoiding the pitfalls you had succumbed to the first time, but the whole experience turns out to be flat. You've seen it all before, and it has lost its freshness, the very essence that made it exciting the first time.

It had been over two days. When Jason sent me back, he had told me it would be for what would seem like a day or two, and I expected to be brought back immediately. Yet, I had this nagging feeling that wasn't going to happen. In my opinion, I had already been back for too long. Jason was monitoring me, or at least he said he was, and he must have sensed that it was time for me to go back. That wasn't happening. I tried to think of ways that I could force it, that I could make myself go back to the present. One way was to put myself in a dire situation, where my life was threatened, but I really didn't want to take that chance.

It was after three, and I figured Rich was home. He wouldn't be too happy with me for leaving him waiting during lunch, and I knew I owed him an explanation for that. I got in my car and headed over to his house, the whole ride there wondering what would happen if I was brought back while driving. The more I tried not to think about it, the more images came to my mind.

"Your grandmother's in the hospital?" Rich asked, his voice rapidly losing the annoyed tone it previously had.

"Yeah, so you see why I had to leave."

"Of course, man, of course. You okay?"

"Yeah, I'm fine."

"You don't look fine. You've got something going on in that head of yours. I can see it."

"Relax Rich, I'm fine."

"You haven't been good since yesterday, since the baseball game."

"Don't worry about it. Hey, listen, can you do me a favor?"

"Anything."

"Keep me away from Tanya, will you?"

"What are you talking about? You're not afraid of Havliceck, are you?"

"Has nothing to do with that. You know, it's just that I find her tough to resist sometimes. Maybe if you keep nagging me about it, if you keep telling me how much of a mistake it would be if we got together, it might help, you know?"

"That's a strange request."

"I know, but can you do it?"

"No sweat, Brett."

"I appreciate it."

"You heading over to the hospital now?"

"No." I wasn't sure if I was going to the hospital or not. The more I thought about it, the more I realized the only way I would find out if anything changed was to be in the center of the action. My parents didn't want me there. Though I didn't really want to go against their wishes, I didn't see that I had much of a choice.

"Where are you going?"

"I have a couple of things to take care of, then I have a little trip to make." The trip, of course, was my expected return to the present. It was starting to bother me that it hadn't happened yet.

"You want company?"

"No, I'll be alright."

"You sure?"

"Yeah."

"Good, because I felt like catching a nap anyway."

"You do that. I'll see you tomorrow."

"Hey man, I hope everything's alright with your grandma."

Despite the fact that I knew everything wasn't alright, I said, "Yeah, me too."

I left Rich's house, and just started driving. I looked around the inside of my car, finding some old cassettes I hadn't seen in years, along with papers and various other things you would expect to find in a teenager's car. I opened the glove box, and something silver fell out. Taking care not to look away from the road too long, I bent down to pick it up. It was my high school ring. I hadn't seen it in seventeen years. I never knew what happened to it. Sometime in June, I would get into a car accident, and I realized right then that one of the guys at the auto body shop must have found it in the glove compartment and decided he needed it more than I did. I had thought it was lost way before that, never thinking to look through my glove box. I took the ring and put it in my jeans pocket. Even if I would lose it some other way, at least the bastard at the body shop wasn't going to get his sticky fingers on it.

I wanted to go to the hospital. I wanted to be there, to see firsthand what really was happening. My parents would filter the story to save us kids the grief, but I wasn't going to find out anything that way. Even if I couldn't save my grandmother, I had to at least find out for sure how she died, and driving around Long Island wasn't going to bring me to any answers. All of my answers were in South Nassau Hospital, in Oceanside, only ten minutes away. I stomped on the gas pedal, and raced over to the hospital, not caring about getting into an accident, killing someone, or killing myself for that matter.

I pulled into the emergency room parking lot, and the attendant put a hand up when I got out of the car.

"This is Emergency Room parking only," the short, white-haired man said to me.

"Yeah, well I just want to take a quick run into Taco Bell. I'll only be a minute." A lot of people tried to use the ER parking lot for the Taco Bell across the street. Yes, people are sick.

"You can't park there son."

"My grandmother is in there. I'm going in."

The old man looked confused, as if he wasn't sure whether I was going to Taco Bell or if I was really going into the emergency room. "Um."

"You want to come in with me?"

"Go ahead, son. If I find out that you are using this parking lot illegally, I'll have the car towed."

I tried to imagine how a parking lot could be used illegally, but I didn't worry, because if there was such a way, I wasn't doing it.

I walked into the ER, a brightly lit room with long benches filled with people suffering from a variety of maladies. One person stood out, a middle-aged woman with a red wig who was holding her stomach. If someone's face could actually turn green, this lady's was about to do it. I didn't want to be in that room when she erupted. It wasn't going to be pretty, but at least she would move herself up the priority list.

"Can I help you?" a young nurse said from behind the window to my left.

"My grandmother came into the hospital today. I'm not sure if she came through the emergency room or not."

"What's her name?"

It actually took me a second to remember my grandmother's first name. I never used it.

"Anne Swenson," I said.

290

The nurse looked at her clipboard, running her finger down the list of names. Hospitals do good business, that much I can tell you.

"She was admitted through the ER, but has been moved to ICU."

"Where's that?"

The nurse gave me a look like she wasn't going to tell me.

"I'll find it myself," I said.

"Young man," the nurse called out, but I didn't hear the rest of what she said because I was already through the double doors leading to the main part of the hospital.

I've read many times about the sterile and sanitary smell of a hospital. Every book, magazine article and newspaper report I read about hospitals made mention of this. The one thing they leave out, and the one thing that I always detect when I am in a hospital, is the reek of both urine and sickness. The sanitary and sterile smells that are always mentioned are nothing more than a cover for this other, more prominent odors. South Nassau was a good hospital. I knew that because my father had chosen to send my grandmother there, and he knew hospitals pretty well. The stench was bad in the hallways of the building, though they did dissipate a bit when I made it to the main lobby, the spot where the lesser friends and relatives wait to hear information on their loved one's condition. Lacking the status to stay in the waiting room on the appropriate floor, these people sat and stared out the window in the main lobby, sipping coffee, and, to my amazement, smoked cigarettes. Smoking laws hadn't been put into full effect. I figured the upper floors, where the sick were held lick prisoners of life, banned smoking but it was allowed in the main lobby.

I walked past the large desk in the center of the room, where two nurses sat, one on the phone, the other working on some sort of paperwork. I thought about asking where the ICU was, but I figured I would be denied such information.

"Can I help you?" the one with the paperwork asked. She looked vaguely familiar. In a sense, it was like a dream, where a face from someone I knew was planted on a person in a dream. I knew I recognized the face, and realized that it was my third grade religion teacher. I decided not to stick around long enough to see if I recognized the name on the tag she was wearing.

"I know where I'm going, thanks," I said, picking up the pace.

The gift shop was empty, and the man in there was busy reading the newspaper. I didn't think flowers were a good idea, only because I wasn't sure of my grandmother's status. I moved past the gift shop, bumping into a few people along the way, and found the sign that listed every area of the hospital. The ICU was on the second floor; the same floor as the geriatric ward. How convenient. Just above that, I noticed, was the nursery. Hell on the bottom, Heaven on top. I wondered if someone consciously made it that way, or if it was just a coincidence. There are no coincidences, I said to myself, opening the doors to the staircase and making my way up to Hell, if that was possible.

If I had thought I received a good dose of bad odor on the main floor, the geriatric ward delivered a heroic one. There was the urine smell I mentioned, the sick smell, and the one smell that to this day I cannot quite understand. It is a smell that comes over the elderly. To my nose, it smells almost like the decay of a living body. When I was younger, the smell was more concentrated, and I, like every other kid I imagine, labeled it as "old people smell." Being older, not nearly as cruel, and moving toward possessing that smell at a rate more rapid than I would prefer, I understood that the smell was just a part of growing older. Like the person who has ten cats and can't smell them or the kitty litter box that desperately needs cleaning. Old people are unaware of their scent. It almost smells like mothballs. Maybe old people have something with mothballs, I don't know. Maybe mothballs are made from old people. Okay, enough of that.

I walked through the hallway of the geriatric ward, randomly taking a look into the rooms as I passed. This was no way to go, I thought, catching a glimpse of an old man hooked up to machines. He must have weighed no more than ninety pounds and probably had to be fed, taken to the bathroom, and bathed. Was that any sort of existence? Though I had been appalled by the euthanasia doctors I had seen on TV, I knew right then that if I was lying there where that man was, and I had my wits about me, I'd be asking for the needle.

At the end of the hallway was a pair of doors with a sign that indicated the ICU was behind them. Along with that sign was another one which stated only spouses and direct relatives were allowed entry. Figuring that a grandson was a direct relative, I walked through the doors, and was greeted by a desk with three nurses sitting behind it. There were beds on either side of the desk, running down the length of the room. Some had the curtains drawn, and some didn't. I didn't want to look at anyone lying in those beds, for fear that I would see something to make my stomach turn. There were a variety of beeps sounding throughout the place, along with the sounds of breathing machines.

"Yes?" the nurse in the center asked. The other two stared at me, like I was trying to rob the place or something.

"Anne Swenson?"

"Excuse me?"

"I'd like to know where Anne Swenson is located, ma'am."

"I'm sorry, but you can't come in here. Only spouses and direct relatives . . ."

"If the sign outside didn't stop me, what makes you think your telling me will?"

"Sir, I cannot let you in."

"Just tell me where she is," I said, my voice growing louder.

"I'm sorry, but . . ."

"Darren!" I heard my father say from behind me. I turned, and saw him standing by the doorway, his arms folded in the manner of someone who wasn't exactly thrilled to see me.

"Dad."

"Come with me," he said, walking through the doors. I followed, and we stopped in front of a door that said "ICU Waiting Room." I had missed that one on the way in. "What are you doing here?"

"I wanted to be here, to see what was going on."

"You have no business being here."

"No business? She's my grandmother, for Christ's sake."

"Your mother and I told you to stay home and wait to hear from us."

"I know you did, but I had to come here."

My father looked at me, then started to say something which I assume would have been some sort of scolding, but stopped. He inhaled and exhaled loudly, then reached to put his hand on my shoulder. "I'm sorry. This is just very hard on all of us. I guess it's hit you pretty hard too, with the dream and all."

"How is she?"

My father didn't say anything, but instead just opened the door to the waiting room. I walked in and saw my mother sitting next to my uncle, both of them holding each other, crying. I realized why my father didn't say anything. He didn't have to.

"Darren, what are you doing here?" my mother asked through tears.

"I just wanted to be here, Mom."

She reached out her hand and I took it. She pulled me down to sit next to her. She leaned over and hugged me, crying even harder. "I know you tried Darren. I know you did."

I was totally confused. Even though I had tried my best to circumvent the past, I had been unsuccessful. My grandmother made it to the hospital hours earlier, and though I had changed that, she had died anyway. No one had said that yet, but I knew it. And she had died earlier. Could that be considered a change? What would be the effects of this change on the present?

"When were you going to tell us?" I asked my father.

"We were going to wait until tonight, when your sister got home from work. We wanted to tell the two of you together."

That made sense. I had found out the first time right after my sister returned from work. Had this been the way it happened originally? Perhaps the events I was witnessing were no different than the original ones, other than the fact that I had been there to see them. If that was the case, then I had no control over the events from the past, and all I could do was experience the pain all over again. I didn't want that.

All of a sudden, something strange happened. I felt someone grab my left arm, but no one in the room had done it. I felt a sharp pain, then my eyes glazed over. For a second, I saw the inside of the room Jason and I had been in, but it was only for a fleeting second. I shook my head, and focused, seeing the ICU waiting room again.

"You okay?" my father asked.

"Yeah, just a little lightheaded is all."

"You should be home and in bed," my mother told me.

"I know."

The door to the waiting room opened, and Alan walked in, holding two cups of coffee. He handed one to my father, then looked at me.

"Darren, when did you get here?"

I lost control. I think it was from the frustration of having to relive this painful period in my life, coupled with the suspicions I had about Alan. I bolted from my chair and grabbed him by the lapel of his jacket.

"You son of a bitch. You did this to her," I said, thrusting him against the wall.

"Darren, what are you doing?" my father yelled.

I didn't reply, but instead just looked into Alan's eyes, which were filled with rage.

"Get off me," he said, trying to push me away with his free hand. I wasn't going anywhere.

"Tell them. Tell them what you did."

"I didn't do anything."

"Bullshit!" I went for his throat. I can't say for sure, but I think I was going to kill him. Looking in his eyes right then, I knew he was guilty. I knew the truth. One thing I'm good at is reading people, and Alan's eyes told me all I needed to know.

I felt two firm hands grab me from behind and pull me to the floor. On the way down, my lip hit the armrest of one of the chairs, and I felt my tooth crack. I ran my tongue across it, and felt a small piece missing.

Both my father and my uncle had a hold of me, and I tried to force myself up.

"He did it. He's the one," I said.

"Stop it Darren. Stop this now," my father said.

"He did it."

"He didn't do anything. You're just making this worse for everyone."

Because both my uncle and my father were a bit off balance, having to bend over to hold me down to the floor, I was able to slip their grasp and get up. My father put both of his hands on my chest, to stop me from going after Alan again.

"You might have them fooled," I said to Alan, "but I know the truth. Just remember that. You won't get away with this." I forced my way past my father and my uncle, and shoved the waiting room door open. I heard my father come after me.

"What the hell is the matter with you?" he asked.

"Forget it Dad. Just remember what I told you on the phone."

"Nan died of congestive heart failure. There was no poisoning Darren. You were wrong."

I couldn't accept that. Maybe that was the effect of what Alan had done, but he certainly had something to do with it.

"Yeah, that's what they told you."

"I'm a doctor Darren. I'd know if anything else happened."

"Whatever," I said, walking away from him and down the hall.

"Come back here," my father yelled after me.

"If I do, I'll kill him," I said, opening the door to the staircase and making my way down to the main floor.

Chapter 21

All I had created was a mess. What was supposed to be a quick trip to the past to change the outcome of an unimportant baseball game had turned into a disaster. My efforts meant nothing. All the tragedies from the past would just repeat themselves, and if I didn't get back to the present soon, I would have to relive all of them. Just seeing my mother grief-stricken again had brought all the rage I had in me up to the surface. I couldn't imagine having to see any more than that.

On top of not being able to change my past, I was making my future life more miserable. My parents must have thought I had gone crazy, and they would want explanations for what I had done. Also, I would have to go to the wake and funeral and see Alan again, and I couldn't be sure that I wouldn't make another scene. I had made it to the age of 34 successfully the first time around, with few problems. The way I was going, I couldn't guarantee that would happen again. I needed to get out, to get back to the present.

Driving on the Southern State Parkway toward home, I figured out a way I could do that. If Jason's research had been based on a Quantum computer created in 1979, then the existence of that computer was what made it possible for me to be sent back. If that computer were to be destroyed, well, then, maybe I would never have been given the opportunity to go back in the first place. This way, all the actions that I took, all the disasters I created, would be erased, and I would go back to living the life I had thought was so horrible. I had originally thought going back in time would make my life better, even in the smallest way, but I realized I was wrong about that. All you can do when you relive your past is make life worse for yourself. If anyone ever offers you the opportunity, don't take it.

I knew I was crazy for trying what I had in mind, but I really had no other choice. For some reason, Jason wasn't bringing me back, and I had to try not to think that maybe I was trapped. Jason might have been experiencing problems in the present, and even if he tried to bring me back, he might not have been able to. The last thing I wanted to do was live another day of this past life.

I went home first, because I figured I should be as well equipped as possible for this crazy adventure. In my room, I gathered whatever money I had, which was about thirty dollars, and stuffed it into my pocket. I took the high school ring out of my pocket and put it in a jewelry box I had gotten when I was five. I then took the small pocketknife I had in there and put it in the back pocket of my pants.

In the bottom of my closet, I found the bowl I had taken from my grandmother's house. Beginning to doubt my theory about Alan and the poisoning, I took it into the kitchen and threw it in the garbage pail. My grandmother was dead, and I knew my father wasn't going to do anything about what I had told him. My actions at the hospital made me seem crazy, and therefore any ideas I had were crazy as well. None of it mattered anyway, if my theory about destroying that computer would work. All the actions I had taken in this past experience would be wiped clean, and I expected to wake up in the bedroom of my apartment, like nothing ever happened.

It would all just be a bad dream.

I went into the hall closet and found the shotgun my father kept there. I wasn't sure if I would need it, but from experience I knew it was better to have a weapon and not need it than need one and not have it. I found the shells on the top shelf of the closet and threw a few into my pocket. I took six more and loaded them into the shotgun. I made sure the safety was engaged, and ran outside to put the weapon in my trunk.

Now loaded up and ready for adventure, I decided it was time to head into the city. It was about seven o'clock when I got onto the parkway again, and the sky was almost completely dark, the last edge of the sun barely visible ahead of me. I drove slowly now, not wanting to get pulled over with a loaded shotgun in the trunk. I needed to carry out this whole operation cleanly, to ensure that I got my hands on the computer and destroyed it.

* * *

It had taken about an hour and a half to make it to the Scitech building. It looked different, without the mirrored windows and other enhancements that would come over the next seventeen years. I found a parking spot across the street. I think it was the same one I parked the Taurus in when I met Jason. I sat in my car for about five minutes, my hands trembling on the steering wheel. I knew I was about to break the law, something I really had never done in my entire life, and I hoped I would be able to get away with it. In the back of my mind, I was certain that the destruction of the computer would wipe all of this clean, but if I wasn't successful in doing that. Well, I didn't want to think about that.

I walked into the building, seeing a man sitting at a different desk located in the same spot like the other one had been in the present. The inside looked old, with worn white tiles on the floor and tan paint on the walls. The whole inside looked completely non-descript, like some ordinary building that houses business offices and the like. No one would ever expect a company like Scitech to be housed there.

"Building's closed," the man said from behind the counter. He looked vaguely like the original security guard, only younger.

"What floor is Scitech on?" I asked.

"Thirtieth, but you can't go up there."

"I figured that. I just wanted to know where it was."

I stole a glance behind the desk, noticing there were no security cameras or any of the other gadgets that had been there on my first visit.

"Something I can help you with?"

"I write for a school newspaper, and I wanted to do a story on Scitech for our science section. Is there someone I could contact?"

The man looked me over for a second, and when he seemed content that I posed no threat, he smiled. "You could try calling Dr. Michael Newbury. He's the head of the company. I don't know if they allow students or anyone else up there, but you could give it a try." The guard handed me a business card, which just read "222 61st Street."

"Is this his number?"

"That's the number to the main switchboard. Whoever is sitting at this desk will answer. I'm not allowed to give out any of the tenants' numbers, but someone here can relay a message to Dr. Newbury, and then he can make a decision about seeing you."

Okay," I said, putting the business card in the breast pocket of my shirt. "Thanks."

"No problem."

I walked out of the building. I figured I would kill some time and come back later at night. I didn't see any alarms on the front doors, and even if there were some at the Scitech area, I didn't doubt I could bypass the old technology. I left my car parked across the street and decided to kill some time in the city before I did my break and entering job, my second of the day.

* * *

Walking around the city wasn't something I ever enjoyed. Even at almost nine o'clock, the streets were crowded with a mix of business people, tourists, and the dregs of society. There were Three Card Monty tables on almost every corner, this being a time before the city cracked down on those thieves. There were also tons of street vendors, hawking a wide variety of what I figured were stolen goods. This was the New York City that had gotten the reputation of being a dangerous, smutty place full of crime. The Three Card Monty tables were crowded, with a circle of people surrounding them, watching the next sucker lose his or her money. Why anyone would think they had a chance at such a game was beyond me, but money removes people of their common sense.

I walked past each table, hearing the cheers and yells of the crowds. People were mesmerized, and I would guess a good percentage of them had their wallets stolen while they were watching someone else lose their money. I kept my hands in my pockets, holding onto the small amount of money I had, not wanting to be victimized myself. I was probably perceived as an easy target, a wide-eyed, middle-class Long Island boy taking a tour of the city.

By the time I made it to the forties, the atmosphere had gotten worse. Times Square, in 2001, was a bustling commercial area boasting Disney stores and theme restaurants. Back in the eighties, it was the center of every sort of adult entertainment, ranging from pornography to prostitution to drugs. Several men, most of them appearing to be homeless, walked up to me and casually asked me if I wanted to buy drugs, a fake ID, or if I wanted the company of a hot woman. I knew that everyone of them had nothing to offer. All they did was ask for the money up front and then run in the next direction. I knew this because Rich and I had that exact experience when we were eighteen. We had come to the city to become men, and when a Spanish guy in a Yankee cap came up to us offering exactly that, we eagerly forked our money over. He told us to wait outside some seedy hotel while he "got the girls ready" and never returned. I figured he walked in one entrance of the hotel and walked out the other, counting our sixty bucks as he did so. We searched the streets for two hours before finally giving up. We actually thought we were going to find him and beat the shit out of him. We were lucky we didn't get killed.

I walked as fast as I could through this section of the city, making my way toward Broadway, where the atmosphere was more affected by the playhouses than the cathouses. On the corner of Broadway, I found the Automat, a self-service restaurant from the fifties where you went up to a wall of windows, inserted your money, and got yourself a sandwich. I had always wanted to go in there when I was younger, and though my father let me take a peek inside one time, he would never eat there, saying the food was disgusting.

I bought myself a roast beef sandwich and a can of Coke, and sat down at a table by the window, eating and watching all of the cars rush by. I saw a few Checker cabs, which had gone out of service in the nineties, and sat there, amazed at this crazy, horrible, mind-boggling experience I had gotten myself into. Even though it had ended in disaster, part of me wanted to see the things that were no longer around in my present.

* * *

I made my way back to the Scitech building sometime around 2AM. I had killed time in the Automat, just sitting at the table and thinking out my plan, and then I had caught a late movie at the theater on Broadway. They were playing *Return of the Jedi*, one of my all time favorite movies. I was surprised they were still playing it. Before the movie, I had called the number on the business card the security guard had given me. There was no answer, so I was confident no one

301

would be there when I attempted my theft.

I had seen the movie a million times, but I got into it again, getting into the theatre experience. I had seen the re-release of the Star Wars movies, with all the extra effects, but I had a hard time noticing a difference between the original and the newer version. In all, I enjoyed seeing the movie in the theater, and I had forgotten about most of my troubles while in there.

What struck me the most was how I wasn't upset over my grandmother's death. I had been devastated the first time around, but this time, it was expected. I felt no real grief whatsoever, other than the regret of not being able to save her. I guess I believed in the back of my mind that I couldn't do that, and had accepted it without even realizing. The only thing that really upset me was seeing my mother so depressed, and not being able to pin anything on Alan. I had seen the guilt in his eyes, and I was somewhat content about that.

The front of the building was dark, and when I peered through the glass door, I saw that no one was inside. For a moment I thought I was headed on a wild goose chase, that a computer of such importance would be protected by high-level security, but I remembered that Jason had told me Scitech operated covertly, and that few people knew what they were really working on. That made me wonder how Jason would know what they were up to. I answered my own question, figuring that he had inside knowledge through his work with the government and the university.

Standing outside the building, I took some time to think about the whole situation with Jason. I hadn't really thought about that in a while, and if things went well, I would be right smack in the middle of that situation real soon. If the president of the university was the one to blame for all the trouble, things would be pretty easy to solve. Hovelle was another puzzling element. Before I took my little time trip, I hadn't gotten enough information to know if he worked for the government or not. If he didn't, then I had to figure he was working with the university president. If he did, then there was a good chance things were going to get a lot worse before they got better. I had Rich on the case back in the present, and I had my other PI friend working on Lowenstein, the university president. Between the two of them, I would have all the answers I needed. I had no idea how much time would have passed when I made it back to the present, and I didn't know what actions I had taken on Jason's behalf would be affected by the destruction of the computer. Most of this was too scientific for my mind to really comprehend, and I removed it from my mind because thinking about it wasn't doing me any good. Whatever was going to happen would, and I'd deal with all of it once I got back.

The door to the building had a simple lock, one that I easily picked with my pocketknife. Swiss Army knives are the most useful creations man ever came up with. I had gotten one of the large ones, with every contraption made, for my sixteenth birthday. My sister got a sweet sixteen party. I got a Swiss Army knife. No, I didn't want a sweet sixteen myself, but I wouldn't have minded my parents throwing a little bit of the cash they would have spent on such a party my way. They'd later pay for my sister's wedding as well, so there is much truth to the idea that girls are more expensive to have than boys. If I ever get married and decide to have kids, I'm stomping on any girls that come out of my wife's womb until we get it right. Easy for me to say, I know.

The door opened with a click, and though I had inspected it several times looking for some sort of alarm, I expected to hear something when the door opened. Nothing happened, so I moved inside and took a deep breath. Committing grand larceny wasn't as exciting as I thought it would be. It was just nerve-wracking.

I didn't want to risk taking the elevator. I didn't know if the electrical system was working, and God only knew what would happen if I tried to use the thing anyway. Besides that, it looked old, and I wasn't a big fan of old elevators. With the prospect of climbing 30 flights of stairs ahead of me, I paused for a moment, built up as much energy as I could muster, and made my way up.

I was an idiot for thinking I could climb that many stairs. Sure, I was in a seventeen-year-old body, but even for someone that young, 30 flights is about ten too many. By the time I hit the fifteenth floor, I was panting, and my legs were cramping up. The only thing that kept me going was the fear of failure, that I would get caught breaking into the building because I passed out in the stairwell. I continued, slowing my pace a little to conserve energy, and made my way to the 30th floor.

When I opened the stair door, I saw the hallway I had been in the first time. Everything looked almost exactly the same, except the writing on the door was different. I went up to the door that Jason and I had entered, and was surprised to find it was open. The lights were off in the room, but I saw some light creeping in from another room. My heart stopped. For some reason, I didn't feel alone. Someone was in the other room. What the hell they were doing there at 2AM was beyond me. I stood in the room for a moment, trying to formulate some sort of plan to get what I needed and get out undetected. Those plans crumbled when I realized that the room which was occupied was the one Jason had taken me into. That meant the computer sat in that room as well.

Before I could even come up with some deranged scheme, the other door opened, and I saw a tall thin man standing in the doorway. He didn't notice me at first, but then jumped when he saw me.

"Jesus Christ, you scared the shit out of me," he said, in a deep voice. "Who are you?"

"Just an interested party," I said, slowly moving toward him. The room was dark, but I did notice a phone sitting at the other end. I put myself between the scientist and the phone, so that he couldn't make a dash for it when he realized I came to steal.

"Interested party? At two in the morning?"

"Yeah. I understand you have a Quantum computer prototype in there."

The guy looked back into the room he had just come from and looked back at me.

"Who told you that?"

"It doesn't matter."

"I should call the police," he said, flicking on the lights. In the better light, I saw that he was scrawny, and wouldn't offer any real resistance.

"There's no need for that. I just want to see it."

"Are you out of your mind? I can't let you do that. Why don't you just turn around and leave, and I'll pretend this never happened, okay?"

"It's not going to happen that way. You see, I need that computer, and the only thing standing in the way of it is you. Now, you can either step aside and let me do what I have to, or I can knock you aside. It's your choice."

The guy eyed me, probably taking note of the fact I was a teenager. "If this is some sort of a prank, you're making a big mistake. I told you to leave and I suggest you do that right now." He made a mistake. His eyes darted toward the telephone, and I knew it was my chance to strike. I lunged at him, swinging a hard right hand that landed squarely on his chin and knocking him through the open door and into the next room. He was shaking his head and rubbing his jaw when I made it to him. I grabbed him by his long hair and bashed his head against the floor a few times until he lost consciousness. I felt bad having to hurt him, but he hadn't given me much of a choice. Luckily for him, he passed out easily. He would probably only wake up with a small concussion.

I looked around the room, and saw three computers in there. Two of them were in the back of the room, but the other one, which had several wires going in and out of it, was on a counter in the center of the room. I was certain it was the right one, the one I had come for, and was further convinced when I saw a pile of notes and spreadsheets sitting next to it. I ripped the wires out of the computer, and lifted it up, slinging it under my arm. It was extremely heavy, but I figured I would be able to make it down the stairs with it. I just had to hope that I could get out of the building quick enough.

I was near collapse when I made it out the front door of the building. My legs felt like they were going to fall off, and my heart was beating at an alarming rate. I tried to breathe deeply to calm myself, but that didn't work. Even if it had, that effect wouldn't have lasted too long. Before I even made it across the street to my car, I heard loud sirens coming in my direction. The scientist must have regained consciousness and called the police. I cursed myself for not disabling the phone to buy some time. I ran across the street, fumbled with my keys, opened the door, and threw the computer in the back seat. I thought about opening the trunk and taking the shotgun, but I figured that would only incite the police if they happened to catch a glimpse of it. It was good that I didn't. Before I even got myself planted in the drivers seat, two cop cars came around the corner and approached the car. I hopped in, started the engine, and pulled away quickly. Ever the quick observers, the two cars decided to follow.

So, that's how I ended up in a high-speed car chase with the NYPD. I probably could have avoided the chase if I had planned my theft a little better, but I hadn't expected to have company. Life doesn't always work out the way you expect it I guess.

There I was, sliding sideways in my car, headed toward the water at the South Street Seaport, wondering if my plummet into the water would destroy the computer and produce the desired effect of sending me back to the present. I saw the rapid approach of the edge of the dock, heard the police cars skid to a stop, and closed my eyes. Time stopped for a second, and I don't mean figuratively. I felt something stir inside me, and I thought I was going to die. I didn't feel the impact I expected, which scared me. Then, I saw the white light that everyone talks about when you die.

Chapter 22

"Jesus, you had me scared for awhile there," I heard Jason say. I opened my eyes, and I was back in the room where Jason had sent me back in time. I wasn't in the machine anymore, but instead lying on a padded bench. I felt dizzy, like I was going to throw up. I dry heaved. "You're going to feel a bit disoriented for a moment."

"What the fuck?" I said, as those were the only words I was capable of saying.

"You had some wild trip," Jason said, standing over me. "You okay?"

"Yeah. Why did you take so long to get me out of there?"

"I tried earlier. You wouldn't come to."

That would explain what I felt in the ICU waiting room.

"How long was I under for?"

"Nine hours."

"Nine hours? That's it?"

"That's it. What it felt like was two or three days for you, right?"

I tried to remember the events from the past, but they were slipping from me as if I had just awakened from a dream. I concentrated on remembering as much as I could, and they slowly came back.

"Yeah, something like that."

"Well, it was a success."

I didn't need Jason to tell me that. I had just experienced the whole thing firsthand.

"Everything go the way you expected it?"

"Not exactly, but I got all the data I needed. Thanks again for volunteering."

"Right," I said, trying to stand up. I felt even dizzier, and lied back down.

"Take it slow. Your mind has been through a bit of overloading. So, did it feel real?"

"Of course it did."

"It didn't feel like a dream?"

"Well, it did in the beginning, like you said it would, but then everything felt as real as it does right now. It was amazing, despite the fact that it was depressing."

"Yeah, you picked a strange time to go back to."

"You saw what I was going through?" I asked, amazed that he could do such a thing.

"Not completely, but close enough."

"Did I change anything? Did I have any affect on the present?"

Jason didn't say anything. He just sighed.

"What?"

"It's sort of a long story."

"What the fuck do you mean it's a long story? Tell me."

"Well, let's just say you went back in time, but you didn't."

"What?"

"That wasn't a time machine you were in."

"What was it then?'

"Okay, let me put it to you this way. Your mind actually believed that what you were experiencing was a real event, an experience no different than you talking to me right now. The machine you were hooked up to tapped into your memories, and was able to extract the specific period you were talking about, and along with your mind, was able to create a scenario which you experienced."

"It was fake?" I asked, sitting up and fighting the dizziness. It was almost overwhelming.

"I told you to take it easy," Jason said, putting his hand on my chest to push me back down. I slapped his hand away.

"Get off me," I said. "This was all some sort of a joke? A trick?"

"No, not at all. Something like this has never been done before. My research on time travel was real, but I don't think there'll ever be a way to do that. So, I decided to take what I knew about that, as well as some research on the mind itself, and blend the two. This machine will be able to recreate your past and let you experience it all over again. Of course, I'll have to work out some of the bugs in it."

"Bugs?"

"Yeah. You had a little too much control over what was going on. On top of that, you got violent a few times, and you hurt yourself pretty good. I think you chipped your tooth."

I rolled my tongue over the tooth I had chipped in what I thought was the past, and felt the small chip I felt earlier. Strange.

"All of the stuff I experienced, everything, it was just my mind playing tricks on me?"

"Some of it was, yes. It's tough to tell, but I think your mind changed some things. If something didn't appear the way you remembered it, you could explain it that way. There are gaps in our memories, and even though our mind records every little detail of life we experience, it isn't so easy to access all of it. Your mind went nuts though, and rapidly changed whatever it needed to fit the situation."

The door opened, and Dave Hovelle walked through it. I tensed, expecting a confrontation to ensue.

"How's he doing?" Hovelle asked.

"What the hell is he doing here?" I asked.

"Oh, yeah," Jason said. "It might help if I explained that, huh?"

"You think?"

"Well, it's sort of complicated. Dave's been working with me."

"You son of a bitch. Don't you know what he's done? He killed Aileen, my friend Mike in Ohio, and one of his goons drove my mother off the road on the parkway. You telling me you had a part in all of that?"

"No, not at all," Jason said. "Calm down. It's not like that."

"Then what's it like?"

"If you'd listen to me, I'll tell you."

"Go ahead, and this better be good."

"I originally worked for the federal government, you know that. I was researching Quantum Physics, along with its effects on time travel, as well as what could be done with it in terms of the human mind. I couldn't get anywhere, and decided that working for the government wouldn't get me the information that I needed. I had heard about the University of Cleveland and what they were doing in this field, and figured they would help me reach my goal. All along, I knew we could somehow meld Quantum Physics and human memories, and find a way to go back in time in our minds. The government was more fascinated with Quantum Physics than anything else, and I knew that it, by itself, would do nothing. So I left my job with the government, trust me they weren't happy about that, and decided to work at the university. There, I found what I was looking for, and along with the help of Scitech, we were able to create the prototype you used. Now, the government didn't know about what I was doing at the university, and the university really didn't know anything about the government. No one knew about Scitech. They were the ones that really understood what I was doing, and how this research could be one of the greatest achievements in the world of science."

"I don't get it. What about the murders? What about the government looking for you?"

"The government was never looking for me. The university was, because they thought I had stolen intellectual property."

"Did you?"

Jason looked at Hovelle, then back at me. "Well, I guess they would say I did. I only combined my two types of research to create my own. That's not stealing. It's just finding a better use for it."

"And the murders?"

"I don't know anything about that. Aileen's death seemed like it was gang related. I didn't know anything about your friend until you just mentioned it."

I didn't believe that for a second, but decided not to say anything so I could get as much information out of Jason that I could. I wanted to know who was ultimately responsible for everything.

"What about all that cloak and dagger stuff? You had a gun in Washington. If the feds weren't after you, why were you so afraid?"

"Darren, this development is going to be worth a lot of money. You wouldn't believe how far the university was willing to go to get a hold of me. They felt that any money I made from this should be theirs. I couldn't let that happen. So, I had to hide out for a while."

"What about him?" I asked, pointing toward Hovelle. "What was up with his following me? Why did he have my friend fired?"

"I didn't have anyone fired," Hovelle said.

"Like hell."

"Mr. Hovelle works for Scitech. He used to work for the FBI, and when he retired, he hooked up with the company to do security work.

He tried to help me with the university, set the whole thing up that the government wanted my research. I figured that way, they would think I took off because I was scared, and not because I wanted to keep the money for myself. I'm not really doing that. I probably won't make all that much. I just know that Scitech would put this invention to better use than the university will."

"And you think you're gonna get away with that?"

"Why not? The university doesn't have much of a leg to stand on."

"I have to disagree with you there."

"It doesn't matter. It should all be taken care of. Once Scitech has possession of a working prototype, which they do, and the data necessary to prove it works, which your volunteering supplied."

"You used me?"

"I didn't plan on it. You just happened to come around at the right time."

"Now, Mr. Camponi," Hovelle said, "I know you have a bad impression of me, but I think now you see I was only doing my job."

"Yeah, of course."

"I don't know why Jason felt the need to tell you all of this, but he has, and I have to tell you that everything we have discussed here is confidential. For your time, Scitech would like to offer you a substantial sum of money. In return, we would expect your complete cooperation in keeping this a secret."

"Hush money," I said.

"You can call it what you want. Listen, you can look at it two ways. You can either take the money and buy yourself something nice, or you can try and notify someone and tell them what you know. If you choose that route, you'll be involved in litigation, and your efforts will be futile. Scitech has the resources to win any legal battle with the university, or anyone else who decides to meddle in their business."

I knew the line Hovelle was taking. Even though my original thoughts about who he was and what he was doing were wrong, I still had the feeling his efforts to keep me quiet covered something up underneath. Even if Jason told me the truth, that the government never had anything to do with this, I figured they would be interested in finding out about it. I couldn't even threaten Hovelle and Jason with that. I had to keep it to myself, and pretend like I wanted to play along.

"How much money we talking about?" I asked.

Hovelle smiled, like he had me. I let him believe this. "I don't know, Mr. Camponi. I would venture to say $50,000 would be an appropriate sum."

"Fifty grand? You guys want me to keep quiet for fifty grand while everyone else reaps in the cash? What do you plan to do with that thing anyway?" I asked, pointing toward the machine.

"There are a lot of uses," Jason said, perking up at the question. "First, it could be like a vacation for people. Just think, you'd be able to re-experience events in your past. On top of that, as you helped to prove, people might even be able to change those events, and see what would have happened if they acted differently. Of course, there are a variety of other uses, such as those which would apply to the justice system. If a guy claims he's innocent of a murder, it can be proven either way . . ."

"Don't bore Mr. Camponi with the gory details," Hovelle said. I could tell he didn't want me to know more than I already did.

"Sorry. Well, anyway, you helped prove some amazing things. I particularly liked the way you handled the whole escape thing, destroying the computer and all that. I think that was why I was able to retrieve you when I did."

"Retrieve?"

"Um, you know, bring you back. Wake you up."

"Okay."

"As you can see, this is a very delicate matter. Dr. Caufield here has come up with an extraordinary invention, and if it falls into the wrong hands, or in this case the hands of people who don't deserve it, it would be a great disservice to the public."

"Of course."

"This virtual time machine can do wonders. Of course, you know, it can't really send someone back in time. But it still is invaluable."

"But not valuable enough to give me more than fifty grand," I said.

"That's not up to me. I was only making a guess. I do, however, need your word that you won't tell anyone anything about what happened here tonight, and what you know about Jason and his past. Deal?" Hovelle extended his hand. I shook it firmly.

"Yeah. I don't want to be involved with this anyway. But, if I don't get the money you promised, more money to be exact, I'll come looking for you."

"There's no need to make any threats," Jason said.

I wanted to punch the both of them, but considering my physical condition, it would be all I could do to get up and make my way out of the building.

"It's not a threat. I was just making a statement. One I wouldn't suggest testing."

Hovelle smiled, then nodded. "There'll be no need for any of that. You'll see. You'll be happy with everything."

"I hope so," I said, making my way to my feet.

"I don't think you should be standing up right now."

"I'm fine. Don't worry," I said. "If I'm not needed here anymore, I guess I will be going."

"You can go," Hovelle said, patting me on the back. "Expect someone from the company to be contacting you within the next day or so. And remember, you gave your word that you wouldn't say anything," he said, tapping a tape recorder he had in the breast pocket of his dress shirt.

"Yeah, everything will be fine," I said, and walked out the door.

My head was still spinning violently when I made my way downstairs and into my car. It was almost noon the next day, but my mind had been through so much in those nine hours that it seemed like it had been years since I had been in my car. I thought about everything Jason had said to me, about the whole trip being nothing but an illusion. I didn't think he was lying about that, yet I was still pissed off that it wasn't real. All of the efforts I made during that experience were for nothing, and on top of that, Jason had deceived and used me. I understood he had to lie about it all being real, otherwise the experiment might not have worked. I didn't appreciate the whole cover up about the government. I knew that Hovelle had me over a barrel because he had me on tape, but that was more of a scare tactic than anything else. I knew what I had to do. I had to inform the correct people about what had been done. I knew right then that Lowenstein was innocent, that he only wanted what was rightly his. And, if things went my way, he'd get it.

I picked up my cell phone, which I had inadvertently left in my car, and called my friend Joe, the P.I.

"Joe here," he said,

"Hey," I said. "It's Darren."

"Camponi. What's up?"

"I need to know if you found out anything about Hovelle."

"Damn right I did."

"Well?"

"Well he used to work for the government, but not anymore. He works for a company called Sci- something or other."

"Scitech."

"That's the one."

"Anything else?" I asked.

"Not much. It doesn't look like he left the government on good terms. He had an IRS audit about a year after he left, and though tax evasion charges were filed, they were later dropped."

"Interesting."

"He seems like a shady guy. Travels a lot. All over the country."

That made sense.

"That's great, Joe. I appreciate it."

"The least I could do."

"I'll call you tomorrow," I said.

"Great."

I ended the call, then dialed Rich.

"Yo," Rich said.

"Hey."

"If it isn't the time traveler. You calling me from the past?"

"Stop it."

"What's going on? Did you go back or what?"

"It's a long story."

"That's what you tell me, 'It's a long story?' You gotta tell me more than that."

"I will, but I can't do that today, Ray."

"What?"

"Forget it. You still got the number for the US District Attorney's office?"

"I do." He called off the number, and I jotted it down in my notepad.

"Thanks," I said. "I'll call you later."

"Leaving me hanging as usual."

"Let me ask you a quick question."

"Shoot."

"Do you remember the baseball game against Baldwin in senior year?"

"The one where you struck out to end the game? Of course."

"What did I strike out on, a curve ball or a fastball?"

"Hmm, that's a tough one. It could have been a curveball, but if I were a betting man, I'd say fastball. He had a really good one."

Though this was interesting, I figured Rich's foggy memory was to blame, and not any effect my virtual trip in time had.

"Okay, thanks."

My next call was to Jim, my PI friend who was investigating Lowenstein for me.

"Yeah," he said, answering the phone on the third ring.

"It's Camponi."

"Well, well. I've been waiting for you to call. You back from your trip already?"

"You could say I never went. Find anything for me?"

"I did. Your man, Mr. Lowenstein, or President Lowenstein to be exact, is one honorable citizen. He pays his taxes, donates to charity, and doesn't even have a speeding ticket."

"I figured as much," I mumbled to myself.

"I thought you said you thought he was dirty?"

"Well, guess I was wrong."

"He does have a skeleton or two. The feds seem to have been watching him closely."

"What do you mean?"

"Let's just say I have a friend in the FBI, and this friend, who doesn't exist as far as you know, told me that the feds have been watching that university closely. He didn't tell me what exactly, but it has something to do with science. What would the government care about a couple of beakers and a Bunsen Burner?"

"A lot," I said.

"Wanna tell me about that?"

"Now's not the time. You know where he is right now?"

"He's at his summer home in Vermont, I would figure. Took a bit finding that. He has it under his wife's name."

"Thanks. You got a number for that?"

"Yep." I wrote this number down on the same page as the US Attorney's office.

"Thanks again. I owe you dinner."

"You owe me more than that."

"Drinks too?"

"Deal."

* * *

I got home, happy to be back in a safe place. I was mentally and physically exhausted, but I knew I wasn't going to get any sleep. My mind was racing, trying to fight off the effects of the experiment as well as to find answers to my current situation. I thought it was interesting that the government was investigating the university, but I figured that was because of Jason. Amidst the little fairy tale he had created lied some truth, though he probably had no idea about it. It seemed that no one knew about Scitech, but that was going to change.

I walked into my living room and sat down on the couch. I stared about the room, amazed that everything was as I left it. I felt like I wasn't even there, that I was dreaming this experience as well. Maybe I was still on the table in the Scitech office, the effects of the anesthesia Jason gave me still not worn off. I shrugged that thought off, got up, and grabbed my cordless phone. I had a friend who worked for the FBI, and even though he only did office work, I figured he could lead me in the right direction. I called him, told him about how I needed information on an investigation into the university, and he patched me over to someone in the Cleveland office who was working on it.

"Agent McCarty," a woman said.

"Hello, my name is Darren Camponi, and I'm a private investigator in New York."

"Yes," she replied in a tone that told me she had no idea why a private investigator from New York would be calling her.

"I understand you are working on an investigation into the University of Ohio at Cleveland."

"I am not at liberty to discuss that."

"I have information for you."

"You'll have to follow the proper procedures. Why don't you visit your local FBI office . . ."

"There's no time for that. I'll tell you what, I'll start saying what I know, and when I'm wrong, you tell me, and we'll end this conversation."

316

"This is highly irregular," she said.

"Just listen. I know that the government is investigating the university in relation to Dr. Jason Caufield, a former employee of the government."

I paused and Agent McCarty didn't say anything which meant I was right.

"This investigation deals with the improper use of research data, and the possible theft of intellectual property from the government."

Again, nothing was said.

"I'm telling you now that you are investigating the wrong people."

"What do you mean?" Now, she sounded interested.

"I mean that the university is just as much a victim as the government is."

"They have been trying to complete Dr. Caufield's research in his absence," McCarty said.

"I know, but that's because they have a couple of idiots over there. Trust me, he didn't leave them with enough to get anywhere."

"How do you know all of this?"

"Let's just say I'm involved."

"Okay, Mr. Camponi. If you are saying we shouldn't be investigating the university, and you are right about that, then who is it we should be looking at?"

"Scitech Corporation, located at 222 61st Street, New York City."

"Okay, what makes you think that they are involved?"

"Caufield is there, testing out his research. He has had a breakthrough, and it won't be long before Scitech reaps the benefits of it. Scitech has been in cahoots with Caufield for some time now, and this has all been a scheme to steal the research from the government and the university so that both parties can get rich."

"Why should I trust your information?"

"Send someone over to Scitech right now. You'll find Caufield, along with a former FBI agent, David Hovelle."

"I don't know if I can do anything about this," McCarty said.

"Trust me. Do it right now. Listen, you have my name. If you think this is some prank, or you find out that I'm wrong, then you can come to my apartment and arrest me, okay?"

"I'll see what I can do. Thank you for the information."

McCarty hung up. Though things didn't go exactly as I planned, I knew she would have to at least investigate the lead I gave her. Once the feds found Jason and Hovelle and discovered their little plan, all hell would break loose. I wanted to be there to see it all, but before I did anything, I needed a nap.

Epilogue

You know, sometimes, if you do everything in your power to make sure that justice is served, it actually is. Agent McCarty did follow up on my information, and the whole Scitech coverup was exposed. It even made the papers, though there was no mention of the sort of technology Jason was working on. I had called Lowenstein before everything hit the papers and told him what I knew. He had no idea who Scitech was, but he certainly wasn't too happy about being duped by Jason. He took the news about who Hovelle was the worst. He did assure me that Aileen Turner's murder was gang related, which was an answer I needed to hear to digest everything in whole.

Jason is currently serving a twenty year term in a federal prison on a variety of charges, the most serious being theft from the government. I don't think they take that sort of thing too lightly. They don't mind stealing and misusing our tax money, but try and take something from them and you rot in a cell. Hovelle disappeared, and when I spoke to McCarty a week after Jason's trial, she told me that the going belief was that Hovelle was dead. I didn't mind that at all.

Darlene never moved to California. She was offered her job back at Sprint. The company had realized they needed her, but she didn't take it. Instead, she went back to school for Creative Writing, and is working on her first novel. The reason why she didn't move to California? None other than the irresistible Darren Camponi. We started dating and haven't stopped yet. Hey, we might even get married.

I never talked to Tanya again. Though I felt a bit of a loss from this, I knew it was for the best. She had called me that one time when she left a message on my machine, but I never called back to find out what she wanted. She did send a letter a few weeks later, stating that someone had come to her house asking questions about me. I figured that was Hovelle. She also told me that I was too immature and unemotional to spend the rest of her life with me. She thanked me for freeing her and, in a sarcastic way, wished me a happy life.

Though I had many questions about what happened with that machine, I never really talked to anyone about it. The technology is now in the hands of the federal government, and though that might not be the best place for it, I figure its better than in the greedy hands of a company like Scitech, which has since gone out of business over this whole debacle. I don't think about my trip to the past too often, but I tell you now, if someone ever offers you the opportunity to experience it, turn it down. It took a good week for my mind to get right.

I thought Jason had told me the truth about my virtual trip to the past. I didn't think he put me in any danger. He just wanted to make his money. I believed that none of it was real, that everything I experienced was nothing more than an elaborate dream. I would have continued believing that wholeheartedly if it wasn't for the phone call I received from my mother about a month after the experience. One day, while she was going through the attic, she had found some of my old things. One thing of interest was my old wooden jewelry box.

Inside was my high school ring.

The End

About The Author

John Misak lives on Long Island, where he studied Creative Writing at Hofstra University and received his Masters in Creative Writing at Queens College. He is one of four children of a former NYPD plain clothes detective. John runs the family billiard hall business when he is not busy writing.

You may learn more about John's books at:
http://johnmisak.n3.net
http://www.barclaybooks.com